D1244696

The Games *of* Ganthrea

ANDY ADAMS

Classic Magic Press

OREGON

www.TheAndyAdams.com

Cover design by Kim Dingwall
Edited by Tim Marquitz
Published by Classic Magic Press in Bend, Oregon.

Library of Congress Cataloging-in-Publication Data
Names: Adams, Andy, 1986—author.
Title: The games of ganthrea / Andy Adams
Description: First U.S. edition. Oregon
 Classic Magic Press, 2020.

Library of Congress Control Number: 2020906055
ISBN: 978-1-7346524-0-6 (paperback)
ISBN: 978-1-7346524-1-3 (ebook)

ISBN: 978-1-7346524-0-6
First Edition: April 2020
Printed in the United States of America

Contents

Chapter One

Windelm

L ike most parents, Windelm hoped camping would create lasting memories. In this case, he was sadly right.

"Dinner's nearly ready," he said, standing next to the day's catch: three pink trout sizzling in a frying pan, caught less than an hour ago from the river in southern Aquaperni. His young son, Seth, was sitting and pointing his mircon at boulders around their camp, using levitation spells to send them airborne and laughing whenever he uncovered an alarmed skink or lizard and sent it scurrying for the bushes.

"I think I'll try-out to be a healer," Seth said, raising a rock and stacking it on another.

"You'd have more fun as a knight," Windelm said, flipping a fish and then cursing as bubbling olive oil spattered his hand.

"Healers get to bring stunned teammates back to life," said Seth. "They're easily the most useful player on the field."

"Wouldn't you rather capture glowbes and lead the charge? As a healer, you'd hang back for most of Zabrani."

Seth now had a small tower of stones six high. "Just 'cause you were a knight doesn't mean everyone wants to be one."

Windelm sighed. "You're right. It's your choice, Seth. I'll have fun watching either—"

What sounded like rocks cracking and a geyser erupting cut him off.

"What was that?" Seth said, standing and flicking his brown eyes at his father.

"I don't know," said Windelm, picking up his wooden mircon and walking lightly to the edge of their camp. Another rumbling sound came, and then their feet trembled. Seth's rock column wobbled and collapsed.

Windelm turned back to Seth. "I'm going to find out."

"I'm coming, too." Seth marched next to him, mircon raised.

"No, you're not. You wait here."

"Oh, come on, Dad."

"We're in wild territory. Could be poachers, or dragons, or who knows what." Windelm put a hand on Seth's shoulder before adding with finality, "Stay back until I come for you. Got it?"

Seth nodded slowly, then looked at his feet.

"Good. See you in a moment."

Windelm, himself an experienced sorcerer, felt his amulet warm as he engaged a flight spell with his mircon and whisked above the bushes toward the sound. After a few minutes, he came to the upper ridge overlooking a small, green valley. He dropped to the ground and crept behind a willow tree. Poking his head out, he saw at least a dozen spellcasters below, circled around a break in the woods. They were shooting their mircons into the ground, out of which rose a blue substance...*is that elixir?* thought Windelm.

Like a fountain of navy-blue wine, the shimmering liquid gushed up in a column from the ground, then floated over and into a large black vault at the foot of a hooded man, who swiveled his head from side to side, keeping a look-out. *It must be.*

As the blue elixir siphoned from the ground, a lifeless, gray color spread outward on the terrain, growing, in a matter of minutes, from the size of a pool to a pond to a lake. Along its path, trees and bushes shriveled like withered, old hands. Windelm sucked in his breath, his heart beating quicker. He had heard stories of elixir-draining, but as it was illegal in each of the seven biomes of Ganthrea, and permanently destroyed the land, he'd never seen it.

If it were just a couple of spellcasters, Windelm thought he could stun and disarm them, but this was a small regiment, too many for him. And he was far from his home biome of Silvalo, or any city for that matter, so sending a distress spell into the sky would only make him an easy target. *Better to remain unseen and return to camp, collect Seth, and fly home.*

He turned from the ridge and flew back toward camp.

Where were these elixir thieves from? Who were they working for? His shoulders tensed when he heard a branch break somewhere behind him, and quickly thereafter a shout from the valley that haunted him ever since.

"Oi! Got us a watcher!"

Windelm whipped around, pointing his mircon toward the immediate trees. There was no one there. But that meant…*Oh no…*

"Seth!"

He raced back to the willow tree at the top of the ridge. Scanning the surroundings, he saw some of the men still draining the elixir. But suspended in midair by a spell from below, a look of terror on his face, was his son.

"Kill him," someone ordered.

"*Seth!*" Windelm called, flying toward him, shooting a release spell at the cocoon wrapped around the boy—*if I can just grab his hand and wrap an Aura around us both—*

His spell hit Seth; the cocoon broke. He was about to catch his son, about to get them both away to safety, when another spell ripped through Seth's chest.

"*No!*"

Seth dropped, lifeless.

Windelm caught him one-handed, and said the words to grow an Aura around them both, as more shots rang out from below and bounced off the shell. He flew fast and hard away from the valley, as if he could take Seth somewhere to be mended.

But this was not a stunning spell, he knew, as hot tears spilled down his cheeks, onto his tunic.

This was death that even a healer couldn't undo.

It took days to get back to Silvalo, and more days until his wife said she forgave him, that it wasn't his fault. But Windelm couldn't forgive himself. He alerted the Silvalo Guard about the murder and the elixir-draining, but it was two biomes away, and they never found the men responsible.

For the next couple years, it felt like cold, corroded chains hung from Windelm's shoulders, and a permanent gloom enshrouded him. He let his hair and beard grow long, and felt aimless in work, marriage, everything. He came close to ending it all, and may well have, were it not for a timely message.

A courier arrived on their doorstep one evening with a trunk. Windelm asked whom it was from, and was informed an old friend had passed on, and left this to him. There was a note. Opening it, he read,

> *"Windelm, don't let Seth's death be the final chapter of your life. Find and nourish the good. Pick up where I left off."*

When the courier left, he opened the trunk, finding an old violin, leather books, furry animal hides, and underneath those, sturdy tubes holding faded, rolled-up scrolls. He pulled one out. The words on it were easily hundreds, perhaps thousands of years old, neatly written in stanzas, and warning of a time where wars raged among the biomes, crippling the people within.

All of which started with someone stealing the elixirs from Ganthrea.

A note scrawled on the margin said, *'there might be a way to stop it.'*

Something tugged within Windelm. He knew he couldn't bring his son back, but perhaps he could honor Seth's memory if he worked to prevent more deaths, to protect life.

As he dove deeper into the scrolls in the coming days, he read about a hidden talisman. And when, two decades later, Windelm felt he may have found the very one, he discovered he couldn't wear it. He needed someone else. Someone who didn't carry his grief, who didn't hunger for revenge, or power…who came from somewhere outside of Ganthrea.

And he hadn't been back to Earth in nearly fifty years.

Chapter Two

Two Colors in the Cottonwood Tower

"Hey, Wheezeridge! Stop littering!"

Book in hand, Brenner turned just as a red car zoomed next to him, a can hurtling out the driver's window. Before he could jump to the side, it hit him in the shoulder, spattering soda on his shirt, backpack, and outstretched book. Brenner stood paralyzed.

"Ha!" Stew Guffman yelled at Brenner as he flicked a finger out the driver's window, his sleek black hair blowing as he drove off into the suburbs of Colorado Springs.

"...freaking... jerk..." Brenner muttered as the car vanished past a bend. He tried, without much success, to clean the Coke off his shirt and book. *What I wouldn't give to watch him get pounded,* Brenner thought. But that was a pipe dream. The older senior had what Brenner sorely lacked: size, friends, and the feeling that oftentimes accompanies those—confidence. He kicked at the can, angry at Guffman and angry at himself for being so engrossed in a story that he forgot to take a quieter route to the woods after school.

As it was a bit over a mile to his tower, it would have been more convenient if he could run—indeed much of his social life would have been better if he could grow four more inches and run faster than a twelve-minute mile. But Brenner Wahlridge was short for a sophomore—short for anyone, really—and to cap it off had asthma, both of which the students at Clemson High kindly reminded him of in gym class…and in the cafeteria …and in the hallways…

He sighed. He still had to survive another two years and three months of this before he could hit restart, and hope for something better in college. He buried himself in his book again and kept walking.

Twenty minutes later, on a trail under tall pines, Brenner had mostly pushed Guffman out of his mind. He liked the afternoon soundtrack of the woods: the early spring wind weaving through the pines and through his short, sandy-blonde hair; chickadees chirruping in the canopy; and if he was lucky, deer brushing through the undergrowth.

For the past six years, the thing that gave him pleasure was a self-made tree tower. Here was a quiet place to think and read away from school, away from bullies, and away from his house.

Ever since he could remember, Brenner's house was a cacophony of noise: his father claimed he didn't have a hearing problem, yet always blared games of football, basketball, baseball, drafts, and any ESPN highlights on the biggest TV; his brother was in the bedroom next to Brenner's, firing live rounds into enemy soldiers in his video games; and his mother (when she was home) added to the din with dramatic, breathless exchanges of her soap operas—turned all the way up to drown out the other two screens.

Perhaps Brenner would've watched one of the TVs, but he grew bored whenever he was not actively doing or reading something, and more press-ingly, he developed headaches whenever sounds grew beyond conversation level or too many noises jammed together, which meant he spent most of his time outside. Even still, there were suburbia sounds of the neighbor's Rottweiler barking, lawn-mowers cutting or, more continuously, cars rumbling at 40-50 mph on the major street behind their fence.

Then one summer before 4th grade, when his older brother was at football practice and his parents were working, Brenner was hiking along the public forest of his subdivision when he noticed a silvery-white tree (an Eastern Cottonwood, he later discovered), thick as a rhino, rising well over ten stories high, and probably old enough that early pioneers would have seen it while heading west.

As he looked at it, an idea came to him for a building of his own. He started drawing an elaborate tower tucked away in the branches of the Cottonwood.

After much asking, his parents, Albert Wahlridge, a no-nonsense accountant, and Miranda Wahlridge, a flashy sales executive, allowed Brenner to use a portion of the small backyard for storing free lumber he collected from the city recycling center—"So long as it doesn't attract rats! This isn't the old Plint farm!" More than once Brenner had overheard them complaining about how they were supposed to have zero children and live comfortably, but instead, wound up with a child, Jeff, whom they regarded as a one-and-done son, and then eight years later, had another setback: unplanned, largely unwanted, and peculiar Brendon, who showed little interest in watching either of the 70" TV screens, instead choosing to go read outside or fiddle with tools in the garage.

For Christmas, they got him some nails and old wood, which would have been okay if they were sturdy, but judging from the dust and spider webs clinging to the boards, Brenner surmised were from the crawl space beneath their house. When the snow melted that year, he hauled wagonloads of his stockpiled lumber to the foot of the cottonwood. He nailed eight steps at two feet intervals on the lee side of the tree, but soon realized that lifting, holding, and fitting the crossbeams together would require another person.

Promising to do his older brother's scrubbing, vacuuming and laundry chores for a week if he helped lift boards for a day, Brenner persuaded Jeff to hold support beams in place while he screwed them to the tree. Jeff worked with him for a couple of hours, mostly muttering angrily to himself, and as Brenner was securing the last of the foundation beams, a horsefly landed on Jeff's neck.

"Ouch!" he yelled, swatting at the bug, "That's it, I quit! Bye, munchkin."

"You can't quit now," Brenner said. "We still have to set up the floorboards and sides."

"No, *you* do. *I'm* going to go meet Steve at his house and throw footballs around with him."

Brenner frowned. "You didn't stick out the whole day. That was the deal."

"Deal-shmeal, you still have to do my chores for a week."

"Two days."

"A week, or I pound you now before I go home."

Brenner glared at his older brother…but he still had plenty of work to do without black-and-blue welts on his arms.

"Fine, a week."

"That's right," Jeff said, then turned and stomped out of the woods.

Brenner lost a couple hours assembling a pulley and rigging system, but moments like those taught him a useful skill: self-reliance. By the following week, on top of doing all Jeff's chores early in the mornings, he had nailed down the floor section and created a trapdoor entrance where the tree trunk met the floorboards. Several weeks later he had four sides and the roof built, which he camouflaged with leafy branches. That summer he became fixated on famous inventors and explorers, reading about Benjamin Franklin, Lewis and Clark, Gaudi, Tesla, and Shackleton. Whenever the sun was out, and he wasn't forced to do chores at home, he was either immersed in a book or adding to his tree tower.

During the summer after 7th grade, after he finished a book on Napoleon's war tactics, he looked out the open window of the tower he had built (now with three zip-lines to other platforms) and felt…different.

To mark the change, he decided to blend his first name, Brendon, with his middle name, Conner, and go by Brenner.

Brenner was nearly at his tower now. His network of cables and platforms had grown substantially over the last six years, crisscrossing through the canopy like steel webs, but the forest had also changed, and not for the better: developers had nipped at the edges of the woods, putting up new homes; and some of the trees in the heart of the forest seemed to be withering slowly, like a disease was choking the land.

At the base of the cottonwood, Brenner climbed the boards up the back of the tree hand over hand, pulled out a key, and unlocked the deadbolt to his trapdoor. The fresh scent of new buds and green leaves greeted him as he swung his legs up and into his chamber. Deciding he'd go for a zip on his cables before finishing his book on John Nash Jr. (*Game Theory: Using the Odds and Unlocking Ultimatums*), he pulled on his harness and clipped in to the steel line, when his dark blue eyes caught a glimmer of sunlight reflecting off something bright yellow.

Curious, he unclipped himself and moved slowly toward the window, where he discovered a shiny, golden necklace neatly placed on his open windowsill. Threaded through the necklace was a glass bauble glowing green and red, whose colorful contents in the light seemed to swirl together.

Brenner picked it up.

In his palm, the spherical amulet was only about the size of a large walnut, but it felt like he was holding a heavy billiard ball. He did a double-take. The two colors were *flowing* like mini-waves within the bauble, but like oil and water, they refused to mix.

Although something inside him stirred excitedly, he was slightly alarmed at how this item had infiltrated his tree tower. He looked around at the shelves in the tower—nothing had been taken. Other than his parents and brother, who hadn't visited since the first day's build, he had never told anyone else about it, and had always bolted the entrance. Either someone threw this up from below—unlikely because the narrow windowsill was more than twenty feet high and the locket was perched precisely on it—or else they had gained entry to his tower. Brenner figured it must have been the latter, *but who would bother to come up, and why?*

He peered around the forest. A couple squirrels chased each other on nearby oaks, and from a ways off, ducks quacked from a stream.

After examining the amulet for several more minutes, he started putting it into his pocket, but decided it would be less likely to get lost if on his neck. He put it on. The amulet almost seemed to resonate against his chest, like a low cello string plucked by a musician. He felt lighter, and the air had a different, pleasant taste to it, like he was enjoying a cool drink with each breath when before he was only allowed one small sip at a time.

Maybe if I scout around the woods, I can find another clue as to who put this here. He went to the zip-line, and after strapping in, pushed off hard from the platform. The unusually warm spring air whipped by as he careened past the trees. He lifted his legs forward to absorb the impact of a small wooden platform, hit lightly, then hoisted up onto the platform.

Footsteps and a flicker of brown and black in the distance caught his eye. *Was that the culprit?*

Unhooking himself from the cable, he descended limb by limb on an aspen tree until he was low enough to drop with a soft *thunk* onto the forest floor. He quietly walked for several minutes until the gentle ripples of the creek came into view. Looking downstream to his right, he guessed the earlier commotion must've been a deer, now gone through trees. His upwind smell probably carried to it on the breeze.

He was about to head back to his tower and read his book when a simultaneous crack and light burst from the depths of the woods, then vanished. A mixture of fear and curiosity swept over Brenner, and his breathing quickened. He wanted to know more, but also didn't want to stumble upon someone with a gun. He turned to hustle away from the creek, when another sound stopped him.

There was a low growl from across the stream, and then out lumbered a black bear, its amber eyes locked on its prey: Brenner.

His own blue eyes widened. Reading about dangerous expeditions was completely different than actually standing in the path of a predator. His body felt rooted to the forest floor.

Gathering every ounce of resolve, he finally broke into a scramble, dashing backward over rocks as quick as his legs would take him, wondering whether his asthma would take him down…or if the bear would. *Or maybe it wouldn't chase?*

A roar ripped through the trees and water splashed behind him.

Nope.

He had maybe a hundred-meter head-start on the bear, and his tree tower was not close enough. Heart pounding, Brenner spotted his only escape: a gnarled Douglas-fir tree with a branch easily twice as tall as himself. At 5'6", the highest Brenner had ever jumped was to skim his fingers against the net of a basketball hoop.

Another roar sounded.

He would have thrown a rock or a stick to stun the bear, but finding one would cost him the small lead. The branch ahead was too high, but it was all he had. He threw a final glance back, and saw the charging bear, teeth barred. Sprinting forward, he launched himself up, arms extended.

The bear bellowed at his back, swiping a paw.

Brenner's outstretched fingers hit and held the high branch as the bear roared past underneath, clawing at his left heel, and ripping off his shoe.

Brenner kicked upward, hooking his legs onto another branch a few feet higher. As he pulled himself up, the bear carved its claws onto the tree and climbed, snapping off the limb below him. It tried a different bough and continued scraping its way up. Sweat dripped from Brenner's forehead into an eye. The bear was almost at his feet. He could keep climbing…or…

He looked down, and timed a kick right as the black bear thrust its head upward—hitting the beast squarely in the snout. That same instant, he could've sworn a beam of light hit the bear.

The bear shook its head in anger, or quite possibly disbelief, and to Brenner's immense relief, scraped back down the trunk. With a last bellow that sent a nest of birds flying, it shambled away from Brenner's tree.

Trembling on the branch, Brenner watched the grumbling bear stalk off to find easier prey. His adrenaline gradually lessened with each passing minute, and the full shock of his narrow escape set in: he had *out-sprinted* and *out-jumped* a black bear. Strangest of all, his asthma hadn't kicked in. Air flowed effortlessly through his steady, rhythmic lungs.

Brenner sat high in the tree, holding up the amulet and staring at the green-red contents.

He became dimly aware that his lower leg hurt. He looked at his foot—thankfully his shoe must've gotten the brunt of the bear's claws. But there was a small tear in his pants where the bear had scratched his ankle. He waited another half hour before he was satisfied that the bear was gone, then carefully descended through the branches, and shimmied down the trunk. He found his shoe stuck in some bushes. The heel was torn. He put it on anyway, looking up at the snapped branch he had grabbed. Yes, it was about twelve feet high, maybe more.

Could I do it again? Or was it a fluke from all that adrenaline?

He was still breathing fine, which was as shocking to him as the high jump, since he couldn't remember a time when he had sprinted for close to two hundred yards without an asthma attack. There was only one thing different: the amulet.

He listened to the woods and watched for any signs of movement. When nothing unusual happened after another ten minutes, he tried another test.

Backing up a hundred yards, Brenner crouched low, and again began sprinting full tilt toward a slightly higher branch on the tree. He expected the usual symptoms of his asthma to flare up: his chest to tighten as though a python squeezed it, his throat to cinch shut, and his head to throb, begging him to stop. But the only sensation he felt was…*joy*…pure joy as his legs practically flew over the ground, kicking up pine needles.

He readied himself for the jump…"*3, 2, 1 – now!*" Springing from the ground as though it were a taut trampoline, his hands outstretched, he watched as they easily rose up to meet the high branch. Grasping tightly, he swung back and forth on the limb, and then did a chin-up, pulling himself onto the branch.

It was not a fluke.

He peered again at the amulet.

Two hours later, Brenner quietly opened the back door to his house, and walked past the living room, where his parents sat on their leather couch, glued to the television. He forgot to step around the middle of the wooden floorboards, which creaked loudly.

"What kept you this time?" his mother, Miranda, asked without looking away from the giant flat screen, while artificial audience laughter rose and fell in the background.

"Oh, I couldn't put this down." Brenner held up the game theory book for them to see, but they didn't bother turning to look at him. He changed the subject: "My homework's done, and I'm not very hungry. I'm going to take a shower if you don't mind."

"No, do the laundry and wash the dishes first," his mother said, gesturing idly with her hand in the air towards the dinner mess she and Albert had left in the kitchen, but still not looking at Brenner, "then you can do whatever you want. I'll be out with clients all day tomorrow," she continued, mainly to the television, "so you're on your own for dinner." Miranda was schmoozing clients more often than she was home, so Brenner was used to fixing his own meals.

But that night, Brenner didn't mind doing the chores. After he was done, he spent several hours on his computer researching one idea to the next: lockets, amulets, healing crystals, unstable elements, record-breaking jumps. But nothing quite explained the strange necklace he was wearing. He was so excited by it that he almost wanted to tell someone, but who would believe him? Not his parents. And even if he did have friends, could he trust them to keep it a secret? *No, better to keep this to myself…conduct some more solo experiments with it.*

He only took off the amulet to shower, afterwards slipping it under a t-shirt and climbing into bed around midnight. He set his alarm-clock forty-five minutes earlier than normal.

Sleep usually came easy to Brenner, but not tonight.

His thoughts kept jumping to what he might do tomorrow: longer runs, bigger jumps…going to gym class, and for the first time in his life, actually playing with a chance to win against other kids. He had always told himself that knowledge and creativity were all that mattered. But there was a part of him that wanted to go beyond mental games and chess and prisoner's dilemnas, and feel that surge of triumph that commanders of old must have felt when they wagered everything on a battle…and won.

He smiled into sleep.

Chapter Three

The Nearly Golden Day

On Wednesday, just to be sure he hadn't imagined the whole bear encounter, Brenner rose shortly after sunrise, checked that the amulet was still underneath his t-shirt, and ran a mile-long route around his neighborhood. He still felt better than ever: no wheezing, and no side aches, as though he had the agility of an Olympian. He came home, ate some eggs, and then caught the bus.

After Biology first hour, Brenner restrained his urge to sprint to gym class.

Mr. Burliss, a past-his-prime gym teacher dressed in a faded track-suit, blew his whistle for the start of class. Since this spring was warmer than years past, their gym class had started playing flag football outside on Monday.

"Shawn, your team will play Tonya's," Mr. Burliss said, as Brenner and the other sophomores assembled into their four football squads on the fields. "Garrett, your team will play Ann's. Winners stay on the same field, and losers —" Brenner felt the eyes of his classmates stare at him, "— switch."

Tonya, the prettiest girl in class and captain for Brenner's squad, sulked, "That's not fair! With him on our team," she gestured at Brenner as though he couldn't hear her, "we're basically playing one person short."

Mr. Burliss said simply, "Then play harder. No trades." He blew his whistle to start the games.

Tonya's team went to the line on defense, but instead of staying as a blocker near the middle like yesterday, Brenner went to the far side, matching himself with Shawn's best receiver, Parker Stevens. Parker, an olive-skinned boy with thick calves, looked at who was guarding him, grinned, and waved to his quarterback, Shawn.

"Get a load of this kid," Parker called out, and the rest of his team glanced over, saw Brenner, and laughed. "Tonya, you're making this too easy!"

"Wheezeridge, what do you think you're doing?!" Dennis yelled at him. "Get back to the line where you belong!"

"That's okay," Brenner said, watching Parker, and predicting the next Hail Mary play to him. "I got this."

"If Parker scores, I'm gonna punch you harder than Shawn does," Tonya shouted, then motioned for Dennis to play deep zone, for when Parker would inevitably fly past Brenner.

Brenner nodded.

Parker leaned across the line to Brenner and sneered, "I'm gonna smoke you."

"Hike!" Shawn called, and Parker took off down the sideline, but for the first time in his life, Brenner stuck with the receiver every step. Ten yards, twenty yards...Parker glanced back at the line of scrimmage, and by his hungry smile, Brenner knew the ball was thrown to him...forty yards out...Brenner was still shoulder-to-shoulder...he looked up to see the football plummeting down just ahead of them, Parker outstretching his arms, ready to catch it in a final push past Brenner, but the ball never reached him.

With a tremendous leap and half-spin, Brenner overshadowed Parker and caught the football with both hands, before landing backwards and backpedaling. Parker skidded to a halt in the end zone. Brenner stopped his backward momentum, looked downfield, and switched to forward gear.

For a long moment, the entire field of players stood frozen like statues, stunned at Brenner's interception.

Then Shawn rallied his team out of their stupor, shouting, "Get him!"

Bursting into motion, Brenner ran past his own 10, zipping past the first opponents trying to rip his flags off.

Six players were now left to stop him, and came at him like a rushing wall. They probably expected him to continue his run up the sideline, content with the interception and thirty-yard return before being pushed out-of-bounds.

That wasn't Brenner's game-plan.

As the play unfolded, and almost in slow motion for Brenner, Shawn's eyebrows lifted in astonishment when, twenty feet before his opponents hit him, he abruptly changed course: he hurtled himself toward the middle of their oncoming wall.

Shawn, well over six feet tall, led the charging brigade at him like a crashing wave towards a lone swimmer.

"Bad choice, Brenner!" Shawn said, a grin pasted on his face.

Brenner sprinted hard. A dozen feet away from the wall of players, Brenner thrust his right foot into the ground and pushed off, vaulting clear over their heads. For a brief moment, he felt like a stuntman flying a motorcycle above a stretch of semi-trucks. He reached the apex—their raised hands didn't even brush his feet—then Brenner hit the ground mid-stride and finished with a trot into the end zone.

Touchdown.

He grinned. An almost giddy sensation overcame him. For a long moment, nobody spoke.

Mr. Burliss's whistle fell from his mouth to the ground. If someone had walked up to the field and been asked to explain the crazed look on the old coach's face, very likely they would have told you his appendix had just burst.

For the rest of that glorious gym hour, Brenner was untouchable. He caught half-a-dozen passes, outmaneuvered tacklers, and when he lost track of the score, tapered back his jumps to be more like a normal 10th grader. More than once he ripped off Shawn's flags, and *accidentally* knocked him to the ground.

Later that afternoon, as Brenner hopped off the bus, he couldn't remember a time he had had a better day. Apart from football, when he was given a surprise examination on the Renaissance, he remembered near-ly every detail from the humorous presentation Mr. Quinn had given the previous day, and answered all thirty questions exactly right.

Two other kids got off the bus behind him, and then the yellow vehicle rumbled down the street. Usually the three students then parted. Russell Wilcox, two grades older, turned left and walked to his house. Susan Sheffield, a slender, pretty girl his age he'd been around since elementary school, usually turned left, too. But this time before they parted, Susan asked, "Do you mind if I walk with you?"

Her question caught him by surprise.

"Sure, that's fine," Brenner said, adjusting his backpack, deciding to take a different route to his house.

They walked for a bit before Susan asked, "So, is what they're saying at school true?" Her light brown eyes flashed at Brenner.

"What are they saying?"

"That you scored six or seven touchdowns, tackled Shawn Ripley, and jumped over a whole team?"

Brenner tried masking his smile. "I don't know about the jumping part," he lied, not meeting her eyes, "but yeah, I scored a couple times today."

"How'd you do all that?"

He considered telling her what he'd told to other students—a change in diet to a daily quart of prune juice—but she was too smart to fall for it. "Well, my doctor did some tests on me," he breathed in, the amulet rising and falling underneath his shirt, "and turns out my asthma has gone into remission."

"That's great," Susan said, looking genuinely happy for him. "But that doesn't explain how you suddenly got to be the fastest kid in gym class." They passed under newly budding lilac bushes and she blurted out, "You know steroids can mess you up, right?"

Brenner groaned. "I'm not taking steroids, okay?"

"I've seen you around our neighborhood since we've been kids. You've never been close to fast."

"Well, I've never had lungs that allowed me the chance."

"Hmm." She was quiet for awhile, then asked, "Why do you go to the woods so often?"

He thought about telling her about the tower...but he'd been so used to being by himself, without noise, without the possibility of being teased... could he tell her about the amulet? *No...what if she told others?*

"I just enjoy the views," he said a little lamely.

"Uh huh..." she said skeptically. "Ever hear the saying, 'no man is an island'?"

Brenner considered her comment, then looked down and said, "Some tropical islands do quite well before people disturb them. I'm at my best when I'm alone."

"If you say so," said Susan.

Low beats from a stereo system boomed past them, and a red BMW pulled into a driveway three houses ahead. Brenner's neck-hairs bristled as he noticed the familiar gelled black hair of the driver as he stepped out. He tried walking quicker in order to avoid facing the senior, Stew Guffman.

Susan picked up her pace, too, but they weren't quick enough.

Standing over six feet tall, Guffman had a thick chin and leering dark eyes, and, for as long as Brenner remembered, always got exactly what he wanted. Right now, from the stare Guffman gave her while pacing down his driveway in his navy blue jacket, it was clear he wanted Susan. His pupils were dilated, maybe because of his hatred toward Brenner, or more likely, because of drugs.

"Hey, Susan," Guffman crooned, taking her hand by surprise, "Warm day, isn't it? You should have a drink with me. Ditch this loser, and come join me inside."

Susan demurred. "I don't think I really need any—"

"Ah come on," Guffman interrupted. "It'll be fun." He started leading her away, his other hand shoving Brenner hard on the chest. "Get lost, little puke. Or do I have to throw something harder at you?"

Brenner stood mute. He'd learned avoiding a fight left him in much better shape than getting involved. Even if he was a fighter, he didn't stand a chance against Guffman. At close-range, with no weapon to defend himself, Brenner knew he would be beat—badly. His fear was amplified by a regret that he had chosen to live with an Mp3 player and not a cell phone. He took a step back.

"Thought so," Guffman said, continuing up the driveway, putting an arm around Susan's waist as they passed a crate full of baseballs on the sidewalk.

Susan protested, trying to pull away, "Uhh, maybe some other time, Stew…"

"Jenny said you had a crush on me," Guffman pressed, pulling her to the door, and then added firmly, "Go inside if you know what's good for you."

Anger and fear pulsed through Brenner. The amulet on his chest radiated heat, and something inside of him flipped open. "Let her go!"

Guffman turned his back to Brenner, grabbed the doorknob, and pushed it open. "Get in," he said to Susan.

Brenner made a split decision—going against his usual choice of self-preservation, he charged up the driveway.

Guffman must've heard him; he shoved Susan inside, grinned, and grabbed a baseball from the crate. He turned and whipped it at Brenner's chest.

Brenner had an instant to react before he was hit.

He leaned back hard, twisting his right shoulder out and away—but not fast enough. *Thwack!* The hard ball pelted against Brenner's left forearm and stung like fire. He cried out and winced. He turned to see Guffman running at him and lunging forward like a prize-fighter, right arm raised with a punch coming straight at his face.

This time, he was ready.

Brenner dipped to the right just as Guffman's knuckles whistled past his head and his torso arced forward, leaving his backside exposed. Brenner channeled his anger into his fist and, rotating his upper body, turned and slammed it hard into the back of Guffman's head.

Wham.

Like a puppet with slashed strings, Guffman collapsed in a heap on the hard blacktop.

The only sound coming to Brenner was his pulse, pounding in his head.

Having never won a fight before, Brenner was speechless, and in quite a bit of shock. Chest heaving, fists still balled, he watching Guffman closely, as if any moment he might spring up from the ground.

"…Brenner…hey, Brenner…"

He looked up. Susan had walked over to him. Her hands fidgeted with the straps of her backpack, and she also looked dazed, as if she couldn't quite believe what she'd seen.

"Are you okay?" she asked.

"I…think so," Brenner said. Then the pain in his arm came back into focus. "Except this." He held up his left arm and saw a large, purplish bruise where the baseball struck him.

"Ouch," said Susan, wincing out of sympathy. "Sorry about that."

"It's alright. Just a big bruise is all." As he said it and tried flexing his fingers, his arm smarted with pain. "Are you doing alright?"

"I'm okay," Susan said, looking from his arm to his eyes. "Feeling a little better now. Thank you."

"Yeah…of course." There was a moment of silence between them before Brenner added, "Now what?"

She pulled out a cell phone from her backpack and said, "I'm going to call the police. That's what."

Before long a squad car pulled up. An officer stepped out, and he checked to ensure Guffman was breathing and stable before he asked them questions about the encounter. Mostly Susan talked, and when it came to his part, Brenner showed the officer his bruised arm. Then the officer called both their parents. Albert was less than thrilled to be interrupted at work with news that Brenner was involved with a fight, even if it was a defensive one. Finally, the officer put Guffman in the back of his car, and said they were free to go.

Brenner went home and took a hot shower. Then he changed and put on a long-sleeved shirt. His parents wouldn't be home for another hour. He went downstairs, filled a canteen with water, put it and some books in his backpack, and then headed out to his tree-tower to process the day's events…had he really fought back against Guffman? It seemed so strange, so unlike him. And he'd actually played football and won…something he had also never thought possible. One thing he did know: walking away as the victor felt a lot better than staring at his feet as the loser.

After hiking through the woods, he approached his Cottonwood and climbed up the worn planks, wincing with each use of his wounded arm. At the ladder's top, he inserted his key into the lock, clicked it open, and lifted the trapdoor, which swung up and thudded down against the floor. Brenner pressed his palms on opposite sides of the entrance, lifted his body, and swung his legs up through the opening.

He turned to shut the trap-door, and froze.

Inside his tower, sitting opposite of him, was a complete stranger.

Chapter Four

An Invitation
Most Strange

With loose, wolf-brown hair that hung past his eyebrows, a beard bristling like steel wool, and a commanding countenance, the man across from Brenner would, even in a public setting, intimidate most people. But here, sitting in his chair with a gnarled walking stick (easily doubling as a club, Brenner thought), up in his tree tower, and a couple miles away from anyone who could help, this stranger unnerved him.

Goosebumps prickling on his arms, Brenner flew through his options: he could turn and back-pedal down; he could make a jump for his zip line; or he could fight, using his fists against a club, and he had an injured arm. There was no time to clip into the zipline, so he swung his legs back through the entrance and clambered down some steps…but as he looked back a final time, he noticed the stranger hadn't moved. He met Brenner's gaze with calm, green-blue eyes, as if this was a routine meeting. Because he was now out of reach, Brenner took a risk and hesitated: he wanted to discover a few things about this man before escaping to safety.

If he had to guess, he would say the stranger was in his mid-forties, had the build of a football player, and was wearing a peculiar, green…*tunic?*

It looked like he'd stolen his shirt off the back of a pirate from the 17th century. Or, more likely, he had just escaped a prison and this was the first thing he had found to wear…

"What are you doing here?" Brenner asked.

The man merely smiled, then said, "I came to have a chat with you, Brenner. I see you've adapted well to the amulet."

Having never laid eyes on him before, Brenner didn't know what was stranger: that this person had gained entry to his tower, or that he already knew his name and about the amulet. Brenner squinted up at him from the floor entrance. "Who—who are you?"

The man waved a hand in the air apologetically. "Where are my manners? I'm sorry, my name's Windelm Crestwood," he said warmly, and when he leaned forward to the floor entrance, extending his arm for a handshake, Brenner noticed a gleam of silver from a necklace under Windelm's tunic. Rather than shake Windelm's hand, Brenner let it hang awkwardly in the air, and moved further down the ladder.

Taking the hint, Windelm turned the failed handshake into a wave. "Right, we'll take it slow for starters. Please, call me Windelm…although, in a previous life my name was…" and he paused, searching the air for a faded memory, then, like a fisherman with a sharp tug on the end of his rod, his eyes lit up, "Plint. Yes, Edwin Plint."

Brenner had heard that last name somewhere…*wasn't it on his mother's side of the family?* A faint memory swam blurrily into his mind, a conversation with his mother. She had spoken of growing up in the city, but that her grandparents had a far different life…*the old Plint farm, that's right…* they worked as crop farmers when her mom, Grandma Laura, and Great Uncle Lester were younger. *But she had never spoken of an Edwin.*

Brenner finally spoke: "I don't know of any Edwin Plint."

"Well," said Windelm, "I'm not too surprised Edwin's story hasn't been told much, seeing as how it must've looked as though he'd run-away, or been abducted."

Brenner's eyebrows raised…*Windelm was talking in third-person, and about abductions, neither of which were good signs…*

Windelm continued nonchalantly, "Thankfully, none of those scenarios occurred. You recall your Grandma Laura, yes?"

Brenner nodded slowly. He had only a few memories of her, as she had died in a winter car accident when he was five…but the fact that Windelm knew of her without prompting was, Brenner noted, a sign that he might be telling the truth.

"She was my sister," said Windelm, "and Lester was my older brother. Before I left, my parents sold their farm and acreage and were moving west to Colorado Springs. Lester was focused on new business opportunities and was glad for the move, and while Laura always had a soft spot for cuddly animals, she, too, was excited for a bigger town."

Windelm's explanation was matching up to what he knew: his great-grandparents had indeed been farmers…and he remembered his Grandma Laura had bought four kittens when her husband passed away…and he knew about Lester, but there was no other boy in that family…and Windelm should have looked at least a little senile if he was their brother, not this forty-something adult who looked like he rock-climbed up fourteeners over the weekends, which made him then wonder why he carried a walking-stick…

"If you're my Grandma's brother, that would make you…" Brenner started.

"Your great-uncle, yes," Windelm said, smiling.

"Pardon me for saying it, but you don't exactly *look* like a great-uncle."

Windelm laughed. "You're right," he said. "The reason I look this way, and why you haven't heard of me, is simple: for most of my life, I've lived in Ganthrea."

Brenner felt a little lost. He knew of many cities, countries, and even habitats around the world, but Ganthrea, he was sure, was none of those. *"Ganthrea?"* He must not have heard correctly. "Where is that?"

"How to explain," Windelm paused, then continued with renewed intensity in his eyes, "Ganthrea is at once very real, yet very separate from this world."

It was at this point that Brenner lowered a foot on the steps—Windelm was certainly crazy. "I'd better be going," he said, edging down the planks.

Windelm held up a hand, "Please, allow me to explain."

"That's okay, I'd rather —"

"Don't you want to know what's inside your amulet?"

Brenner's neck hairs stood on end. The amulet on his chest seeped with warmth like a baked potato, as if affirming Windelm's words. Brenner paused. He did want to know. As long as Windelm didn't do anything sudden, he decided to hear him out. "Alright."

"To understand your amulet, you have to understand Ganthrea," Windelm said, taking a foreign-looking, golden coin from his pocket. "Imagine that Earth is represented by one side of this coin, and Ganthrea, the other. While they're quite separate when it's still," he showed both sides to Brenner, then flicked the coin into the air with one hand and pointed at it with his walking-stick—it continued spinning in midair, and eerily, didn't fall. "When it spins, the two use the same space. So, while we share similar landforms, the sea, the soil, the mountains, we live distinctly parallel lives. And," he stopped pointing at the coin, and it fell into his outstretched hand, "only Ganthrea has retained the deep magic."

The floating coin trick was about as bizarre as the last words Windelm had said. Brenner voiced the next question welling up inside, "What exactly do you mean, 'magic'?"

"What else did you think was in that amulet of yours?" Windelm said, turning his head to the side with a coy smile. "In Ganthrea, magic collects together into a fluid-like substance called elixir, which can be bottled into amulets, like yours. It's the lifeblood of spells, and the reason why I look about half as old as I am."

The amulet, Brenner knew, *had* amplified his speed and jumps… and cured his asthma. "Okay," said Brenner, "I believe you about the amulet …just how did you get it so perfectly on the ledge?"

"I could have done it multiple ways," Windelm said, "personal flight, or controlled animal assistance…but this time I chose a simple Movement Spell." To answer the next question ready to spring from Brenner's lips, Windelm pointed his stick towards a corner of the tower filled with a stack of Brenner's books and said casually, "*Levitulsus.*"

One of the heavy books twitched, and then leapt up from the stack high into the air, as if gravity was now optional. Then another strange thing happened: like the coin earlier, the book didn't fall. What's more, it flew around the chamber, twice, before calmly landing in Windelm's outstretched hand.

Brenner's eyes nearly popped out of his head.

Windelm watched his flabbergasted expression with the knowing smile of a parent teaching a child how to command a dog to come when called. "Yes, that first encounter shatters your reality, doesn't it? And that's just one of the easier spells you can learn in Ganthrea. Which reminds me, hold up your arm."

Slowly, Brenner raised his left arm up. Windelm pointed his walking-stick at it. Although Brenner couldn't see his bruise beneath the bandage, he felt his skin pulling together, and a tingling sensation tickled his arm briefly. He pulled up his sleeve and peeked under the bandage—the purple and yellow bruise on his arm had returned to healthy, normal skin.

"Woah…" Brenner said. Now convinced that Windelm was more than some street performer, he climbed up into the tower and sat on the floor. "So…why did you come back?"

"Every now and then, I check on Earth. Partly out of nostalgia, and to see how the environment compares to what I left…and also to see if there are others ready to experience the other world. By the way, your escape from that black bear yesterday was carried out quite well."

Brenner's eyebrows arched incredulously, "You saw that?"
Windelm chuckled. "Oh yes, the jump, the tangle in the tree…and I was there to ensure the bear didn't do any permanent damage. But what I was most pleased to see was how you used your skills to help someone else, not merely keeping them for yourself."

Brenner realized he'd seen the fight with Guffman.

"She would've been hurt," Brenner said.

"I'm glad you stopped him," Windelm said sincerely. "You know, Brenner, you're not the first I've tested with an amulet. But unlike the others, you didn't use it solely for personal gain." Windelm's expression softened, and he continued, "Brenner, I think you are meant to come with me. You have both the cunning and compassion necessary to thrive in Ganthrea."

"Come with you…?" Brenner echoed, lost in thought.

"Indeed."

"But…why me?"

"Because I've seen a glimpse of what's inside of you, Brenner. How many books have you read in the past year?"

"I don't know…two or three a week…so…well over a hundred."

"And over eight or nine years, that's around a thousand books, and a thousand more ideas. Those biographies and stories and essays have shaped your thinking…given your experiences into how people behave, how battles and game strategies work, and how nature ebbs and flows. After you spend a couple years at the academy in Silvalo honing those thinking and athletic skills, you will possess enough talent to make an *extraordinary* life."

Brenner leaned forward.

"There are dangers of course," said Windelm, "but in my opinion it wouldn't be fun otherwise. For starters, Ganthrea's inhabitants don't cage wild creatures, and at some point, you'll likely be confronted with them. Also, the larger cities have their share of thieves and swindlers, but you'll learn how to protect yourself against those, too.

"And of course, there are the Games, which, with any luck, you'll get into during your second year at the academy. Since you are already twice as agile with just the amulet, imagine what you can do on the Zabrani field with a mircon and a spell or two."

Behind Windelm the sun was setting, giving him an orange silhouette.

"My bet is that you've longed to be elsewhere for quite some time, Brenner. The door to Ganthrea hardly ever opens, and right now it could use somone like you."

Brenner sat transfixed by his words, weighing the pros and cons on a mental scale. Part of him tried to figure out what 'Silvalo' meant and what these Zabrani games were like, while the other tried to imagine what sort of wild creatures lurked in Ganthrea.

"Or, if you'd like," Windelm said, "you can stay here in Colorado—you do have a nice tree tower," he gestured to the walls and zipline, "and I'm sure you'd grow to lead a perfectly normal life, which for many people is fine. If you choose not to come, I'll understand. But I'll need your amulet back, to find another holder."

That got Brenner's attention. Now that he had tasted the magic of the amulet, could he really give it back? To go through his life with raspy, deflated lungs?

"How long would I be there?" Brenner asked.

"Two years at the academy to start. Longer if you'd like."

"Would I be able to talk to anyone here while I'm gone?"

"Unfortunately, no," said Windelm. "Aside from myself and a small handful of others, people of Earth do not know of Ganthrea. Most wouldn't believe it if you told them. To avoid unnecessary wars, that's how it should stay."

Another question bubbled to the surface of Brenner's mind. "How do we get there…to Ganthrea?"

Windelm looked to choose his words carefully. "I've brought enough elixir to make a path for us—a rabbit-hole, so to speak. It's not the most comfortable…but it doesn't need to last long."

There was one last thing nagging at Brenner: uncertainty. What would happen to him there? Would this academy be any different than his current high school? His fingertips drummed the back of his knuckles as he mulled it over. Was it possible to reinvent himself there…and instead of being ridiculed, actually compete? Gain not just knowledge…but, maybe, acceptance? But, the rational side of him argued, perhaps it was better to play it safe, give back his amulet, return to what he knew: books, security, and solitude. He played that choice out like chess: In ten years he'd be even smarter, in twenty, financially secure, in fifty, retired, older…and at his current pace, alone, looking back whistfully and wondering…what might have been?

Brenner breathed out deeply, nearly arriving at his decision. "If I say yes, when would we leave?"

"As soon as we inform your parents that you've been accepted to a top-secret government program."

"Brenner, what's this about?" his father, Albert, said Thursday evening while brandishing an envelope he evidently had just torn open. "It's bad enough you got in a fight yesterday, now this?"

Brenner had just returned home after an afternoon in the woods, thinking hard on Windelm's offer. Last night he searched boxes in their crawl-space under the house and scoured an old trunk, which contained spiderwebs, old photographs, papers and mementos. Sifting through old letters, he found a few faded pictures at the bottom, of his Grandma Laura at a school in Colorado Springs, of Lester playing basketball, and of not two but *three* younger kids in front of an old barn.

There were no names on the back of that one, just small print that read, 'White Rock, AR.' While he recognized the faces of Lester and Laura, there was a boy between them with dirt on his pants, holding a fishing pole—*could it be…Windelm?*

He looked over to see what his father was waving about.

"Says it's from the *government,*" Albert continued gruffly. "Dear Mr. and Mrs. Wahlridge…we are pleased—right, *pleased,* when are they ever pleased unless there's more taxes involved? *Hmph*—to announce that your son, Brendon, has been chosen to enroll…in a two-year training school for future CIA operatives…What?" he paused, squinting at the page, clearly uncertain whether he had read the sentence correctly.

He shot Brenner a look of accusation, before continuing in a baffled voice, "Because of the confidential nature of this program, I will need to share more with you in person at your residence, at 5:00pm on Friday, April 3rd. "

His irritated tone swelled into exasperation. "*What?!* That's tomorrow!" he shook his head, then continued in a mocking voice, "Congratulations on this prestigious opportunity. If he accepts, Brendon's training will begin immediately. Sincerely, Lt. Col. W. Crestwood."

Brenner was almost as surprised as his father. He almost thought he had dreamed the whole offer. He was interrupted by his father's loud, irritated sigh.

"Brenner, what have you done now at school?"

"Gone to class like usual," Brenner said defensively, "and I still have all A's and B's."

"Then why do we have this?" said Albert, brandishing the letter at him, "Why is the federal government suddenly interested in you?"

Brenner could see through his words. By 'you,' his father meant himself. He was always paranoid another IRS audit was looming around the corner.

"*Well?*" his father demanded. "What in blazes is this about?"

"I suppose," Brenner said, thinking on his feet, "Since the government *is* monitoring pretty much everything, maybe they liked my civics essay on why the U.S. should increase their quotas of annual immigrants."

Albert shook his head, "I don't buy it." With each year, Brenner failed to live up to Jeff's normal interests. And now here he was getting the government tangled in their affairs.

"What are you doing in the woods all the time?"

"I've told you, working on my tree tower."

"Right…right…" Albert said, rolling his eyes, "your tree fort. Listen, I'm not sure what this is, but it had better not be some prank of yours," he said, a warning look in his eyes. "If it is, plan to be grounded for the summer. Since I've already planned to be home early tomorrow to set up for Poker night—you're lucky—we'll just see what sort of *government official* turns up at five."

He threw the letter on the counter. With much restraint, Brenner held his tongue. Here his father had been given a letter praising his son's merits, and Albert had warped it into some government surveillance plot.

Yanking open the fridge, Albert grabbed a can of beer and ended the conversation by huffing down to the den to watch ESPN highlights, leaving Brenner alone with the letter.

He picked it up. The handwriting on the envelope was cursive; the letter was typed and formal, crisply formatted with date and emblem of the White House on top. Brenner was impressed: for being crafted, sealed, and delivered in just a day, it looked quite official.

His mother, Miranda, got home an hour later. Glancing at the letter with mild distaste, she walked over to Albert and said dryly, "Well, if they want him, they can have him."

Brenner looked up from his book to see his father's crossed arms and stormy expression, and Miranda adding in what she evidently thought was a quieter tone, "What are you so worked up about? It's either a fake or we get him off our hands." Albert's demeanor softened. Miranda reclined on the couch with her tablet, idly clicking on little candy pieces to burst as she rummaged through a bag of gourmet cookies.

That night his parents slept soundly on their waterbed, Albert snoring deeply, as if they had gotten a letter that Brenner had been selected to the Honor Roll, rather than one inviting him to leave for good.

Brenner looked out the window to the clear night sky, holding the amulet aloft and comparing the red and green swirls of it to the pale yellow of the moon. He ran a hand through his sandy-blond hair.

While he didn't know what would happen once he joined Windelm and somehow got to Ganthrea, he knew that his life with the amulet was better than his life without; hopefully, with the same grit he applied to building his projects and understanding strategies, he could harness some of the magic that Windelm conjured forth so effortlessly. His eyelids started drooping shut, and he drifted to sleep hoping that he wouldn't have to face the worst thing of all: that he would wake up, and discover that this unexpected adventure had been a fleeting dream.

Chapter Five

Through the Rabbit Hole

Friday morning his parents didn't say much to him, probably still thinking he had concocted the letter. At school, Brenner sat quietly through his classes with tempered restraint, determined not to disrupt some cosmic balance that might ruin everything. In gym class he told Mr. Burliss that he'd pulled a muscle and needed to sit out. Mr. Burliss seemed to buy the excuse, as prior to Wednesday Brenner had been entirely unspectacular.

Although he was the target of stares and whispered rumors for the rest of the day, Brenner succeeded in keeping his excitement to himself.

When he got home, the minutes seemed to crawl by. He busied himself with his weekly chore of vacuuming, noticing that for once in his life he didn't mind it now that his lungs were working. He looked at the clock—only 3:45. Walking onto the soft carpet of his room, he wondered what he may need for the trip.

Glancing at his alarm clock, desk lamp, and computer still open to a screen of a 3D building he was rendering, it struck him that Ganthrea probably wouldn't have electrical outlets. *With magic, why would they?*

He opened his closet and looked at his hanging shirts. Since he didn't know what to expect, he emptied his backpack, then packed both thick and thin shirts, socks, underwear, and his metal canteen.

Shortly after four o'clock he heard footsteps below: his father was home. He continued packing some of the smaller essentials—his knife, compass, journal, pen—and deliberated if he needed matches, finally packing them in case he got separated from Windelm. He looked at his bookshelf, and got absorbed in guidebook on wilderness survival.

Light conversation came from downstairs. His mother, Miranda, must be home early. Brenner looked at the clock, and his stomach fluttered. It was ten to five. *What if Windelm didn't come? What if he changed his mind, or found someone else? Or...what if my parents say no?* He slung his backpack over a shoulder and went downstairs.

His mother was lounging on the sofa, watching TV as if nothing was different. His father had fixed himself a bacon and ketchup sandwich in the kitchen, lifting an eye to look out the front window between bites.

Albert turned as Brenner entered the kitchen, and asked suspiciously, "Well, what do you have planned next?"

Brenner wasn't sure how to reply. "You saw the letter. It said five. There's still a couple of minutes," he said, giving an imploring look out the window.

"Yeah, a whole two minutes," Albert said, his mouth half-full. He swallowed and took a sip of beer. "Boy, if I find out you've been pulling my leg, I—" but at that moment he was interrupted by the sound of a car engine purring up their driveway. Brenner bounded to the living room window.

A black sedan with tinted windows rolled to a stop; the passenger door clicked open. A tall man in a black suit exited, flattening his sleek blue tie with one hand, and clutching a leather briefcase in the other. He strode purposely toward their front step and pressed the doorbell.

Albert muttered something in disbelief.

Opening the door wide, Albert found himself face to face with a clean-shaven man with trimmed brown hair, removing his dark sunglasses.

Brenner heard a familiar voice from the entryway say, "Mr. Wahlridge?"

"Yes…" his father said suspiciously, the usually proud tone from his voice checked, "…that's me."

"Lieutenant Colonel Crestwood," the man said confidently, extending his hand, "pleased to meet you." Albert gave a limp shake.

Crestwood, seeing Brenner walk over from living room behind his father, said, "And this must be Brendon, yes?" A glimmer of light from the entryway chandelier caught his green-blue eyes as he smiled at Brenner.

"You should know who he is," Albert said, his distaste for government rising to the surface, "since he's been selected to this 'elite program' of yours."

"It's a pleasure," Crestwood said, ignoring Albert's comment and reaching out to shake Brenner's hand. Seeing Windelm's clean-shaven face, military-trimmed hair, and silver necklace, Brenner found it hard to believe this was the same man to whom he had spoken two days ago.

From the way Albert was warily eyeing Crestwood, it looked like he was being forced to choose between getting a finger removed or a lobotomy. After a tense moment standing on the threshold, Windelm asked Albert, "May I come in?"

"I suppose," said Albert grudgingly, and then he called to the far living-room, "Hey, Miranda! Turn the TV off and get in here. The…uh… corporeal is here."

"Lieutenant Colonel," Crestwood corrected him, stepping into the foyer.

"Right," Albert said, looking away.

"May we please speak in your dining room?" Crestwood continued, covering for Albert's lack of manners.

"Fine, take a seat in there," Albert motioned.

Crestwood went in, set his briefcase on the table, then sat with perfect posture, folding his hands together in front of him. Albert, Miranda, and Brenner pulled up chairs.

"Mr. and Mrs. Wahlridge," said Crestwood once they all were seated, "You should be thrilled that your son has been selected for our elite academy. We only take one or two recruits each year from around the country."

Albert and Miranda raised their eyebrows, seeming to find it strange that anyone had selected Brenner for anything at all. "Just *how* did you pick him?" ventured Miranda.

"Through a combination of aptitude and merit tests. Every other year, students across the country take standardized tests, and we see which students score high in multiple areas." While this cover story was interesting to Brenner, as soon as he had mentioned tests, Albert and Miranda's faces glazed over.

"This year Brendon scored brilliantly in many categories, from science to math to psychology and others."

"Have you seen him run?" Albert asked with a scoff.

"We have," said Crestwood, "And if necessary, that is something that can be improved. But because of his strong mental qualities, he has been selected to enroll at our academy for future CIA officers."

"And just where is that?" said Albert.

"I'm sorry but that's classified information. We need to take every precaution to protect new officers, one of our nation's most precious resources." Miranda and Albert looked at each other in astonishment: this man had just referred to Brenner as both brilliant and precious.

Albert cut to the chase. "How much is this elite academy going to cost us?" He crossed his arms.

"Brendon's room, board, and tuition will all be paid for by the U.S. government. You won't be billed a dime."

As if he had won the lottery, Albert's head perked up and his eyes widened. He tried to compose himself. "Where do we sign?" he asked, pleased as though he had just single-handedly negotiated the deal. Miranda, too, had a faraway look, as though a masseuse had melted her cares away on a tropical island.

"I'll get the papers," Crestwood said, reaching to his briefcase. "But just a couple more items to discuss," he said, placing a small stack in front of Brenner's parents, who were now nearly beside themselves to grab pens and sign him away before the deal was snatched from them. "Brendon will have access to top-secret information, and both he and you will not communicate for two years' time to protect the integrity of the program. After that, if he decides to come back, he may, or, he may choose a different name and begin his career with the CIA."

Albert and Miranda paused only slightly at this, and Brenner could see the gears in their heads whirring at full speed, probably planning cruises and wine-tastings abroad.

Crestwood continued, "We will also inform his high school that he has been enrolled at a new educational institution, and will no longer be taking classes there. You'll need to sign an agreement document for that as well. Brendon's complete care, his clothes, food, and welfare will all be provided for."

He slid the papers over to them. Clicking their pens, they started signing on every agreement line they could find. Finally, seeing no more places to scribble, they looked up. Crestwood was watching both them and Brenner.

With an eyebrow raised at them he broke the silence: "Aren't you going to ask Brendon if he wants to go?"

Albert blustered, "With an offer like this, why in the world wouldn't he?! Anyone can see how…how *important* it is to serve our country, and especially when they are going to provide for your *every* need"—again Brenner read between the lines, that Albert was really talking about having all of *their* needs met—"How about it, boy? Are you going to step up and do something with your life? I don't know why they picked you, but you better grab this opportunity!"

"You heard how it's free," said Miranda, "You might as well."

Brenner had already made his decision before his parent's half-hearted comments. It would be difficult, but it would be harder still to let both the amulet and Windelm be yanked away.

Brenner looked from his parents to Windelm. "Yes…" he said. "I'll go."

"That's the ticket!" his father said.

"Good choice," chimed in his mother.

Windelm smiled and nodded.

"So, when does he leave?" Miranda asked expectantly.

Windelm stood up and, as though talking about the evening's weather forecast, said, "Right now."

Brenner had half-expected this, once he saw how quickly the letter had come, and the date for their meeting. Even though Windelm did not rush through conversations, once a decision was reached, his actions were resolute. Brenner stood, left the table, and picked up his backpack. *It's really happening...*

His parents stood and followed Windelm and Brenner to the door. "Well, good luck then," his father said, glancing down at him, "and don't do anything stupid to get us in trouble."

"Yes, sir," Brenner said.

His mother's phone vibrated and she looked down at the message. "Have a good time, Brenner," she said absentmindedly, as if he was leaving for a sleepover at someone's house.

"I will," Brenner said. And then, despite his parents' absence from his pursuits for the majority of his childhood and adolescence, or maybe because of it, Brenner felt a tinge of sadness. "Well..." he said, "goodbye then."

With that, Brenner and Windelm walked over the threshold, then down the sidewalk to the black sedan that started its engine as they approached. Looking extremely pleased with the deal, his parents grinned at each other in the doorway, nodded once to Brenner, and shut the door after them.

Brenner climbed into the backseat, Windelm into the passenger's, and a chauffeur drove them away.

"Brenner," Windelm said, as they coasted through his neighborhood, "this is Terry." He motioned to their driver, a stocky, middle-aged man, also in a suit. "Terry, please take us to Culver Street and follow it until you reach Noble, about three miles north of here."

Terry nodded eagerly.

As the car drove on, Brenner watched his familiar haunts pass by, and then the woods. Yesterday, while walking through the woods after school, it started to sink in how he'd be gone for two years, maybe more. He had stopped at his tower, and decided to do something he'd never done before: he stuck one of his trapdoor keys under a piece of tape on the top step. Hopefully someone would discover it, and enjoy his tower while he was gone.

"Terry," said Windelm, "pull over by that blue collection mailbox."

The car slowed. Windelm opened the lid and deposited a sealed envelope with the words 'Clemson High School' on the front. The metal lid clanged shut. Then he turned back to Brenner and said, "That will notify your school that you're no longer enrolled due to an academic transfer." Brenner nodded; the last tie to his ordinary life was severed.

"Carry on, Terry," said Windelm.

Terry, who wore a beige colored shirt and an even duller expression, remained mute for the drive, like he was on auto-pilot. This was confirmed later when Brenner saw a fly land on Terry's ear, and rather than swat at it, he just kept looking straight ahead. As they were driving by another grove of pine and aspen, Windelm said, "Terry, this looks good. You may stop."

The car eased next to the trees and green shrubs. Windelm exited the car, and Brenner followed.

Windelm grabbed something from the trunk, and before shutting his door, pointed his walking stick at Terry. A thin blue streak of energy floated around Terry, then returned to Windelm. Windelm shut the door. Through the window, Terry looked dazed, as though waking from a nap.

"Come along," Windelm said to Brenner, turning on the spot, and ushering him along the path and into the woods.

"Windelm," Brenner asked when they were no longer within range of the road, "who was that man?"

"Terry Brocklehurst," he said, "a fine fellow who was kind enough to be my chauffeur for the afternoon."

"What was that blue stuff you directed at him?"

"A mental spell. I saw him leaving for work this morning and planted the idea in his mind that he really needed a new suit in my size, and that he had important work to do from home in the afternoon." Pinching the lapel of his black suit, Windelm added, "he did a fine job selecting this one."

"Wait, you controlled his mind?" Brenner asked.

"Of course," said Windelm nonchalantly. "Magic isn't just all bursts of fire and enabling books to fly, you know. I merely suppressed some of his other desires and implanted ones that involved being a chauffeur for me, keeping quiet unless spoken to, and doing what I instructed. And as I haven't the slightest idea how to drive one of your automobiles," he waved his hand in the air, "I needed a suitable escort."

Brenner felt a little guilty: because of him, Windelm manipulated an innocent person.

"Did it hurt him?"

"Heavens no. Don't worry, Brenner, I checked to see he wasn't a surgeon scheduled for operation, or a parent responsible for watching his kids for the day. He was a salesman for an insurance company, and his afternoon was hardly dashed. He'll just have to reschedule golf and drinks with managers for next week. With no recollection of the afternoon, his life will continue as normal."

Brenner breathed easier, then asked, "When did you have time for that haircut? You look more like a drill sergeant than a wizard."

"Oh right, that," he said, and bent his head forward while aiming his staff at it. The short, cropped hair immediately sprouted before his eyes like tendrils of kudzu vines, and his beard grew until the bristles were thick like the muzzle of a bear. Try as he might, Brenner could not help himself from gaping like an idiot each time Windelm performed another bit of magic. "Much better," said Windelm, "And I'm not yet a full-wizard, I'm a sorcerer, just one notch below the the highest spellcaster rank."

Brenner and Windelm walked briskly for another twenty minutes, then left the path and came to a rocky ledge. Windelm used his staff to levitate and move a coffin-sized boulder away from the others. Behind the rock was a small cavity, where Windelm had stashed his boots, pants, cloak, and tunic.

"If you don't mind," he said to Brenner, pointing his finger away and making a swirling motion.

Brenner turned and admired the forest while Windelm changed. The last rays of sun were striking down through the thick glen. He would miss the fresh air and peaceful atmosphere of the pine forest. *Would Ganthrea have such beauty?*

Windelm walked past Brenner in his cloak and started making a couple marks in the ground. Brenner turned to see Windelm's former suit, dress shoes, and garments scattered pell-mell by the rocks.

"You can't just leave them there."

"Leave what?"

"Your suit and stuff. It will look like some weirdo came out here, stripped down, and went on a rampage through the woods."

"So it may," Windelm replied nonplussed, continuing with his efforts to draw a few more symbols in the dirt.

Brenner crossed his arms. "I thought we were supposed to be inconspicuous?"

Windelm paused and sighed, "If you insist." He turned to the pile of dress clothes. Shooting a spell at it, he animated the suit to fling itself up from the ground, then grasses zoomed up and stuffed themselves inside shoes, pants, and shirt, and then crunched together into a well-dressed scarecrow before launching upwards and sticking itself onto a pine tree.

Windelm used another spell from his staff to inscribe a title on a rock standing knee high next to the tree: "Suit Yourself, on Pine #3."

He smiled at how absurd it looked, and then said to Brenner, "That should turn a few heads." A few minutes more of drawing symbols on the ground and he was finished. "You have your backpack and items you wish to take with you?"

Brenner patted his pockets and backpack, and his hand brushed against a folded photo he'd almost forgotten about. "Windelm," he said, pulling out the barn photograph he found a few days ago, "what can you tell me about this?"

Windelm leaned over, and holding it up, gave a soft smile. "That was the summer my father borrowed the neighbor's Kodak to take a few pictures of farm equipment to sell, and got one of us kids, too: Lester, Laura, and me. I was going off to the river, hoping to catch more smallmouth bass. Lester and Laura preferred staying around home. The last time I saw them was a couple years after that photo..." He gave it gently back to Brenner. "Thanks."

Brenner put it back in his pocket, and then checked his necklace to see the amulet. "I'm ready."

"Great," said Windelm. "Now, the next spell I cast is going to be unlike anything you've ever seen. In fact, you won't see it." He chuckled at himself. "What you'll hear is the sound of rushing rapids."

Brenner steeled himself, and turned to look at Windelm, "So this is it, huh?"

"Yes, and try not to worry about the pressure. It will be over sooner than you think. Now grab onto my hand, and whatever you do, don't let go."

Brenner took his hand, and Windelm scanned the perimeter once more. He said something under his breath, and suddenly the air in front of them split apart with a loud, low grind, as though two ships collided, scraping their metal hulls against each other. Their legs shook from the tremor of energy.

In front of them hovered something translucent, the size of a small window, blurring the trees behind it.

Involuntarily, Brenner squeezed Windelm's hand.

Windelm had to shout over the noise that engulfed them, "On my count, Brenner, we jump!"

Brenner's felt like he was standing on a wooden plank above an angry sea. The portal had something like a magnetic pull, tugging his sweatshirt and jeans forward.

"Steady now..." Windelm commanded over the noise, "three...two... one...*jump!*" he shouted, yanking Brenner's hand as they leapt headfirst into the abyss.

And then they were gone.

The roaring portal vanished, along with any earthly trace of Brenner Wahlridge.

Chapter Six

Ganthrea Unveiled

Moisture pooled in Brenner's eyes—they were flying at such dizzying speeds, spiraling through the portal toward a distant horizon. Breathing became difficult: Brenner's body felt squished, like he was diving leagues under the ocean.

They were traveling away from misty grays and pale greens, flying towards a convergence of rainbow colors, with a white bulb at the center of the horizon, growing and growing like the headlight on a locomotive chugging full throttle at them.

The pressure magnified against his bones—the light ahead grew to the size of a whale, its mouth open wide to swallow them, its whiteness nearly blinding—Brenner started to lose focus—the collision now seconds away, the white sphere rushing at them head on—

Then, like twin bullets breaking a pane of glass, Windelm and Brenner shot through the portal and onto the jungle floor. Unlike Windelm, who landed on his feet with the alacrity of a gymnast, Brenner belly-flopped with an "Oomph!" into a tangle of bushes.

Gingerly, he moved his arms; every muscle in his body felt bruised, as though he had just rolled a car into a ditch. After much effort, he sat up.

"We should be grateful," Windelm said, smiling. "At least our entrance portal wasn't smack in front of an Ironclad tree. Last time through that's *exactly* what happened to me. Took five spells to get my nose straightened out."

Brenner was wondering how Windelm stood so easily, and flinched as Windelm pointed the wooden staff at his chest.

"Wait a sec—" he started to protest, but before he could finish, a green bolt shot forward from the staff, wrapped around Brenner, and then returned to Windelm, taking his aches and pains with it. "That's incredible!" he said, eyeing Windelm's stick and rising to his feet. "I feel like I could run for miles."

"Well, that's good," Windelm said, glancing around the immense forest, "because that's what we're doing next."

No longer focused on his fatigue, Brenner took in the surroundings. "Windelm...where are we?"

"Thought you'd never ask," Windelm said with a smile. "Brenner, welcome to Ganthrea."

Like a child marveling at the magnitude of the sky for the first time, Brenner's mouth gaped open as if he could drink in the scenery. Huge, lush, mossy green trees shot up so high he couldn't see where they ended—making his Cottonwood in Colorado seem like a seedling. Faint tropical birdcalls whistled down from the canopy, and a breeze brought the fresh smell of citrus to his nostrils. Brenner took several steps on the soft forest floor toward the nearest tree. He placed his palm on the thick bark, noticing the strong smell of cinnamon. The trees' girth was astounding: each was as wide as his garage, and this one, even larger. If someone carved a tunnel through the thick layers of bark and heartwood and then out the other side, two semi-trucks could pass one another with ease.

"To be more specific," Windelm said, "we are in the middle region of Silvalo, the healing land of forests, one of the Seven Biomes of Ganthrea."

"You...live...here?" Brenner said, staring at the trees, and then at Windelm.

"I live in a place similar to this, yes, but closer to Silvalo's central city, Arborio." Seeming to sense Brenner's next question, Windelm added, "But I didn't want to draw attention to ourselves by shooting out from a portal in the middle of a packed marketplace. So, we trek on from here."

Brenner nodded, looking at the shimmering beds of vase-like plants around the jungle floor. Even if Windelm showed him nothing else in Ganthrea, he felt he could be content for a long time.

"Come," said Windelm, waving a hand in front of Brenner's eyes, "we have about two hours before sundown, and then we'll need to make camp for the night."

Windelm found something like a deer trail, and Brenner followed. As they walked, Brenner tried identifying the strange noises, what sounded like primates calling in baritones to each other high above, birds chirruping unusual melodies from all heights, and adapting to the colossal size of everything. Windelm pointed out some of the trees, some Brenner had heard of—acacias, rubber trees, mahogany—and also explained new ones: the largest, which smelled faintly of cinnamon, were called oakbrawns, others were ironclads, dragonbarks, and magnayans, which had multiple twisting trunks that braided together like thick ropes. Despite his age, Windelm moved with surprising agility—with one hand jumping over giant roots, the other gripping his staff.

"Windelm, that wooden staff of yours…is it some sort of wand?"

"This?" Windelm said, holding up the staff. "It's called a mirconduit, or mircon, for short. It's similar to what you probably think of as a wand, but only works when the spellcaster using it has elixir to draw upon." He pointed to Brenner's chest. "That's where your amulet comes into play. When you've mastered the physical enhancements of your amulet, you'll be trained to channel elixir into a mircon to form spells, which travel like a loop to your target and back. Learning how to handle a mircon without damaging yourself is one of the reasons why you'll want to attend Valoria."

"Valoria?"

"Yes. One of Ganthrea's premiere academies of magic."

Brenner had mixed feelings about that. Although he performed well in his classes at Clemson High School, he had failed miserably at making social connections. He could count on one hand the number of people that talked to him. *Would this academy be any better?* He pulled out the amulet from under his shirt, watching the elixir swirling crimson and green.

"Windelm…what is elixir?"

"Elixir is the liquid-like magic generated in the heart of every land. While it's usually concentrated underground, at rare intervals it swirls up in atmospheric storms, like aurora borealis."

"The Northern Lights?"

"Yes. The storms are brief, and the elixir quickly dissipates into the air or soaks down to a groundswell."

"So…this elixir in my amulet is why I was able to sprint, jump and breathe so well—its magic was coursing through my body!"

"Precisely," said Windelm, "And usually it takes people several weeks to adapt to the elixir. You developed an affinity for it fairly rapidly."

"Thanks," Brenner said, following Windelm and climbing over canoe-sized roots. He tried to guess just how old these ancient trees were…*easily a thousand, maybe two thousand years…* Looking up at the oakbrawn's tree limbs, some forty or fifty stories overhead, he had a sobering thought: *What if a branch snapped off? It'd be like a water tower breaking off its posts and plummeting hundreds of feet down, crushing anything or* anyone *unlucky enough to be there.* He shuddered and kept alert for any creaking sounds overhead. Windelm turned and saw him eyeing the treetops.

"Anything the matter?"

"No…just, how much do you think the branches above us weigh?"

"They're probably several thousand pounds per limb, but they're very sturdy. You can relax."

Brenner tried, but found that Windelm's suggestion gave him the opposite feeling.

They walked another hour through the forest until the light filtering through the leafy oakbrawns was getting dim.

"We can make camp here," Windelm said, motioning towards a section of mossy ground, sandwiched between two huge tree roots. Sitting himself against one of them, Windelm reached into his cloak and pulled out a tan satchel, about the size of a magazine. He loosened the leather cord cinching it shut, then reached his hand in…and kept reaching…past his elbow— "It's in here somewhere," he said, rummaging until, somehow, he was up to his shoulder.

"Here," said Windelm finally, pulling his arm up and out of the satchel, "have a few bites of these." He tossed Brenner a soft, doughy ball, and a stick of something dark.

Brenner caught them, noticing the rumbles coming from his stomach. He bit into the soft bread and smiled: it tasted like semi-sweet buttered rolls. "What's this?" he asked, holding up the stick of what looked like dark meat.

"That will be your biggest obstacle yet, Brenner," Windelm said, holding up his own piece and tearing off a hunk with his teeth. "It comes from an animal that has an insatiable appetite for living things," he said spookily, "and it uses its cunning to blend in with polka-dot birch trees."

Brenner looked cautiously from Windelm to the piece of meat. *Do I really want to eat this?*

Windelm waited another moment and then broke the silence. "And that magical creature is called… a cow! You've had it before, yes?"

Brenner shook his head and laughed under his breath, "Jerk."

"Jerk-*y*, Brenner, Jerk-*y*," Windelm corrected him, clearly amused with himself. "Plenty of our diet is similar to what you have had back on Earth," he said, chewing his last bite, "but the parts that are different are usually— in my humble opinion—far superior."

Glancing around the roots and tree, Windelm said, "Oh good!" and pointed up. Brenner saw a large cluster of silver and spaghetti-red mushrooms, each the size of a large plate, staggered up along the tree bark.

"Rombell mushrooms!" Windelm said with unmistakable delight, "My *favorite*. If you please, Brenner, we'll need two long sticks for these."

Brenner took to his feet and scoured the grounds. Walking across the forest floor, he saw giant logs and some prickly bushes, which contained a clump of red fruits that smelled alluring, like raspberries.

"Are these edible?" he asked Windelm.

Windelm looked over to him. "Ruberia somnums? They are, if you want to spend the next week in a coma."

"Hmm...I'll pass on that," he said, collecting a few sticks to bring back to their camp. Windelm had gathered some dry logs into a pile, and pointed his mircon at them. A small stream of light came from the staff, and the wood started to flicker, then smolder with flames.

"Those will do," he said, as Brenner handed him a stick, and Windelm traded him one of the big mushrooms. It had good heft, like a sirloin steak. Brenner imitated Windelm by spearing it through the middle and rotating the mushroom over the flames, which eagerly licked at it.

Windelm's mushroom soon was golden red, and he took a bite of the crispy edge. "Mmmm," he said, smacking his lips, "nothing beats a plump Rombell mushroom."

Brenner pulled his mushroom back from the fire, blew on it and took a bite. He found himself agreeing with Windelm when a rich umami flavor met his tongue.

"Windelm," said Brenner, "About that portal you took me through. Do they happen often?"

"No, the natural-forming flare portals are rare. I haven't seen a flare portal since the first time I came to Ganthrea."

"Did you come with someone else?"

"That was a solo accident. When I came to Ganthrea, I was disoriented and unprepared for magic—especially the creatures. If a basilisk, wurm, or dragon had found me first..." Windelm looked into the fire. "I wouldn't be with you now."

"How did you know where to go?"

"I didn't. A group of spellcasters on their way to Arborio noticed me on their path: waving my arms, speaking to them in what they thought was complete gibberish."

He took another bite of mushroom before continuing, "One of the full-magicians on the trip, DeFarras, took pity on me as their caravan went by. Through him I learned the Silvalo customs, and after many foggy months, the language, and after training and practice at Valoria, the spells. Which reminds me."

With a flick of his wrist, he pointed his mircon at Brenner, then closed his eyes, and channeled a white, vaporous spell at his face.

Brenner felt his forehead tingle with cool then warm sensations, as a flow of words and images came to him. Like a gentle stream, a language washed over him, meshing with his memories and thoughts like molecules bonding together. Then the warm sensation stopped; Brenner's pupils dilated and shrank. His mind swam with activity, and he looked up at Windelm with wonder.

"You just…taught me a new language."

"Indeed. I thought I'd catch you up to speed—it certainly beats the months of hard study which I had to do. I've found that the language here, Gentril, is quite descriptive. Since I've already assimilated it, and know the structure of English, I can pass the knowledge to you."

"Thanks," Brenner said, playing with the word associations in his head, his lips and tongue forming the new phonemes. "Can everything be learned that fast?"

"Spells can transfer simple logic and linguistic patterns between minds quite easily. It's only the harder stuff—physical dexterity, muscle memory, or magic usage—that I can't imprint directly into you."

The two finished eating their roasted mushrooms, and then Windelm reached his whole arm into his satchel and pulled out a blanket.

"Here," he said, tossing it to Brenner, "The nights get cool."

"Thank you," Brenner said, pulling his backpack off and padding it into a pillow. He laid back on it and looked up to the dark canopy above, from which came rustling sounds and ruffling feathers of nocturnal creatures. "Windelm," he said with a yawn, "do you have family here?"

There was a long pause from the other side of the root alcove. "Yes, I have a wife. Her name is Sherry; she's beautiful and caring—the love of my life. You'll meet her when we reach home."

"Any kids?"

Windelm took a deep breath. "I…had a son…" he paused, and when he spoke again his voice had lost its warmth, "…but he has passed on."

Brenner said gently, "I'm sorry, Windelm."

A gulf of silence hung between them as if a canyon had opened up.

Finally, Windelm spoke again. "It's in the past and can't be changed. Tell me, do you like games, Brenner?"

He brightened. "I've always loved strategy games, yes."

"And athletic ones?"

Brenner thought back to that golden day of football.

"Now that I can run…yes."

"Good. Over thousands of years, Silvalo—and all of Ganthrea—has developed and played games that test spellcasters' wit, speed, and cunning."

Brenner propped himself on his elbow to listen.

"There are individual and team games. At Valoria, they'll have you start with the game of Agilis, which tests your daring against obstacles and other players. Later, you may get the opportunity to play Zabrani, which is on a changing field with teams of twenty-one players, each vying for land control, glowbes, and attacks on the other king. After you've shown expertise with that, and control with your mircon, you will be allowed to duel others in the martial art of magic: Contendir."

Brenner tried picturing the games…Agilis sounded like an obstacle course…Zabrani sounded like paintball mixed with chess, and Contendir sounded like Kung-Fu…"Why do they play them?"

"Several reasons: games are the real application of magic learned, games test spellcasters' daring and inventiveness, games determine who is promoted within Valoria, and who gets the best offers after Valoria. Reputations are won or lost. And of course, they're some of the most fun you'll have."

"Have you played all these games?"

"Many times."

"Which was your favorite?"

Windelm smiled and looked up past the fire. Brenner caught a glimpse of a few twinkling stars past the dark treetops.

"They are all engaging…but I excelled at Zabrani. I liked forming landscapes that kept our treasures defended and positioning my squads to make gains into our opponent's territory.

"Anyway, we should get some sleep. Your mind and body need a rest before the remainder of the journey. At daybreak we'll continue to my home." He pulled his cloak over himself and leaned back against the tree. "Sleep well, Brenner."

Brenner turned over to his side, still trying to make sense of all the new things: the forest, food, magic, language, and games, but above all, he was most grateful for his new companion, who, though he had only known him for three days, already seemed more familiar…and more caring, than the parents he'd always wished he'd had…

"Goodnight, Windelm."

Chapter Seven

Silvalo Flight

Brenner was jolted awake only once during the night.

Crack!

What sounded like steel-toed boots kicking a windshield echoed around him. When he looked up, cold terror flooded his veins: eyes like burning candles stared down at him from the root above, then the creature—something like a black panther—bared its fangs and snapped its paw down at Brenner. He covered his face.

Crack!

It should have struck him, but for some reason, didn't.

"Windelm!" Brenner shouted, scrambling over to him. "Wake up!"

He grabbed Windelm by the shoulder, just as the giant tiger scraped over to the other side of the root and swiped at him again—

Whack!

Thankfully—it missed again. Instead of leaping into action, Windelm merely looked up and said, "Don't worry, it will hold. The Nightshade should tire soon."

"What?!" said Brenner. "What will hold?"

"The Aura," Windelm said calmly, pointing up.

55

Double *thuds* rang out around them. Brenner's heart was pounding…but Windelm was right. The giant black tiger swiped a few more times, but each time was blocked by an invisible wall. It leapt away and padded off, growling behind the oakbrawns.

"How did you…?" Brenner began.

"The Aura? It's protective magic…acts like a cocoon," said Windelm. "Conjured it before we went to sleep. As long as we don't get a barrel-wurm or a dragon crushing down on it, we'll be fine. You can go back to sleep now." Windelm rolled over and, within a minute, was snoring.

Brenner tried…but it was another hour before he could fall back asleep.

A hand gently tugged on Brenner's shoulder. He stirred, blinking his eyes to the warm sunlight filtering through the canopy.

"Didn't much care for that Nightshade, did you?" Windelm said, holding something out to Brenner.

"That was— No, not at all…"

"They're actually quite beautiful—when they're not trying to eat you, of course. Not to worry, they're nocturnal. Mostly. Here, try some of this." He handed Brenner a soft, red fruit the size of a pear. Brenner bit into it, and a sweet taste like pomegranate filled his mouth. In a moment, he devoured the pulpy fruit, and Windelm tossed him another.

"Not bad, huh? It's a tangy red-nectar, a treat of the Silvalo forests."

"I'll say," Brenner said, nodding his approval.

"We should get going. I'd like to get to the cottage by lunch."

They trekked on through the deep jungles, Windelm leading, and Brenner kept watch for any sudden movements in the treetops. After a while the colossal trees thinned, and Brenner could hear the sound of water rushing through a gorge. They climbed past ferns, and emerged on a rock outcropping overlooking a great river shimmering blue with froths of white. Windelm turned to Brenner.

"How are you feeling?" he said, resting on his staff.

"As good as ever," said Brenner, unscrewing the lid from his canteen, and taking a swig.

"Excellent. In that case I propose that from here, we fly."

Brenner gave him a dubious look and said, "So, I just spread my arms like this?" He fanned them out and stood at the edge of the rock.

"If your brain has been replaced with one from a bird, yes. But for someone traveling with a sorcerer, that's not necessary."

"Oh?" Brenner said quizzically.

"Now," said Windelm, "you will feel an odd sensation as the magic surges around both of us, but by now, you should be used to that."

Brenner looked over the edge and felt a mixture of fear and excitement swell within. Windelm continued, "Above all else, *do not let go*, because I only have enough elixir to fly as a whole unit, and not to gravitate both you and I separately. I would hate to have your final lesson in Ganthrea be one of unassisted falling."

"That makes two of us," Brenner said, trying to shake the nervous tension in his body by kicking a few loose pebbles over the edge, and watching as they plunked down the canyon. "Just one question."

"Yes?"

Brenner turned back and grinned, "Why didn't we do this yesterday?"

Windelm gave a loud laugh. "You certainly *are* my great-nephew. Well, I did have some reasons: first, your body had to acclimate from the portal crossing to Ganthrea; second, you needed to experience how the ecosystem of Silvalo lives and breathes; and most importantly, in the half-light of the evening, it's quite easy to fly headfirst into the gossamer web of a giant Demon-Spider. Am I correct in guessing you don't like to be smothered in webs and eaten alive?"

"Yeah," Brenner said nodding, scrunching his face at the thought of a man-eating spider, "that's a safe assumption."

"Do you have your amulet?"

"Of course," said Brenner, pulling it from underneath his shirt.

"Good. Keep it close always. Others would snatch it in a heartbeat if they could."

Brenner looked again at the swirling reds and green inside the amulet, then slipped it under his shirt and tightened the straps to his backpack. "I'm ready," he said.

Windelm looked east; the sun was now a couple of hands high over the green horizon. He turned right and slightly southward. With strong fingers, Windelm took hold of Brenner's hand, and then the spell surged into him—warmth racing up his arm, into his chest, then splitting into every artery and permeating his whole body like liquid-pleasure.

Brenner looked at his feet, which were no longer on the ground, and let out a shout, "I'm flying!"

Windelm smiled. "Hovering, really," he said, and then with a hint of showmanship added, "*This* is flying."

Windelm tilted his chin up, and immediately their floating bodies careened off the rock ledge and hurtled forward through the air. Like swallows, they dipped and banked and soared above the blue waterway. Below, he could see rapids swirling and frothing. Then, in a pool off the main channel ahead, he saw a herd of deer bending down to drink by floating logs.

As they flew overhead, Brenner did a double-take when one of the logs lunged forward with a splash, clamping onto a deer, and dragging it underwater. Beneath the surface sunk the tail of an alligator.

Windelm increased their speed. The trees and river and rocks began whipping by below. Then he realized Windelm was shouting at him.

"I should have asked earlier! But do you—" a gust of wind from ahead hit them.

"What?!"

"DO YOU," Windelm hollered, "Have a HEART condition?!"

Brenner furrowed his brow. "NO!" he shouted back. "WHY?!"

The pattern of river, rocks and trees that had repeated beneath them suddenly ended mid-air. With his stomach lurching and trying to eject itself from his body, Brenner realized why.

Windelm flew them lower to the waters' edge as the roaring headwall of a giant waterfall approached. Then they were soaring over the edge of a terrifying wall of water, the white-blue cascade falling probably a thousand feet into distant mists below them, as Brenner's heart also attempted to escape up his throat.

"The Pearlescent Waterfalls!" Windelm called over the airflow.

Safely beyond the edge, Brenner looked back and marveled: there was not one, but three waterfalls carrying their shimmering currents down to the lake below. Windelm had taken them over the tallest waterfall, like the top level of a podium, with the other two falls flanking it.

He looked forward, and Windelm guided them higher, up above the tall crowns of oakbrawns that stood like dignified skyscrapers. Brenner estimated they must be at least two thousand feet above the ground—the only benefit to a drop from here would be a *quick* death, which would be a shame because, at that moment, he was feeling very much alive.

Brenner looked to his right past Windelm, and saw the dark green splotches of trees continuing to the horizon, with copper red mountains edging above the curvature of the land. He looked left, and saw lime-green groves stretching into a distant band of orange sand. Windelm now accelerated such that the treetops below blurred together. Their feet floated behind them as they flew parallel to the clouds above. Gushing air currents blew into their faces, making Brenner wish he had packed one other item: goggles.

Several hours later, the trees seemed to grow more massive and interwoven into hundreds of monstrous buildings of the city on the distant horizon.

Windelm pointed, "Arborio."

They flew above a scarlet flock of birds, beneath which Brenner could see a few curving roads, like little brown veins crisscrossing through green toward the heart of the region: a large city to the east. Windelm steered them further south.

"Aren't we missing the city?" Brenner called.

"We're not headed to Arborio…not just yet. We're going to Vale Adorna."

Windelm zeroed in on a dirt trail below, flying lower until they went beneath the canopy line on either side, and then, as gracefully as a swan touching down on water, he landed them on the path.

Windelm released his hand, and Brenner sensed the flight spell trickle from his body.

"How do you feel?" Windelm asked.

"Like my legs are bloated," he replied, steadying himself against a tree. "Give me a sec."

Windelm turned his head to the side as a breeze swept toward them, then announced, "No time. Follow me, and keep quiet."

He moved off the path behind some trees. A group of military men with matching dark tunics and bright green capes came flying round a bend in the distance, hovering ten feet over the path. Only when they were out of sight did Windelm speak again. "You never know which convoy of spellcasters might be flying through. That one, thankfully, was part of the Silvalo Guard. Overall a useful regiment, provided leadership has the right motives. Strange, they're not usually in our village."

Brenner stared after them as they disappeared behind a bend.

"We'll be at Vale Adorna momentarily—" he looked over at Brenner and chuckled. "And you will stand out like a black sheep."

"What's wrong with me?"

"Hold still," said Windelm, pointing his mircon at Brenner.

A faint light streamed into his blue jeans, turning them midnight black and velvety, then the zipper and teeth on his gray sweatshirt fell off, at the same its hem grew longer and the material morphed to a soft, flax texture. His tennis shoes lost their neon colors and became brown as beaver fur.

"That's better," said Windelm. "We have a twenty-minute walk before us, or a two-minute flight. Which do you prefer?"

"Definitely the flight."

"Some people get sick after their first prolonged flight. I'm glad to see that you don't." He extended his hand to Brenner. Magic tingled through him, and again they were levitating and then flying forward, following a rutted path that wove through the trees. After a couple stretches and crescent turns, Brenner saw a central avenue with dressed-stone shops lining each side, not unlike pictures he'd seen in history class of Medieval towns, in front of which strolled men in tunics and women in long, colorful robes.

They flew away from the shops, and Brenner saw children playing next to a large, sparkling fountain, and others running up and down wooden ramps that coiled up and around trees, with bridges linking platforms. The maze-like, wooden structure overlooked parents and grandparents chatting on benches below.

Windelm glided them past the youthful fountain and park, along a street dotted with rustic cottages of wood and stone. A moment later, after branching off the main road and down to a less-worn, dirt track, their feet touched down, and Windelm let go of Brenner's hand. They stood in front of a large elm tree, around which an entrance path meandered through rows of cheerful yellow and robin-egg blue flowers, up to a handsome, two-story house.

Windelm gestured up the path, saying, "Brenner, welcome to Crestwood Cottage."

Chapter Eight

Crestwood Cottage and Agilis

"Sherry," Windelm called, his bright voice bouncing around the many rooms of the house. "I'm home, and with a new friend."

Stepping past the front entry, Brenner saw wood carvings of animals on either side of the door, and a finely crafted handrail that led to the second floor.

A woman emerged from the next room, beaming. She wore a comfortable green dress, had dark mahogany hair that flowed past her shoulders, a slender nose, and a sunny smile on her face. Like Windelm, she looked to be in her forties.

"Hi, dear," she said affectionately, hugging Windelm. "Glad to have you back." Then she turned to face Brenner, asking Windelm warmly, "And who is this young man?"

"This is my great-nephew, Brenner Wahlridge," Windelm said, "and I'm proud to say he has inherited the better parts of my family's dispositions. Already I've seen him outrun a wild bear, and—"

"A wild what?" Sherry asked, her head cocked to the side.

"A bea—Oh right. It's...a smaller version of our Golden Ursa."

A look of admiration came to her eyes, and she nodded. "*Very* good. And how did he do with flight?"

"More than three hours of it, with little ill-effects."

"Excellent. Oh, you will like it here, Brenner," she said, her brown eyes twinkling at him. "Welcome to our home, and welcome to the family."

"Oh…uh, thanks," he said, blushing, and looking at the floor. Realizing he should say something more he added, "It's nice…very nice, to be here."

"You'll stay with us for several days," said Windelm, putting a hand on Brenner's shoulder, "and learn the Silvalo culture. Then you'll travel to hone your spell skills with the sages at Valoria, after you've passed their entrance examination, which I don't see you having any trouble with."

"Let him relax a moment, dear," said Sherry, and then to Brenner, "come in the kitchen and have some spiced tea. I'm sure you're quite ready for some real food after eating rations in the woods."

They followed her into a sunny kitchen with smooth wood floors and large windows overlooking an expanse of gardens and trees. Actually, Brenner had enjoyed eating the rolls, jerky, mushrooms and fruit in the woods very much, so was wondering what she would have to top it, but didn't have to wait long before a steaming plate of food was put in front of him, and he was biting into the best steak sandwich he'd ever eaten, along with roasted green and orange vegetables, and sipping from a mug of sweet apple tea.

"I've never met someone named Brenner before," Sherry said, sitting next to him, and handing a plateful of food to Windelm.

Sherry then took a kerchief off a basket, reached in, and offered him a piping hot muffin, which he accepted. "Brenner—it has a nice ring to it. Your parents must have given much thought to naming you."

"Actually, I sorta made it myself," Brenner said, biting into the sugary muffin, and breathing in the warm steam that enveloped his face.

"Hmm," said Sherry, taking a sip of tea, "People don't usually rename themselves in Silvalo, Windelm here being one of the exceptions. If they do, it isn't until they have mastered several stages of using their mircon."

She turned to Windelm and glanced at his carved staff resting against his chair. "You didn't allow him to use yours already, did you?" She shot Windelm a stern look.

"I'm not *that* careless, honey," Windelm said pausing from his sandwich.

"Good," said Sherry, and to Brenner added, "Spellcasters new to mircons have been known to discharge all their stores of elixir at once, with explosive results."

Seeing Brenner's worried expression, Sherry said, "Right. So, wait until you get some instruction. What else would you like to know about here? About us?"

"So, you're not from Earth then?" he asked.

"Correct," said Sherry. "My family has been living in Silvalo and in Ganthrea for countless generations, and I've lived in Vale Adorna here with Windelm after we graduated from Valoria."

Windelm spoke up, "Brenner, outside of this house, please do not mention Earth. If people ask you where you come from, tell them you grew up in the farming community of Cormith."

Brenner felt his face turn hot. "Oh, right. I'm sorry," he said.

"It's alright," said Windelm, "I trust my wife, but there's probably not another soul in Silvalo, and maybe a few in all of Ganthrea, who know about Earth. Let's keep it that way."

"Got it." Brenner said. He looked from Windelm to Sherry. "Since Windelm is my great-uncle," he said, doing some math in his head, "that means he's at least seventy years old. How old are you?"

Sherry laughed, "I suppose I did say ask *anything…*" she looked at Windelm and continued, "Windelm is seventy-two and a half years old—and looking handsome as ever—but I am far younger…"

"That's right," said Windelm, "a youthful seventy-one."

They chuckled. Brenner was trying to reconcile that with the fact that they both had hardly any wrinkles, and looked like they wouldn't get a second glance at a dinner party with his parents.

He thought of the shops he saw on the main boulevard: there had been a café, and what may have been a bank…

"So, with all of your magic, do you have to work at all?"

Sherry smiled. "Yes, both Windelm and I work. I work in botany, making potions, and discovering uses for magical plants, herbs, and occasionally, critters.

"Windelm works in the Council of the Sovereign as the steward sorcerer. His team is responsible for charting territory, deciding how spellcasters may use the land, and designating areas for growth and cultivation."

"You're welcome to tour the Ironclad Assembly in Arborio," said Windelm. "It's where the government of Silvalo meets."

Brenner had finished his meal and was sipping more of the spiced tea, when a flash of movement outside caught his attention. Something like a red fox was climbing a large tree in the backyard, stopping to gather nuts from the branches. A moment later, Brenner noticed something else on the tree come to life: a yellow and brown serpent began slinking diagonally upward. His chair scuffed against the floor as he stood up to have a better look.

"What's that on your tree?" Brenner asked.

Windelm put down his sandwich and turned, but by then the snake had disappeared. "Ah, the striped coati—foraging for nuts, no doubt. Friendly little buggers, even if they cause trouble in the fall when they make nests on the house." Smiling, he added, "There's a lot more back there than just trees and critters. You should try the community Mindscape."

"Windelm," said Sherry, "He just got here."

"It's the best part of our Vale!" Windelm said good-naturedly, "And he should get a feel for one before the entrance examination at Valoria. Some folks say they're actually *trying* to kill newcomers these days. Brenner, would you like a tour of our acreage?"

"That'd be great," he said, but was a little startled by Windelm's comment. *Why would the school want to kill newcomers?*

They stepped outside onto a soft stretch of grass and began walking on a wood-chipped path. Then he saw the yellow serpent again. "What is that?

Not the coati—that snake going 'round the tree?"

Windelm let out a low grunt as he spotted the neon yellow head of a snake wrapping around the tree, edging closer to the coati, which was nibbling a nut, its back turned to the serpent. "Poison-coat python," muttered Windelm. "Beastly thing."

He disappeared back to the kitchen, then reappeared in the doorway, mircon in hand. Windelm aimed it at the tree and said, *"Parsplodo!"*

A bolt of red energy shot from the wooden staff, flying hundreds of feet across the yard, and blasting a cannonball-sized chunk off the tree just below the open jaws of the snake.

"Fewmets!" Windelm cursed. "Missed it."

At the sound of the mini-explosion, the red coati rushed madly across the limb, leapt to the next tree, and scampered out of sight. The python hissed at them and coiled around the backside.

"Usually I let nature take its course," said Windelm, lowering his mircon, "but those devil Poison-coats are just as dangerous to humans as they are to animals."

"Do they have venom?" Brenner asked.

"Yes, but not in their mouths," said Sherry, "their skin is coated with a slick, toxic substance. When it gets on its victim's skin it stings and paralyzes the muscle beneath. As soon as the python strikes—or lands on its victim, which it prefers—it goes for the chest and neck. If it can get a solid coil around you there, you'll be dead in about a minute."

As Brenner had always had a healthy dislike of snakes, he was getting second thoughts about touring the acreage.

"Most of the Poison-coat pythons are deep in the jungles," said Windelm. "Whenever the citizens of Vale Adorna see them, they blast them on the spot. So, the snakes usually keep their distance."

Brenner stayed close to Windelm and Sherry as they walked through the jungle for half an hour, the dense forest gradually thinning to reveal parts of jagged columns, ancient statues, and strange stone formations. There must have been people playing on the course ahead, because he saw flickers of movement and heard shouts.

"Right this way, Brenner," Sherry said, ushering him under a stone archway that read, 'The Mindscape of Vale Adorna.'

"You're in for a treat," said Windelm, leading them over to a tall spiral staircase, and motioning them to follow him up. "Playing Agilis on a Mindscape takes a tad more effort than whacking a ball and riding after it in a cart. Today you're gonna see, in my humble opinion, one of the finest Agilis performances."

When Windelm wasn't looking, Sherry whispered to Brenner, "Try to restrain yourself. Any compliments and Windelm's head will swell up and float off his shoulders." She gave him a wink.

They reached the top of the staircase, which opened to a long wooden platform some forty feet high, and stretching out before them was a huge greenway filled with giant sculptures of magical beasts, a steep pyramid, marble archways that soared a hundred feet high—some even looping—clusters of columns forming the frame of a skyscraper, a waterfall that fed into a blue lake, and a brook winding into the deep woods beyond. Here and there players were sprinting up and around the obstacles, trying to grab onto brightly colored, floating balls.

On the platform were numerous wooden trunks, and Windelm reached down to one, tapped it with his staff, and its lid popped open. Seven gleaming white orbs, each about the size of a baseball, floated out of the trunk and towards Windelm.

"Glowbes," said Windelm, in response to Brenner's puzzled expression. "The goal of Agilis is simple: capture as many of these as you can, as quickly as you can."

He pointed his mircon at something else in the trunk, and out hovered an hourglass.

"I usually set it to five minutes," Windelm said, changing the dials on the front. Half the crystals inside the hourglass dissolved. The glowbes began bumping into each other midair, as if impatient to get the game started.

Windelm turned his attention to them and said, "Agilis, moderate intensity." Obediently, like a charm of finches released from their cage, the cluster of orbs flew in loops across the field, until finding nesting spots in high places. They alighted near the peaks of the structures, at the top of the marble loops, on some tall oakbrawns, and over a giant sphinx. One even hovered over the middle of the lake. Then white beams of light radiated from the glowbes.

"Sherry, please hold this," Windelm said, handing her his mircon and then turning the hourglass upside down. "Brenner, enjoy the show."

With that, he leaped off the wooden platform to the ground, racing towards the first obstacle with a speed Brenner wouldn't have guessed someone in their seventies capable of.

He came to the columns stacked into a pyramid frame, where, five stories up, an orb shimmered like a tiny star. Brenner leaned forward against the deck railing, curious to see how Windelm would manage to scale it. There were no stairs, and the stone columns seemed too wide to wrap one's arms around. Windelm sped ahead anyway, and launched himself at a column. As he soared toward it, he extended his feet forward. His soles landed against it with a soft *thump*; then he pushed off and vaulted up at an angle to another column, landing and rebounding up like a jumping spider until he reached the first horizontal level of planks, where he grabbed one and hoisted his legs up and over it. He jumped and performed the nimble routine up four more levels until he reached the top columns, where four planks made a square with a hole in the middle.

Above him hovered the glowbe, glimmering like the top of a lighthouse. Windelm looked up, then jumped from one side over the middle, snatched the orb, and landed deftly on the narrow scaffolding, rocking slightly as he held his balance. The orb turned green, and Windelm tossed it aside. Immediately it flew back to the trunk by Brenner and Sherry's feet, wriggling into place like a family dog returning to its favorite cushion.

Then, less like a man and more like a graceful orangutan, Windelm swung down from platform to platform, until he was close enough to drop to the ground. He made a mad dash for the lake, where another orb hovered above the water's midpoint. As he approached the bank, Brenner waited for Windelm to dive into the water, but the splash never came. Instead, Brenner watched with mouth open as Windelm's legs became a blur. He raced from the bank *onto* the water and then, *across* the pond, like some sort of water-lizard. In a second he was at the middle, his arm outstretched and grabbing the orb, his feet kicking ripples across the water as he finished his sprint and leapt to the other bank of the lake.

Aside from water on his ankles and up the backs of his legs, Windelm was completely dry.

Brenner shook his head.

Windelm tossed the now green orb into the air, and it floated dutifully back to the trunk as the first had done.

Windelm used the same fierce running technique to dash up the twisting, corkscrew archways and grab another orb upside down at the peak, then he ran back to Sherry and Brenner.

"A little wetter than usual, dear," Sherry said, rubbing a hand across Windelm's shoulders. "But not bad."

"Thank you," Windelm said, chest panting as he turned his gaze to Brenner. He picked up the hourglass, where crystals were still streaming down. "Alright then, Brenner, would you like to grab a glowbe in Agilis?"

Brenner's heart beat a little faster, both thrilled and nervous at the opportunity. "I'd love to try."

"Dear," Sherry said sternly, her brown eyes fixing on her husband, "do you think it's wise to have him run the course the first day he gets to our Vale? After a full morning's flight?" Her crossed arms told Brenner she clearly thought otherwise.

"Oh, he'll be fine," Windelm said, waving her suggestion aside. Reaching for his mircon, he tapped the trunk. Immediately, the captured glowbes flew across the field, hovering above different obstacles.

Before Sherry could interject with more sensibility, Brenner bounded off the platform and ran to the column pyramid.

"See, he wants to give it a go!" Windelm said.

When Brenner reached the base of the columns at full speed, he tried to rebound from one to the other as Windelm had done, but they were further apart than he realized. His arms wind-milled as he collided with the base of a column and slid dejectedly down it.

He tried wrapping his arms around it and climbing, but just as quickly was slipping down the smooth column.

Okay…how about…the lake? He raced towards it with what he thought was break-neck speed, but when the tips of his shoes touched the clear surface as Windelm's had, they plunged through, creating a terrific splash that frightened a nearby flock of ducks into flight.

Coughing and spluttering lake water, Brenner grabbed for the plant roots on the side of the bank, pulling himself out onto the grass. He gave another glance at the orb in the middle of the pond, considering if he should swim for it, but since it floated six or seven feet above the surface, he knew he couldn't jump high enough from the water to snatch it.

Sopping wet, he looked around the field for easier glowbes. Ahead, there was a large marble sphinx statue some forty feet high, with the body of a lion, the wings of an eagle, and the face of a woman. A white orb glowed above its head, giving it a sort of angelic presence.

Pushing his wet hair back, Brenner walked toward it, planning his climbing route. When he was at the front of the statue, at the base of its front paws, he jumped for the top of a foot to hoist himself up, but was backhanded twenty feet by the stone paw. Thoroughly discombobulated, Brenner slowly rose to his feet, looking at the sphinx.

It was still. But, it seemed to be watching him.

So, the front paws are off-limits. He gave the sphinx a wide berth and circled behind it. Then he ran towards the statue and leapt onto the stone tail.

He was lucky to have gotten strong handholds on the tail, because it suddenly whipped to life, thrashing back and forth like an angry fire-hose. It was all he could do to hang on. By sheer determination, Brenner shimmied foot by foot up the tail towards the back of the creature, the whiplash becoming less severe the higher he climbed.

Finally, he hoisted himself onto the sphinx's back and stepped along the spine and had half a second to duck before the massive wings swept across the creature's back, hoping to catch him like a ship's boom swinging across the deck. He crawled along the remainder of the stone back, as great air gusts from the wings blew at him. The sphinx had strands of long, chiseled hair dangling down, and Brenner used the cracks between them as grips to scale the final wall.

The sphinx, in a last effort to buck him off, violently shook its head back and forth and up and down, but Brenner clung harder with each new handhold. As soon as he reached the crown of the sphinx's head, he jumped upward as high as he could, and felt his fingers wrap around the warm sensation of the glowbe.

He landed off-kilter, skittering to the edge of the sphinx's head—"*No!*" he cried out—barely stopping a few inches from a sheer, four-story drop. If it had given just one more buck, he was sure the resulting fall would have cost him the use of his legs.

Surprisingly, the sphinx had gone stone still, as though it was a begrudging stallion finally broken-in. The glowbe in his hand turned to an emerald green, and as he uncurled his fingers, it flew merrily back to Windelm and Sherry, who were applauding and shouting from the platform.

"Yes!" cheered Windelm, his voice magnified across the field, "That's the spirit!"

"Good show, Brenner!" Sherry echoed.

Sweaty, bruised, and chest heaving, Brenner nonetheless felt a surge of triumph rush down his spine and a smile grow across his face. He slid down the hair of the sphinx and began walking across its flattened back, when its wing abruptly rose up to strike—then stretched itself to the ground, offering him feather-chiseled, stone steps to descend. Tentatively, he walked down, and after jumping the last step to the ground, the wing gracefully swept back into place above the sphinx's back. Brenner could have sworn there was the slightest wisp of a smile on its face.

He jogged back to Windelm and Sherry, who were still grinning at him.

"Great start, Brenner," said Windelm, clapping him on the back. "Your perseverance paid off."

Brenner wasn't sure if it was perseverance or just thick-headedness that had kept him trying to scale the sphinx.

"You sure…made it…look easy," Brenner said, breathing hard.

"Well, I've had *years* of practice, my boy!"

"Brenner," Sherry said, a look of concern on her face. "Are you hurt?"

He glanced at his bruised arms and felt a dull ache in his lower back. "A little, but I think I'm alright," he said.

"Are you sure? Let me perform a mending spell," Sherry said firmly.

"Okay then…"

She pointed her mircon at him and a green jet gushed forth; he felt cocooned in a warm, pleasant glow. The stiffness left his joints; his muscles relaxed. It felt as though he'd just soaked in a hot bath. "Thank you, Sherry."

"It's the least I could do," she said, "seeing as how Windelm hardly lets you rest before throwing you into more danger." She cast a reproachful look at her husband.

"Come now," Windelm rebuffed her, "he threw *himself* into the Agilis challenge. He could have said, 'No thanks,' and we would have understood."

"Mm-hm," Sherry said, unconvinced.

"He could've," Windelm insisted, "but then he wouldn't really be related to me, would he?"

"Quit it, you," Sherry said, swatting him on the chest. "Let's help Brenner settle in."

Windelm summoned the rest of the glowbes back to the trunk, and then they headed back to the cottage.

A few hours later, after the three finished a scrumptious dinner and were sitting on sofas and armchairs in the living room, Windelm asked, "Would you like to tour Market Boulevard tomorrow?"

A tour sounded a lot less exhausting than today's flight and Mindscape running, so the choice was easy. "Yeah," said Brenner. "That sounds like a good change of pace." He had another thought: for so long, he'd been used to doing his own solo-activities…but it was kind of…nice…to have adults who wanted to include him. "Count me in."

"Very good," Sherry said. "You can tour the village with Windelm, get some supplies, and see some of Vale Adorna's historic places. Unfortunately, I'm needed at the shop tomorrow morning, new shipment coming in. But you're more than welcome to visit."

"Market's a bit busy on the weekend," Windelm said. "Still, you'll enjoy it." He looked at Sherry. "I've heard that Lincomb & Leavitz recently got their hands on some new carrier carpets. How's yours been holding up?"

Brenner listened as his head drooped to his shoulder.

"It's a bit frayed around the edges, but as long as the cargo is not too big, it will suffice."

Brenner sunk further into his cozy armchair. The combined effects of a full stomach and a whirlwind day were starting to overpower his consciousness. It was hard to keep focus…bits and pieces of their conversation were coming to him…his heavy eyelids closed…

"…we've been speaking Gentril all day and he understood *everything*…"

"…you saw how he climbed the sphinx…I have full-magician friends who *still* can't get up that shrewd statue…"

His thoughts were drifting to dreams of fountains, rivers and flight, and from the faint edge of reality came the words: "…are you sure he's ready for Valoria? And the test?"

Then he was asleep, hardly stirring when strong hands carried him upstairs and placed him on a soft bed.

Chapter Nine

The Boulevard of Vale Adorna

Brenner awoke to sunlight streaming onto his face, and a modestly furnished room with paintings of birds migrating, a bookshelf, and carved wooden statues sitting along a shelf. His nose told him that something savory was baking downstairs.

He stretched his legs, and noticed his backpack in the corner of the room. Pulling his journal from it, he made a couple of notes about flight, creatures, and Agilis from the previous day, then headed downstairs.

"Ah, good morning, Brenner," Windelm said, as Brenner walked into the kitchen. "You can select some of these to eat along the way to the market." He produced a basket filled with fruit and warm pastries. Brenner took a bite of a muffin. "But first, you may as well stuff any other jeans and t-shirts you've packed into the closet for good, as I don't know a better way to put a target on your back that says, 'Look at me, I'm from a different dimension.'" He gestured to a brown tunic, cloak, and plain black pants hanging on a chair. "I picked these out for you."

"Thanks," Brenner said, as he took the clothes and headed for an empty room. He opened the first door in the hall, stepped in, and shut the wooden door. Then he smelled something peculiar, like pickled fish. Turning around, he saw a shelf full of colored vials, powders, and potions, with containers holding floating objects in murky, green liquid. One looked like tonsils. Brenner crinkled his nose. *Must be some sort of ingredient room.* Quickly, he changed, and then exited the malodorous storeroom.

He found Windelm waiting by the main entrance. "Splendid," Windelm said, giving Brenner's wardrobe an appraising eye, "now you look like a regular spellcaster. Let's be off then."

Brenner walked with Windelm through the doorway, and down the front path. His tunic felt thick and just a tad coarse, while his pants felt as though something slick and smooth was woven into the fabric.

"Where's Sherry?" Brenner asked, before popping another one of the muffins into his mouth.

"She had to open the potions shop early this morning. We'll see her along the market boulevard. Now then, would you like to walk, run, or fly this morning?"

Brenner thought back to Windelm's Mindscape performance yesterday, and wanted to know how he stacked up to the sorcerer. "Let's race!" he said, breaking into a run.

Brenner started in the lead, but not for long. His amulet bounced lightly against his chest, and Windelm blazed ahead of him, like a panther shooting past a pack mule. He tried sprinting faster along the path—the arching trees forming a tunnel overhead, but Windelm was soon out of sight.

A voice called from the distance, "Had enough?"

Brenner caught his breath, then called out, "Yeah!"

He jogged forward, and finally saw Windelm, sitting on a bench. Between large mouthfuls of air, Brenner asked him, "H-how do you do that?"

"What?" said Windelm furtively, "The running?"

"No," said Brenner, "the dancing— Of course the running!"

"Same way you do, I put one foot in front of the other and repeat as necessary until—"

"Oh, come on," Brenner said, giving Windelm a shove.

"Well, what do you think?" Windelm asked, joining Brenner on the path. They passed a spellcaster outside her cottage, pouring a foaming liquid on the base of a plant, which then sent ivy tendrils shooting up the side of her chimney.

"Your amulet," Brenner guessed. "It's better than mine."

"It is different, but they contain about the same amount of elixir. That's only a part of the reason. What else?"

"You used your mircon to propel you faster."

"I could have, but I didn't. Did I have it yesterday in the course?"

Brenner mentally replayed the events of yesterday and then said, "No."

"So, what is it then?" Windelm said, looking at him with his eyes shining. "How does one get better at anything?"

"Practice," said Brenner.

"Yes, but even before practice what needs to happen?"

"You must have…seen it somewhere?"

"Seen, and then imagined."

"Imagined what?"

"Imagined myself doing what I had observed," said Windelm. "Hmm, how to phrase it…when a spellcaster sees a human or even an animal doing something, he learns from it. He internalizes the action, believing himself capable, and imagines himself doing it. Then, after perfect practice, he can perform it."

"How long did it take to learn to run on water?"

"I had to learn many other skills first, and those took years, but once I set my mind to water skimming, oh, about three days."

"Three days?" said Brenner in awe, imagining how long it would take him to run as Windelm had on the water.

The path wound around sweet lilac trees and white birches, and through the trees Brenner could see buildings ahead, with more people trickling onto the path, walking toward the marketplace with their families.

"So," said Brenner, processing Windelm's advice, "what did you see that was so fast?"

"During an expedition I caught a glimpse of a Nightshade sprinting at full speed. At first, I just saw the grasses part in a swift line as it sped by. Then I saw its sleek black body dart toward the riverbank, and rather than stop, it just catapulted itself onto the water and somehow kept on running, clean over the surface, as if it was a water-bug. I knew that if something *that* size could do it, I could do it."

"Impressive," Brenner said.

"Thank you," Windelm said, and looked to carry himself a little higher. "Well, here we are, the Boulevard of Vale Adorna."

They walked between the outer stone buildings, around leafy trees, and the sounds of the marketplace gushed forth: people laughing and bartering, carts creaking as they wheeled over cobblestones, and footsteps clattering on the stone street. They passed by vendors showcasing tiered rows of neat purple fruits and red-nectars, craftsmen displaying metal pots and assorted jugs, and artisans with tables decorated with furs and intricately shaped clay vases.

Then Brenner noticed a curious thing: when people saw the two of them, they gave Windelm and Brenner long stares and a wide berth as they walked past. Brenner got that ugly feeling he had in school when people tried to disassociate from him in the hallways, especially after gym class.

"Windelm," he said discreetly, his face flushing a slight shade of red, "I think people are noticing me."

"Oh that," said Windelm in an unruffled tone, "It's nothing. Some folks are just…uneasy…when sorcerers walk by, that's all."

But Brenner noted that it was not just some folks but nearly *all* folks who watched them longer than normal. "Why would they be uneasy?"

"Habit, I suppose. Many years ago, before sovereigns were elected and the city guard wasn't as effective as it is now, magic communities were loosely held together and dominated by the strongest spellcasters — individual sorcerers and wizards, who oftentimes didn't care what was wrong or right, so long as they got—"

"Windelm!" a hearty voice cried out from a throng of people.

Brenner and Windelm turned their gaze toward the call, and a large, ruddy-faced man with a tousle of red hair waved from the side of a stall and strode over to them.

"Ah, Rimpley!" Windelm said. "Good to see you!" He clasped the man's outstretched hand and then motioned to Brenner, "Rimpley, this is Brenner, my great-nephew. Brenner, this is Rimpley Cagginton."

Rimpley nodded genially and stuck out his hand to Brenner as well. When Brenner gripped it, Rimpley shook his whole arm so vigorously it was like shaking hands with a polar bear.

"I can see the resemblance already, Windelm!" Rimpley boomed, letting go of Brenner, who rubbed the feeling back into his squashed hand. "He's got your strong shoulders, and a confident chin, too. Going to teach him to become a steward sorcerer then? How's he liking Valoria? I still remember those gutsy Zabrani plays of yours—'full tilt, never back off!'—you were a *great* flyer, I always said."

Windelm smiled, clearly flattered, and said, "Thank you, Rimpley. I haven't pushed him into my vocation. That's for him to decide. And, actually, he hasn't started at Valoria yet, we were going to take him to the academy—"

"Hasn't started yet?" Rimpley cut in. "Don't they still start young spellcasters around nine or ten? That's when we went."

"He grew up with his parents in Cormith—they wanted him to be a farmer like them. But the harvest has been light in recent years, and there's enough talent in him that they couldn't pretend not to notice anymore. So, they finally allowed him to study at the academy, and live with us between terms."

"He'll be far behind his peers, then, won't he?" Rimpley said, crossing his burly arms together.

Windelm looked at Brenner, shaking a carefree face, "No, I've seen him in action already. He's a quick learner and a natural on his feet. I wouldn't be surprised if he advances to a conjurer's rank in a year's time."

"Hmm," Rimpley said, thoughtfully. "How old are you, son?"

"Sixteen," Brenner said, feeling pleased with himself after Windelm's compliments.

"Well there's odds I'd bet against," said Rimpley bluntly. "I was stuck at the apprentice level for the better part of my schooling. I didn't move up to the conjurer rank till I was seventeen, and that was *with* full schooling."

"Rimpley," Windelm criticized, "some of us were already mages by his age, and you didn't exactly help yourself by pulling pranks and picking fights in school. You hardly applied yourself to your studies—"

"Ah, didn't need 'em, did I?" Rimpley cut in. "Still landed where I wanted to be—got my own Pegasus freight business in Arborio, and set my own hours—couldn't be happier. Sure, I'm not a full-blown sorcerer like *you*, Windelm," he said with what sounded like a touch of envy, "but being a solid mage suits me fine. And now I get to sample all the imports first!"

He stopped and put his hand into one of the many leather pouches tied to his waist, pulling something out. "Here, Brenner. Doubt you've had one of these before, I just got a shipment of 'em—came all the way from an Aquaperni island—Lotropius, I believe."

He dropped some colorful balls the size of olives into Brenner's hand. Brenner nearly dropped them when, by their own power, they started rolling around his palm.

"Go on, have a bite of the moltifrutes," Rimpley urged him. "Somehow those Aquaperni artisans can pack eight, nine or even ten fruit flavors into each ball, and a bit of wild plant temperament, too—they claim. But personally," he leaned in to Brenner, "I think they just cast a Twitching Spell on 'em."

Brenner popped one of the moltifrutes into his mouth, and a burst of sweet strawberry hit his tongue, followed quickly by other tangy fruits, as though an entire berry pie had been shrunk to the size of a marble and now pleasantly rolled around his mouth. He crushed it with his molars and immediately honeyed juices filled his mouth.

"Thanks, Rimpley!" Brenner said, relishing the treat.

"Ah, don't mention it," said Rimpley, grinning back at him. "But if you need to, put in a good word for my couriers."

The sound of loud, rhythmic flapping came from overhead—with more power than what Brenner thought could come from a bird, and he looked up in time to see a large, black-winged horse veering high overhead. He ducked, although neither Windelm nor Rimpley did, as the animal swooped down, following the boulevard, and Brenner noticed a rider guiding it, and a harness off the back connecting the winged-horse to its barge: a large, decorated chariot the size of a sportscar. Brenner straightened back up.

"Ah, that would be the next shipment from Aquaperni then!" said Rimpley excitedly. "I better go supervise the unloading. Windelm, great to see ya."

"You too, old friend."

"And Brenner," Rimpley said, backpedaling into the crowd, "If you ever want to get away from that old bat sometime, or just want an up-close view of a Pegasus, come over to my shop—Rimpley's Sky-Couriers." With that he gave a final wave, then turned and walked up the busy street.

Windelm motioned them onward, and the two continued down the avenue. Brenner looked past the bustling crowds, fruit stalls and tents to the regal stone buildings with strange symbols printed above the doorways, and was surprised when his brain translated them readily. Above one doorway read, "*STERLING & GOULD'S*, MAKERS of AMULETS, MIRCONDUITS, & FINE MAGICAL TALISMANS since 4771 A.E." A group of children emerged laughing from the next store—"**Dandilop's Sweet Eats, Treats and Confectionaries**"—carrying orange drinks that foamed and fizzed over their hands. One of them bit into a giant hunk of brown candy bar that Brenner guessed was chocolate, until it shimmered magenta and changed into a long, wriggling tube, spinning like a windmill in the boy's hand.

Across the street, Brenner saw a wide building made out of slab stones, emblazoned with the large title: "**OBERFELD'S HOME DESIGN, CREATION, and OBFUSCATION**."

He turned to Windelm, "What does that mean, obfuscation?"

"The art of concealment," Windelm replied. "Oberfeld and his architects can hide a residence so well you could walk face-first into the chains on the drawbridge before you realized a castle was there."

As they passed by a glass window, Brenner looked inside and nearly fell backward as a red rug whipped through the air like a banshee toward him, the last second changing course and careening up out of sight. He put his hand cautiously on the cool glass, leaned his face in closer, and another orange carpet zipped through the air inside the long shop, carrying a smiling family of six, with the two youngest children happily tugging the tassels on the edges. Looking at the doorway, Brenner read, "LINCOMBS & LEAVITZ, *LEVITATORS* & *AIRBORNE SPECIALISTS.*"

Brenner tugged Windelm's sleeve. "Windelm," he said. "Are those *magic carpets* in there?"

"Indeed," Windelm replied casually, "A carrier carpet is an easier way to transport large groups and families. They don't have as much power as winged-horses, but they offer more space, less mess, and limited behavioral problems."

Brenner gave the shop a final look: a boy was punching a roll of carpet standing on end, when suddenly the carpet uncurled itself and wrapped around the boy, who let out a muffled shriek. Immediately, a clerk appeared, wrestling with the rug and trying to pry the boy loose from the mischievous carpet.

They came to a corner boutique shop with a carved wooden sign hanging from the side of the second story: "**Potions in Motion**" it said. The exterior glass further read: **Bewitched Ingredients, Botanical Solutions, and Potions-a-Plenty.**

Windelm held the door for Brenner. As he walked inside, a familiar face with deep mahogany hair came around a shelf filled with purple vials.

"Brenner! So nice of you to visit."

"Hi, Sherry," said Brenner, feeling at ease despite the assortment of ghoulish containers on either side of the aisle, one of which housed a writhing mass of tarantulas.

"How's business this morning?" Windelm said, striding up and giving Sherry a quick peck on her cheek.

"I sold three cases of Security Tendrils to the Laddocks this morning. Said they are getting too many Needlewing Bats and a Poison-Coat Python around their place."

"What are Security Tendrils?" Brenner asked.

"Oh, they're quite useful," Sherry said animatedly, "Simply plant a few around a house perimeter, or at the base of trees, and within a few days, they will have perched themselves high in the boughs or up on the rooftop and be ready to ward off intrusive creatures."

Brenner tried imagining just how they could subdue the yellow python he saw yesterday. "How would a plant move fast enough to stop a snake?"

"That's part of what makes them so dangerous," said Sherry, "they appear quite docile, but when they're really hungry, they can shoot at you as fast as a chameleon's tongue. They would be quite noxious themselves if they didn't have certain altruistic properties. You see, the tendrils naturally protect the tree or house they live on. They want the organism they're rooted on to grow stronger and taller in order to attract larger bugs, birds, and creatures, so whenever a pest comes within range of them, they ensnare it, and after a day or two, digest it."

"Wouldn't they attack humans?" Brenner asked.

"Yes, but if you harvest them young enough, or use an Entrapment Charm, you can transplant them to another home. When you do, you mix a small part of yourself—a piece of hair or drop of blood—with Rathflower petals and feed it to the plant. The Security Tendrils associate the Rathflower with dragon-fire, and will recoil at the touch of you from then on."

"Oh," said Brenner, fascinated. He looked on the back shelves and saw a few snakelike vines wrapping themselves around a bug that had wandered too close.

"Sherry!" someone shouted anxiously from the back store room. "Sherry, it won't stay still!"

"Coming, Margery!" Sherry said. "Boys, please excuse me."

"Do you want any help?" Windelm asked.

At the back hallway Sherry called over her shoulder, "We'll be fine, just a new arrival of a Seven-Silk Spider."

Brenner looked at Windelm with wide eyes, thankful that he wasn't the one tasked with holding down a magic spider. As they browsed around the store, the frequency of Margery's shrieks died down.

Something nagged at Brenner. "Windelm," he said. "Rimpley made it seem that going to Valoria wasn't the only way to succeed here. Couldn't I just learn with you?"

Windelm let out a knowing sigh. "I wish it were that simple, but I've already used much of my yearly time-off with you on Earth, and if I want to hold on to my job, I'm needed back at my work as steward sorcerer."

"I see."

"Rimpley is a good man, don't get me wrong, but I wouldn't let his average experience guide your decision. Every young person in the greater vicinity of Arborio is allowed a chance to try out for the academy, but not everyone has the desire or means. It's considered a supreme honor among spellcasters to learn at an academy—every biome in Ganthrea boasts several competitive schools. Your amulet is only part of what you can do, Brenner, but a mircon, which in time you'll get at Valoria, transforms everything."

"So, what do I need to bring to the academy?"

"Once you pass the Agilis entrance examination at Valoria, they'll provide you with the appropriately-colored tunic, plus room and board. But you'll need extra clothes, walking boots, books, a toothbrush—"

"I have that at least."

"Ah, good. That just leaves an amulet, which you have, and once you pass the first three levels, a mircon."

"How many people *don't* pass the examination?"

"No need to dwell on it, Brenner. You'll do fine," Windelm said, picking up some vials of potion.

While he wanted to gain entrance to a place Windelm held in such high esteem, he still had some doubts…

"But say I don't pass?"

"You will," Windelm said firmly, looking into Brenner's eyes. "You have what it takes. And as your peers have already been in school for seven years, the sooner you gain admittance to Valoria Academy, the better."

Brenner looked away; he still felt uneasy.

"Tell you what," said Windelm, "I'll give you three extra weeks to train on the Mindscape course. I'll check on you during my lunch break."

Brenner felt a knot in his stomach loosen. "Thanks."

Windelm reached for something on the shelf, "Hey, this potion might help, too." He held up a green-yellow vial. "Alacritus – for nerves."

"Ugh!"

Sherry had returned from the storeroom, putting a large glass jar filled with glimmering white strands onto a shelf, and wiping a hand across her forehead, "Getting silk from those beasts these days—there must be some mutation among them, I've never had so much of a struggle."

"What do you use the spiders for?" Brenner asked.

"The silk of course," Sherry said. "The Seven-Silk Spider has different types of silk: web-building, digestive, radiant, invisible, attraction, hardened, and of course," she tapped the jar, "regenerative silk. Great for bandaging open wounds—can sanitize and heal them in just a couple of hours." She strode over to them, then produced from her front apron a vial. "For your apprenticeship at Valoria," she said, putting the blue vial of swirling liquid into Brenner's hand. Like a firefly, it flickered yellow. "Essence of Spungelite—an uncommon extract that will allow your mind to behave like a rare organism that stores sunlight during the day and radiates light at night. But you may not even need it," Sherry added, winking, "I can tell you absorb ideas quickly."

Brenner examined the vial in his hand, smiling at her kindness. "Thank you, Sherry," he said, touched by how in only a few days he had received more hospitality and warmth from the Crestwoods than from his parents during his entire childhood.

"I'd like to buy this too, honey," said Windelm, holding up the Alacritus potion and attempting to give Sherry some coins.

"Put that back," she said, pushing his hand away. "We're never going to make any money if you keep buying everything in my shop. And I can make Brenner a vial of Alacritus from our home supplies.

"Now, I have to help some customers and assist Margery in bottling the rest of the spider-silk while it's fresh. I should be home later this afternoon."

There was a clinking of glass bottles behind them. A severe-looking lady with a large waist and a hooked, parrot-like nose approached the counter, her basket full of fragrant magenta bottles that jostled together. She gave Windelm a flirtatious look.

"The potions won't work on him, dear," Sherry said to the lady, noticing the contents of her basket and giving her a wink. "That one's mine."

"Oh—I uh—sorry," the woman said, blushing.

"Boys, you get along now. I need to help a customer."

Sherry shooed them off, and Windelm blew her a kiss as they departed the store.

Back on the boulevard, Windelm said to Brenner, "We should pick up a few supplies for Valoria."

The two walked back through the throngs of people. Soon the sounds of stringed instruments filled the air. A small gathering of teenagers and adults clustered around a couple men in bright costumes strumming two-necked guitars, while behind them an assortment of drums were played rhythmically by floating drumsticks—striking the taut drumheads by themselves.

They strode past a prominent bank made of marble, then a boisterous tavern called "The Surly Spellcaster," when a tall, black-bearded man with sinewy arms exited the door, saw Windelm and gave them a pleasant look of surprise.

"Oh—hullo, Windelm," he said affably.

"Patrick," said Windelm, "Fine seeing you. This is my great-nephew, Brenner."

"Nice ta meet you," Patrick nodded and smiled.

"You too," said Brenner.

"Haven't seen you round here a'fore," said Patrick, "First time in our Vale?"

"Yeah," said Brenner.

"Figured so. Been neighbors with Windelm for's long as I can remember, we go way back. You lucked out, Brenner, as far as sorcerer's go, he's one of the saner one's we got in our village, but not by much—" he jabbed Windelm with his elbow good-naturedly.

"And you're one to talk?" said Windelm, smiling.

"That's different," Patrick said, raising his hand in mock disdain. "I ain't a sorcerer, am I? And spellcasters expect a bit o' zest from me, since I remove pesky critters for a livin'. Hey, Windelm—"

Patrick motioned them away from the tavern entrance to the side alley, and then asked, "Did you hear about the McRorins?"

"No," said Windelm, "What's happened?"

"The city guard came through yesterday," said Patrick, "interviewed the *whole* family. Phillip McRorin *is missing*."

Windelm stiffened and turned his head to the side, "Missing? How?"

"Well, he was out huntin' with a group of other mages, far out on the western region of Silvalo, and they were supposed to have picked up more supplies from Barringer Point two weeks ago, but thing is, they never came back."

A concerned look swept over Windelm. "I saw Phillip at Oswald's Outfitters a month ago...and he never showed up?"

"Nope," said Patrick. "The Guard did their own search of the Silvalo wilderness in that area, but you know they can't check everywhere. The jungle stretches out for leagues in every direction, it could take a man a good year to walk the sand border with Arenattero, let alone the whole southwestern side of Silvalo."

"My cartographers are due to classify some of that region this summer. I'll be sure to have them on alert for any evidence of his expedition."

Patrick's voice lowered, "You don't think they were overtaken by Arenattero spellcasters, do you?"

Windelm paused, seeming to choose his words carefully. "It's been over a century since the last battle between Silvalo and Arenattero, and their sovereign wizard, Amal Jadula, had just visited Arborio last year. He seemed to be on good terms with our sovereign, Donovan Drusus. I don't think he'd be stupid enough to start a war with us, especially with the Games of Ganthrea happening in a little over two months."

Patrick shifted his weight. "It had to a'been spellcasters. McRorin is a seasoned hunter and a mage; he's too clever to be taken down by a creature. Could be slavers…or assassins, maybe…"

"Maybe," said Windelm, his eyes looking off in the distance. "Stop by the cottage later this week, or the Mindscape, and we can discuss more."

Patrick nodded, then stepped back to the street and put on a cheerful facade, "The Mindscape? Ha! You just want another excuse to show off."

"I'm just trying to keep you young, Patrick! Doing my part to help work off that gut you've been feeding over the years."

"You old goat! We all know Sherry pumps you with potions to keep you running like a young buck."

"Nonsense!"

"I'm on to you, Windelm. Alright—my missus needs some boar meat and moltifrutes, and is probably wondering what's keeping me so long. Windelm, one last favor."

"Yes?"

"Don't mention the Surly Spellcaster, eh?"

Windelm chuckled. "Consider it forgotten."

"Great. Best be off!" He turned, raised a hand, and waved back at them. "Watch out for that one, Brenner!"

Brenner suppressed a smile.

Windelm shook his head and laughed. "Come on," he said. "Let's buy your supplies and head back to the cottage. You've got some practicing to do."

Chapter Ten

The Entrance Agilis

The extra three weeks staying at Crestwood Cottage felt like a mix of vacation and boot camp: quick meals in the morning, dinner at evening with Windelm and Sherry, and the rest of the day, tough challenges in what was quickly becoming Brenner's favorite place: the Mindscape.

He scraped his sides badly the second day while trying to climb the pillars, and then got a black eye on the third day when he was caught off-guard by the sphinx's tail. Even still, he kept at it each day that Windelm and Sherry worked, testing the limits of his jumps, stretching his upper body climbing up and over walls, turrets, and ledges. He took Windelm's earlier advice to heart, and whenever Windelm joined him on the course, he studied how his great-uncle practically flew around grabbing glowbes, skimming over water, and Brenner imagined himself doing the same.

The second week brought fewer injuries, and the third week, none. Now, his body quickly did what his brain told it to, and when he saw himself in the mirror after a bath, he was surprised to see a lean, strong, flexible young man staring back at himself.

During his meals, Brenner listened to Windelm and Sherry share about Silvalo customs (people here didn't give handshakes: men locked right hands on another's shoulders; women put their right hand on the other person's waist), and what their work was like (Windelm scouted places where the government should add vias, or roads, and noted where resources were flourishing or dwindling; Sherry, the entrepreneur, made, bottled, and sold potions). With Windelm he also rehearsed his own 'story' about his previous sixteen years in a farming community called Cormith.

At the end of April, Brenner stood outside the Crestwood cottage in the warm morning sunshine with Windelm and Sherry, ready to give the Entrance Examination a shot.

He wore the usual tunic and garb of spellcasters, and also fine leather boots that Windelm had bought; they were firm yet lighter than any shoes he'd had. Sherry had given him a new rucksack, packed with spare clothes, a couple spellbooks, homemade toothpaste and brush, as well as the Essence of Spungelite and home-made Alacritus potions. He was delighted to discover the rucksack had the same magical, inner-expanding ability as Windelm's satchel.

"Do be careful at the academy," Sherry said, catching him off-guard with a firm hug, "And you're welcome back here whenever you'd like!" She beamed at him.

"He'll be just fine, dear," Windelm said. "And I should be back for supper." He gave his wife a kiss on the cheek.

"Thanks for everything, Sherry," Brenner said.

"Our pleasure!"

Windelm said something under his breath to engage their flight spell, and in an instant he and Brenner were soaring above the green trees of Vale Adorna, past the cottages, marketplace, and fountains, and north toward Valoria Academy, which lay within the giant city of Arborio. Wind swept across Brenner's face and his feet floated behind him. Windelm's green cape fluttered behind him. In the distance, Brenner could see massive oakbrawn, magnayan and mahogany trees rising up like a thousand water towers, standing shoulder to shoulder.

Brenner noticed other things flying toward the vast city. A shimmer of white wings in the distance proved to be a winged-horse hauling a caravan filled with goods. A blur of green came into focus as a pack of spellcasters, flying with mircons in hand.

But something flying to the west made Brenner twist his head in a double-take: jumbo eagles with enormous wingspans circled down to their nests, clutching limp deer in their talons. He tugged on Windelm and pointed. "Should we be worried about those?"

Windelm looked to where Brenner gestured, and then turned back to him, saying calmly, "Aviamirs. And yes. But they've already captured their meal, and at this distance we can out-fly them."

Brenner breathed out a sigh. "Well, that's good news."

Giant stone pillars, built about half a mile apart all along the city's perimeter, grew on the horizon. They looked like space elevators ascending up to the cloudline. While he couldn't see the end of them—the city curved for miles on each side—they probably formed a ring around it. Windelm flew them down through the treetops to a wide, well-trodden dirt road—"Via Arborio," he explained—and hovered to a stop on the ground. They walked toward one of the stone pillars, above them city guards perched on its balcony.

"We'll fly again in a moment," Windelm said, "but walking gives you a better perspective of the city. Here," he motioned to the pillar, "is one of the Shell Towers." He led Brenner off the road. The height of the pillar, and the trees behind it, made Brenner feel insignificant. "The magic in them forms a powerful Aura field that, when activated at night, keeps spellcasters and beasts out of the city."

Brenner reached his arm tentatively toward the air by the base of the structure. "Is the field invisible?"

"It's not on."

"Oh, right," said Brenner sheepishly. "What happens if you touch it when it is on?"

"You ever touch a bolt of lightning?"

Brenner cringed.

"No one needs to be reminded twice of the painful electrical energy the Aura field releases. Come along."

The two walked back to the path and past the Shell Tower into Arborio, weaving between a couple of trading caravans, as city guards inspected the back of a wagon.

Monstrous trees—mahoganies, ironclads, redwoods, and oakbrawns—stretched up five hundred to a thousand feet tall. He could see canopy bridges built between the giant trees, a flurry of people crossing them, as well as apartments built onto the side of the trees. There was a small stream of people flying just above street level, and some spellcasters were so high up they looked like hummingbirds flitting through the open air. The streets around them were more crowded than Vale Adorna.

"Why doesn't everyone fly?" Brenner asked.

"Couple reasons," said Windelm, "First, they need an amulet with elixir to power their magic, which costs more money than half of the residents can afford. So, they travel by foot, animal, or pay for magical transport. Second, you need spell training for flight, which is a physical type of magic usually learned around the mage levels. And not everyone gets that far in their education."

Brenner rubbed the back of his hand, feeling a little daunted.

"With the right training, you'll get there," Windelm said, putting an arm out to stop Brenner before a group of horsemen cantered across their path. "That way," Windelm pointed. "Take my hand. Valoria Academy lays on the east side of Arborio." He levitated them off the street and soon they were flying between the beautiful trees.

As they flew above the crowds, Brenner noticed that important-looking spellcasters flew solo or in pairs above the street, along with some families on carrier carpets, while merchants and most people walked between buildings and trees. Below, shopkeepers held up leather sandals and touted their soft rugs; chefs piled steaming yellow rice with curry onto plates; in the shadows of alleys, men pulled their cloaks close. Twice Brenner spotted a pair of city guards patrolling through the air.

Finally, the two came to a set of tall, wrought-iron gates with a centerpiece of spirals and trees.

"Welcome to Valoria," Windelm said, landing; then he tapped his mircon to the gate, which swung backward. "After you."

Brenner stepped forward, and lifted his gaze to Valoria. With tall turrets, green-tinted windows and dormers scattered like jack-o-lantern faces atop walls of turquoise limestone, Valoria Academy was a grand castle, but what fascinated Brenner as he walked up the mossy stone path, was how its rock walls merged into living oakbrawns and cedars, so that it was hard to tell where nature stopped and the castle began. Many of the turrets, he now realized, were actually built around giant trees—some carved with windows and spiral staircases.

They came to a brick booth, where an old man in faded green robes was writing on a scroll. He looked like he'd entered into a competition to grow the biggest beard—and with the wisps of his silver-white beard nearly reaching his belly button, Brenner thought he was clearly winning.

"Good morning, deputy, I'm Windelm—"

"Crestwood, ah," said the man, looking up. "Thought it was you. Made it to rank of sorcerer, if I'm not mistaken."

Windelm looked pleased. "That's right," he said. "My great-nephew, Brenner Wahlridge, would like to apply for entrance to Valoria."

The deputy looked down at a different sheath of papers on his desk, muttering to himself, "Wahlridge…Wahlridge…hmm…this will be his first attempt then." He looked up. "Brenner will need to take the Agilis entrance examination."

"We know," said Windelm.

The deputy turned his gaze from Windelm to Brenner. "And how old are you?"

"Sixteen," said Brenner.

The official shook his head, "Sixteen…my, that will make it harder… yes, much harder. Usually students apply when they are eight, nine at the latest…he will be placed in the eldest entrant category."

He consulted another piece of paper and looked up with solemnity. "And are you aware of the dangers for older entrants?"

"We are," said Windelm, pointedly ignoring Brenner's sideway glance.

Brenner's eyebrows furrowed. If Windelm *had* known the dangers, he certainly hadn't shared them with Brenner.

"Very well," the deputy said, handing them a long piece of parchment. "You will need to sign here as his guardian, and Brenner, you sign here."

Brenner tried to read the tiny words as Windelm hastily scrawled his name.

At first the language was foreign…then goosebumps rippled on his arms as he read unmistakable warnings:

You accept all responsibility for mental and physical dangers of the Agilis Entrance Examination, which include but are not limited to: partial or full paralysis, loss of appendages or limbs, blindness, mind-warping, death by falls, death by impalement, death by drowning, death by fire, death by mauling, death by…

And the list of 'death by's' went on and on for another three paragraphs.

Brenner's insides lurched. "Windelm," he said. "Are you sure I can do this?"

Windelm put an arm around his shoulder, "Of course you can! Brenner, sure, the test is a bit harder for older entrants, but you are capable of handling it; I've seen you succeed on a tough Mindscape for the past three weeks. Just sign here," and he pointed to the bottom left corner which read, *'Applicant's Consent to Agilis Examination, All Liability Hereby Waived'.*

Gingerly, Brenner scribbled his name.

The deputy took the parchment dispassionately, then said, "As you're his guardian, you may come along to the observation level with me, and watch if you'd like. Follow me."

He turned and marched them from his brick station to a dark tree painted on the limestone wall of Valoria, which, once he put his mircon on it, melted away and revealed a long corridor. Windelm and Brenner followed him through the tunnel, lit with glowing torches.

Brenner picked up his pace to be closer to the deputy, then asked, "How often do you get older entrants?"

"Older entrants?" he laughed. "There are so few. Most have calculated the odds against themselves…" he held up a fist and started raising fingers one-by-one…"Hmm…in the last twenty years…five entrants."

Brenner grew warmer. "And how many have passed?"

"Let's see, who passed…" he started curling down his fingers, "Two were impaled…one drowned…another was crushed…and one boy yelled for help a quarter through the course. The last time I've seen someone your age pass…goodness," he brought a finger to his chin, "it must have been forty or fifty years ago."

Brenner felt a heaviness settle across his shoulders. Combined with the blunt death warnings, this was probably the most discouraging news he could've been told.

He was silent for the remainder of the walk. Their footsteps echoed in dark tree tunnels, then across a long pavilion. Finally, they followed the deputy through a wide doorway onto a gray stone platform, the entrance to an open-air stadium under the cloud-speckled sky.

Brenner's jaw dropped from the immensity of the field. It was like standing in a Coliseum built for giants.

The oval stadium walls stretched far and away until he could only see a blurred blob of brown seats in the distance; in the arena itself was a lumpy woodland filled with hills, gnarled trees, a rockslide, a scattering of stone structures, and that was only before the midway point. Beyond it, he could only see treetops.

He exhaled and looked at his feet, and then noticed a thin line of darkness just beyond the lip of the platform. His heart thumped irregularly.

The deputy held up his hand.

"Windelm, this is as far as you may go." He pointed to another archway near the wall, and motioned to Windelm. "Brenner, this is the beginning of the Agilis test. You may use your amulet, abilities, and whatever you can find along the course to make it to the other side. I will be judging you based on technique, speed, and glowbes captured. And, of course, you must survive the Agilis course to gain a place in the academy. You may call for help at any time, but doing so will immediately disqualify you from acceptance to Valoria."

Brenner rubbed his clammy hands against his pants. "How do I know when I am done?"

"If you reach the other end of the field," the official said, "look for this crest." He motioned to a silver emblem on the wall, consisting of a shield bordering a tree with two mircons crossed in an X. "Touch the Valoria crest, and you have finished the Agilis examination."

Brenner nodded slowly.

"One last thing," the old man continued coolly, "the more glowbes you reach, and the faster you get through the ordeal, the higher your initial placement will be in the school. Well, good luck to you then."

He turned and disappeared under the archway.

"Brenner," Windelm said, walking to Brenner and putting a hand on his shoulder, "This is just a larger version of Agilis at the Vale Adorna Mindscape. You have what it takes. You can beat this."

"Okay…" Brenner said, wishing he could share Windelm's confidence.

Windelm turned, strode back through the door, and a moment later, the two older men were peering out an open window overhead. The deputy swept his mircon in a spiral and called down loudly, "Begin!"

As Brenner surveyed the landscape, a small pack of glowbes shot out from behind him like ghostly will-o'-the-wisps and darted through the terrain, some remaining visible like lanterns in the distance, while others zoomed past the treeline and out of sight.

He took a step onto a carved image of a hunter, and a ripple of energy flooded out from his pedestal into the arena. Strange noises and growls emanated throughout the woodland, as if beasts had awoken.

Brenner clenched and unclenched his hands, trying to suppress the urge to turn around and flee. *It just keeps going and going...* he thought, looking at the vast arena ahead of him. *How am I supposed to get through the whole—?*

A ghastly shriek from deep in the distance interrupted his thoughts. His neck hairs bristled; he took a step backward. *Is this worth it?*

*If I don't do this, I'll never get a mircon, never fit in with the Crestwoods, just be another outsider again...*he looked at the doorway behind him. *I could just tell Windelm I quit, save my skin, hand back my amulet, go back to Earth...and to what? To parents who don't really care? A school where I'm practically invisible? A life alone...*

"Brenner!" Windelm's bright voice called from above. "Just take one obstacle at a time. You can do this!"

Brenner tried to distance himself from his darker thoughts. *Okay, if Windelm thinks I can...*he steadied himself, placed his hands on his hips.

Then I can. I must.

With great effort, and against the advice of a small voice in his head, he walked to the edge, looked down, and forced his body to jump off the stone platform into the gamut. The air whistled against his face as he fell ten feet to the rocky base of the first stage. Brenner landed on his feet into a crouch, and then straightened up. His brain entered high-alert mode; his amulet warmed against his chest.

Then he saw the first obstacle. It didn't assuage his nerves.

Directly ahead of him stretched a dark chasm, emitting a musky, dead smell. Longer than an Olympic-size swimming pool, the forbidding pit stretched from the left side of the arena all the way to the right. It was much too far to leap across in one bound, and looked...bottomless.

He walked closer to the edge, searching for anything he might use. Dreary clouds blocked the sun, and a moment later his eyes adjusted to the dim light. Then he noticed gray objects scattered throughout the chasm, and his mind made the connection: stepping-stones. They looked like over-sized toadstools; only, they weren't supported by anything, just hovering over the inky darkness.

Brenner saw a floating stone not far from him. He walked to it and tested it with one foot, straddling the pit with his other foot firmly on the ledge. The stepping-stone held him. Cautiously, he shifted his full weight onto it, and after a moment, sighed in relief. *Good, it can support me.* He lifted his gaze to the chasm. *I wonder where the next...*

The stone began to tremble. Suddenly it fell.

"Aghhh!"

Brenner jumped backward and caught the edge, pulling himself back up, breathing fast. A distant, dull *thud* echoed up the walls of the canyon. *So, there* was *a bottom.*

Surveying the whole chasm again, he noticed an assortment of stepping-stones on one side, some as large as shields and others more like the plate-sized, Rombell mushrooms. He was confident he could run across that side without too much trouble—provided the footing held long enough for him to step and rebound.

And then a glimmer of light caught his eye. On the other side of the pit, where it stretched widest, there hovered a glowbe in the middle of the canyon. There was only one problem: it hung between two stepping-stones, which looked more than twenty feet apart.

Brenner gauged his ability, remembering the giant leap he performed at football...undoubtedly, this would be on the edge of his range...but his intuition told him that he could it, and if he had to cross the canyon anyway...

He jogged over to the far side, clutching his amulet against his chest. There were six toadstools before the middle chasm, and six after, looking like dull, gray mirrors. He would have to pace himself. He backed up, then looked ahead, focusing his mind.

Go.

His feet pumped into action across the rocky ground and to the edge of the abyss; he jumped out easily to the first stone, about five feet away, caught it square in the center with his left foot, and sprang to the next one.

Brenner's foot rebounded not a moment too soon, for he felt the resistance of the stepping-stone fall away the instant he left it.

His right foot landed on the next one, six feet away. His left found the next at seven feet, then eight feet, nine feet, ten feet…*NOW!*

He pushed himself as hard as he could go, shooting up across the gap— his fingers slapped against the glowbe and it shimmered from white to green—his mind already moving to the landing of the next stepping-stone. His arc descending, he felt the sickening suspicion that he was coming up short—his arms wind-milled—

His hands lunged for the toadstool, caught it, and instinctively he swung himself hard underneath and kicked his legs up, letting go and arcing up toward the next platform. Midair he saw that he was on track to land on it, and stretched his foot forward. It was large enough to give him two quick steps; he caught it and jumped away as it fell to the abyss. *Focus. Four more.* Jump—land. *Three more.* Bound—land. *Two more*—leap!—one—

As he flew toward the last toadstool, it suddenly flipped on its side, making the once manageable landing like aiming for the back of a snake. Brenner pointed his foot and barely hit center, wobbling him off balance for his final jump to the other side of the canyon.

VAULT!

But it wasn't enough. The approaching wall was too far for his feet; he would come up short—

Crack!

His body smacked the wall, his fingers scraping onto a rock under the lip. *Just. Hang. On.* He struggled, pulled, then heaved himself onto the ledge. Rolling onto his side, he exhaled.

He had made it. *One down.*

Blood pumping, he tried to refocus his mind as he entered the second stage, jumping down to a level of packed, red clay. The ground ahead looked as though a giant had scraped out a long, sloping bowl about three hundred feet across. As the sides were all steep and smooth, there was no other route but down.

Brenner watched his step while descending into the canyon, and when he looked up, he noticed a white glowbe hovering in the middle. Unlike the first obstacle, it was too high to jump for.

But, in front of the glowbe and leading above it, a couple of poles floated.

Suddenly a deep, grating sound filled the air, as though under the earth plates were grinding angrily against one another. Brenner's neck hairs stuck straight up. High on the walls behind him, he saw stone archways slide open, one on either side of the arena, revealing black caverns. In the darkness, figures loomed closer, and then came rushing into the light.

Boulders the size of bull-elephants rolled down both sides of the course behind Brenner in two furious waves, causing the ground around him to quake.

The rocks funneled to the center, smashed, then gathered energy as gravity hurtled them all the same way down the canyon: directly at Brenner.

Brenner's eyes widened; he turned and sprinted. The rumbling boulders pounded the ground behind him, quickly gaining. He was nearing the center of chasm but didn't see how he would make it out before being crushed by the rock-balls. Up ahead, a small network of floating poles hovered just out of reach.

Then he saw a small hope: one of the poles from above had broken off, leaving a fifteen-foot piece on the ground. Grabbing it, he ran forward until he saw a crack in the ground. He slammed the end of the pole into it, and used the momentum to vault upwards—grabbing one of the poles above, just as the boulders crashed into his stick and bashed against his feet, sweeping them forward.

His feet shot clear over his head from the force of the impact, and then a wave of boulders stampeded underneath like a herd of mammoths. He climbed hand over hand; his heels throbbed.

The boulders charged through the middle of the canyon and far up the other side of the bowl before losing energy, pausing, and then tumbling back down the course towards Brenner again.

Brenner hoisted himself onto a levitating bar, about as thick as a stop sign-post, balanced upright, and then stepped along it heel to toe like a tightrope walker. When he got to the middle of the canyon, he stopped. There was a short vine hanging down, directly over the glowing orb.

He lowered himself down on it, holding with both hands to the last piece of vine. He stretched with his foot…the glowbe was just out of reach. The boulders were now arcing back around for another rush towards the middle. If he stayed in his dangling position for more than ten seconds, they would certainly smash into him.

He rocked his upper body back and forth, creating a swinging motion, then lunged and kicked out his leg again—the glowbe was still a foot away. The rock-balls hurtled towards him, thirty feet and gaining.

He let go with his left hand, swung back, kicked forward—

He hit it!

Then the boulders bounced up, about to bash into his torso—

He reached up with his left arm, grabbed the vine and with both hands swung his legs up—

The boulder grazed his exposed back and then barreled away, up the hill.

Quickly, Brenner seized the vine and pulled himself back up to the safety of the bar. A few moments later, he had navigated to the end of the pole, jumped down, and was safely on the other side of the canyon; the loud clanging of rock smashing against rock behind him reverberated around the giant stadium.

He saw the next obstacle, and understood now how the previous entrants had been impaled.

Below him stretched a pit filled with swords, glinting silver as their blades pointed eagerly towards the sky; in front of him were more floating poles, some round and long like javelins, others thin and sharp. The only problem was the grid didn't start before the edge of the pit: it started a good ten feet after.

Knowing he would get one shot at this, he chose his first target carefully, and then ran and hurled himself over the chasm of the swords, willing himself to latch on to the bar. He swung forward, then back, lifting his torso to the bar, and pulling himself onto the pole.

The first beam was as thick as a staff, and he walked across without difficulty. The next, however, was narrow, like sticks of dynamite fused end-to-end. Thankfully, there seemed to be a guard rail running parallel to the beam at waist-level. He proceeded cautiously, but halfway through his foot slipped off the thin beam. Falling to his right he instinctively grabbed for the guard rail—and cried out as an icy stab of pain shot through his hand.

His first instinct was to let go of the bar. But with all his willpower he fought this urge, knowing that doing so meant plummeting to the daggers waiting below.

Each second was excruciating as the razor rail cut into his palm and fingers. With his feet on the main pole, and one hand on the razor beam, he pushed against it, winced, and like a pendulum swung back over the middle, then quickly wrapped his body around the thin, main pole.

For the remainder of the obstacle, he clutched the pole upside-down, legs crossed over the top, and struggled hand over bloody hand toward the end of the grid. His eyes caught the familiar glitter of a glowbe hovering over a particularly nasty section of razor poles, and he decided this orb was not worth it. At the end of the bar, he righted himself on the top, then jumped the final gap over the swords onto a stretch of grass.

His right hand was still bleeding. He made a fist to try to staunch the flow, then plucked blades of grass to stick to it as a makeshift bandage.

He now realized that beautiful string music was faintly playing ahead, emanating from behind bushes and a thick stand of trees. He plodded ahead, keen to not be caught off-guard by more dangers. Poking his head around the last tree, he saw from where the gentle notes were coming: a small pond lay to his left, and in it, an even smaller island. There, a shining, golden harp was being strummed by an angelic woman.

Brenner gazed at her, forgetting his stinging hand. She had long, red hair, a carefree smile, and was wearing a dove-white dress. When she saw him, she blushed, and continued playing the harp. He thought he spied a light coming from near the harp. Without another thought, Brenner ventured towards the water surrounding her little island.

A cloud passed overhead, and Brenner saw a rowboat in the water not far from him along the grass. He put his foot onto the wooden boat, rocking it slightly, then sat down. Brenner pulled an oar from either side toward himself, then began rowing towards the island; *The glowbe must be behind her harp,* he thought, rowing through the placid waters, looking at the radiant musician.

The soft spell of music grew lovelier still; the red-haired woman was now standing and walking towards the beach he would soon land upon. He paddled harder; the cloud above passed on and sunlight now reflected on the water, warming his face, and he chanced to look on the rippling water toward the island—and jolted upright.

Where the reflection of the beautiful maiden should have been, instead was a dreadful, hooded banshee with blood-red eyes and a wide, wicked grin.

He gripped the oars harder and immediately started backstroking. The smile of the maiden faltered; she beckoned to him once more, and then, when he did not change direction, her mirage dissolved. In its place stood a grotesque, dark-robed woman with a sharp-toothed grin, looking more dead than alive.

She shrieked like a bird of prey and then dove into the waters toward him.

Brenner redoubled his rowing efforts. Sweat trickled down his brow as the banshee swam with surprising alacrity through the waters. As quickly as he could, he beached the boat and jumped from the deck; then the shrill cry of the woman pierced his ears, momentarily disorienting him and triggering a headache. Trying to regain focus, he fled from the water, looking over his shoulder and shuddering to see the ghoulish woman had reached the shore and was gliding towards him. He saw a bright light coming from the other sidewall of the stadium, and noticed an orb floating along the rocks by the wall. He rushed towards the outcropping. A mixture of limestone and granite boulders formed a ledge, and he bounded up the rocks without thinking, only hoping the path would continue. The banshee reached the rocks beneath him, and as he ascended to the final plateau, she let out another ear-splitting screech. Instinctively he clapped a hand to his ears, causing him to lose his grip.

No! Before he could gain a strong hold, he slipped and fell a few feet, hitting his head hard against the granite wall.

The next scream sounded like it came from an arm's length away.

Brenner focused his energy, hung on, and climbed upward despite the screeches that assailed him. His head throbbed.

At last, he reached the plateau where the orb waited, jumped to touch it, and when he did, the screeches subsided. But he didn't dare look at the ghoulish figure again, fearing that another scream would drop him to his knees. Spotting a flight of steps carved into the sidewall, he followed them briskly up to a higher level.

Panting, Brenner walked out onto the next section of field. His headache pulsed, but with the relative quiet of the new stage, it thankfully started to lessen. Ahead of him, piles of granite boulders and red slabs littered the field as though a mountain had shattered to pieces here. Rocks rose up like huge tombstones, casting shadows into a labyrinth of chasms below.

Brenner scanned for movement around the rocky landscape. There was none—so far—only wisps of smoke puffing from the dark pits, and faint echoes of stones tumbling down the sides. In the distance hovered a familiar, white glow of an orb.

He made his way slowly at first, navigating across a heap of rocks, then leapt across a ravine. Finding a path, he took it, scrambling up, hugging against a wall, then squeezing between boulders. Because it seemed the quickest route across, he wanted to keep on it as far as possible before being forced to descend into a chasm. Climbing onto a pile of rubble, he looked to the end of this obstacle, when a whooshing sound filled his ears and he flattened himself to the ground. A giant, vulture-like bird swooped down on him—"Argh!" Brenner yelled, as its talons grazed his shoulder. He ran his palm across it and looked down. *Good, no blood.*

The bird squawked angrily. Speeding through the air, it doubled back to take another dive at Brenner.

My only choice now… Brenner thought with a sigh, *is down.*

A high-pitched whistle grew louder, but before the giant vulture could sink its claws into him, he leapt into a fissure.

He fell for about ten feet before hitting one slanted ledge, then another—his momentum propelling him forward—finally coming down on all fours on the cold, blackened ground. Groaning, he peeled himself off it and surveyed the chasm floor. The giant vulture was still cackling high overhead, but it refused to fly lower to get him. *That isn't good…* he thought as his eyes swept the area, *that means there's something down here it fears more…*

Rustling and scuttling echoes caught his attention, sounding like a suit of armor being dragged across a courtyard. He crouched low, ready to run, but didn't see any creature.

Ahead, a T in the canyon wall gave him the options of going left or right. Recalling the orb to be distantly left, he ventured to that side. He trekked for ten minutes, watching his back every other step, but realized after a couple switchbacks and bends that he couldn't reliably determine which way he should go. He needed to go back up.

He turned the corner around another stone wall, and saw where the smoke he'd seen earlier was coming from: a black land-dragon twenty feet away leered at him with coal-fired, yellow-orange eyes, a plume of acrid smoke rising from its nostrils.

"I bet you're a friendly one, aren't you?" Brenner said.

In response, it sent a jet of hot orange flame directly at him.

Brenner leapt back past the corner, the heat from the fire warming his side. He scanned the rock ledges for a way up. He saw one not too far, and bolted for it. By the time he was on the second ledge, the wingless dragon had rounded the corner, its heavy claws scraping against the rocks as it sped toward him. A bright scarlet stream of flame shot at him, and Brenner ducked behind a rock outcropping. It began to glow red.

He wiped the sweat from his forehead, forcing himself to stay calm. All he needed to do now was climb a switchback…which required him to dash back the way he came, giving the dragon a wide-open shot at him. That wasn't going to work. So, he waited for the dragon to move.

It didn't.

Instead, it rocked back on its haunches like a guard dog, knowing full well where the exit was.

Brenner thought quickly. He grabbed a nearby rock, and ricocheted it across the canyon walls behind the beast. He heard the dragon's tail slapping against the rocks as it turned a corner below. *Yes!* Wasting no time, Brenner leapt from his cover, bolted across the rock path, and up the switchback. Suddenly heat and smoke licked his heels. *Go, go, go!*

Hand over hand, he scaled the rockface, as another burst of fire struck the wall just below him. With a tug up and over the lip, he rolled onto the top. He sucked in clean lungfuls of air. *I'm not out of this stage yet…*

His eyes darted across the upper landscape to find the giant-vulture before it found him. Thankfully, it had not ventured far from where he'd left it, circling and peeking its head down the cracks. Turning forward, he realized he was now closer to the final wall of rock, and also, the glowbe. Slowly, he positioned his body onto his knees, lifted his torso, and calculated the shortest zig-zag route. Capitalizing on his headstart, he sprinted across the boulder tops, jumping from crag to crag over the gaps.

A raspy bird-call pierced the air behind him. *Here we go again!* It would be a few seconds before the vulture was bearing down on him.

But he couldn't stop now: there were no shelter stones, and the white glowbe was only fifty feet away. He spotted a rock ahead the size of a shot-put, and grabbed it before he jumped another fissure. When he landed, he tumbled forward and spun around—just as the vulture's outstretched talons were bearing down upon him. Adrenaline coursing through his veins,

Brenner aimed and chucked the stone at the head of the diving-bombing bird.

A sickening *thunk* told him he had aimed true, but the vulture was still careening at him in a frenzied spin. Brenner rolled to his right, and the massive bird whammed past him into a wall, then ricocheted off and fell back into the chasm. *That was too close,* he thought as he rubbed his hands together and scrambled to his feet. As Brenner summited the next rockpile, he heard the dragon below crunching the bones of the vulture.

Moments later, he stood in front of the white glowbe, then reached out and touched it, causing it to shimmer green. He smiled, and another sight ahead gave him hope: he could see the curving sides of the stadium coming together. The end was getting near.

He walked down a stone-cut, spiral staircase, and stood before a grassy field, in which was a fountain, a glowbe surrounded by rings, and beyond which rose a partition, stretching from wall to wall. A door cut into the far end of it. *That's my exit.*

His muscles were tense and sore, but at least his hand had stopped bleeding. This next challenge…seemed surprisingly straightforward. On the right side, he saw five concentric rings painted on the ground with a white glowbe hovering in the middle, and on the left, a fountain shot up shimmering splashes of colorful, delicious-looking water.

While the fountain looked tantalizing, he had doubts about the reliability of the water, given the tricks of the banshee he had encountered earlier. And the fact that the glowbe was nowhere near it.

Warily, he ventured towards the glowbe. When he passed over the first ring in the ground, he paused.

What am I doing here? He looked at the fountains and arena walls and, far above, the empty stands. *I've never been inside a vast stadium like this before.*

There was a shimmering orb not too far from him, and pool of rainbow water the other way. He was thirsty. *Maybe a drink will jog my memory.* He turned away from the orb and strode towards the pool. He came to its edge, dipped his hand in the soothing water, and brought a cupful up to his lips. Just as he was about to drink, he saw the cut in his hand, remembered the razor pole, realized what he was doing and dropped his hand. The water splashed into the pool, and he jerked away from it. *No,* he thought, *I better not drink from that.*

He started toward the glowbe again, and had a moment of déjà vu as he passed over the first line. Again, he couldn't remember his purpose. Why was he striving for this glowing sphere? He backed up, past the line, and then it hit him: the line unleashed a power that was interfering with his mind. He looked around for some dirt…spit on it, and then dabbed his finger in the mud to write on his arm the words 'Get glowbe.'

Steadying himself, he walked again past the first line…*Where am I going?* He turned around, about to give it up, when he saw the muddy message on his arm. He nodded.

He strode forward and passed the second line, and as he did, he felt his energy sap. His legs had to be dragged with all his might to move an inch; his shoulders felt like they were loaded down with heavy stones. *Okay, the first one was a memory charm, the second was a strength remover, but I can do this,* he thought, looking up, *I can get to the…*and then he cringed. There were three more lines he needed to cross before he could reach the glowbe.

After much slogging forward, he came to the third black line marking the ground. He pushed his body to move past it. Suddenly, voices called out from the stadium on every side.

"You pathetic boy!" one snapped.

"Give up!" a high-pitched girl shouted. "You're getting nowhere!"

"Hey Wheezeridge, no one likes you!" a voice leered. "You'll never be good enough!"

Brenner realized the ploy of this ring. Again, he pushed himself forward. But it was hard.

Each jeer and verbal spar stung like ocean water in an open wound, eroding his determination. Hours seemed to pass as he trudged to get to the next ring. When he crossed it, he heard a commotion behind him.

Looking back at the rainbow pool, he saw himself holding a mircon and wielding extraordinary power. He was clad in golden robes, shooting jets of magic that made the ground burst as new plants shot forth, magic that forced enemies to cower before him, and magic that attracted throngs of admirers to line up for a glimpse of him. And all it took was a drink of water.

No, he thought, *I have to gain admission to Valoria to get a mircon. That isn't real. It's another mirage.*

He turned back towards the glowing orb, now only a dozen feet away. He edged closer to the last line. His weary foot stepped over it. And the day plunged into night.

Instead of the white orb in front of him, it morphed into blue fire, shifting between frightening images: the banshee shrieking and clawing him, Stewart Guffman coming at him with knives, Windelm dying— Brenner fell to his knees—his forest and tree tower burning in a blazing inferno, inside an old, sallow man that looked eerily like himself, but this person was babbling to himself with vacant, defeated eyes. He stopped, unable to look further.

He retreated. When he crossed the thick line in reverse, the horrible blue fire stopped. It transformed back into an orb. Daylight returned. Though jarred, he was okay. *It was just in my mind.* He breathed deeply. *Just my mind…and I've come this far; I can't stop now.*

He willed his feet to step forward again.

Immediately the fire came back, even stronger, and feelings of helplessness and fear washed over him. He felt sick; he needed to turn back, make it stop. And then a faint voice rose from within.

No. I will not be beaten by my fears.

He trudged forward, one step at a time, despite the images tearing at his soul.

He reached out his hand towards the flame. It crackled against his skin, burning hot and painful. He pushed his fingers to touch it, blisters forming on his skin, and then—

The fire extinguished, turning into a cool, green orb; the vise grip on his body abated. He walked backward; the jeering ceased; his energy returned; his memory refreshed; once again, his goal was clear.

He jogged to the door on the far side of the partition, opened it, and walked into the final stage. He passed under a gnarled olive tree, and, to his relief, saw that the gray stadium wall was only a couple hundred yards away. He walked slowly across the flat field, past piles of rocks, checking the sky for any winged-threats, the ground for suspicious holes, and the walls for booby-traps. The only unusual thing about this field was the enormous bull-like statue standing next to a large wooden door in the stadium wall with a green symbol on it.

The statue was life-like in its carving, and held a giant battle-axe in its hands. Although he had never seen one outside of his mythology books, Brenner was sure the creature he was staring at was none other than a minotaur.

He looked to either side of the door, and spotted the white glowbe on the far left. He changed his stride toward it, when a husky voice nearly blasted him off his feet.

"MOVE NO FURTHER, OR YOU WILL DIE!"

The stone minotaur had come thundering to life, swinging its axe above its head.

Dumbstruck, Brenner very nearly wet himself.

It took three large strides toward him, each shaking the ground. Brenner looked around earnestly for some rock or stick to grab, but nothing was close-by. He backed up, eyes wide with fear.

"To reach that glowbe, and the door behind me," the minotaur said in a loud voice that sounded as if the earth itself was speaking, "you must defeat me in a physical or mental match."

Brenner's hands trembled, and he tried to make himself sound much more confident than he felt. "What are the rules of each contest?"

"The physical match is a test of strength," said the minotaur. "Whoever can lift the biggest rock after three tries is the victor. For the mental match, you must answer a riddle correctly."

"How many guesses do I get?"

"ONE," snorted the creature disdainfully.

Brenner weighed his options: with its towering physique and bulging muscles, the minotaur was clearly stronger than him; the riddle could be about anything, and would probably be magic-related, in which case he didn't stand a chance of getting it right. The minotaur was setting him up for a contest he had no hope of winning. He panicked.

"CHOOSE!" the beast said irritably, rolling the shaft of the axe in its hands.

*With these rules, I can't outwit the minotaur, can't get around it without being bludgeoned, certainly can't move the rock...*he tried looking at the problem differently...*I doubt I'm even faster...unless...*an idea came to him.

"I challenge you to a physical contest," said Brenner.

"So be it," said the minotaur, thundering towards a pile of stones.

"On one condition," said Brenner.

The minotaur paused, eyes narrowed in annoyance, "What is *that?*"

"We have a race," said Brenner, with what he hoped was a convincing tone.

The minotaur arched his head back and chortled, which Brenner surmised was laughter. "That isn't a contest at all," it said. "Of course, I will win."

"Then prove it," said Brenner, stepping forward. "See that tree over there?" he said, gesturing over his right shoulder toward the lone olive tree by the gate. It stood about a hundred yards from them.

"Yes," the minotaur snorted impatiently.

"The first one to touch it," said Brenner, raising a finger, "wins."

"You've sealed your fate, human," the creature replied. "Once I win, I will cleave you with this," he said, brandishing his giant battle-axe.

"Perhaps you will," said Brenner. "But if I win, you must let me advance past this stage...and you—you can't carry any weapon with you during the race."

"Accepted," said the beast with a wicked smile, using its axe to carve a deep line in the dirt. "We start here," it grunted, letting its axe fall to the ground with a clamor. Brenner cautiously stepped over to the line. The breath of the beast smelled like rancid meat. With the minotaur standing twice his height, he realized just how futile this race would be.

"On my count then," Brenner said, jockeying himself forward. The minotaur leaned his torso and gave a huff of impatience.

"Three…" said Brenner, "two…one… Go!"

The two set off sprinting, and immediately the raging minotaur took an enormous lead. The beast bellowed with satisfaction as it thundered trium-phantly toward the tree. With twenty feet to go, the minotaur turned back to gloat as it closed in on certain victory and Brenner's certain death—

But by then, Brenner was off in other direction, halfway to the final door.

The minotaur ripped up earth with its hooves as it stopped, turned, and charged back towards Brenner, screaming "NOW you're going to get the AXE!"

What did he say finished the Agilis?! Brenner feverishly thought, sprinting towards the door. *How do I open it?!*

The minotaur was now racing up to their starting line, hardly slowing to pick up his battle-axe as he trampled toward the teen.

Brenner reached the giant wooden door; there was a metal knocker on it. He raised it and hammered it down—nothing happened. He looked desperately for a knob—there was none!

He glanced over his shoulder.

The minotaur was closing in, battle-axe raised high above its head. In a few seconds, it would be upon Brenner.

Panting, Brenner scanned the whole door one last time. *No handle—no hinge—no flap.* Something green glittered above. *The insignia!*

Brenner leapt up and slapped his hand against the symbol.

"YOU are *MINE!*" the minotaur roared.

In a split-second, the door whooshed open; Brenner leapt inside; it closed, and then—

THWACK!

The blade of the minotaur's battle-axe hammered the door. The frame vibrated angrily, but did not yield to the axe; Brenner let out the biggest sigh of his life. Chest heaving, he looked around to find himself in a candle-lit, stone anteroom.

Blood pounded through Brenner's body; and then, ever so slowly, a blissful thought floated through his mind…*I. Did. It.* The realization felt like sunlight warming his skin; he grinned wider than ever before.

I made it! I've beaten the odds. I'm in, and better yet, I'm alive!

"I'm ALIVE!" he shouted euphorically, pumping his fists high above his head, "Yeaahhh!"

Just then footsteps echoed in the chamber; Brenner brought his fists in front of himself like a boxer and watched the door. Only when he heard muffled, familiar voices, and was certain it wasn't another creature hell-bent on destroying him, did he lower his arms.

The deputy walked into the torch lit room first. "You performed quite well," he said in a formal, approving tone.

From behind him, Windelm came bursting into the room, and practically threw the academy official aside.

"You did it, Brenner!" Windelm shouted, running up to Brenner and lifting him up off the ground, and into the air. "I knew you could do it! Absolutely knew it!" For a moment Brenner couldn't breathe due to Windelm's great bear-hug. "But that was even better than I'd expected!" Windelm finally set him down, his green eyes twinkling brightly.

Brenner had never seen someone smile so hard at him, or for that matter, be so proud of him. Although extremely stiff, sore, and exhausted, Brenner grinned back at his great-uncle—grinned wide and long.

Chapter Eleven

Valoria

"Brenner," the old deputy said, "you are now welcome to join the spellcasters of Valoria." He pulled a forked wood mircon from his tunic and directed a spell toward Brenner's hand and upper body. Immediately the gash on his palm and fingers closed. As though manners suddenly occurred to the official, he nodded and added, "You may call me Caster Greaves."

"Thank you," Brenner said, still feeling fatigued, but no longer in pain.

Greaves led Brenner and Windelm up from the lit stone room to a spiral staircase, up and up hewn rock steps, and then they emerged onto a sunny concourse.

"How did I score?" Brenner asked, no longer able to hold back his curiosity.

"No one here expected you to survive," said Greaves tartly, "but since you did, and finished the Agilis, you earned admission to the academy."

"Knew you would!" Windelm said, clapping him on the back as they walked across a corridor filled with plants and paintings.

"Every glowbe on the Agilis course required quick thinking and bravery," said Greaves. "Of the few applicants that I've seen finish the course, most scraped through with only their lives. Sometimes they'd hit a single glowbe. A long way back someone snagged two orbs. You," Greaves said, turning to look at Brenner, "got five." He raised an eyebrow, studying Brenner as though there was a second head growing out of his shoulder.

Hoping to break the odd disquiet in the air Brenner asked, "...And that's good, right?"

"I'll put it this way: many students here still can't get three glowbes."

Greaves walked over to an arched window and showed them groups of teenagers training across a courtyard several stories below. In the golden rays of evening, Brenner could see one group of youngsters leaping across tops of what looked like telephone poles, and another group of older teens shooting spells at targets in the distance. Brenner watched as one wooden target swelled to the size of a buffalo and then exploded loudly. Scanning the rest of the courtyard, Brenner noticed a mixture of young adults sitting quietly, focusing their mircons on levitating rocks, wood stumps, and writhing plants.

"Valoria is structured on teaching and rewarding young spellcasters for mental, physical, and magical achievement," Greaves said. "Here, performance determines your level, not age. There are twelve levels of rank at the academy. All students, unless they show considerable proficiency, start their training on level one, and some won't even make it past that. Very few reach level twelve. You completed the Agilis course in fairly quick order, and captured glowbes under some of the most difficult scenarios, demonstrating considerable mastery of your amulet, and also good reasoning and risk analysis."

He took them to another door, opening to reveal a large chamber room with an oak table, around which were black cushioned, winged armchairs. The three sat down. Greaves pulled out a piece of parchment and shot a spell at a feathered instrument, which flew to life and immediately began scrawling neat words across the paper.

"Brenner," he said. "I am awarding you placement at Valoria on level four."

A shiver of excitement rippled through Brenner, causing him to sit up straighter in his chair.

A broad smile stretched over Windelm's face. "That means he gets access to a mircon, right?"

"That's correct, Windelm," Greaves said with a nod.

Images popped into Brenner's mind of shooting spells and flying— unassisted—above the forest. *This is going to be even better than getting my driver's license...*

Windelm nudged Brenner out of his daydream, "I didn't get rights to mine till after a year of training. That's a very good start."

Greaves continued on: "The academy will supply trainer-mircons for him to practice with over the next several weeks, but he will be responsible for securing one for himself."

"Of course," said Windelm.

"He already has an amulet," Greaves said, nodding at the quill which made a small checkmark on his paper, "We will supply his outer green tunic. I trust you brought a few additional clothes?"

Windelm procured Brenner's satchel, a leather pouch no bigger than a sketchpad, and opened it enough so that Greaves and he could see. Inside was magically enlarged to hold multiple outfits, black pants, socks, toothbrush and paste, his knife, compass, journal, pens, the potion vials Sherry had given him, and what appeared to be croissants wrapped in a red kerchief.

"Good," said Greaves. "In that event, Brenner, you may join the rest of the apprentices for supper this evening, and your spellcaster training begins tomorrow morning after breakfast."

Brenner's initial excitement about new spells was now waning as he thought about being around new students. His stomach grumbled, and not just because he was hungry.

Greaves slid the parchment from his side of the table to theirs; the feathered pen finished drawing twin lines at the bottom of the contract, then floated like an obedient pet toward Windelm, waiting for him to take it.

"Any questions?" Greaves asked them as Windelm scrawled a signature.

"Where will I stay?" said Brenner.

"Here of course," said Greaves. "Each level has boy and girl assigned dormitories, where you will live for the first month of training. After that, you are permitted weekend visits home, until you advance to the next level."

"How many years will I be here?"

"That varies for each individual," said Greaves. "You may choose to quit at any time, but that will be the end of your training, and you may not return," he said solemnly. "As students are called to different professions, they may complete training at different ages, or take a gap year. All are allowed to learn at the academy until the Ganthrean Games of their 18th year."

"When and what are those, exactly?"

Greaves gave him a quizzical look, as if Brenner had said something terribly stupid. Windelm jumped in.

"Forgive him," he said hastily, "Brenner's family is from the farming outskirts of Silvalo, and every day's spent on agriculture. Not a lot of time for travel, you know."

Greaves seemed mildly convinced. "The Games rotate host biomes each year," he said, "but traditionally are held around the peak of summer."

Brenner did the math and realized he had, at most, a little over two years in Valoria.

"Anything else?" Greaves said.

He wanted to ask about a typical day, but was interrupted by something knocking against his hand. He looked down and saw the magical pen hovering in front of him, impatiently bumping his wrist. Obligingly, he took it and started signing the document of admission.

"You still run regular Zabrani and Contendir matches, right?" said Windelm.

"Yes," said Greaves, "and have added several variants since you last played as a knight, what, forty years ago?"

"Closer to sixty," said Windelm. "But who's counting?"

"How fast the years fly," Greaves said, looking wistful for a moment. He saw Brenner finished signing, collected the paper, then added, "But new talent keeps the games fresh." He stood up. "Time to check you in then."

Windelm followed suit, and as Brenner got to his feet, he felt a tingle of apprehension as he realized, *this is it. Windelm is going back to Vale Adorna, and I'm staying here. Alone.*

Greaves walked to the door, then looked back and said to Windelm, "If you'd like a short word with Brenner before you leave, that's fine." He excused himself, shutting the door.

"Brenner—level four, that is remarkable," Windelm began, clapping him on the back again. "You're going to love it here. The spells, the games, the sages, the friends."

"Yeah," said Brenner, before adding a little reservedly, "I hope so."

Windelm must've sensed Brenner's bittersweet emotions, for he put an arm around his shoulder. "You feeling alright?" he asked. "I know you just went through one heck of a challenge."

"I'm okay," said Brenner, feigning a smile, "It's just…" He couldn't bring himself to explain his sadness at Windelm's departure, the loss of his one sure link to this new place…he didn't want to come across as clingy, or worse, afraid.

"Remember," said Windelm leaning in, "After a month, Sherry and I are only a short flight away." He straightened up and smiled. "And besides, you'll enjoy the independence—you didn't want to hang out at our place forever, did you? Here you'll be meeting all sorts of friends and interesting spellcasters your age, I promise!"

That's what I'm afraid of, Brenner thought, looking into Windelm's hopeful eyes.

"Don't worry. The sages here will teach you everything you'll need to know, and you'll be flying through the courses in no time. Literally."

"That…sounds good," Brenner said, then thought, *I can always keep to myself and focus on studying. I'm good at that.* A gentle rap on the chamber door told them their time was up. Brenner slung his bag over his shoulder

117

and they joined Greaves, who ushered them down another stone corridor.

"Windelm," said Greaves, "I will need to show Brenner to his new quarters. I trust you can find your way back to the academy entrance?"

"Indeed, I can."

They soon came to a fork in the passage, and Greaves held his hand toward the right causeway for Brenner to continue down.

"You've got good instincts, Brenner," Windelm said, turning down the hall, "Make me proud!" He broke from the group and was almost around the corner when Brenner said, "Wait!"

Windelm turned and paused.

Something inside of Brenner wavered, like a willow bending in a rainstorm, then became resolute. "Thank you," said Brenner, jogging toward him, and reaching out his hand. "For everything."

"You are *always* welcome," Windelm said, clasping Brenner's hand and in one quick motion pulling him in and thumping him on the back. Releasing Brenner, he said, "Have some fun now. See you soon." And then his green cape swirled behind him and he strode off down the tunnel.

"This way," Greaves said.

Brenner followed, hands tucked in his pockets. Their footsteps clicked lightly against the stone floors; Brenner observed how the passageway narrowed and then widened into a grand hall, where Greaves selected yet another tunnel to trek through amid dozens.

After following the passage for ten minutes, Brenner heard the sounds of teenagers laughing and talking, and then a pleasant aroma of roasted meat and baked bread wafted into them. Greaves led him out of the tunnel and into a large, domed expanse.

"The Banquet Hall," Greaves said as they walked into the cavernous space. The number of students before him made his hands sweaty and his shoulders tense. Seated at about thirty big tables, hundreds of young spellcasters dressed in different clusters of green chattered loudly as they ate the evening's feast. On the walls, Brenner saw high windows and exquisite tapestries that depicted what must have been historical battles and contests, where wizards of brilliant green tunics shot spells at invading armies. In each of the four corners of the Banquet Hall stood massive tree pillars, their mighty trunks stretching up to the ceiling and then disappearing beyond.

Twenty feet away, Brenner spotted something white floating above a full table—*a big wad of cotton, maybe?* He looked closer, then realized it was a blob of mashed potatoes, hovering and circling above a group of youngsters. A passing teacher shot a spell at it, breaking the floating charm and sending the clump down with a squishy plop onto its owner's plate, spattering his face with white flecks.

"Brenner, help yourself to the evening meal," Greaves said, motioning to a far side of the Banquet Hall where a buffet was laid out, "and then please speak with Sorian."

He then turned from Brenner and nearly knocked him over when he called in an amplified voice, "SORIAN SELTICK!"

The chorus of happy conversations dwindled for a moment as everyone turned their heads to view Greaves and the new boy standing awkwardly by him. Brenner shoved his hands deeper into his pockets.

"Go along then, Brenner," Greaves insisted.

As he lurched forward and began to shuffle past them all, Brenner felt like he was in gym class again: hundreds of pairs of eyes scrutinized him, watching his form, likely judging if he was someone to take note of, ignore, or bully. Brenner did his best to keep his attention forward and act as though he didn't care one way or the other.

Gradually, the conversations resumed. As Brenner headed toward the other side of the Banquet Hall, he noticed a dark haired, teenage boy walking toward him. The tall teen looked about his age, and strode towards Greaves with a hard look on his face. As they passed each other, the boy's narrow eyes shot towards Brenner, daring Brenner to meet them.

A real gem, I'm sure. Here's someone I don't need to see again.

Brenner approached the counter, and saw a stack of finely carved wooden plates. The food next to them, he was glad to see, looked delicious. He helped himself to sweet potatoes and a savory meat stir-fry, then turned, looked at the sea of tables, trying to decide where he was supposed to go. As he stood at the end of the buffet, a girl in bright chartreuse green robes came over to pick up a dessert. She selected a slice of lemon meringue pie, and was about to leave, when she noticed Brenner standing awkwardly with his plate.

"What group are you in?" she asked. When Brenner didn't immediately respond, she added, "Are you a level one apprentice?"

"Uh…no," Brenner had to think a moment, "I'm in level four."

"Four?" she said curiously, brushing her brown hair behind her ear. "Oh. You're at those tables over there then." She pointed to the other side of the hall, then headed back to her own table in the middle of the hall.

Brenner advanced to a long rectangular bench that must have held around forty boys and girls, all of whom wore matching robes of apple green. Most of them looked younger, he guessed around thirteen or fourteen. A few stole a glance at him as he approached. Brenner slipped into an open spot at the end of the bench, hoping to keep to himself. But as he sat, the students around him gave him frosty looks.

At least the food is welcoming, he thought, bringing a piece of roasted meat to his mouth.

"You're in *my* spot," said a salty, irritated voice from behind him, and when Brenner turned, his shoulders drooped. It was the same boy who had just stalked past him. "Get up."

Oh great…this must be Sorian. Dark-hair slicked back, broad-shouldered and taller than most, Sorian looked like the type of bully who enjoyed throwing his weight around.

Slowly, Brenner got to his feet.

"Tell me your name," Sorian commanded.

"Brenner Wahlridge," he said.

"Okay, Brenner," Sorian snapped, putting his hands on his hips, "I'm Sorian Seltick, and as you're now in my squad of level four conjurers, let's get a few golden rules down. First is simple: *do* as I say, *when* I say. Got it?"

Brenner decided to play it safe and acquiesce. He nodded.

"Answer when I speak to you."

Brenner exhaled. Had he really worked his tail off just to find himself in another school like his last? He spoke slowly, "I understand."

"How old are you?" Sorian's eyes narrowed.

"I'm sixteen."

"Sixteen?" Sorian scoffed. "Must be poor then, aren't you? Family finally scraped together enough coppers to send you here?"

Not expecting the insult, Brenner said nothing, but clenched his fingers and felt his neck grow hot. This was not at all the warm welcome that Windelm had promised.

"That's what I thought," Sorian said. "I'm this squad's captain, and my co-captain"—he pointed to an athletic, auburn haired girl who sat across the table—"is Kendra Valencourt."

Kendra met his gaze and nodded the tiniest bit.

"To have a chance at leveling up, and who knows, someday earning more than a fruit vendor," Sorian said to the amusement of the table, "you better follow our directions, and know your place in the squad." He jabbed a finger at Brenner. "Understood?"

Brenner didn't know what came over him, but said, "If your directions are better than your introductions, I understand completely."

Like an alpha wolf, Sorian leaned toward Brenner. His next words were quiet and icy: "Try that again, and I'll have to break-in that face of yours."

Brenner weighed his options: he felt like calling Sorian's bluff, since he doubted the captain would throw a punch in front of the whole academy; then again, he'd likely be better off not fighting his squad's captain when he didn't know how long he'd be stuck under him.

So Brenner kept quiet, looking away.

"That's right," said Sorian. He pointed down the table. "Eat on the other end, unless asked to be seated by the premiere players. Now get out of my spot."

Brenner grabbed his tray, and Sorian curtly turned his back to him as he sat down to talk with his squad.

What kind of leader is so scared he has to bully a newcomer on his first day? Brenner thought as he headed to the other part of the long table, still wrestling with the urge to give Sorian a piece of his mind. As he neared the end, a ruddy-faced boy scooted over in his seat and motioned Brenner to sit by him.

Relieved to see that not everybody was hostile, Brenner placed his tray down and joined him.

"Our esteemed captain give you the standard tongue lashing then?" the red-haired boy asked.

Brenner nodded.

"Don't let it get to you. Old Sorian has been trying to lead this squad for too long, and he gets way too much pleasure from his power trips. I'm Finnegan Hutch."

The boy held out a hand, and Brenner shook it. "I'm Brenner."

"Good to meet you," Finnegan said, releasing his hand and giving him a quick glance. "You must have been stuck as a level three apprentice awhile. Which group did you come from? Pazinsky's? Dagman's?"

"No, actually. This is my first day," Brenner said, taking a big bite of stir-fry.

"Your *first day?*" said a teenage girl across the table, her mouth hanging open. Brenner looked up from his food and noticed that the kids nearby were now all watching him, too.

Brenner finished chewing and said nonchalantly, "Well…yeah, I just completed the entrance test."

"The Entrance Agilis? At your age?" said another boy sitting kitty-corner to him. "You must be, what, fourteen?"

"Sixteen," Brenner said.

The teens' eyes widened, and they exchanged looks.

"*Sixteen?*" said Finnegan with disbelief. "The sages increase the hazards at every birthday, maxing out at age seventeen." His curly red hair bounced slightly as he shook his head. "Crown me a sovereign," Finnegan said admiringly, "My cousin couldn't do that stage until he was a level ten magician. You must be *wiped out.*"

Brenner smiled. "Yeah, you could say that. How old are you, Finnegan?"

"Just turned fourteen," he said with pride, and then in a lower voice, "and well on my way to getting up to a level five conjurer and away from *that* dictator." He gestured towards the other end of the table, where Kendra and the premiere players laughed at something Sorian was saying.

"Where are you from?" the girl across the table again spoke up. She had soft brown hair, a sharp nose, and hawk-like eyes.

Brenner quickly tried to remember the story he and Windelm had rehearsed.

"By...the three waterfalls near Cormith."

"Oh, I've been there many times," said the girl, "Those waterfalls are absolutely gorgeous, aren't they? My parents and I go at least twice a summer to them, and again for the foliage in the fall. My name's Maureen, by the way."

Brenner smiled at her.

"How come you came to Valoria only now?" Maureen asked bluntly.

"My parents...finally let me," Brenner said, hoping that would suffice.

"That's strange," Maureen said. "My parents signed me up as soon as I turned nine."

"Your parents would buy you a team of winged-horses if they thought it would turn you overnight into a magician," Finnegan cut in.

"Oh, quiet, Finnegan," Maureen said. "You're only jealous since my family owns the Russwell Suites, and what are your parents, barkeepers?"

"Oh! You're *right*, I am jealous," Finnegan said in oily tones, and with feigned sincerity, added, "Please, do be *generous* and drop some hints to them that I need a sky-blue Pegasus, too? Then we can braid their tails together!"

The boys and girls around them laughed. Maureen crossed her arms, looking thoroughly unamused.

"Brenner," Finnegan said. "You'll find that while, yes, there are plenty of oafs in our squad, there is a core of students who know how to have a good time."

"Oh, please," said an olive-skinned girl sitting next to Maureen. "If you listen to Finnegan, you'll be cleaning out the academy beast stalls every night. He gets yelled at by Sorian at least once a day."

"Portia, that's because I teach the squad the *right* way of doing things!" Finnegan said. "Sorian can't handle being corrected, is all."

"You'd do better letting someone else do the correcting for once," said Portia, raising her eyebrows.

"If someone else wants to accept that noble task," said Finnegan, his hands raised in mock-surrender, "I'm all for it."

"How do you get to be a captain?" Brenner asked.

"The sages decide," Finnegan said. "Mostly it depends on how well you perform on the previous level classes and games, but for some unknown reason, kids from rich families are usually given special treatment and more captainships." He glanced again at Sorian.

"How long has he been captain?" Brenner asked.

"At least a year, that's as long as I've been here," Finnegan said.

"Closer to two years," Portia said. "And that's longer than normal. Usually, captains only go six months to a year before they move up to the next level."

That would explain his inferiority complex, thought Brenner.

"He doesn't even have much responsibility," said Finnegan, "his official role is to lead the squad during games of Agilis and other practices, but I think he's trying to break the school record for most orders barked out."

Brenner was now about done with his meal, and noticed many students had placed their trays back near the buffet table and heading toward a large archway on the other side of the Banquet Hall. *Where to next?* he wondered, deciding it best to follow one of the level four's, hoping he wouldn't be asked more personal questions.

"Here," said Finnegan, interrupting his thoughts, "come with me, and I'll show you the better ways of getting around."

"Oh...thanks," said Brenner. *Maybe having a guide here would be better than getting lost in the corridors by myself.*

The two rose from the table, and Brenner followed Finnegan's lead as he put his wooden tray and utensils in a wall-opening near the buffet table, and instantly they floated up and zoomed into a foamy sink with a splash, then began scrubbing themselves.

Finnegan, although younger and a little shorter than Brenner, had a spry walking pace. He led them underneath the Banquet Hall's tall, pointed archway, a beautifully carved leaf and rose design, with dozens of green emeralds studded in vines that laced up the door sides.

"Valoria is hundreds of years old," Finnegan said, "and full of changing passageways when roots bore through the old tunnels. Stick close, so you don't get lost." Ahead of them, students funneled into a dozen different corridors. Finnegan wove through a pack of them, leading them past a palm tree that Brenner could swear was swaying back and forth, even though there was no wind.

"Once when I was ten," said Finnegan, "I got quite lost, and found myself way off on one of the ramparts overlooking the Agilis course. When I went to turn around, a thick oakbrawn tree root suddenly ripped out of the ground and collapsed my return tunnel. I had to wait hours before a sage noticed me waving from the ledge and used a floating spell to bring me down."

"Who are sages?" asked Brenner.

"Sages? They're the ones who teach us the magic concepts. Most went through all twelve levels of the academy, and are senior sorcerers. Usually we have two or three sages that work with each squad. You'll meet them tomorrow. Sage Shastrel's my favorite."

They ducked under a low hanging leafy branch, and came to a dead end. Nonplussed, Finnegan traced his finger around a circle on a red stone in the wall, which then slid back into the wall, prompting the ones around it to cascade into neat piles, revealing an isolated corridor that overlooked a courtyard.

"That was cool," said Brenner.

"Ah thanks," said Finnegan, "but I just directed the elixir in the wall."

They walked through the now open wall, which reassembled itself a moment later. Evening sunrays dwindled across the courtyard, and after a few more turns, they came to a passage rimmed with apple green stones that matched Finnegan's robes, and a large door with the numbers four, five and six engraved into it.

"Welcome to the conjurer's community room," said Finnegan.

He pushed the door forward, and inside Brenner found an inviting room illuminated by torches on the walls, flickering with not orange but green fire. It was tastefully furnished, with mahogany tables on soft embroidered rugs, as well as plush chairs and long benches, upon which several teenagers chatted, their robes identical colors, with some wearing gold or silver belts.

Finnegan led them past the benches and tables, and Brenner overheard conversations about flight. The room split off into two hallways, and he saw two girls chatting to each other in the left hallway.

"Hello, ladies," Finnegan said to them, who continued talking as if they hadn't heard him.

He escorted Brenner down the right hallway. At the end of it stood a thin, rectangular door, above which there was a painting of a wizard warrior running headlong into battle, mircon raised and casting a blazing spell into soldiers and a horde of beasts. "Boys' room in here."

Rows upon rows of bunk-beds stretched before them in a large grid, and Brenner was certain a hundred boys could fit comfortably inside. The smell of all those teenage boys, however, was not so agreeable.

"New robes can be found on this rack," Finnegan said, motioning to a neat stack of pale green clothes. Brenner put a couple underneath his arm, and the two made their way towards the back. Finnegan pointed out an open bunk adjacent to his own.

"You have a couple options in the evenings, Brenner," Finnegan said. "Most people talk or play games in the conjurer's common area—I could teach you Dragon's Duel—you can also practice in the Agilis training zone, or use your mircon in the Zabrani arena if it's free."

"Thanks very much," Brenner said, still trying to make a mental map of all the castle corridors and tunnels they marched through. "But I think I'll just get an early rest."

"Makes sense," said Finnegan, "I'd be pretty beat, too, if I just completed one of the hardest Agilis courses. What did they put you through, anyway?"

Brenner's head swam, recalling the course. He used his fingers to count as he spoke: "They tried to fling me to my death, crush me, impale me, have a banshee rip me apart, a dragon smolder me to ash, peel apart my mind…and oh, have a minotaur hack me to pieces."

Finnegan's eyes practically bugged out, and then he said, "Well, hey, at least they didn't try to *strangle* you. I mean, that's when *I'd* start to take it personally."

Brenner laughed. "Hey, thanks for showing me around, Finnegan.

"Anytime," Finnegan said, turning to go. "Oh, and our first lesson is at 8 o'clock tomorrow."

Brenner looked around for a clock. "How do you tell…" he began.

"The time?" said Finnegan. "Easy. Just find the appropriate time-numeral you want on your bed frame, and tap the raised knob for it with your hand."

Finnegan showed him twenty-four different carved numerals, and Brenner pressed the one for 7 o'clock.

"Well, goodnight then," Finnegan said over his shoulder, wandering back to the community room.

"Thanks, Finnegan. Goodnight."

He heard sounds of water splashing against stone, and followed them till he found the washroom, where he thought a hot shower would be delightful. After toweling off, Brenner put on some shorts and went back to the bunkroom. He had intended to make a few journal notes from his Agilis ordeal, but within minutes of laying on the bed—made, he figured, out of soft, woven hemp—he fell into deep, well-earned sleep.

Chapter Twelve

Conjurer Training

Aminiature earthquake jostled Brenner awake. He jerked up, his mind on high alert, and wondered how anyone in his dormitory could still be sleeping. The vibration became stronger. He leapt off his bed and onto his feet and was surprised to find the floor completely still.

His bed, however, continued trembling. *Ohhh*, he thought.

Brenner cautiously put his hand against the wooden dial that Finnegan had shown him yesterday, and at once the shaking bed turned dormant. He put on his trousers, boots, checked his amulet, and then donned the apple green tunic. He smiled. Wearing the official robes made him feel more confident. Across from him, Finnegan's bunk was empty.

He exited the boys' dormitory, went down the hallway and into the conjurer's community room. A couple of students there were reading. He decided not to bother them, and try navigating the passageways himself: retracing his steps from yesterday, and hoping for the best. After back-tracking twice—first when the tunnel he was following suddenly sealed shut from a stone wall sliding out from the side, and second when he pass-ed under a tangle of plants, and anaconda-like tendrils snapped at his cheek—he finally found the Banquet Hall. Sunlight streamed through arched, stained-glass windows between the wall tapestries. Food was already laid out on the long buffet table, and Brenner helped himself to fruit, tea, and hot porridge, before walking to the end of a table to sit by himself.

"Hey!" he heard a bright voice from a couple tables away, "Over here!"

Brenner was so used to eating in cafeterias by himself it took a moment for him to realize Finnegan was motioning to him. It felt strange going against his usual habit, but he willed himself to walk over to Finnegan's bench with the other classmates.

"You found us, eh?" Finnegan said. "No hallway trouble?"

"Not too much," said Brenner, "Just a tunnel that suddenly dead-ended, and some carnivorous plants that tried to bite my head off."

"Oh, tendrilsnakes!" said Finnegan, slapping his hand against his head. "I'm sorry, I meant to warn you about those. Didn't bite you, did they?"

"They would have, but I ducked," said Brenner, spooning into his mouth a warm dollop of porridge that tasted like pure vanilla.

"Good show," said Finnegan. "I figured you made it out okay. If not, we would have seen your ballooned figure clogging a whole passageway. Tendrilsnakes' venom causes their victims to swell to huge sizes. And then if they're not found in a few hours, well, what's the word for it...they explode." At this, Finnegan laughed.

"What's so funny about exploding students?!"

"Oh, it's just survival of the smartest. In my first week at Valoria, a young apprentice tried showing off by slapping his hand on their thickest archway. The tendrilsnakes bit him so many times, he grew to the size of a mammoth. Probably would have burst apart too, if a sage hadn't quickly counter-acted the venom and rolled him to the infirmary for potions treatment."

"Wasn't that the idiot, Baldspur?" a boy laughed from across the table.

"Yep," said Finnegan, "You'd think he'd learn, right? But he as soon as he got better, he tried showing off in the Agilis course jumping between the high posts. Cost him the use of his arm for a month."

Brenner made two mental notes as Finnegan talked—be wary of plants and passageways in the academy, and also, since Finnegan knew of mammoths, there must be some overlap of creatures between Ganthrea and ancient Earth.

"Those tendrilsnakes…" said Brenner, "Just what does Valoria gain by having harmful—"

"Deadly," Finnegan corrected him.

"Okay, deadly plants draped about their passageways?"

"Keeps young spellcasters away from the more dangerous potions rooms," Finnegan explained, "And also out of the magician and sorcerer's quarters."

"I suppose that's one way of doing it," said Brenner, taking a drink of warm, spiced tea.

"I don't know how they taught you back at Cormith," Finnegan said, "but that's the way of life around here."

"Yeah," said Brenner, "Learn quick or die."

"Not *necessarily* die. Just hang around with people who know the ropes, and you'll be fine. Finish up your breakfast and we can go down to the training grounds before Sorian bursts a blood vessel ordering the squad to march there in lock-step."

After they'd eaten, Brenner and Finnegan joined a group of other similarly dressed apple-green conjurers. As they walked, Brenner noticed that the students around him were all holding things in their hands: some carried sticks, some had small scepters, and a few had carved antlers. Brenner thought for a moment before concluding they must all be mircons. Although different in style and thickness, most were about the size of an orchestra conductor's baton.

The group meandered through the well-lit passageways, then exited the wide castle doors. The warm morning sun lit up their faces, causing Brenner to sneeze, and they strode down a large grassy hill. Finnegan directed him to one of the fields at the bottom, with towering trees forming a natural wall on the eastern periphery. To the west, beyond the castle, the roar of the city he had walked through yesterday was reduced to a hum.

"Conjurers, take your positions," an adult voice came sternly from behind them.

Brenner turned to see a well-built man with brown, parted hair walking along the path towards them. He wore a long, silver robe, and strode confidently to the front of the class, who hastily assembled into four rows, each with about a dozen students. Brenner fell in next to Finnegan in the second row.

"Fair morn, young spellcasters," the man said.

"Fair morn, Sage Shastrel," everyone except Brenner echoed together.

"I hope you have been practicing your Apellatum spell," the sage said, taking a large black rock from his pocket and placing it on the ground next to him. "To see who has, we'll start with a challenge: who will be the first person to summon this rock to them?"

Shastrel's sterling eyes swept over the whole assembly.

His voice rang out, "Begin!"

Brenner noticed as all around him, the forty-plus students stretched their arms forward and pointed their mircons towards the brick-sized rock, muttering "*Apellatum,*" apparently attempting to channel their desire for it to come to them. Brenner would have liked to try, too, but realized that without a mircon, it would be pointless.

Shastrel walked through the ranks, giving advice. "Travarius, use the *mircon* to summon, not your arm...Witkins, *enunciate* the spell... Maureen, think about what the rock wants, not just what you want..."

The rock began rolling slowly one way, then seemed to change its mind and swivel the other way. When Shastrel saw Brenner, a look of curiosity came to him.

"Ah," Shastrel said. "You must be the newest member of Valoria. Brenner, I believe?"

"Yes," Brenner said quietly and nodded, not wanting to stand out as the straggler of his classmates, who were all loudly muttering in concentration.

"You're not attempting to get the rock," said Shastrel, "Why?"

Brenner awkwardly held up his empty hands.

"Ah, that *would* make it hard to summon," said Shastrel, turning to walk briskly over to a leather satchel. He pulled out a sapling stick about an inch in diameter and the length of a hammer. It had a spiral carving running down its back, and a faint glow against Shastrel's hand. Without missing a beat Shastrel turned and flicked the dark, wooden mircon over the first row's heads, and Brenner shot his arm out, catching it.

"Good," said Shastrel, "Your reflexes are still intact after yesterday."

Brenner smiled, and gripped the mircon firmly with his right hand. The surface of it was smooth, as though recently polished, and Brenner's arm tingled as he took a few practice waves with it. His chest felt strange. It was as though someone pressed a hot mug of cocoa against it, and looking down, he realized the amulet underneath his tunic was glimmering brighter: one moment red as a ruby, the next, a dazzling green emerald. The dark heartwood mircon in his hand hummed contentedly, creating something like a strong magnetic force between the amulet and itself.

When Brenner turned his attention toward the stone in front of the class, it was too late: another student manifested a forceful spell and the stone flew threw the ranks, narrowly missing a girl's head, before it stopped, hovering midair in front of a smallish boy in the back row.

"Batterby, well done!" Shastrel called from the front of the class toward the boy, who managed a smug smile. "However, that three-minute spell needs to be wheedled down to a three-second one."

Batterby's smile waned. Shastrel turned to the rest of the class. "Some of you have been here quite long, and I do wonder why you can't perform a simple Apellatum spell with such a straightforward object as that rock." He pointed his mircon at Batterby in the back row, and immediately the rock zipped back to himself. He flicked his mircon down, and the rock landed at his feet.

"You have all mastered your amulets by understanding how your body moves, breathes and thinks," Shastrel said. "Now to master the first stages of physical magic with your mircon, you must understand how an object thinks."

Brenner wondered if he had heard correctly. *How an object 'thinks'?*

"Conjurers, tell me about rocks," Shastrel continued. "What do they want?"

"To be big," said a girl in the front.

"What if they are already big?" Shastrel questioned.

"To not be crushed," said Finnegan.

"Good, Finnegan, closer to our goal," said Shastrel, "but how often do rocks get crushed? Unless there is a Montadaux Dragon nearby, not very much. What else?"

"To be aloof?" ventured a girl in front, whom Brenner remembered as Kendra.

"Not necessarily, Kendra," said Shastrel. "Think of mountains, aren't they composed of giant ledges stacked on top of one another?"

When the class was silent for a long moment, Shastrel let out a sigh.

"Think of rocks in terms of human qualities. They are big, come in groups, are frequently admired for their ruggedness…"

Brenner's mind lit up. *They don't want to change. Rocks love constancy and predictability.*

He looked up, but no one else seemed to share his excitement.

"Think about that," said the sage, "as you do, I will prepare your next challenge."

Some students craned their necks to see what Shastrel was getting out of his bag, while others whispered "*Apellatum!*" to sticks and pebbles nearby, giving out whoops when they succeeded in making small rocks jump over to them.

Shastrel turned back towards the students, holding something blue in his hand. "Follow me," he said, then turned and jogged across the field into the trees in the distance, his silver robes rippling against the light breeze. The large group followed, first over green grass, then to the mouth of the forest, which funneled them into a single file. If an eagle happened to be looking down at them from high in the sky, it would have seen what looked like a segmented, green-yellow snake chasing after a gray mouse.

133

A moment later in the trees, Brenner heard splashes of river water lapping and fomenting through rapids. Sage Shastrel stood waiting for them on a large limestone outcropping next to the dark blue river. The students fanned out into a large semicircle, with Brenner and Finnegan climbing up a caravan-sized boulder for a better view. In his left hand, Shastrel held out a shimmering, cobalt blue stone.

"This stone," he said, "is rare, and not like most others. Can anyone tell me what it is?"

"A compass-stone?" a girl next to him asked.

"Good try, but no," Shastrel said.

"A flame-starter," Sorian said, on the ledge below Shastrel.

"Does it look red to you, Sorian?" Shastrel admonished. "No, it's not a flame-starter."

Sorian muttered something and looked away. Finnegan elbowed Brenner and grinned.

"Well, I don't want to waste the whole lesson on guessing. This," Shastrel said, holding it high above his head, "is a repulsion-stone."

Many of the students let out impressed ahs.

"Allow me to show you how it acts upon water," Shastrel said, then he leaned back and cast the repulsion-stone far into the middle of the roaring current. When it should have hit the surface, it instead plummeted down to the bottom of the riverbed entirely untouched by the current. A wall of impenetrable air engulfed the stone. The water that would have gushed over it was instead driven straight up into the air like a geyser, flowing ten feet up before streaming back down the curved sides of the air radius.

"Now," Shastrel said, "this type of rock thinks very differently than ordinary ones. Let's see who can work a summoning spell on it. I would be surprised if you can budge it, especially when it is engaged with another element."

The teenagers brought their mircons in front of them, and Brenner could faintly hear their cries of "*Apellatum!*" over the din of the rapids.

Different than ordinary ones, Brenner thought. *Stones love constancy...so this one must thrive on solitude and different levels of unpredictability…and the water wants to cover it up, which it won't allow…it must prefer openness and transparency.*

"*Apellatum,*" Brenner said calmly, pointing his wood mircon at the middle of the river.

In a flash, a thin ray of blue light streamed from his mircon towards the frenzy of the water geyser in the middle of the stream. The ray of blue hooked onto the stone and pulled it back; the waters frothed and parted with a splash as the repulsion-stone plowed through them and flew to Brenner. Finally, an arm's length in front of him, it stopped, hovering expectantly.

The class lowered their mircons to their sides; some gaped at him.

Brenner reached out with his left hand and made a cup with his palm; the repulsion-stone landed obediently in it.

"*That's* how you do it!" said Shastrel, beginning to clap, "Well cast!"

Brenner looked over at the teacher, then at the other students, who did not join in the sage's clapping.

"Now, how did you summon it, Brenner?" Shastrel said. "Explain, so that your peers can see your line of thinking."

"Umm," Brenner began, not knowing exactly what to say, "I just figured the stone would prefer solitude and openness—not wanting to be covered by the water."

"Right," said Shastrel, "repulsion-stones hate being smothered, and desire elevated vantage points. Now then, each of you pair up, and with your partner, select three stones here ranging from the size of a bird's egg to a dragon's egg. Then practice your summoning spells back on the field." When it was apparent the whole class was still staring at Brenner and hardly stirring, Shastrel raised his voice and added, "Get on with it, then!"

Only then did Brenner feel the eyes of the class leave him, and the tense atmosphere slowly dissolved into a more casual one as boys and girls scrounged the wide banks of the river for stones.

"That…*was*…sublime!" Finnegan said to Brenner, leaning over to get a stone. "Now I suppose you're going to tell me that was your first time handling a mircon, too?"

"Well…" said Brenner lightly, smiling to himself, "Yes."

"Buckets of balderdash," Finnegan said, eyeing the gray stone in his hand before deciding it wasn't quite big enough and pitching it into the stream. "What are they feeding you at home? Elixir-soaked spinach?"

Brenner laughed and tried to deflect the praise. "I'm sure you could do it, too," he said. "Just imagine what the stone wants."

"Right," Finnegan said sarcastically, "As soon as you start fixing my meals." He grinned and tossed a stone to Brenner. "That one big enough?"

"Fine by me," Brenner said.

They worked together to pry a melon-sized rock free from a crevice, and walked back on the trail through the woods. By the end of the lesson, Brenner had summoned all three of the stones from short ranges of five feet to as far as a block away. Finnegan was getting the hang of controlling the egg-sized stone, and could fly it to himself from as far as ten feet away, but further than that and it flopped around erratically like a newborn chick.

Peals of iron bells rang out, and Brenner looked up high above the academy ramparts to see one swaying in Valoria's high towers.

"Together then," Sage Shastrel called the students, who congregated around him. "I want all of you to take the time to practice your summoning spell this evening." He looked into their eyes before continuing, "And if more of you can cast your *Apellatum* spells as well as Brenner, so much the better. Class dismissed."

Students turned again to look at him, some with respect, many with jealousy, and then the squad ambled across the grass toward the castle doors. As they did, Sorian strode past, and Brenner briefly caught his eyes. Sorian threw him a withering glare, muttering, "Lucky start, rookie."

"Forget him," Finnegan said. "let's get some lunch."

"Hold on," Brenner said, going up to Sage Shastrel and holding out his mircon.

"Thanks for letting me use this," Brenner said.

"Not a problem. It's the standard one I lend to all students," Shastrel said, picking up his leather satchel. When he turned, Brenner was still holding the mircon out towards him. The sage waved him away. "Hold onto it until you get your own. Point it away from people's faces," Shastrel said, then added, "And if you break it, you owe me two."

"Deal," said Brenner.

Shastrel smiled at Brenner, then disappeared through a smaller, camouflaged castle entrance, which Brenner judged must be just for the sages. Finnegan and Brenner made their way back to the Banquet Hall, where platters filled with stacks of honey ham and roast beef sandwiches lay waiting on the buffet table. Throngs of students joined the Banquet Hall, and Brenner looked more closely at individual groups: they were clustered in pockets of different shades of greens. The girl who had originally asked him about his level was walking with a group of younger looking students, whom Brenner guessed to be around ten or eleven years old; with their bright green robes, they looked like a brood of startled chameleons. Apart from their identical robes, a handful of older ones had belts of silver, fewer still, gold.

His group all had the more subdued, apple green robes; looking closer, he saw that none of his group had belts, while four tables over, the whole lot of pupils had silver ones. *So, the older the students are, the darker their robes.* He noticed now that the Banquet Hall was mostly organized by age: the biggest group in the hall was composed of the youngest students, clad in bright chartreuse green and easily filling a dozen tables, then the apple-green colors of his own squad seated across eight tables, then four or five tables of students wearing rich, forest green clothes, smaller still a group clad in jade green, eating sandwiches at three long tables, and when he looked to the furthest side of the hall, he noticed one solitary, round table with the most experienced students. All wore deep, bottle green robes.

"Finnegan," he said, grabbing a sandwich, "why do some students have belts?"

Between mouthfuls of roast beef Finnegan replied, "Mmm—ranking."

Brenner nodded. "So, if someone has our same color robe on with a silver belt, that would denote level five or level six?"

"Five," Finnegan said. "Gold's level six."

"So, robe color represents the different stages…what are their names?"

"You skipped over the three apprentice levels where we mastered our amulets; our level four—and the next two—are at the rank of conjurer, the level sevens and eights are mages, then two levels of magician. If students get to level eleven or twelve, then they have earned the highest title of sorcerer."

Brenner looked again to the small group of seventeen and eighteen-year-olds in bottle green robes eating together. "Why aren't there many sorcerers?"

"Easy," said Finnegan. "Some students quit early; some go work abroad; some hit their 18th summer and have to leave; many discover they are not talented enough to get past being a level five or six conjurer; and some spellcasters," he looked at Brenner and shrugged as if he was explaining a fact about the seasons changing, "die trying."

Brenner remembered his Agilis examination. "They sure make it easy to get killed around here."

"It's what the academy was founded on," said Finnegan nonchalantly. "It takes real danger and courage to create conditions for valor. Students decide how far they are willing to go. The pay-off is once they're out of the academy, trained spellcasters have more prestige and earn significantly more golders than non-magical citizens."

While he liked that factor of self-determination, Brenner wasn't sure if he agreed with the all-or-nothing trial of Agilis, where a minor slip-up would be the end of you.

A loud voice from the end of the table interrupted his thoughts. "Conjurers!" Sorian said, standing at the head of their table. "Finish your lunch. We are meeting in the Arena for our Agilis regimen."

Brenner glanced over to Finnegan.

"We do it every other day," Finnegan said. "Sorian likes to spring it on us as though he thought it up, but every squad does group practice."

Brenner chased down his sandwich with a swig of pomegranate juice, and joined Finnegan as the squad walked together through the inner castle corridors. They passed through a large hall that had towering brown statues on either side. Brenner looked at one of the winged-horses standing twice his height, and marveled when he realized the Pegasus was carved from a single, giant trunk.

"What color is your amulet?" a soft voice asked behind them.

He and Finnegan turned around to see a small group of pretty girls staring at them, one of whom he recognized as Maureen. Brenner wasn't sure who asked. The girls looked back at him expectantly, continuing their walk.

"Why's that matter?" Finnegan cut in.

"We just wanna know," said a taller girl with crow black hair. "It's not a big deal."

"What color is yours?" Brenner asked them.

"Green," the girl said, which the others echoed in turn.

"Right," said Finnegan, "All of ours are green, so what's your point, Evie?"

Brenner peered down at his tunic. "Mine is green...and red."

The girls let out a small squeal of surprise. "See?! I *told* you he had different elixir!"

Brenner felt a flush of embarrassment rise to his cheeks. "Don't other students have red elixir?" he asked.

"No," said Evie. "Students with red elixir never come to Valoria. Why didn't you go to Boldenskeep Academy in Montadaux?"

"Course they have!" Finnegan jutted in. "Lots of dual elixir students come here. They're just usually blue or yellow in addition to green. Don't act like you've never seen a double colored amulet."

"He's right, Evie," Maureen said, as the group went down steps into a dark passageway illuminated by hanging lanterns.

"Fine, but why didn't you go to the other school?" Evie said, pressing her point.

"This is where my family always went," said Brenner coolly.

"What's your last name?" said Evie.

"Wahlridge."

"I've never heard of that name before," said Maureen.

"And I'm sure you know *every* spellcaster that has graced these halls, right?" said Finnegan dryly.

Some of the girls laughed at his comment.

The students filed through a large door into a large space about half the size of the Agilis stadium. Before the girls could question Brenner further, Kendra and Sorian strode to an elevated platform and addressed the squad.

"Today you train on the rods," said Sorian, "until all of you finish without error. Then you will scale the crag wall. Boys, follow me!"

"Girls," said Kendra, "come with me to the wall."

Brenner looked up and saw two large castle turrets on either side of the training space. Between them a dozen tall, narrow poles stood like stilts and stretched across in a line for probably a hundred yards.

The groups split, and Sorian directed the boys towards a high turret, with a winding, exterior staircase spiraling upward like ivy. In a minute, they had scaled the steps and waited on the roof of the turret. In front of them stood about thirty poles staggered some ten feet apart and, more importantly, they rose up fifty feet from the ground.

"Travarius," called Sorian, "show 'em how it's done."

A tall, dark-skinned boy with intimidating muscles strode towards the front. Quickly he leapt from the turret, landed on the first pole with his foot and launched towards the next, nimbly jumping across the flat tops of the thin poles, as carefree as if he was sprinting down a track. In less than a minute, he had reached the turret on the other side, turned, and crossed his arms smugly as the next teenager walked to the ledge.

Sorian nodded his approval, then yelled, "Witkins, you're next!"

Witkins, a chubbier teen with spiky hair, stepped forward and gulped.

"Get on with it."

Witkins nodded tentatively to Sorian, pumped his legs and started crossing the poles. Arms out and wobbling like a tipsy panda, Witkins was nowhere near as graceful as Travarius. On the fifth pole he missed the mark and sprawled forward, screaming. His hands flailed, grasping for something to cling to, but it was too late: he fell through the columns, halfway down bashed into another rod—Brenner held his breath—and then…an unexpected splash hit Brenner's ears.

A splash? Brenner let out a relieved sigh. He hadn't seen the thin layer of water before, and up until that moment presumed the poor kid would be dashed upon the hard ground.

"Pathetic," Sorian said, peering over the edge of the turret. "Batterby," he called out.

A mouse-like boy shimmied through the group and stood at Sorian's side. "Yes?" he said meekly.

Still looking at the floating body, Sorian said, "Go pull Witkins out of the water. Make sure he's breathing."

"Yes of course," Batterby said obediently. He leaned over the other side of the turret, grabbed onto a metal pole, and quickly slid out of sight. Brenner walked over, and saw an enormous fireman's pole that hugged against the turret and stretched down to the ground.

He heard the sound of water sloshing below, and saw Batterby prodding Witkins to the side of the pool with a long pole.

"Next!" shouted Sorian.

With group morale shaken, it took a moment before anyone ventured forward. Brenner considered volunteering, but thought that Sorian would perceive his confident act as brazen showmanship, which he didn't feel would help his already icy relationship with the captain. Finally, another boy took to the starting ledge.

By Brenner's count, only five teens finished the course, while eight unfortunate others stumbled and fell headlong fifty feet down into water, which, judging from their arm-flailing shrieks and belly-flops, couldn't have been too pleasant. Nevertheless, if they weren't completely knocked out, Sorian ordered them back up the turret to do it again.

Brenner stepped to the ledge, watching the current runner. The boy nearly completed the course, but missed the last pole by inches, and before his cries of fright were cut off by the water, Sorian turned and directed Brenner.

"You. Go."

Brenner looked across at the stone columns, tried to push away the tense feeling of being watched by the other conjurers, backed up, and hustled towards the edge of the stone turret.

He jumped.

The first pole was as wide as a dinner plate, and he caught it easily with his left foot and then leapt to the next. The rest of the field melted: he was in his element now, calculating each jump quickly and flawlessly. He felt like a mountain lion leaping along a well-trodden path…this was even becoming fun. When the surface of the last poles shrunk to the size of a fist, requiring precise footing and balance, Brenner still sprinted as though on solid ground. Then he landed upon the roof of the other turret, and slowed to a stop before the back wall. He grinned.

"Nice run," said one of the boys. "That looked as fast as Travarius."

A couple other teens nodded, and Brenner heard some shouts from the other turret. Travarius bristled and gave him a cold look.

"Thanks," said Brenner, walking the perimeter. His Mindscape training over the past weeks had paid off: he felt hardly winded.

"You! Brenner!" Sorian's voice called from across the poles, "Do it again."

"What?" one of the boys asked incredulously.

"You heard him," Travarius sneered, closing in on Brenner. "Do it again, or you'll find yourself falling."

"Get on with it!" Sorian called out loudly from the other tower, "Or everybody has to do the course again."

Brenner could see Finnegan shaking his head and motioning something, but he didn't want to cause more of a commotion.

"Fine," he said.

Brenner backed up on the platform so that he could begin with speed, and again raced towards the poles, leaping across the gaps.

Jumping the course in reverse actually was slightly easier, as the pole footing started small and became larger. He was nearly halfway through when something unexpected happened: a bolt of white light struck a pole three places ahead of him—it shattered in two and fell towards the ground far below. He landed. Only one pole stood between him and the huge gap. He surged his strength. He landed and vaulted, and careened over the gap as the huge pole whacked like a dragon's tail against the water below.

He grimaced, it would be close—

His foot connected with the pole-top. *Yes!* The forward energy surged down to the ball of his foot and he became like a spring, uncoiling itself and rebounding for the final stretch of poles. *I'm going to make it!*

Then his face fell.

Two more spells rocketed into the next poles in his path, which let out groans as they toppled over.

Brenner didn't have enough time to plan this next jump.

He bounded forward into the gap—his arms whipped in panicked circles as he began his free fall—there was no chance of making the jump—*this is gonna hurt*—

Then he froze, midair.

"That's *enough*, Sorian!" a stern voice called from below.

Brenner tried to move. He couldn't. It was like he was stuck to invisible fly paper. Presently, he felt himself being lowered to the ground. He saw Sage Shastrel, a deep scowl on his face, directing a steady beam of magic at him, but speaking with an amplified voice toward the upper deck of the turret.

"Sorian," Shastrel said firmly, "the next time you try to sabotage a member of your own squad you will be stripped of your captain's rank. Squad dismissed."

As they walked back in the tunnels from the practice field, Finnegan came alongside Brenner. "That piece of scum," he said, scowling towards Sorian. "You alright?"

"Yeah…" Brenner said slowly, still shaken from the fall. "I think so."

"It's one thing to stun an opponent during Zabrani, or Contendir, but your own squad?" Finnegan said, shaking his head. "Sorian's sunk to a new low."

"There's one in every school," Brenner said, more to himself than to Finnegan.

"You've been to other schools, then?" Maureen asked unexpectedly from behind.

"Uh, no," Brenner thought fast, "Just in general, there's a bully in every group."

Maureen's look told him she was not convinced. "How did you get so good at Agilis?"

"I just practiced a lot…" Brenner said, trying not to meet her eyes, "a Mindscape in the woods."

"Hmm," Maureen said. "Should be interesting to see you play Zabrani tomorrow."

They entered the Banquet Hall, where the tumult of other students talking and laughing covered for him as he followed Finnegan to the buffet table. He and Finnegan sat together by the rest of the conjurers, and eagerly started eating.

In mid-bite, a sharp jab to Brenner's back caused him to cough. A low voice came from behind.

"Don't think I'm through with you," said Sorian coldly, continuing past Brenner so that the sages on the edges of the room wouldn't notice.

Anger coursed through Brenner, but he forced himself to remain seated.

"Great lesson in Agilis, *Captain*," Brenner called after him. "Now we know how to promote fear *and* failure in our squad."

Sorian stopped and turned to stare at Brenner, shooting a scowl at him. Brenner stared defiantly back, knowing that Sorian wouldn't dare do anything brash in the middle of the Banquet Hall.

"Lucky break for you, rookie. Tomorrow's Zabrani may be too much for you to handle." He turned on his heels and joined the other side of his squad.

Finnegan's attempts at humor later that evening in the common room helped his spirits, but Brenner's mind kept returning to Sorian, and how to outmaneuver him.

"What do you want to do tonight?" Finnegan asked.

"Depends," Brenner said. "How well do you know Zabrani?"

"Been playing it since I started in this squad."

Brenner smiled. "Mind teaching me?"

Chapter Thirteen

Zabrani

"You'll like the next class we have," Finnegan said the next morning.

"What's that?" Brenner asked, sipping his pomegranate juice.

"Mental magic with Sage Erlynda. And I believe this time I'll have an advantage over you."

"Oh, really?"

"Of course! I've been toiling at it for twelve months longer than you. You won't be able to walk into *this* class and blow everyone away."

"You're probably right," Brenner said. Although if mental magic required the same intuition that physical magic did, he reasoned, he may grow to rival Finnegan fairly soon.

Ten minutes later, Finnegan guided them into a sun-lit courtyard that Brenner guessed was in the middle of Valoria. Students were already seated in a circle around a lady with dark, raven hair, darker eyes, a thin physique, and silver sage robes.

"Please be seated," Sage Erlynda called in a clear, high voice, pointing to woven-reed mats.

Brenner and Finnegan sat on the mats next to stone columns.

"Fair morn, spellcasters," she said to the group.

"Fair morn, Sage Erlynda," the group dutifully responded.

"Today we will continue our foray into mind reading. Using what you learned about *mentalidium*, you will read the image presented in your partner's mind. Now, look at your mat."

As she spoke, luminescent yellow lines from their mats grew on the ground like tendrils, curling across the circle toward other vines until each found a match. Brenner followed his light-line until he saw who he had been joined with. He gulped. He was paired with Kendra.

"Now that you've been partnered," Erlynda went on, "Boys, picture an animal in your mind's eye, and maintain eye contact with your partner. Girls, let your minds see the reflection of their thought. Raise your mircons. Begin."

Around the courtyard, spellcasters called out, "*Mentalidium.*"

Brenner didn't know which was more awkward: having to stare into a girl's eyes for what seemed like forever, or knowing that she was trying to see inside his thoughts. He pictured a green chameleon, perched on a branch.

Nervous giggles rang out from the class, and after a moment, animals started being called out.

"Leopard!"

"*Nightshade!*"

"Golden Ursa."

"Very good," Sage Erlynda commented, walking around the students, and pointing her mircon at their foreheads.

So far, Kendra wasn't having much luck getting into Brenner's head, but she was certainly causing discomfort. Brenner felt something like a vice grip squeezing his mind.

Kendra's eyebrows furrowed, and she continued scowling as the two made the most unwelcomed and forced eye contact Brenner had ever been part of, broken only when a fly landed on his arm and bit him. He winced and batted it away.

"It's something green…" Kendra said, as the sage passed next to her.

Brenner gritted his teeth, unwilling to let his concentration lapse again.

After another long minute, Erlynda thankfully called out, "Stop."

Kendra lowered her mircon, and Brenner felt like a magnet stopped tugging at his head.

"This time," Erlynda said, "visualize the mental defenses of your target. See beyond the physical person in front of you." She raised her arm and said, "Again."

Brenner pointed his mircon at Kendra, said, *"Mentalidium,"* and although he was watching her eyes, they turned into a hazy mist, and pushing through that, he found a solid mental wall erected. He knew he'd have to do more than just put pressure on it.

*How does she think? Confident, controlling, proud, an alpha…How would she defend with a wall?…she'd expect brute force…so if I can distract her, I might just slip around it…*he didn't exactly know how, but he sent her a picture of an army…first it attacked a section of the wall, which held fast, then it divided in two and tunneled at opposite ends. Then it divided again and tried scaling the walls…and now a war broke forth, with Kendra's own army appearing at the tops and pushing his soldiers back…his mental energy fading, he gathered his army into one mass again except for a scout laying low to the ground, and after failing at breaking the front entrance, bowed before the wall and turned back in retreat. Then it happened. The back of the wall faltered, likely because Kendra felt she had won and relaxed her guard, and his lone scout saw beyond the rampart to a scaly creature flapping its wings.

"A dragon," Brenner called out.

Sage Erlynda pointed a mircon at Kendra, checking for herself. "Very good, Brenner."

Kendra scowled at him once more before breaking eye contact.

Brenner made a note to add to his journal: *Mental magic hinged on knowing character.*

Next to him, Finnegan was focusing his attention on Maureen, trying to find her animal. Beads of sweat formed on Finnegan's forehead. He heard other students calling out animals—"Owl!" "Hydra!" "Coati!"

Sage Erlynda circled the group a few more times, before calling out, "Conjurers, you may stop." Finnegan let out an exasperated sigh, while across from him Maureen smiled in triumph to her friends.

Erlynda didn't offer the thorough explanations behind magic that Sage Shastrel had given yesterday; she spent the next hour asking the students to think about crafting their mindwalls, and hinting that the next level of mental magic would be to look into another's thoughts, motives, and memories.

After Sage Erlynda adjourned the morning session for lunch, Finnegan was quiet. But when Brenner offered to bring him a chocolate éclair that the cooks had just placed on the buffet table, he reverted back to his usual self.

"Thanks," he said, taking a bite. "Ready to play some Zabrani?"

"Hopefully," said Brenner. "We'll see how well you taught me."

The two hustled through the corridors of Valoria, past the courtyard where a group of level six conjurers were practicing mental magic, up to the northern part of the castle.

When they walked through the grand archway to the west entrance of the field, Brenner saw a rocky terrain so vast he thought it must have been a trick of the eye.

It was like the stadium had swallowed a dozen football fields, or was built to be a holding dock for a convoy of supertankers. Although it seemed impossible, it was even larger than the Agilis stadium.

Around the giant oval field, tens of thousands of seats rose up in tiers so high they blurred together. Finnegan and Brenner walked from the archway to the large, buzzing crowd of students congregating on the field at one end of the oval.

More than just his level four conjurers, but not the entire academy, there must have been around a hundred teenagers in different shades of green, the younger with brighter colors, and the older with darker hues.

Just then a middle-aged man with matted brown hair, a body the size of a stuffed recliner and neck strewn with golden necklaces, walked up to the spellcasters, and casually floated ten feet in the air. Like the other sages, he wore a silver tunic.

"Fair noon, spellcasters," he spoke in an amplified voice, "You've probably noticed it is not just your squad here today for Zabrani." He gestured to the large crowd with fingers the size of plump sausages. "We are trying a new method of training. You will play in blended ability groups, so that we can see if new leaders emerge, and observe how you handle unexpected situations."

Murmurs rippled through the crowd.

"Who is he?" Brenner said, leaning to Finnegan.

"Sage Vicksman."

"As always," Vicksman continued, pointing to the small crowd of adults in silver robes in the stands, "your instructors and I are watching how you integrate your education into the arena; your performance shows us who is ready to advance to the next level."

Brenner looked up and down the sideline. His hands fidgeted, poking the ends of his mircon. The other students looked much more confident than he felt.

"You may test your mircon on those targets," Vicksman waved toward three stone statues in the distance, "and then select a shield for yourself." Behind Vicksman, back against the rampart, stood a large rack that held a couple hundred glimmering, silver shields.

Brenner joined the throng of students walking up to the edge of the field. They immediately started shooting bursts of spells at the targets. With the barrage of sounds bouncing off the arena walls, Brenner felt as though he had entered a firing range.

He pointed his mircon at the first chipped, marble statue of an archer about a hundred yards away, recalling the spell that Finnegan had taught him last night, as he had explained rules while they practiced by the forest before dark.

"Arcyndo!"

His amulet warmed against his chest, and a bolt of red shot out of his mircon, streaked downfield, and kicked up a clod of dirt five feet from the archer. He steadied his aim at the next statue, this one a centaur made of dark obsidian; Brenner guessed it to be double the distance of the first target.

"Arcyndo!"

Again the red energy burst from his mircon, flew like a phoenix across the field, and this time it just nicked the tail of the centaur: the whole statue shimmered from black to pewter gray. Other shots pelted the ground all around the statue, making faint sizzles. Brenner glanced at the higher ranked spellcasters, and realized that they weren't saying anything at all as they cast their stunning spells. Only his cohort was saying the spell trigger.

Brenner squinted to make out the last distant target: a warrior statue made of red sandstone, standing halfway across the field—at least three hundred yards away. Colored zaps of spells hit the grass all around the statue; a few wild shots hit the far walls. Brenner calmed his thoughts and pointed his mircon, then, louder than he intended to, he said, *"Arcyndo!"*

His mircon shot a current of red light, which soared downfield past the other statues, and found its mark in the chest of the warrior. Its whole body rippled dark then light red. Brenner smiled; his confidence ticked up a bit, even though his next several shots missed.

"Looks like you're ready to go," said Finnegan.

"I think so," said Brenner, "just trying to refresh myself on the rules: fire at opponents to stun them, use my shield to block, and if possible, try to stun their king or grab one of their three glowbes, right?"

"Right," said Finnegan. "Score points for hits, more for king or healers, partial points for shielded blows, and twenty points per glowbe captured. Once all three of the opponent's glowbes are captured, or one team is immobilized, the game is over, and the team with the most points wins."

"Are those the best ways to win?"

"Those are the tried and true methods. Unless you're feeling lucky, then there are a couple of gambits."

"Gambits?" Brenner said, turning from the firing range with Finnegan, and following the other players walking to the wall of silver shields.

"Yeah," said Finnegan, "you don't really need to know them yet. They're different types of offense, and there's one that can technically earn points, but it's probably the stupidest thing you can do."

The two walked over to the shields and Brenner asked, "What's that?"

"A Wizard's Gambit," said Finnegan, "It's when you gather all three glowbes from your side, take them across the entire field, and deposit them in the opponent's tower. If you do, you gain 120 points. But if you don't get all three in the tower—most of the time the player won't even reach the tower—it adds to your opponents' score and you're done for. Once opponents see you running with three glowbes, you're guaranteed to be spell-bombed. So, no sensible player tries it."

"I can see why," Brenner said, picking up a shield, which was about as large as his torso. He slid his left forearm into it, and his first thought was how surprisingly light it was. It weighed even less than his amulet, like a sheet of air had thickened and bonded together. He rapped it with his knuckles. It was quite solid.

When the students walked back to the field with their shields, Vicksman turned and called out, "*Scindo.*"

Immediately the sound of an earthquake filled the arena, and a large wall of rock erupted from the ground on one end of the stadium. Like a train speeding from a tunnel, it grew across the arena, neatly cutting the field into two extremely long corridors. Vicksman pointed his mircon at the three statues, and they rose into the air and soared off the field into an open tunnel entrance, which swiftly closed. Then he turned to the players.

"*Aperio.*"

The shields all around Brenner flickered and the silver colors changed to new ones: goldenrod yellow, brilliant blue, zest orange, and royal violet. Brenner looked at his own: it had morphed into orange. Beside him, Finnegan's shield shone bright blue.

"Darn," Finnegan said, looking in disappointment from his to Brenner's. "I was hoping we could team up."

"Yellow shields will play blues," said Vicksman, "while oranges will battle against violets. Yellow and orange, your territory is at the far end of the field."

"Good luck then!" said Finnegan, turning to join the blue shields.

"Thanks," said Brenner, hustling the opposite way; he had to hurry if he'd get there in decent time, as it was going to be a *very* long run to the other end of the field. But when he and a group of younger players were about fifty yards out, Vicksman's voice called out with impatience:

"Spellcasters, make use of the launch."

Brenner stopped, looked around, and then saw students with yellow shields filing towards the left edge of the stadium, while those with orange shields jogged to the other side, up to some sort of black square behind two green poles.

Spellcasters strode to the back of the launch, jumped lightly onto it, and were catapulted the entire length of the field. Brenner made sure to put plenty of teammates between himself and the magic transporter, watching tensely as one by one they sling-shotted across the field.

Am I missing something? Did they recite a spell to do that?

Too soon, it was his turn. He gripped his mircon and shield, and walked to the edge of the black surface, wondering what in the world he was supposed to say.

"Hurry up then," an annoyed voice called from behind.

"Who's holding up the line?"

Brenner forced himself to jump nervously onto the magic mat. The good news was that he wasn't given any more time to guess what to do.

Like being hurled from the hand of an angry giant down the length of a par-5 hole, Brenner flew some six hundred yards in the air gripping his mircon and shield—wind whipped against his face—the entire field blurred past him—and then hard ground rushed toward him, and he braced for a painful landing.

At the very last second, he passed between two poles, and some magnetic force slowed him: it felt like falling through thick, invisible gelatin, and then he was deposited gently on the black square. Relieved, he jumped off the mat, and looked back to the device. *The poles—ohhh, they must have been responsible for my stop.*

"Who's captain then?" someone asked.

The last students landed on the launch pad, trotting to join a large cluster of new teammates holding orange shields. Vicksman's voice emanated throughout the vast arena: "The most senior spellcaster in each group is captain, and they choose the team's three healers and king. Since the field is split, we won't be using the spiral towers, therefore winning is through total team stunning or glowbe capture only. No Wizard's Gambits. In five minutes, I will ring the brass bell to make your landforms, so quickly decide your formation and plan of attack."

Brenner looked to the students, trying to find one with the darkest shade of green robes. An older boy with short hair, bottle green robes and steel blue eyes stepped to the front.

"Looks like I'm the only level twelve sorcerer. Am I missing anyone?"

The spellcasters remained silent, so the older boy continued.

"My name's Maverick. I'll be your captain, and I'll choose the healers based on rank as well. Is anyone level eleven?"

Again, no one spoke.

"Level ten?"

Three teenage boys and one girl who looked about Brenner's age raised their hands and stepped forward through the small crowd. They all wore jade robes.

Maverick looked at each of them, sizing them up. "What are your names and game strengths?"

"I'm Juma, and I am the fastest in my squad," said the first youth, tall with a dark complexion. With his strong calves showing below the hems of his jade robes, Brenner believed him.

"I'm Berlin," said the next boy who sported a blond crew cut, "And for the last five games, I've only missed my target once." He crossed his arms and looked smugly at Maverick.

Maverick nodded, then looked to the third youth, a hulking figure with a shock of black hair, standing a head taller than Juma. "And you?"

"The name's Hector," he said, "and if you couldn't tell—" he turned unexpectedly and grabbed a younger spellcaster from the group and in one swift motion lifted him over his head. "I'm strong."

Maverick chuckled, and motioned for Hector to put down the boy, who looked uncertain whether he should struggle to get down, or prepare to be thrown over their heads. Brenner looked at the other level ten spellcaster: a girl with long, chocolate-truffle hair pulled back into a ponytail, with a slender nose above cherry lips, who met Maverick's gaze with confident, green eyes.

"And you?" he asked.

"I'm Gemry," she said coolly, "and I know when knights should push ahead for an advantage, and where we should set traps."

This seemed to satisfy Maverick, who said, "I need swift, precise, and strategic healers; so Juma, Berlin and Gemry, these are for you," he said, handing them three white cloaks and specially marked mircons with white tips. "And Hector," he added, noticing that Hector's lip was curling in resentment, "I need you to help lead on offense."

"All spellcasters who can fly—the knights—over here," Maverick continued, pointing to his right.

Three quarters of the group joined him on the right. Only Brenner and five other students remained. Brenner's hands clenched when he saw that Sorian was one of them. Sorian glared back.

Maverick turned to the group of six. "So, you're my groundlings, eh? Well, make yourself useful and stun at least one opponent before you get zapped. I'm adding five knights to your group to cover your flightless limitations." Maverick turned, divided the group of knights into three groups of five, assigned a healer to each, and gave them territory to cover.

Brenner was relieved that five skilled flyers were with his group, since he wasn't sure how he'd fare against a swarm of opponents.

"Juma, Berlin, Gemry—take a glowbe and place it in the rear of your group. You are responsible for directing sub-teams. Since I'm the highest level, I'll be the king."

Then Maverick turned toward a pedestal in the back of their territory, grabbed something from the top of it, and wordlessly flew up in the sky, hovering above their half of the field. Next came the part Finnegan explained to Brenner multiple times, yet he still couldn't quite wrap his head around it.

In the distance, Brenner could see the violet shields of his opponents and three purple glowbes shooting faint columns into the air. If it weren't for what Maverick would do next, Zabrani would be too simple: just shoot across open terrain until the other team was stunned.

A deep, brass bell rang, and Brenner felt the sound reverberate in his feet. Maverick threw a handful of pebbles on either side of him, but when the stones hit the ground, something strange happened.

Where the pebbles hit, giant hills, as big as Egyptian pyramids, grew out of the ground, forming a rocky ridge between the two teams. Maverick then soared over the tops of the miniature mountains, scattering more seeds as he went. Seconds after he flew over the ridge, tangles of trees and bushes sprouted forth, accomplishing more growth in a few seconds than what a forest often achieves in a century. He circled back towards the team, forming pockets of trees on the two sides of the field right up to the dividing wall that Vicksman had created. Then he tossed three blue stones onto the open plain in the center, and when they hit ground, it was like a gushing artesian well burst forth, creating an enormous lake in the middle of the field.

A moment ago, what had been a rocky and flat land was now a rugged, multi-featured landscape with forests, hills, and a wide lake before the rocky midpoint ridge. Brenner's eyes felt dry; he realized he hadn't blinked in some time.

"Center formation, follow me," Gemry called out to her group of eleven spellcasters, and Brenner had to sprint to keep her in sight as she flew towards the back of the lake. Only he and the five other flightless students had to run and navigate the trees, the five knights simply flew over them.

"Watch where you're going, Wahlridge," Sorian said, brusquely shoving past Brenner as the group raced toward the meeting spot in the distance.

By the time the six students reached Gemry, she had already given assignments to the flying knights. Scanning the field, Brenner noticed them hovering by treetops on all sides of the lake.

Gemry herself hovered about seven feet off the ground, facing the flightless students. "If they're brazen, they're going to come from the high peak on the right," Gemry said, motioning to the towering hill in the distance. "So, you three, station yourselves within view of that pass." She pointed to Sorian and two other spellcasters, and they headed out. "If they're smart, they'll try to sneak through the lower pass by the trees, so there's more obstacles to cover them. You two," she said, pointing to the remaining two, a boy and a girl, "flank the left side of the lake and find a good vantage point in a tree to keep that pass in your sights. Signal me if you see them trying to sneak through."

"Can do," one of them said as they hustled away.

As the only flightless player left, Brenner waited for instructions. He felt awkward as Gemry floated above him, probably deciding some leftover spot to assign him. Suddenly she flew down to the ground, standing as tall as he did, her hands on her hips.

"I saw you during the practice shoot," Gemry said, her green eyes meeting his.

Oh great, Brenner thought, bracing himself, *she saw my misses, and how I have to say the spell out loud to make it work. Sorian's bad enough, now she's going to grill me, too?*

"There's not many lower level conjurers that can hit the red warrior a full league away."

Huh? His cheeks warmed; he hadn't expected a compliment. "Oh… thanks…" he said, and awkwardly realized he'd forgotten her name. "Was it Gimery?"

"No, Jem-ree, like a gemstone. And what's your name?"

"Me? Brenner."

"Just Brenner?"

"Brenner Wahlridge."

"Well, Brenner Wahlridge, I saved you for last because along with the high and low passes, I need you to guard the sky."

Unconsciously, Brenner's shoulders straightened back. "Thanks," he said in what he hoped was a dignified voice. "I'll do my best."

"Make some good stuns, and prove me right," Gemry said, as two loud peals of brass bells sounded.

Sage Vicksman flew above the middle ridges, sent a pulsing light from his mircon that touched every part of the stadium, and shouted, "Zabrani matches—begin!"

"If you can keep up with me," Gemry said, "press forward to take more land and, eventually, the glowbes. Now, play hard and win," Gemry added, flying towards a high elm tree on the right side of the lake.

She hadn't assigned him a fixed spot, just an objective. He liked that.

Brenner took off around the left side of the lake, so that he could watch both of the likely entry points that Gemry predicted.

Flashes of light flickered over the ridge and through trees ahead: the battle was upon them.

Coming to the last stand of trees before the hills, Brenner hid behind one and peeked out to see three flyers with violet shields sending a continuous volley of stunning spells at a trio of his orange teammates behind large boulders, pinning them in place. His teammates, two flightless groundlings and one knight, shot back, and succeeded in hitting the leg of one of the flyers. He let out a sharp cry, and his leg went rigid, yet he still hovered in the sky.

Brenner pointed his mircon around the tree and was about to shoot, but saw he'd only hit their shields, and worse, give up his position. *I can do more damage if I get around them…get a clear shot at their backs.*

One of his teammates let out a yell, and the orange knight fell from the air to the ground with a sickening *thud*, immobilized.

"Gotcha!" a violet flyer yelled.

They were now down, two groundlings against three flyers, when the odds got worse: two new violet knights flew from over the left hill.

It was now or never.

Brenner made a run to the far right of the melee, sprinting across the open hillside and diving for cover behind a grey boulder. He held his breath. The shots of spells continued…but they weren't directed at him. He stuck his head around the side of the boulder. The five flyers had picked off another of his teammates, and they started to fan around the rock to finish the remaining orange groundling.

Brenner leaned to his right around the boulder, and as hard as he could, thought, *"Arcyndo!"*

His spell streamed out from his mircon, struck a knight in the back, and as he fell, Brenner pointed to a red-haired girl flyer and shot again.

"Aaaaagh!" shouted the first boy as he dropped to the ground, catching the attention of the two closest fliers to him. As they turned, Brenner's second spell hit the next knight, and she plummeted to the rocky hillside. *Yes!*

"There's one over there!" a violet knight called to her two teammates, who had swooped around and stunned the last orange spellcaster.

Brenner's adrenaline kicked in: they'd be coming for him now. He looked up the hillside—briefly saw a sage in shimmering silver flying far above, watching the field—then saw two boulders wedged together, forming a narrow cave entrance. Knowing the three knights would surround him, he sprinted for the cave, holding his shield back to defend his shoulder and blindly shooting spells at the flyers.

Hot bursts of light cracked into the rocks around him, and two blasted hard into his shield as he ran the last twenty feet to the cave, diving in headfirst. Chunks of stone showered his feet; then he whipped around and placed his orange shield in the entryway, which barricaded most of the cave-mouth. This gave him a narrow opening between his shield and the upper rock, much like an arrow loop in the walls of a castle, through which he could see two flyers coming towards him—*where was the third?*—then it felt like his shield was slammed with sledgehammers.

If he could only hold his shield still during their shots, he could figure out the flying pattern of his opponents…

…the girl seemed to loop in place with aerial cartwheels…the boy darted side to side, but his legs drifted lower than his shield could cover…*Yep, there's his weak spot.* Brenner waited for his twist to the left which would leave him open, and shot a spell through the mouth of his cave—it stunned the knight's legs, which surprised him enough to throw his shield arm up in the air—and by then Brenner had already loosed a second spell at him—WHAM!

Got him! Just one more left.

But when he looked for the violet flyer, she was gone. An eerie quiet filled his cave; he could only hear faint spells firing in the distance.

"*Parsplodo!*" a voice rang out.

The walls around him started shaking, and rocks from the ceiling smacked onto his shoulders. She wasn't shooting at him: she was shooting at the boulders *above* him.

He had to escape, even though he'd be an exposed, easy target. Another explosion rocked the cave, and a jagged rock hit him in the calf. If he didn't jump now, the crumbling walls would crush him. Whether he could be healed from that or not, he didn't want to find out.

Turning his shield sideways, he lunged out of the cave, falling backwards in midair, and shot up at the hovering violet figure.

That same instant, her spells rocketed into his chest, and his body froze. His back landed hard on the rocky hill, and his chest ached with a fiery pain.

A moment later, a dull *thud* sounded from the hillside.

Yesterday, Finnegan had said anyone in danger of dying would be removed by an official. While he wasn't worried about dying, his mind was fixed on the immediate pain of two things: his calf was bleeding from the rocks, and his chest felt like he'd been shot at close range with a paintball—and it didn't help that the stunning spell left his whole body feeling constricted. He wondered if he could muster enough energy to send a surrender spell into the air, which, if an official found him, would eliminate him from play. But hopefully take away the pain.

While he was still deciding if he should wait around or send up a spell, a white mist enveloped his body...then his pain...melted away. The stunning spell dissolved. He could move.

"Pretty impressive for a conjurer," a feminine voice called over to him.

Brenner looked up the hillside to see Gemry floating above him, her long brown hair rippling behind her like a ribbon.

"Careful!" he shouted, "There's one more left, behind the boulder!"

"You mean that stunned flyer over there?"

Gemry pointed uphill, and when he jumped up to look, he saw that the violet flyer had been immobilized from his final spell.

"Oh..." Brenner said. "It worked."

"I'll say. Where's your teammates?"

"They got picked off behind that rock," he said, pointing, "over by the wood's edge."

Gemry flew over to the pacified players. A moment later, the three of them joined Brenner at the crest of the hill.

"You got all five of those knights?" asked the boy in dark green robes, looking around at the frozen violet players.

"Well, the first two were busy shooting at you," Brenner said, "so I had a couple of easy targets."

"Very good," Gemry said, "but we haven't won yet. While you were skirmishing on your side, the right side was overrun; our king, Maverick, was stunned—"

"There goes twenty points," said a knight at Brenner's side.

"It's worse," said Gemry, leading them to the top of the ridge. "They also grabbed our first glowbe. Now, nearly all the violets are surging toward the center glowbe. There are about six teammates left to guard our last two glowbes, so we need to move fast. Their right glowbe may be unguarded. You two," she pointed to the flyer and the groundling, "go take it as quickly as you can. We—" she gestured to Brenner and another boy, "will go for their center glowbe, and then converge on the remaining one."

They split up: the two teammates ran to the right side of the ridge, toward a purple light shooting behind the rocks from a thick stand of trees. Brenner and the other boy bolted up the center ridge, while Gemry flew ahead to the grove of trees.

When will I learn to fly? Gemry covered the same ground in a fraction of the time. As they ran downhill, jumping over bushes and crags, the other boy called to him.

"So! *You're* that new kid—the one who aced the Agilis test!"

"Yeah," Brenner said, vaulting over a rock, "I s'pose that's me." Suddenly a streak of white light shot into the hill behind him. They picked up their pace.

"Nice job back there! I'm Girard, and I—" Loud spellfire sizzled past. Two violet knights were shooting at them from the far left.

"Over here!" Gemry yelled to them.

They burst through some bushes, and the shots on the ridge behind them ceased. Gemry nodded ahead, then glided silently above them. Brenner followed her, with Girard behind, breathing hard from the sprint, which triggered an old memory for Brenner of burning lungs. But so far, he gratefully felt fine.

As he and Girard crept through the woods into enemy territory, the middle glowbe came into view; then a loud snap filled the air. Brenner looked back twenty feet to see Girard grimacing as he lifted his foot off a broken twig.

A flurry of spells shot toward Girard; Brenner dove behind the closest tree.

Girard froze in place, then fell with a loud *thud*. Brenner artfully jumped up to a high bough, careful to avoid sticking his limbs out, then peeked through a clump of leaves at the scene below. Five players soon pressed around Girard, mircons at the ready.

"Where's the other one?"

They were within a dozen feet of Brenner's tree. Another moment and he would be forced into a firefight. Then he saw Gemry.

Hovering across the clearing and behind a few maple trees, she was directly behind the violet knights. As they strode away from her, mircons pointed toward Girard, she rained stunning spells down on them. Two players were knocked out. The rest of the team scattered, regrouped, and then fired back, pinging her shield, and forcing her lower into the trees for thicker cover.

In their haste to attack her, their backs were now exposed to Brenner: a golden opportunity.

Arcyndo! he thought, shooting jets of light at two of the knights, hitting them squarely in the shoulders.

When the last knight realized he was pinned between Brenner and Gemry, he made a mad dash from the clearing. But crisscrossing spells from both of them finished him off.

"Good timing," Gemry said to Brenner, hovering in for a graceful landing next to him.

"You too."

"Would you like the honors?" she said, gesturing towards the purple glowbe floating nearby.

"Sure," Brenner said. He leapt up and grabbed it. The orb changed from a misty violet to a vibrant orange in his hand, then levitated high in the sky with its new color-beam. Scanning the woods, they saw another light in violet's territory flicker and turn orange. Two glowbes gained, one to go.

"Can you go back and thaw Girard?" Brenner asked.

"Uh-oh," Gemry said with alarm. "No time."

"What?"

"Look back at our territory."

Brenner raised his eyes over the hills, and noticed two of the three distant lights from their home glowbes now shimmered purple.

"We need to move," Gemry said, and with a sweep of her hair, was flying again.

Brenner bolted through the woods after her.

The two came to the edge of the forest, about thirty yards from the last violet, shimmering glowbe, which inconveniently floated behind a ring of opposing spellcasters. His heart sunk: four flying knights and six groundlings. He and Gemry were severely outnumbered.

"I have an idea," said Brenner, catching his breath. "How far can your healing spell shoot?"

"If I can see you, I can heal you."

"Good," Brenner said. He told her his idea, and then the two moved to opposite sides of the woods.

As the ten violet knights circled their glowbe, watching for movement from the hillside back near Orange's territory, Brenner climbed, listening to their conversation.

"—should clinch the game any moment now," one of the older boys was saying, "I came back to check our defense as Kuehl was on his way to grabbing the second glowbe."

"How many are guarding the third?"

"No more than a handful. Dozens of stunned Orange spellcasters were on—"

Suddenly Brenner burst from the treetops in a flying leap toward the glowbe, falling fast toward the prize behind the circle of spellcasters.

He was shot five times midair.

His body froze in place, but gravity continued to do its work, and this time there was no sage to stop his long fall to the ground: time seemed to drift lazily as he fell like a ragdoll, and then fast-forwarded as he built up speed to the hard earth—*WHAM!* Briefly, he landed on his feet before crumpling hard on his side, between the ring of knights and the shimmering glowbe, about fifteen feet away.

So, this is what a bruised rib feels like.

"Well, that was obvious," one of the violets called.

"See any more?" a groundling called back, casting glances to toward the forest where Brenner had emerged.

"No…was it just him then?"

"I dunno—"

"*Ah!*"

Pulses of spellfire burst into the violet players, knocking one to the ground.

"There!"

Counter-spells rang out: the violet band of knights concentrated their fire at Gemry on the other side of the clearing. From his sideways view on the ground, Brenner could tell their firepower was too much for her to make forward progress. The whole gang swarmed towards her, forcing her to fly behind a large elm.

Now, they flanked her, rounding on all sides, giving her one last shot. She popped out behind the tree trunk, cried her final white spell—"*Mobilus!*"—which cut through the ranks of the knights, unfortunately missing them completely—and then she was hit.

The pandemonium ceased, and the violet knights smirked at their handiwork.

What they didn't realize was that her last spell wasn't aimed at them: it had surged the last hundred yards over the clearing and into Brenner, freeing him from his frozen bind.

One knight happened to turn back, saw Brenner rising to his feet, shouted, "Oh…*no!*" and fired wildly at him. Brenner blocked this with his shield, and ran forward as mircons aimed and shot at him.

Brenner made one good leap—straining for the glowbe with his hand, spells converging upon him. He touched it and was stunned.

The glowbe shimmered and turned orange.

A loud voice echoed across the arena: "North field! Your Zabrani is finished! Orange team has claimed victory!"

Within a few moments, silver and white robed officials flew through the area, sending revitalizing spells into those who lay immobilized. Brenner felt the magical bonds of the stun spell loosen, and he stood up, smiling.

Sage Vicksman's voice emanated from above the stands, "Convene at the stadium entrance for individual scores and game recap!"

The violet players looked at Brenner, shaking their heads in disbelief, and then trudged off toward the entrance. Striding from the trees over to Brenner, Gemry appeared, eyeing him quizzically. Brenner saw her small smile, and tried to read her expression.

"That *actually* worked," she called to him, "Frankly, I thought you wouldn't land half as close to the glowbe as you did."

"Yeah, it worked okay," Brenner said, cradling his arm against the shooting pain in his side, "whether or not it was the best strategy is up for debate. By the way, great healing shot under pressure."

"It's what I've learned to do."

As Gemry came closer to him, she grimaced, probably at the sight of his swollen face and cut up arms. "You don't look so hot after that fall, Conjurer. How do you feel?"

"Oh, you know, like I fell forty feet onto a pile of rocks. Terrible."

"Here," Gemry said, "hold still." She looked into Brenner's blue eyes, then sent a spell into him with her mircon.

Soothing energy poured into Brenner: his head, arms and back stopped throbbing.

"*Woahhh.*" It felt as though he had taken a relaxing bath. "Thank you."

"No problem," Gemry said, casting another curious glance at him. "How old are you, anyway?"

"Sixteen."

"Hmm. Me, too. So, what took you so long to join Valoria?"

Here, Brenner decided to stray from the truth. "My family wanted help on the farm…and initially thought I could do without formal schooling."

"That's strange," she said. She nodded her head toward the base to indicate they should start walking; Brenner followed her lead. "I asked to sign up for Valoria as soon as I came of age," said Gemry. "I knew since I was six that I wanted to become a sorcerer, actually do something with my life…although my family wants me to just stick with Zabrani. Think I can earn the most money for them that way."

Brenner's eyebrows arched. "For them?"

"Of course. All Games of Ganthrea winnings go to parents until tuition and debts are paid…which for my parents will probably be never."

"Tuition?"

"You *are* new around here, aren't you? Of course, tuition. You don't think an academy like this is free, do you?"

Windelm hadn't mentioned a cost involved with Valoria, just passing the entrance Agilis.

"Right, of course not…" he muttered. "How long did your family have to save?"

She laughed. "Save? That's a foreign word to my parents. I do know that tuition's more than a year's worth of wages as a pawnbroker, which is what my father does."

"Well, you played great out there," said Brenner, changing the subject as the two walked up and over the midfield mountain crest. "Healing teammates at a critical time, ambushing that group before the center glowbe…I think you could dominate at the games."

"Thanks. If I can win Zabrani at the Games of Ganthrea…the prize money might finally pay for my tuition and make a large dent in their debt." She was quiet a moment. "They don't seem to care that professional Zabrani games can be fatal."

"How so?"

"You haven't seen one, have you?"

Brenner shook his head, realizing he was ruining his chance of creating a suave, sophisticated image. "No. Not yet."

"You saw the sages on the field, right?"

"Well…the announcer sage at the beginning…" he thought back, *wasn't there someone else in white flying around?* "I think I saw one mid-match."

"Right. There are at *least* four sages at Academy games," she said, matter-of-factly. "But in the Games of Ganthrea—there are none. Stunned players are left alone when hit. If they're lucky—a healer from their team finds them soon. If they're not—they hope for the game to end quickly, when the moderators and officials fly around to dissolve stunning spells."

He jumped around the boulders that had nearly crushed him a half hour ago, and had a chilling thought. "You mean—"

Her raised eyebrows confirmed his suspicion. "Yep. Death. Our bones are strengthened by elixir, so while most flight falls are okay, there are limits. If you fall from way too high—or you plummet into a lake—you better hope your healer is nearby, or you're gone."

"That sounds...barbaric." He wanted to ask why they didn't just play soccer, football, rugby—or any other of a dozen *non-fatal* sports. Gemry seemed to read his mind.

"That's why only the best and often the most desperate play during the Games of Ganthrea, and why crowds pay so much to see live games—every match may be the last game their favorite knight plays."

"And your parents *want* you to go pro?"

Gemry shrugged. "I didn't say they were great parents."

Brenner gave a short, hollow laugh as they walked along the edge of the lake. "They sound like mine."

Gemry arched an eyebrow. "How so?"

"Well—my folks, they just cared—er, care more about themselves than about me. With just about everything."

"But they sent you here though—that's something."

"Yeah," Brenner nodded...*if only she saw their ecstatic faces when they heard I would be taken off their hands...*

"What do they expect of you after the academy?"

Brenner thought on his feet. "Use my magic to enhance the crops...help the family business."

"Oh," Gemry said. "So, they want you around to use you...I can relate...but what do *you* want after Valoria?"

"After?" he said, not having the faintest idea. Then he had a wonderful thought: *when you know how to fly, what else could you want?* "For now, just survive each day." As he said it, two things just occurred to him that made him smile: one, that a beautiful girl was talking to him longer than the record of five seconds back at high school, and two, while Gemry could have easily flown back to their base by now, she instead chose to walk next to him. She seemed different than girls at his school—more perceptive, more friendly.

"Anything else?" she asked.

"I do want to develop better control of magic—and fly half as good as you do."

Gemry blushed a little. "Tell me, what are you doing after evening meal tonight?"

"I was thinking I might practice my mental spells in the courtyard."

"Oh," she said softly.

"Why?"

"Well," she said, brushing a strand of hair behind her ear, "if you wanted…I could try teaching you how to fly."

Brenner's heart raced. "Really? You'd do that?"

"Sure," Gemry replied, as they came closer to the buzz of talking teenagers ahead. "Just be prepared to fall." She raised her eyebrows. "A lot."

"Don't worry," Brenner said. "In that department, I'm an expert."

"So I've seen. Let's meet on the eastern side after dinner."

"Okay," he said, not believing his luck.

They joined the crowd of teammates at the base of their tower, where their orange teammates congregated below Maverick, who was floating above. From the bursts of colors shooting in the air over the wall, Brenner could tell the other match was still being played.

"Hey," Gemry called to him, "Tap your shield and mircon over here." She gestured to a silver metal sphere at the foot of the tower. Following her lead, Brenner touched both items to the smooth orb. It pulsed with life and sent a flicker of light along a coil, growing up the sides of the tower like ivy.

"All players have reported," Maverick called out.

As he said that, from the silver sphere a pulse of energy shot up and around the tower. Then a plume of white mist emitted from the top of the tower and floated down, forming a tall ivory wall. Letters started to appear in bold oranges, bunching together, and Brenner realized that names were coalescing from the mist, creating what looked like a giant scoreboard. He started at the bottom, scanning the list of players for his own…there was Sorian's name…a little later was Girard's name…muffled murmurs broke out among his teammates…he was halfway up the list when a voice interrupted his reading.

"Well played, spellcasters!" the now familiar voice of Sage Vicksman rang out from the arena. "A very close match! For team Violet, the first glowbe was captured by Mage Lanera Meyero for twenty points, and the second by Sorcerer Sullivan Kuehl. Their high scorer was Kuehl, with his sharpshooting of Orange's king and several knights bringing him up to forty-six points."

From across the arena, there was a subdued cheer for Kuehl.

"And now, our victors—team Orange!" Vicksman proclaimed.

The players around Brenner raised their fists and let out rowdy shouts.

Vicksman built off their energy, adding, "The first glowbe captured was done by a *conjurer*—Brenner Wahlridge!" The orange spellcasters applauded, but looked unsure where to direct their attention until Maverick flew down and clapped Brenner on the back.

"The second glowbe—caught by Mage Juma Oswanna."

Students rallied around Juma, shouting louder. Juma stepped forward and modestly waved to his teammates.

"The final glowbe capturer," Vicksman boomed, although students chattered in knowing groups, pointing, "and *high scorer* for the team—well, that's unusual—was also Brenner Wahlridge! With forty-eight points!"

The applause was louder this time; most students had either their mouths hung open or their eyebrows scrunched at Brenner, all seeming to wonder the same thing: Who was this kid?

"Excellent match! Great work!" Maverick shouted to him.

"Thanks," Brenner said, feeling pleased, but also uncomfortable from all the attention of his teammates. He shifted his weight from one foot to the other.

"How did you do it?" Maverick asked, and the shouts died down to hear his response.

"Well—it was three of us, really." He described the effort Gemry, Girard and he had put into getting the second glowbe, and then the push toward the last one. Someone clapped Girard on the back.

"And the final glowbe?" asked Maverick. "How many did you stun to get it? Five?"

"Well, none actually—I just jumped for it," Brenner said.

"That's all?" said a teammate.

"Did you snag it mid-air?"

"No, I didn't get it at first—I wouldn't have, without Gemry."

Gemry stepped forward and the players shifted their attention to her.

"He looked like a dragon whelp trying to fly for the first time: leaping out from the trees a good twenty feet forward…floundering…getting shot by a bunch of spells midair—and falling to the ground like a rock. I've seen a lot of falls—I thought he was unconscious."

Several teammates laughed good-naturedly at this.

"Anyway, I acted as a decoy for the ten orange fighters," continued Gemry, "and when I knew I couldn't hold out any longer, I used my last healing spell on Brenner. He had a second to turn, jump and grab the glowbe before they realized I invigorated him. And somehow, that worked."

The players nodded their approval, encouraging shouts began anew, and the students surged around Gemry and Brenner, clapping their shoulders and offering them high-fives. To Brenner it felt surreal, like a hot spotlight beamed onto him.

"Bold move, Conjurer!"

"Good goin' out there!"

Having never been the center of such attention, let alone triumphant cheers, Brenner wasn't quite sure what to do next. In a brief gap in the crowd around him, Brenner saw there was only one teammate standing away from the group, studying the score-cloud with a scrunched nose, as if it was a most-disappointing magic mirror: Sorian.

After ten more minutes, the other match finished, and all the players massed together near the entrance tower to hear the results. Finnegan approached with a couple younger spellcasters, cradling his arm; he gave Brenner a curious look as he walked into the middle of the smiling group of spellcasters.

"How'd it go then?" he asked.

"Pretty good," Brenner said offhandedly.

Finnegan looked up and read the giant score-cloud, which now posted all players' results. Then he looked at Brenner, shaking his head with a smirk and a look of utter disgust.

"I—don't—believe it," he said. "*High scorer?*"

Chapter Fourteen

The Girl Unafraid
of Heights

After Zabrani, the students rejoined their ranks, and in talkative clusters walked from the stadium through the corridors to the Banquet Hall. As their squad ate evening dinner, Finnegan shared the details of his own Zabrani game.

"Our king, Riswalt, lumped all nine flightless groundlings together and made us go on a suicide mission up the middle hills. The first two over the crest were stunned immediately by flyers, but another guy, Lucian, and I were able to take cover by some boulders. We kept the yellow groundlings and flying knights busy while our blue knights flew stealth to both sides—the rockwall and forest barrier."

"Hit anyone?" asked Brenner.

"I was just getting to that part."

"Carry on."

"A yellow flyer sped past us and stunned my teammate, but he wasn't expecting two groundlings, so I was able to stun him midair, and since he had so much momentum he made a *spectacular* fall into the ravine on our side." Finnegan mimed the boy's crash landing with his hands and said,

"Thoom!"

"Nice going, Finnegan."

"Thanks, then just as I turned around to blast the next knight, some girl jumped over my boulder and froze me."

"Ouch."

"Yeah…thankfully, there was still a healer left on our side. After fifteen minutes, he found and thawed me, and I was able to help in the final push for the yellow glowbes."

Brenner didn't need to ask if he got one. He saw the second score-cloud for the blue spellcasters, and knew that Finnegan racked up just two points.

"What was the final score again?"

"41-98."

"Bummer," said Brenner. "Better luck next time. Hey—there were a couple scoreboard numbers I wasn't sure about."

"Yeah?"

"So, the first number after your name is glowbes captured, then stuns, then some mystery numbers and a total."

"You mean the stun number for a full hit—chest or head—then the partial stun numbers—like a leg or arm for a quarter point each. Stunning the king's an extra twenty, healers an extra five. And the amount of spells successfully shielded, rounded down, gives one point per five shielded."

*Oh…*Brenner thought to himself, visualizing the numbers next to his name: the large 2 for both glowbes—each netting him 20 points—then 6 full stuns for an equal amount of points, 0 partial stuns, 11 shielded spells for 2 points, creating a grand total of 48 points. Finishing the mental calculations, he realized that he loved playing this game: challenging terrain, fluctuating battle strategy, game-play of near infinite possibilities, and best of all, he now had control over his performance. If only his parents could have seen him play this…*I wonder, have they even thought about me much since my departure?* Their rapt expressions came to mind, when told Brenner would be gone for two years. *I doubt it.*

"So, tonight," Finnegan said, licking the last traces of vanilla custard from his spoon, "you want to join some of the guys and me shooting spells during open practice?"

Gemry's face crystallized in Brenner's mind's eye. "Actually…one of my Zabrani teammates wanted to teach me something."

"What? Who?" Finnegan looked around their table, pointing and guessing.

Brenner shook his head. "They're not from our conjurer group."

"Huh? Unless your older sibling is at the academy, students usually don't mix ability levels. Which group?"

"Well…she's a…" and Brenner had to think back to the start of the game, to her jade green robes, "magician."

"Okay, woah—it's a she? And a magician?" Finnegan stared, not knowing what to jab Brenner about first. "What's her name?"

"Gemry."

"Gemry…you mean Gemry Gespelti? She's good. And that's weird. Upper level magicians and sorcerers don't associate with apprentices and conjurers like us. Why did she offer to teach you?"

"I'm not sure, but I told her I'd meet her."

"Okay, well," Finnegan said, putting his palms out, "just…be careful. There have been instances of spellcasters sabotaging each other."

Brenner narrowed his eyes. "Why?"

"Simple: eliminate the competition, and there's less contenders for spots in Agilis and Zabrani during the Games of Ganthrea."

"Hmm," said Brenner, wondering if he should second-guess his plans with Gemry, "Well, I suppose I'll be on my guard then."

"You better," said Finnegan. "And if not, tomorrow I'll inform the sages of the reason for your demise."

Brenner gave him a light shove. "Thanks, Finnegan. You really go out of your way for your friends."

"No problem at all! And while you're gone—I hope you don't mind—I'll just be rummaging through your trunk, looking for secret spy potions, spellbooks, and whatever else you've stolen to get your skills."

Brenner's smile widened. "Finnegan, you know I'm not a spy. I'm too clueless to be a spy."

"That's *exactly* what a spy would say."

"Look, how about we have our own practice—tomorrow during a break, or after dinner?"

This seemed to cheer up Finnegan, "Yeah...alright then," he said, then composed himself, adding, "That is, if you feel you need it. Maybe I'll let you in on a few tricks I've been keeping secret."

"Sounds good," said Brenner, standing, "Well, have fun at target practice tonight."

"Have fun *being* target practice tonight," Finnegan said, eyebrow raised.

Brenner waved him off and set out for the east doors of the Banquet Hall.

*He's just jealous...*Brenner thought, passing next to the huge, carved winged-horses...*Gemry* had *seemed friendly earlier, didn't she? Or was she just trying to make him think that?*

After walking across stone concourses, and through the castle passage-ways, he found his way out the same heavy oak doors that took him to Sage Shastrel's class the other day.

The sun drifted lower in the sky, but thanks to the long days of summer he reckoned he had at least an hour until it dipped below the horizon. As he strolled along the path, he noticed a few students sitting underneath giant willow trees, poring over old scrolls. But no sign of Gemry.

He stopped and waited. Long minutes passed.

He slowly turned in a circle on the path...*Where exactly had she wanted to meet? The eastern rolling hills, right? She couldn't have meant to meet in the forest—or did she?*

A thought crossed his mind that he had gone straight from Zabrani to dinner and then to this meeting without the one thing he needed most: a shower. *Duh...that's probably what she had in mind. Evening meal, then shower,* then *meet on the eastern side. That's why she's late.* As inconspicuously as he could, he gave his armpit a quick sniff. He crinkled his nose.

Great, as soon as she gets within arm's length of me, this lesson's over.

He contemplated running back to the dormitories, but he'd hate to risk her arriving to an empty field and thinking he had purposely stood her up. So, Brenner sat with tense shoulders on a grassy knoll, the evening sun at his back, watching the east woods and the occasional parrot-like bird gliding between trees. He rolled the ends of his mircon between his hands. A burst of movement in the forest caught his eye: a poison-coat python fell from the trees and wrapped around a now motionless rabbit, gulping it down and then slinking out of sight behind bushes. His forehead creased in worry.

Had Finnegan been right? Was this just some set-up for failure? Or worse?

A whooshing sound met his ears—something dropped from the sky, landing at his side. Instinctively, Brenner jerked back to face the intruder, ready to use his mircon more like a baseball bat than a wand.

"Sorry I'm late," Gemry said, dressed in a forest green top and smiling in amusement at her startling effect upon Brenner, who relaxed his grip and lowered his mircon from above his head. "I had to get this from my room." She pointed with her mircon at the tattered, rolled up mat under her left arm.

"Oh—hey—no problem," Brenner said, attempting to compose himself. "What is that? Family picnic blanket?"

She rolled her eyes at him. "Yes, I couldn't help myself; I simply *adore* evening picnics on old rugs. Did you remember the wicker basket full of sweet meats?"

Brenner gave a little laugh. "Sorry, no wicker basket," he said, trying to play along. "I was too busy…memorizing poetry for the occasion."

"Wonderful—what would you like to recite for me?"

Brenner looked into Gemry's lively eyes and thought hard. The only line that came was about love being a red, red rose, which he thought would come across as pathetic, desperate, or both. He held up his hands. "Okay, you got me."

"Shoot, I wanted a poem," Gemry said, unfurling her mat on the ground and tapping it with her mircon. It floated up to her knees. "Preferably one about enchanted islands, aviamirs, or twist endings."

Brenner stood up next to her. "I'll have to find one for next time."

"Deal. Now, hop on."

Brenner looked at the mat, gently rippling like an underwater fern. He wanted to make a good impression on Gemry, not like his failed lake run that got him drenched, or his indecision before the transporter launch where he backed up the line—so he decided the best thing to do was gingerly put his foot on the outer edge of the rug; then he shifted his weight onto it.

Suddenly the mat shot out from under him, sending him toppling backwards onto the ground. Like a spooked animal, the carpet flew up and zig-zagged violently in the air above.

Gemry let out a great belly laugh, which caused some of the students nearby to look up from their spellbooks and squint their eyes at the commotion. Still giggling, Gemry reached down and extended her hand to Brenner.

"So then, this is your first trip on a carrier carpet?"

Brenner looked up at her grin, and brushed the dirt off his pants. "Yep." Taking her hand, he said, "Thanks," and stood up.

"For starters," she explained, "you have to step on the inner portion of the rug, not the tassels. That's like stepping on someone's fingers. And Velvo hates that." She shot a thin spell at the carpet still circling them; like an obedient dog it glided down to Gemry and waited patiently, hovering at her knees.

"Velvo…?"

"Yes, Velvo. Our carrier carpet. You didn't get out much in the boonies, did you? Here, watch," she said, turning and stepping on the rug's midsection of brown and green diamond embroidery, which barely sagged from her weight.

She met Brenner's eyes and said in an overly-reassuring, motherly voice, "Now *your* turn. *Eeeeeasy* does it."

178

Taking great pains to avoid the tassels, Brenner stepped aboard the carpet, which was soft yet surprisingly firm, like a door laid flat, and stood next to Gemry. When he got his footing, he realized the space between the two of them was embarrassingly intimate—less than an arm's length. Her green eyes sparkled; this close, she was even more stunning. He hoped he didn't smell as bad as he thought.

"*Much* better," Gemry said, lightly applauding, and not seeming to mind the close proximity.

"Thank you," he said, still feeling foolish. *Could this evening have gotten off to a clumsier start?* "So…where to?"

"First, let's see if you can hold your bearing. Velvo, forward please."

Like an excited sparrow, the carpet jolted forward, which sent Brenner flying backwards. He would have flown off, too, if Gemry hadn't firmly grabbed his wrist, pulling him back on the carpet.

Now on high alert mode, Brenner steadied himself, and breathed a little quicker, not least because he was now face to face with Gemry, and she had both her hands fastened on his arm.

"Thanks…a second time."

"My pleasure," Gemry said, releasing his arm as though she did this all the time. "I'm sure it won't be the last. Quick tip: You need to lean forward into the ride."

He did so, and noticed his wrist tingled from where she had gripped it. She was stronger than he had thought, which reminded him that he wasn't the only amulet-amplified teenager.

"Got it. I'm ready now," he said.

The carpet rotated a quarter-circle so that he was now riding in front of Gemry, and in many ways it seemed like riding a large surfboard, which he had never done. He turned his stance sideways, bent his knees a little, and twisted his torso forward, bracing himself for the coming wave.

"Velvo," said Gemry firmly, "increase speed.

The rug raced forward in the evening air like an uncaged animal: first grazing the ground and then ascending to ten feet above the blurring green grass. Brenner was sure Gemry had planned this height so that his next fall wouldn't be quite so painful—likely just a mild concussion.

Wind whistled past his ears as they raced over the knolls surrounding the castle. They surged toward the forest trail entrance—and abruptly pulled up, above the path, above the trees, and soon well over the canopy. Brenner lowered his stance. He could see the eastern ramparts of Valoria: a mix of towers, turrets, and stone walls stood vigilant, cemented into oakbrawn trees, resembling old illustrations he'd seen of medieval fortresses.

They whisked up and north, until they came to the outer stone perimeter of the Zabrani field. Giant stone columns rose up higher than them, and while Brenner appreciated the magnitude of the colossal field, he also took a moment to pray, *Please don't let me slip. Please don't let me slip.*

Rounding the northeast side of the oval stadium, they veered left. While they had flown over the shorter treetops nearby Valoria, they now coasted along at only half the height of the five-hundred-foot trees of Arborio, which was still *plenty* high for Brenner. *It's like zip-lining,* he thought, *but with none of the reassurance that a trusty harness clipped you in for safety. A fall from here would be the end.*

Majestic, mysterious, and seemingly endless, the tree-city of Arborio was like a beehive humming with activity: spellcasters flew between high-rise buildings and wooden additions made to the sides of redwoods, oakbrawns, Douglas firs, and new kinds of trees he'd never seen before.

As they glided between the huge trunks, Brenner felt as if he was flying among respected elders. Each tree looked ancient and somehow even proud: it was as if they had graciously permitted humans to live under the protection of their regal, green crowns. Caught up in the moment, Brenner temporarily forgot his fear.

"Looks like you're getting the hang of it!" Gemry's voice called from behind.

"Maybe," Brenner replied, briefly turning back, "but that *doesn't* mean I want you to speed up." He saw her lips pull into a smile.

"Okay then," Gemry said, "how about some bank turns?"

"I think I'd rather—*ahh!*"

The carpet swooped left, then cut right, as though carving up and down a half-pipe. Brenner's heart leapt to his throat. At the apex of each turn, gravity forced his body to lean over the void, beyond the fluttering tassels of the carpet, so much so that his amulet dangled out from his shirt, and his eyes bulged at the distant street some two or three hundred feet below.

"Hey!" he yelled. "Take it easy!"

Despite his suggestion to the contrary, they flew faster around tree trunks, underneath elevated skyways, and each time he began to fall off, the rug—earning Brenner's eternal thanks—seemed to sense his feet leaving it and swung underneath just in time to save him from a free fall.

"*Woohooo!*" sang Gemry in a high voice that was far too cheerful for Brenner's nerves.

At the peak of their sharpest turn she yelled, "This is great, isn't it?!" which was when Brenner decided to stop leaving his fate in the hands of a berserk carpet, and crouched low, gripping the side of the rug for dear life.

"Awww," Gemry said, a tinge of playful disappointment in her voice, "something tells me you're not enjoying yourself."

Brenner tried to get a word out, but they banked hard left again, this time to avoid an oncoming Pegasus mail carrier—and his body nearly somersaulted off the side.

"I *suppose* we can cut back on the thrills," Gemry said.

The carpet stopped its hairpin turns and sailed gracefully through the sky like a schooner over the Caribbean. Although there were interesting sights above and below them, Brenner wasn't watching: sprawled on his knees with his face planted firmly against the rug, Brenner had locked his hands in a death grip around the edge, probably looking to passing spell-casters as though he was practicing a very uncomfortable type of yoga.

"You're awfully quiet up there, Conjurer," Gemry teased.

Still grasping the edge of the carpet, Brenner forced his gaze from the bottom of the carpet back to Gemry. "I thought…we were going to practice the art of flying."

"Oh—" she smiled innocently, resting her cheek in her free hand, "*not the art of flinging people to their death?*"

"Exactly," said Brenner, "not that art."

Gemry clicked her tongue and shook her head, chiding herself.

"So, *that's* why no one wanted to take flying lessons with me twice."

She leaned over and sat down cross-legged next to Brenner, smiling lightly as her brown hair fluttered gently behind her. Slowly, his wits returned to him, but he kept his guard up.

"And here I thought everyone was just avoiding me," said Gemry.

"Funny, I thought the empty carpet seats on the return trip would've clued you in."

She laughed. "Well yes, but those occasions were for the *unwanted* guests."

Brenner turned forward just in time to see a large flock of yellow and blue birds flapping straight at them—

"Look out!" he shouted, shielding his face, and felt a whoosh of wind as feathers fluttered and wings beat on all sides of them. He peeked through his fingers to see the last stragglers of the flock hurtle at them, then peel away and fly off.

"So," Gemry said, unruffled, "what have you learned about flight so far?"

At first Brenner thought she was being facetious. But when she was silent a moment longer, he realized she was actually serious.

"Well, start low until you get your bearing…push into the wind, don't let it push you."

"Sometimes let it push you, but right, not usually."

"Okay. Hmm…watch out for trees, mail carriers and other flying objects…"

"Always."

"…and…I don't know, what else?"

"Imagine you are…what?"

"The wind?"

"Too unpredictable. Too whimsical."

"A...bird?"

"Now you're thinking. Which one? And please don't say pigeon."

Brenner had always enjoyed watching the birds from his tree tower...swooping and soaring...

"A hawk?"

"That works," she said, nodding approvingly. "Personally, I think of being an eagle. The initial take-off is hard work: you're fighting the bonds of gravity before the spell takes hold and you're harnessing momentum and air currents...then once you get your wings beating—"

His quizzical look paused her.

"Figuratively speaking, of course—then the flight spell carries you forward, and you're exerting a fraction of the energy you did during lift off."

As she spoke, she pointed her mircon down, steering their carpet lower around the massive tree trunks, passing by what appeared to be apartments built against the mid section of trees...yes, through a window he could see a family eating dinner...and on they continued, with the tree-houses hugging tightly in spirals to the oakbrawns, their steps and sometimes railings connecting to others, looking like a giant sequence of toadstools dotting the sides of the great trees.

A breeze blew from behind, and a faint, sweet smell of honey and hybrid tea roses came to him. Gemry's hair and clothes blew towards him, but she didn't seem to notice the fragrance. *Oh.* He smiled as he drew the connection, making a mental note of the similarity between her and the rare climbing roses he sometimes saw in his old forest...*that's her.*

They flew lower toward the streets below until they were about thirty feet high, above the foot traffic making evening errands after work. Brenner realized this was a popular level to fly at: spellcasters and carrier carpets whisked at them until Gemry steered them to one side of the street, joining a throng of airborne people, allowing flyers to pass safely on the other side.

"It's more crowded here on the air-via, but there's less birds and animals to run into, and we're nearly there," Gemry said. "Velvo, to the village square please."

Brenner decided the rug must have an affinity for the grassy lawn that lay ahead, because it flew forward with renewed energy, darting like a puppy this way and that. Now that he wasn't intensely focused on gripping the sides for self-preservation, Brenner ran his hands across the top of the rug. It felt plush, not unlike the coat of a shaggy, silky terrier.

"This is a nice carpet you've got," he said. "Softer than I anticipated."

"He *is* one of the finer carrier carpets, thanks. And just what were you expecting? Sandpaper?"

"Haha, no," Brenner said, running his fingers across the fine material. "But most rugs are a little coarse, that's all."

"I see. When I bought it, I thought it felt almost like velvet, but firmer, so I named him Velvo. He's held up very well over the years."

"So, it's a 'he' then, is it?"

"He took longer to tame than the average carrier carpet—spellcasters usually refer to these stubborn types as males."

"Male and female rugs?" Brenner said with amusement. "Do they date then?"

"It's just an expression," Gemry said, shoving him lightly. "Don't make me flip this carpet upside down."

Brenner's fingers reached to the edge for safety. He knew—or thought he knew—that Gemry was joking…but just in case.

The two of them coasted down to a grassy stretch illuminated by waning rays of golden sunlight, and Brenner noted how their surroundings felt like a campus mall area: manicured green grass, meandering walkways; ornate stone buildings on the outer perimeter, most of them artistic restaurants, pubs and bakeries with names like 'Tasty Delicacies—*done by Marie*', 'Forest Foragings', 'Drink-o-the-Woods', and a peculiar shop called '*Greater Ganthrean Game Supply*', with a sign beneath that boasted 'from Agilis *to* Zabrani.'

"Have you been in that one before?" Brenner pointed to the game shop.

"Several times," Gemry said. "Some of the best strategy books came from there. One summer I spent so much time with one, I could recite full pages of Dietrich Dashmettle's *The Zen of Zabrani* by heart. The way I figure it, if I'm going to play the sport, I better learn how to be the best."

"Cool," Brenner said, trying to guess the cause of a flashing purple lights flaring in the store. "Dietrich Dash…who?"

"Dash*mettle*. You know, the famous Zabrani player of the last century? Who's won more professional Zabrani games for Silvalo than the next two highest players combined?"

"Right. That's the one. Just wanted to make sure."

"You know," Gemry said, giving him a look like he had just used his mircon to pick his nose, "you are surprisingly good at Zabrani for having no clue what is going on."

"Hey, I have some clue," Brenner defended. "And I learn as I go."

"Let's hope so," she said. Gemry directed her mircon at the mat, "Thanks, Velvo, you may land." The carpet obligingly hovered onto the ground beside a bubbling fountain and fell still.

Gemry and Brenner stepped off the carpet. She flicked her wand at Velvo, which curled up by her side, then she turned to him, hands on her hips.

"Alright, show me what you can do."

"Okay, but it's not much," Brenner said. He pointed his mircon to a fist-sized rock nearby the fountain, said, "*Aperio*," and the stone zoomed over to him.

"Not bad. Now, try to move this." She stepped over to a fountain, channeled some of the water out with her mircon, and directed the stream to the ground. She spun her mircon in a small circle, and the water mixed itself into the brown dirt, making mud.

"You want me to move that?"

Gemry nodded.

Brenner tried the spell again, but only solid flecks of dirt grudgingly lifted from the mixture and flew to him. The watery mud stayed put.

"Okay, that tells me what you're capable of," Gemry said. "If you can get a mixture of mud moving on its own, you'll have a chance at flight."

"That means I have to think like a liquid, right?"

"Sort of—liquids *and* solids. For starters, how does water think?"

Brenner imagined himself drifting along a river, always moving, always changing, gathering new parts as it moved along, being able to change into gas or solid, but *did it want to? Maybe it just wanted to stay as a liquid.* He directed his mircon at the mud and tried again: this time, a little of the watery mix flew up from the ground.

"Better," Gemry said. "What were you thinking about?"

"Curiosity. And playfulness."

"That is part of a liquid's essence, yes."

"What am I missing?"

"Think of the fountain. If it could talk, what would it say?"

Brenner watched the jets of water spurt up from the centerpiece, creating rivulets of water that splashed almost cheerfully on the water surface.

"It's saying: 'Look at me'?"

"There you go. What's that quality?"

"Attention seeking? Flashy?"

"Right. A key part of water. Along with that ostentatious desire for attention there is also a confidence: it *knows* that it is vital for life, and enjoys being sought after."

Brenner was trying to mesh all these qualities together in his mind.

"Okay, so I have this idea of what water wants, now what?"

"Now you need to combine that with your knowledge of solids."

"Does it matter what the solid is?"

"Of course. Broken-down compounds like dirt have small desires and are easier to understand and move than more complex, organic objects. With living creatures, the level of knowledge needed to manipulate, or levitate, is increased again.

"Start by trying to lift just water."

Brenner directed his mircon at the pool of gently purling water, pretended that he was an attention-seeking performer, and thought silently to himself: *Levitulsus.*

To his surprise, a thin jet of water jumped over the outer stone wall and splashed onto the ground and his boots.

"I did it!" he whooped.

"Good," Gemry said with a slight nod and smile. "Now, try moving the wet mixture of mud."

Brenner directed his mircon and channeled his mental energy at it. As though carried by an invisible frog, a small portion of the mud slopped forward.

"That's it," encouraged Gemry.

Brenner steadied his mircon and applied more thought: the portion of hopping mud grew in size and now jumped a few feet at a time. As he continued his spells, Gemry's voice carried to him, "Once you understand how airborne creatures work, and can move mixtures, levitating them wherever you want, then you can fly. At your pace, I'd be surprised if you don't manage personal flight before the Games in June."

The words energized Brenner. He smiled, looked up from his work, and caught Gemry studying him. Redoubling his efforts, he tried spell after spell, driven in no small part by the fact that a cute, confident girl was working with him, actually interested in helping his spell and flight development. *What had Finnegan been so worried about?*

He kept at the training until Gemry mentioned that the sun had set. She stood up from the side of the fountain.

"Nice work tonight," she said. "We'd better be going back to the academy."

"Okay," Brenner said, looking up, now noticing the cooler tones of the evening shadows. "You know, you're good at teaching."

"Thanks," Gemry replied. "I doubted it at first, but you *do* seem to pick up on things fairly quickly." She pointed her mircon at the carpet. "Velvo, float, if you please."

The carrier carpet unfurled, lifted itself up from the ground, and approached her knee.

The two of them stepped onto it, with Brenner again taking extra caution to avoid stepping on the tassels; once aboard, Gemry rotated the carpet so that they sat side by side, looking over the shops that had extinguished their inner lights. Scattered high above them, yellow flickers of light dotted the trees.

"Ready?" Gemry said, with a growing smile that Brenner didn't quite trust.

"As much as I can be," he said, reaching for the outer tassels of the rug, the reins of this wild horse.

Gemry nodded, and the carpet zoomed ahead, speeding with what could only be pleasure. Brenner used one hand to stow his mircon inside his shirt, then gripped the sides firmly with both hands. The faster they traveled, the louder the air current whistled in their faces. Soon a great wind was blowing against his face and chest, causing Brenner to squint. Gemry's hair flew wildly behind her.

"Do we have to go at a breakneck speed?!" he shouted to Gemry over the air whipping past them.

"Of course not!" Gemry yelled back to him, "Just like we don't *have* to do barrel rolls!" Then she laughed and called out, "Velvo, barrel spin!"

Brenner flattened his forehead against the carpet and prayed for the best. As he did, he felt a warm sensation briefly envelop his body, and then the carpet spun hard. He hung on tight as the rug rolled three times, like a roller-coaster shooting along a corkscrew track.

When the carpet finished the last spin and righted itself, Brenner was—miraculously—still on.

He chanced a peek at Gemry: curiously, she sat calmly upright. Her hands and mircon lay nestled neatly in her lap; she looked over at Brenner and giggled. Without warning, the carpet barrel-rolled again—and while Brenner clenched the carpet with all his might, he saw Gemry didn't use her hands at all, and yet, apart from her long hair dangling straight down like a brown curtain, she wasn't in the least bit affected by gravity.

"Wha—?" Brenner said in bewilderment.

The carpet returned to right-side up.

"How are you *doing* that?" he asked with a flabbergasted expression.

"What?" she said coyly. "Sticking to the carpet?"

"*Yes!*" he said, gaping at her.

She gave a shrug. "It's easy."

"No, it's not! I was falling off before!"

"Here, let me show you." She tucked her mircon under her leg, then reached over and removed his hands from the carpet edge, holding them with her warm hands. She looked him in the eyes.

"Velvo, barrel spin!"

Her eyes glinted devilishly; his expanded wide with terror—too late.

The carrier carpet spun, and as it flew upside down, Brenner sucked in a gasp of air to scream as he fell to the forest floor, but instead of plummeting, he remained stuck to the carpet, as though super-glued.

Riding upside down through the night air on a magic carpet, Brenner found himself more dumbfounded than he had ever been.

Gemry's soft hands squeezed his twice, and she said gently, "Remember, keep breathing."

Then the carpet finished the rotation and they sailed along right-side up.

With considerable difficulty, Brenner forced himself to speak: "*What— just—happened?*"

"We barrel-rolled," said Gemry cheerfully.

"Thank you," Brenner said sarcastically, as she continued to smile bemusedly at him. "I gathered as much myself. Why didn't I fall out?"

"I placed a spell on you."

"You what?"

"Put a small counter-gravity spell on you, or rather, a sticking spell. Sure makes carpet flying a whole lot simpler."

"But I nearly fell off before, and this time, I didn't budge at all!"

Slowly Brenner started to piece together what had happened, remembering the warm feeling that swept over his whole body when he had put his head down.

"You mean you could have put that spell on me the whole time?!" Brenner's eyes flashed at hers.

"Well of course."

"But you didn't?!"

She smiled at him. "You wanted to know how flight feels, right?"

Brenner shook his head at her slowly, his mouth open.

"Oh, relax," Gemry said, trying to diffuse the tension. "I wouldn't have let you fall—too far, that is." She pushed his shoulder. "Part of being introduced to carrier carpets is having a learning session at the expense of your image—and to the delight of the pilot."

As the victim of a potentially lethal practical joke, Brenner said, "Not so funny."

"Sure it is! And now that you *know* you're securely fastened, flying is a blast! Velvo, show us some tricks!"

The carpet twirled suddenly and loop-de-looped. This time, Brenner's heart didn't leap into his throat—still, it beat twice as fast. The carpet veered on its side and they flew past a cottage built onto the middle of an oakbrawn; their heads almost brushed against the wooden deck rails jutting out from the house.

Brenner didn't want to admit it to her just yet, but Gemry was right. Now that he knew he was safe, he was actually starting to enjoy this. Velvo soared under some thick branches, and then over a flock of bright orange birds.

"See?" Gemry called to him as the carpet pulled out of a dive.

"Fine. You're right."

"I knew you'd like it."

They flew along the giant trees, passing yellow orbs of light floating at different heights.

"What are those?"

"Elixir Lanterns, or Elixterns. You didn't have them back home?"

"Uh…no."

"You really *did* live in the boondocks. They're everywhere in Arborio. The city permanently puts a spark of elixir into the lanterns, casts a long-term hovering spell on each, and as twilight sets in, the guards ignite the evening spell to illuminate them."

The little lanterns, yellow and white, flickered all over the city, looking to Brenner like hundreds of fireflies. They made him feel at home, like he was back in his tower. He looked at Gemry.

"You know," said Brenner, "apart from the whole trying-to-kill-me-thing, I had a good time tonight."

"Me, too. And don't worry, there's still *plenty* of time for that."

Brenner found himself laughing at last. Gemry joined in.

"Aren't you supposed to be the one healing people?" he asked.

"Sometimes," said Gemry, "but I'm just as good at stunning."

Brenner wanted to say something about her looks also being stunning, but something told him that that was what a dork would say. "I getcha. Either way, I'll just hope you're on my team."

"Smart choice."

They rode past the giant trees, toward the outer perimeter of the Zabrani stadium.

"Hey," Brenner said. "Why didn't we just practice on the hillside next to Valoria?"

"Silly, you would have missed the whole flight simulation."

"Oh, right."

"And you never know who's watching at the academy. Some people are more receptive to personal lessons, others resent them, or worse."

"Worse?"

"It's not often a magician helps someone so low in rank, like a conjurer."

"So, why did you?"

"You're not a regular conjurer then, are you?" she smiled.

"I suppose not."

He thought about her comment as they rounded the edges of the stadium, and then hovered over the treetops, back to the eastern ramparts of Valoria, where the carrier carpet brought them in for a soft landing. The night was coming to a close, and Brenner knew he had to ask a question before they went back to their different quarters.

"Gemry," Brenner said, stepping off the carpet and then holding his hand up to her to step down.

She took it, even though he knew she didn't need to, and stepped gracefully off Velvo. "Yes?"

"Would you mind teaching me again?"

There was a moment of uncertainty, or appraisal, that, to Brenner, seemed like forever. Gemry gave him a curious look.

"Even after the whole nearly-killing-you-thing?"

"Yes," he laughed. "Even after that."

"If you're *sure* then…" she raised an eyebrow at him. "I'd love to."

Brenner wanted to pump both fists into the air and jump, but again, he composed himself.

"Great," he said. "Thanks again."

"No worries," she said, tapping Velvo with her mircon, who rolled up and curled under her arm. They walked to the castle doors. "I have to work for my parents over the weekend, so how about Monday night?"

"I am completely free."

"Good. See you then."

The two walked through the broad castle entrance, and Gemry motioned her quarters were down a different passageway.

"And Brenner?"

"Yeah?"

"Next time, see if beforehand you can sneak in a quick shower."

His face puckered. *Ouch…she* had *noticed.*

"I can handle that."

She laughed. "Alright, see you Monday," she said, waving as she glided down the passageway to the magician quarters. "Sleep well."

"Goodnight, Gemry."

He wound his way through the halls, his path illuminated by yellow wall lanterns. While walking, he couldn't decide which was luckier: that Gemry had said yes to meeting with him again, or that she had said yes despite the fact that he had worn sweaty clothes the whole time and she hadn't run away repulsed.

Either way, one thing was clear: on Monday night, he would be going on a date.

On a date with a girl who was clever, cute, vivacious…and fun.

He decided not to tell Gemry that this, for him, would be another first.

Chapter Fifteen

Mental Games

J olts from beneath him awoke Brenner from deep sleep. His body was sore. In a happy flash, he remembered the glorious events of yesterday—the Zabrani game, capturing two glowbes, flying through Arborio next to Gemry on her carrier carpet—it had been almost too wonderful. He had showered late the previous evening before bed, and so only needed to select new robes for the day. After dressing, he headed down to the Banquet Hall.

As he entered the spacious room, he noticed more attention was given to him than normal: eyes darted in his direction, only to flicker away when he met them.

"Nice game yesterday, Conjurer," someone sitting at the mages' table said behind him.

"Thanks," Brenner said, looking over his shoulder. "Oh hey, Girard!" he said, his mind registering the friendly teammate with whom he had bolted down the ridge, before the violet knights attacked.

"You gonna pull fancy tricks like that every game?"

"They weren't anything special," Brenner said, trying to brush the compliment aside. "And it was a team effort; I wouldn't have gotten any glowbe if not for you and Gemry."

"Gemry yes, but all I did was a great job of getting myself stunned," Girard said as his friends chuckled at the table with him. "Anyway," Girard continued, "I hope we can join together again. Only next time, I'll work on stealth. See if that can save us from an ambush."

"Deal," Brenner said. He turned and loaded his tray with hot pancakes and fruit, making his way to the conjurer table by Finnegan.

As soon as he sat down, there was a subtle shift of students at the table: about half turned away from him, pointedly talking to others, while another group gave him curious looks.

"How was the date?" Finnegan said, handing him a glass vial of ruby syrup.

"Thanks," he said, pouring the red-sweet syrup on his fluffy stack of cakes. "But it wasn't a date. It was a training session."

"Of course…" Finnegan said with amusement, putting his chin on his fist.

"It *was*," Brenner said defensively. "She just showed me how to levitate water, and play around with mud mixtures. Except for pigs, I don't think anyone would call that romantic."

"Mud wrestling, huh? You sure know how to charm 'em!"

"You weirdo," Brenner said, shaking his head. "Although, you were partially right."

"About what?"

"About watching my back. She nearly threw me off her carrier carpet."

"Knew she would—the beautiful ones are always the deadliest. So, you almost wound up as one of these?" He grinned and held up his fork: balanced on the end was a large pancake, dripping with syrup. "Personally, that's not my top choice for moving on to the afterlife."

"Same here," Brenner said with a laugh, before taking a bite of food.

"So, that's all then?"

"Of my night? Well, yeah."

"Hmm, okay," Finnegan said, clearly unconvinced. "Well, you missed an epic target practice session last night. Payton and I each nailed the red statue from half-field."

"Nice going!"

"Thanks. Maybe I'll let you in on a tip or two today."

"Fine by me," Brenner said. "By the way, what are we learning today?"

"We're back with Sage Shastrel, and then afternoon skirmishes with our squad."

"Wonderful. More drama with psycho Sorian."

"Right. We'll see how much flak he sends your way. I hear he had a most disappointing performance yesterday at Zabrani."

"Yeah, I think I saw his name towards the bottom of the scores, which will probably make him yell at me all the more."

"Absolutely!" Finnegan said brightly as though predicting sunny skies. "Well, they say this school hasn't turned out a flabby spellcaster in centuries. Sorian's just doing his part to help fulfill that mission."

He stopped, then pointed to the far corner of the hall: "Hey, Brenner."

"What?"

"Is that her?"

Brenner looked. At the other side, with other students in dark green robes, Gemry sat smiling at her magician's table, brushing aside her brown hair as she ate her breakfast.

"Yeah."

Finnegan let out a soft whistle. "I'm impressed."

"Come on," Brenner said.

"Too bad you only got one *training* session with her." He took a bite of an apple.

Brenner smiled. "Who said it was only one?"

Finnegan looked like he wanted to say something, but choked on his fruit. He coughed hard to dislodge it. "Whaddya mean? You gonna see her again?"

"Maybe."

Finnegan punched him in the arm. "Rascal. When?"

"In a couple of days. Another flight lesson."

Finnegan shook his head, then went back to his plate, muttering to himself, "I don't believe this guy…"

Brenner stared past the spellcasters a moment longer, and, as if she could sense it, Gemry looked away from her peers, across the hall, and into Brenner's eyes.

She gave a slight smile that showed her top white teeth: a rush of warmth filled Brenner's head, and immediately he felt foolish and self-conscious. He half-lifted his hand in a clumsy wave, but by then Gemry had returned to her conversation.

Finnegan pretended not to see any of this.

"Come on, let's go."

Outside the castle walls, standing on grassy knolls, the group of conjurers began Sage Shastrel's class flicking their mircons, practicing a spell to cast away objects.

Brenner pointed his wooden mircon at a mossy stone next to him.

"*Repello,*" he thought, and was happy to see the stone skitter backwards as if he had kicked it.

"Make certain you are aiming your objects *away* from other conjurers," Shastrel said as he flew above them, circling the class from the air. "Yesterday I had to send two students to the infirmary because a careless boy blindsided both of them with a two-ton repelled log."

That reminded Brenner. He looked around to locate Sorian, and breathed easier once he saw him on the other side of the field with Travarius. When Sage Shastrel's back was turned, Sorian and Travarius cast repulsion spells into an unlucky boy nearby them—Batterby from the looks of it—who yelped and shot backwards twenty feet before falling with a *thud.* Batterby's cry caught Shastrel's attention, and he hovered more closely to Sorian's side of the group.

"You will channel your spells at objects only—not each other," said Shastrel sternly. "Further disobedience will result in evening demerits."

The students snapped back to their best behavior, while Brenner wondered what exactly the demerits consisted of...*maybe scrubbing stone floors, or cleaning hundred-foot chimneys? Perhaps watering those vicious tendrilsnake plants?* The thought made him shudder.

As class continued, Brenner got the hang of the spell, while Finnegan made some progress. So, Brenner branched out, practicing his spells on simple organisms. He had just gotten a couple blades of grass to uproot themselves and fly to his hand, when Shastrel called from behind him, "Brenner, let's see your repulsion spell."

He looked up, slightly jarred from Shastrel's noiseless approach. "Sure thing."

Brenner aimed his wand at the mossy stone, now thirty feet away.

Apellatum, he thought, and the stone obediently flew to him and dropped at his feet.

Repello, he thought again, and, as though an invisible fishing line yanked it from far away, the stone jerked and threw itself backward.

"Very good," Shastrel said, nodding. "I'm impressed you've progressed to nonverbal spells. Two observations: First, you may choose to think or speak your spells in my class, as spoken words add some power to spellcasting. Second, as you repel your object, imagine either its greatest fear or greatest annoyance, to shoot it further away."

Brenner nodded. "Thank you."

"Quite welcome. Now, Finnegan, let's see your spells."

Finnegan waved his mircon, pressing his lips firmly together and squinting his eyes, but nothing happened, except that, after a long moment, his face turned a nice shade of beet red.

"Try saying the spells aloud," Shastrel directed.

"*REPELLO!*" Finnegan blurted, and the rock in front of him scooted like a startled mouse a few feet backward.

"Not bad, Conjurer. Keep going till it jumps a good ten feet, as that's the average distance I expect from your group today."

"Yes, Sage."

The teacher flew to the next group of students, and Finnegan looked at Brenner, cocking an eyebrow. "Seriously, were you born in a pool of elixir?"

"No," Brenner chuckled, "but if you find one, I'd be happy to push you in."

"I'd throw you in in a heartbeat," Finnegan said with exasperation, "but knowing you, you'd probably walk across the top and finish dry as an Arenaterro desert."

Class continued without any major incidents, except when Sage Shastrel went to help Evie get unstuck from a tree after she repelled herself into its upper branches.

Sorian glanced over to ensure Shastrel was occupied, then shot a repulsion spell at Brenner. Thankfully, Brenner had been keeping an eye on Sorian. He dodged the spell, and then rebounded with magic of his own that blasted Sorian down the hill flat on his back. Seeing their squad leader coughing for breath, more than a few of his peers let out surprised laughs.

"What's going on here?" Sage Shastrel demanded as he turned from levitating Evie down from the tree.

There was a tense moment when the conjurers looked between Brenner and Sorian, and he wondered whether Sorian would call him out, but that would mean showing weakness in front of his squad. The thought seemed to cross behind Sorian's eyes, too.

"Nothing," Sorian said, rising to his feet, and dusting off his green robes.

"Nothing?" Shastrel repeated skeptically. "Not going to say what or *who* knocked you down, Sorian?"

Sorian glowered, but remained silent about the humiliation. Brenner figured he was using the time to think of ways to retaliate.

"So be it," said Shastrel. "Given your earlier behavior, I imagine it was not unprovoked then."

Sorian just shrugged, so Sage Shastrel nodded and said, "Spellcasters, continue your spellwork."

In no time at all, the sun was shining directly overhead, and bells tolled from the castle. "That will do," Shastrel said, "Conjurers, you are adjourned to lunch."

When they were only halfway through their meal Sorian stood up at the end of the table and yelled, "Squad! Forks down. Plates to the wall. Go to the southern stadium!"

Finnegan frowned and elbowed Brenner. "He's a real charmer, isn't he?"

"You can say that again."

"Now!" Sorian said, noticing that some of his squad hadn't immediately jumped to their feet, and instead were trying to cram extra food into their mouths.

After a brisk march through the walkways and tunnels, they came into a giant stadium, and as they did, Brenner's hairs bristled: this was the Agilis Arena from his entrance exam...*was that screaming banshee still in there? And the minotaur?*

But, apart from being incredibly vast, it looked completely altered. There was no chasm at the beginning, no floating bars, no trees, or lake. He realized the sages must repurpose it as needed. It would certainly be a waste to let it lay dormant except for the few Agilis entrance examinations per year.

"Squad!" Sorian barked. "Listen up!"

The group of conjurers turned to give him their attention, except Finnegan, who leaned against the back wall, crossing his arms. Sorian jumped onto a carrier carpet, which flew above them, swishing back and forth as he, probably intentionally, talked down to them.

"We will play modified Agilis this afternoon," Sorian said. "Rules are simple: collect as many glowbes as possible without being frozen or knocked unconscious. I will drill you until you all show that you are capable of catching one. Since this is Agilis, you won't be using your mircons; set them aside. Am I understood?"

Murmurs of yes rippled through the squad, and they placed their mircons in a pile by the door.

Sorian shot a red spell from his mircon to a symbol on the wall, and a low grating sound filled the stadium. The walls on either side of the vast arena opened, and from each side protruded three statues. The six stone statues looked like solemn, tall spellcasters, holding two mircons and pointing them at different angles across the arena. The next moment, the air lit up as their mircons shot a steady barrage of spells like yellow and red laser beams, crisscrossing each other and then smacking the opposite stadium wall, where they were absorbed by black, felt-like material.

"As usual, the spells are set to stun," said Sorian. "If you fall, get yourself up. If you can't, wait until I choose to unfreeze you." He gave a nasty smile.

Sorian's carpet flew down to a wooden chest on the side of the arena, and he tapped his mircon to it.

About twenty white glowbes darted out of the box, zipping through the crossfire of spells and then stopping, hovering both low and high, but keeping to the first third of the vast arena.

"Line up!" Sorian shouted.

The forty some students approached a glowing line that stretched from one side of the arena to the other. As Brenner stepped to the line, a quick calculation told him that there were too many students for each to nab a glowbe.

"You want to run together?" Finnegan asked.

"Thanks, but not this time," said Brenner.

He thought back to his books on game theory. He had two choices: go immediately for the few close, attractive orbs, or try for the larger clusters past the barrage of spells. This was like the Nash simulation of too many guys pursuing one blonde lady and blocking each other instead of factoring in the others' choices and striving to meet one of several available brunettes.

He knew what to do.

Brenner's leg coiled back, primed to spring with his knee just above the ground. His fingers twitched at his sides.

"*Go!*" shouted Sorian.

Immediately the squad of students darted across the rocky arena. Brenner joined near the leaders in the front, and out of the corner of his eye, Brenner saw Travarius and a pack of students shoving towards the same glowbe. One of the boys tumbled down, shouting. Instead of joining them, he set his course on the first line of spellfire, which formed a solid jet of energy at eye-level. He slid underneath, unscathed, and ran towards the next two lines of spells, which together crossed at knee and shoulder level.

With a great burst of energy, Brenner ran and jumped as high as he could, arcing over the top of the yellow spells and landing with a roll on the other side. Only he and four other students reached this point of the course so quickly, and in the middle of them shimmered an unclaimed glowbe.

Batterby and another spellcaster raced for it while Brenner passed, deciding to press forward to the tantalizing cluster of glowbes just beyond the next fence of spells.

A faster boy from his class got to the fence before him, and attempted jumping over. With a cry, he fell to the ground stunned, and Brenner saw why. This blockade of spells didn't just fire in a straight line—it rotated in circles.

He and another student that skidded up to him, Kendra, watched the looping shots of magic. Behind this obstacle, at least half a dozen glowbes hovered enticingly.

Brenner watched the movement of the two spinning mircons. The statues fired nearly constant spells, and Brenner followed their trajectory, hoping to discover the pattern. A moment later, he had found their weakness: a fleeting gap in the red spells occurred at chest level every five seconds.

Before Kendra could spot it, too, Brenner dashed for the opening, counting down…5…4…3…2, *jump!* He dove just as the hole appeared, and felt the air behind his feet crackle with heat—then he was tucking and rolling on the ground. He sat up, examining his body.

Success!

But now Kendra was running for the same spot. He had to act fast.

Brenner looked to his right and sprinted for three glowbes. He tagged each in succession, and they switched colors from white to gold and whisked to the side of the field. Spinning around, he saw Kendra coming out of her tumble, rising, and sprinting from him for the other three glowbes, which were staggered in two areas. Brenner raced for the glowbe away from Kendra—tucked behind a lone boulder in the clearing—and was only a few feet away from getting his fourth glowbe when his shoulder throbbed with pain—a spell had struck him, and his body went rigid. He fell forward and, unable to use his hands, watched with a mixture of fear and confusion as he struck the ground with his face. Warm blood trickled around his eyebrow, and a throbbing pain filled his head.

He saw Kendra's feet jog past him, and heard the glowbe lightly sizzle as she captured it. He vaguely replayed the scene in his mind: Had he missed a stream of spells? No…the last section of glowbes was well past the rotating shots…he was out in the open…someone must have fired an Arcyndo spell…but his squad surrendered their mircons before Agilis began…except…

Sorian.

With his head tilted slightly off the ground, only one eye could see downfield, away from his squad, so Brenner had to wait to be unfrozen, in pain and anger, as the other conjurers picked up the final orbs. And the stunning spell prevented him from speaking. He could only listen to the sounds of spellfire ricocheting around the arena.

At last, the shots stopped ringing out.

"Squad!" Sorian was calling something in the distance, "…to the starting line."

Again, Brenner waited for a thawing spell…none came. Then he saw a shadow growing and heard the swish of the carrier carpet coming from behind him around the boulder. Sorian's voice was quiet.

"That's for acting like you're something special."

He heard Sorian clearing his throat; then a warm glob of spit hit the back of his head. Brenner's eyes squeezed shut. *Ugh…that awful punk!*

"And that," said Sorian, "is for thinking you're on my level. You're no better than one of my family's slaves." Sorian hovered lower and said, "If you report it, worse things will happen." The carrier carpet rustled away.

He felt a warm spell sensation strike his back, and his limbs were once again able to move. He turned to shout at Sorian, but he'd already flown over to the rest of the conjurers, saying, "*Identifio!*" and shooting a spell at the flock of hovering glowbes on the sidelines.

Brenner flicked the spit from his hair, grimaced, and brought his other hand to his forehead to help stop the bleeding. *Hadn't anyone seen Sorian?* He looked back…no, unfortunately he had been hidden behind a boulder *…so that's the price I pay for going solo with an enemy around…*

As he walked back to the starting line, he noticed glowbes floating themselves to the spellcasters who captured them. Three came to hover in front of Brenner.

"What happened to you?!" Finnegan exclaimed, a glowbe hovering by his furrowed eyebrows.

"Stunned in the back," Brenner said, throwing a glare toward Sorian. "From him."

Finnegan shook his head. "That sleezy…"

"Squad!" Sorian shouted. "Round two of Agilis starts now. If you didn't get a glowbe, line up."

"Brenner needs to go the infirmary," Finnegan said. "I'll take him."

"Did I give you permission to go?" Sorian rounded on him. "You'll wait on the side until the group—" Sorian looked past Brenner at the entrance door and suddenly changed his demeanor.

Brenner turned to look, too, and saw a sage entering the arena.

"Fair noon, Sage Vicksman," Sorian said warmly. "I was just directing these two to the infirmary after our first round of Agilis. One of the statue's Arcyndo spells got Brenner."

"Ouch," said Vicksman, surveying Brenner's bleeding forehead, "That was a nasty fall. Looks like it paid off though," he added, noticing Brenner's three glowbes. "Nicely done."

"Thanks," said Brenner. He gave Sorian a glare, but decided it would be pointless to accuse him without any evidence that it was Sorian's shot. And he just wanted to get cleaned up and have his headache go away.

"Come on," said Finnegan, handing him his mircon and leading him out of the arena.

Walking to the infirmary in the heart of the Valoria, Brenner considered his options: he either had to get out of Sorian's squad, or strike back when it was a fair fight with just the two of them.

"In here," Finnegan said, opening a door to a wide room with high windows and white beds. There, a sage named Penelopi channeled a healing spell at Brenner's forehead, and gave him strong tea to drink, saying, "This should help replenish some of the blood."

An hour later, after showering and finding some clean robes, Brenner felt much better, and walked from the boy's dormitory to the spacious, ballroom-like conjurer's community room. A quick scan told him that Sorian and Kendra weren't present, just three or four mixed squads of conjurers.

A bookcase twenty-feet tall spanned across an entire wall, its shelves full of colorful tomes; in the corners by the windows grew living gingko and acacia trees; spellcasters sat at carved wooden desks, writing on parchment; others chatted softly in luxurious armchairs; still more played games with levitating marble pieces.

He strolled to the vast bookshelf, and a shimmering, gold spine enticed him. He plucked the book off the shelf. It felt worn and looked to be at least a hundred years old. He cracked it open to read, but was baffled by strange characters with delicate swoops and detailed clusters of script. He considered asking Finnegan, who was one of the conjurers immersed in a board game that looked like Risk (but with hovering pieces shooting light beams), what language the book was written in, but decided that would raise undesired questions: "What do you mean you don't know what language this is? You're speaking it!"

Fortunately, as he started skimming the page, something in his brain flicked on like a gate lifting in front of a water reservoir, and he was both surprised and delighted to find the words pouring into him.

The title was printed in elegant letters, and read, *"Elixir: The Essence Within All."* He found the first chapter fascinating—it contained a mixture of diagrams, spells, and explanations, similar to Da Vinci's sketchbook of inventions that he had once read. The lessons reinforced his studies so far, specifically the notion that to use magic on anything, one had to understand the desires or qualities of the object itself.

After reading the first chapter, he flipped the pages until a heading caught his eye and stopped him: *Properties of the Seven Elixir Colors.*

He was about to read more, but had the uneasy feeling that he was being watched. Sure enough, he saw Sorian and Kendra had entered the room. Rising from his chair, he glanced around the community room for an exit and noticed a doorway by the windows, with sunlight streaming in. Clutching his book, Brenner strode to it.

White light grew brighter as he ambled through the tunnel and into the warm room. Sunlight filled the conservatory, and Brenner stood smiling at the assortment of tropical trees and blooming pink flowers that filled it. Through tall glass ceilings and outer walls, he could see pristine blue sky. The air tasted sweet and faintly of citrus, no doubt amplified by the oils of the yellow and orange buds and glistening leaves all around. He strolled to a small circle of chairs, sliding his hand across one of the deep green plants along the way. He raised his palm to his face: the fragrance smelled strongly of aloe and ginger.

Brenner plopped into one of the armchairs and flipped again to the chapter about *Properties of the Seven Elixir Colors*:

While naturally spellcasters prefer the elixir of the biome they are raised in, there are distinct spell advantages that each color of elixir affords, since each is influenced by the landscape from which it originates. Ganthrean spellcasters may grow their spell-abilities for physical, mental and Aura magic, and often focus their strengths on the color of their elixir.

Physical magic is capable through all elixirs, but especially promoted by three colors. Owing to cliffs, mountains and canyonlands, Red Elixir bolsters strength, boldness, and ideals of fortitude. From the sweeping deserts and tropical oases, Orange Elixir enhances resilience, as well as shrewdness and beauty. Elixir of Green, from jungles and forests, increases growth, rejuvenation and enhances charity...

...Two colors assist with Aura magic: Violet Elixir—generated beneath bayous, everglades, and marshlands—refines power, adaptation abilities, and influence; Yellow Elixir, from savannas, steppes, and plains, increases Auras of protection, as well as faithfulness and synergy...

...Welling up from reefs, islands, and coasts, Blue Elixir boosts mental magic, especially ingenuity, empathy, and persuasion. Growing deep beneath glaciers, permafrost, and fjords, Indigo Elixir also increases mental spells, growing knowledge, self-control, and eloquence...

With training from senior mages and wizards, and direct experience within the biome, spellcasters can tap into the strength of their amulet's elixir color. Colors can and do occasionally mix together in amulets—usually through a wizard's forging—although amulets don't normally allow for additions past two elixirs, as they become more unstable with each new elixir. Sovereign wizards of each biome are known to own multiple elixir amulets—though many prefer a dense amulet heavily imbued with their own elixir color...

Contently reading, Brenner spent a relaxing hour sipping the knowledge of elixir that his peers had been steeped in since birth.

After dinner, Brenner asked Finnegan to show him his shooting skills in the Zabrani arena. A group of spellcasters of all levels joined them on the field, and Sage Vicksman arrived shortly after, unlocking a large chest next to them: a flock of glowbes zoomed around the stadium like excited doves, hovering above white statues near and red and blue ones farther on, while others flitted and spiraled in loops, perpetually mobile. Brenner looked to Finnegan.

"Are we supposed to catch those?"

"Watch *and* learn," Finnegan said with bravado.

He aimed his mircon, and a strange thing happened: two jolts of red light sizzled out, one from the tip of the mircon shooting fifty feet ahead and striking a glowbe, and a wild jet of energy that sparked from the mircon's side—flying inches past Brenner's face before hitting a wall.

"Sorry!" Finnegan said. "Didn't stun you, did I?"

Brenner put a hand up to his face. "You nearly froze my nose, but I'm okay."

"That was definitely not supposed to happen. Sorry mate." He looked down, inspecting his mircon. "Yeah...there's a nice crack here. Gonna have to get this fixed. Corsmith's might have something for it. Well, do like I did with the first shot, just without the extra firepower."

Brenner started with the stationary glowbes, then focused his shots on the close-moving orbs, which was much like taking a BB gun and trying to hit baseballs as they smoked back and forth in line-drives. As the hour passed, his shot pelted glowbes more often. Brenner then worked on long shots at statues the rest of the evening, and noticed Sage Vicksman hovering above the better shooters, congratulating them on their skill and talking about some after-term internship they should consider doing.

As night set in, he felt much more confident: his *Arcyndo* spell was quite accurate at close range with the glowbes, and even though the red statue was half the distance of the colossal field, every so often, his shots struck it.

The next morning, Friday, Brenner filed into Sage Erlynda's with the rest of his conjurer class. They spent the first part in the courtyard thinking of emotions, while their partners attempted to peer past mental walls and identify the hidden feelings. Brenner was paired with Batterby, the small, mouse-like boy, and was surprised to find that he had a strong mental barrier. It took ten concentrated minutes of applying the mental spell before Brenner found a weak section that hinged open and revealed a calm, glowing yellow emotion: admiration.

Brenner was curious. Batterby had never spoken a word to him—perhaps this was his way of saying he was on Brenner's side?

"Is your emotion admiration?"

Batterby gave a flustered nod, and from his crossed arms, Brenner could tell he'd hoped to stump him.

Batterby tried to slip past Brenner's mindwall, but by imagining a fortress with a closed portcullis—and not letting his attention drift—he was able to keep it firm. He knew that one look too far, and Batterby might see a hint that he wasn't of their world. He didn't know what would happen if someone besides Windelm and Sherry knew his past, other than it couldn't be good.

After a second half of class spent on reading future thoughts—which Brenner enjoyed, seeing Evie's imagination of harvesting summer strawberries in her family's orchards—the group ate lunch and then spent the afternoon on the forest ropes course.

Brenner swung from rope to rope and came up to a platform rigged against a humongous baobab tree, where Finnegan was taking a breather before entering the next stage.

"Hey," said Finnegan, "we have the day off tomorrow. Want to explore downtown Arborio?"

"Sure," Brenner said, leaning back against the rough bark.

"Great."

"That reminds me, I need to return my mircon to Sage Shastrel once I get my own, is there a good place to look for new mircons?"

"Of course," Finnegan said. "I was already planning to swing by Corsmith's Mircons and Amulets."

It then occurred to Brenner that, unfortunately, he didn't have any Ganthrean coins. *Well, it wouldn't hurt to browse.*

They finished the rest of the ropes course that afternoon, and since they were careful to let Sorian and his favorites climb far ahead of them, they didn't have to suffer any of his power-trips, or worry about being sabotaged from behind.

At dinner that evening, conversation turned to plans for the weekend. Spellcasters chatted about using Saturday for leisure, schoolwork, or exploration, and for Sunday some would return home to see family, meditate, or relax on the castle grounds.

Later, as he settled into his bed, he thought about his first week at Valoria: the good news was that he'd survived it, despite the entrance exam and Sorian's attempts otherwise. And having Finnegan and Gemry to talk to made it much better than his old school. Still, it would be nice to have a few days off and explore the forested city of Arborio.

Surely it couldn't be as bad as dealing with Sorian.

Chapter Sixteen

Dangers and Deals of Arborio

"Shall we run or walk?" Finnegan asked Brenner as the two exited the broad castle doors of the western entrance of Valoria Academy. A sunny Saturday morning greeted them, and a wide smile grew on Brenner's face at the prospect of seeing more of the city with a friend.

"How about a light run?" Brenner suggested.

The two jogged at first with plenty of space down Via Valoria, but the further they ventured into the city, the thicker the crowds became. Between the skyscraper trees and multistoried shops, Brenner noticed bottle green banners waving on posts. Pictured on them was a tree ringed by a circle of seven colored diamonds, with six white dots in a hexagon pattern on the tree, and on either side waved a glowing mircon, and in the middle shone a large, bright glowbe.

He concluded the six dots symbolized Zabrani, the middle glowbe stood for Agilis, but what of the rest?

"Finnegan," he said as they ran, "Are those banners for the upcoming Games of Ganthrea?"

"Right you are." "So, Zabrani, Agilis, and the mircons are for…"

"Contendir."

Since his squad hadn't practiced it yet, he concluded that the sages must think them unprepared for that game.

"What are the seven colors for? On the edges?"

"Those are the different biomes of Ganthrea."

"Ahh…right." He looked at the pattern of colors, starting with green. "Green for Silvalo…and the rest?"

Another banner came to view, and Finnegan gave him a look that said even-though-I'm-incredulous-I'll-still-humor-you.

"Blue for the ocean clans of Aquaperni…" he said between breaths as they ran, "Indigo for the cold tundra civilization of Gelemensus…violet for the marshland people of Vispaludem…"

They passed under a tunnel formed by interlocking branches of two monster mahogany trees.

"…Red for the rocky empire of Montadaux…orange for the desert palaces of Arenaterro…yellow for the savannah society of Safronius…and green you thankfully picked up on."

"I'm getting there," Brenner said, sparking a connection between the elixir colors he read about and the biomes. *Hadn't Windelm mentioned Montadaux producing the fiercest dragons?* And he remembered the strawberry tang of the moltifrute balls at the boulevard of Vale Adorna…*didn't Windelm's friend, Rimpley, say they were from an island? They must be part of the blue biome, Aquaperni.*

"Like all young citizens of Arborio," Finnegan cut in, "I knew Ganthrean geography *before* starting at Valoria. Biomes are basic—didn't your parents teach you anything?"

"They taught me the essentials—farming and jungle life. Enough to be useful."

"Pretty low standards of usefulness if you ask me."

The heavy wings of a Pegasus mail carrier beat above them, making Brenner wonder how long it would be before he could join the spellcasters flitting above them in the canopy.

"Just what is the errand we're off to this morning?" Brenner asked.

"Remember when I nearly stunned you point blank?"

"How could I forget?"

"Right. I need some Lumarlin Oil to fix that."

"Good call. And where do we get that?"

"Follow me."

Finnegan threaded them past inviting fruit stands, jewelry booths with dazzling metal arm bands, and intricately carved storefronts that reminded Brenner of Vale Adorna's bustling boulevard, the only difference was here—past *every* corner—lay yet another cobblestone street packed with more shops, more merchants, larger trees, and occasionally, dark alleys. Unlike his old home of grid streets, where nature was excavated to make way for perfectly crisscrossed intersections, the roads in the forested city of Arborio were purposely built around living trees, twisting and forking pell-mell as the trees dictated. Finally, Finnegan stopped in front of an ancient store that felt like a rustic timber lodge.

"Welcome to Corsmith's," said Finnegan. They pushed open heavy maple doors, and walked past a burly man with folded arms and a mircon. He nodded curtly at them.

The store smelled of pine and earthen minerals, and for its expansive size it was surprisingly tidy; a moment later and Brenner could see why: wooden brooms swept dirt into neat piles as if guided by invisible custodians, then, after brushing the piles into animated dustpans, the pairs flew off and out of sight.

Brenner was drawn to a large display case at the front of the store. Behind thick glass, ancient-looking silver and gold amulets held swirling colors—mostly various shades of green, but a few held different colors: maroon, indigo, and shimmering violet. Brenner noticed nearly all of the amulets held only one swirling color. Only a few in a special section behind the counter had more than one color swirling around inside, and of those, only one had three. The numerals below the solo colored amulets seemed foreign for a second, but then his brain made sense of the puzzling runes, and he understood the amounts. He gaped.

"Finnegan," he said in a hush, not wanting to draw attention. "These amulets cost *over seven hundred golders!*"

"What do you expect?" Finnegan said, walking up to his side. "Elixir is power, and power isn't cheap."

Brenner gazed at the dual colored amulets in the case behind the counter. His eyes bulged. A green and amber amulet in the crystal glass display cost twelve hundred golders. He brought his hand to his necklace, making sure that the amulet was hidden safely under his tunic. It was. *Windelm's trusted me with a great treasure.* While he had obviously never planned to lose the amulet, his protective instincts now magnified.

"Over here," Finnegan said, pointing to a wall filled with colored stone rods, animal horns, and carved wooden wands, most around the size of a hammer. Brenner approached the wall, lingering at each section of mircons as energy pulsed from their collective magic like waves washing around him.

What intrigued him was that the mircons were fashioned from all types of natural substances: aspen, cherry, yew and mahogany woods, followed by a section devoted to all colors of molten metals…then antlers, ivory and horns…conch and spiral seashells…*bones?*—Brenner cocked an eyebrow, and his spine tingled—*that's different*…even long rocks and stalactites had been carved into intricate, spiraled mircons.

The prices for the magic-conducting mircons, while less than amulets, were also not cheap. He found himself drawn to two types of mircons: jagged quartz wands that looked like solidified lightning, and a type of wood mircon that reminded him of the forests back in Colorado—thick evergreen wood that was polished smooth. He sighed—each was anywhere from thirty to over a hundred golders. How was he going to earn that? *Maybe Valoria allowed summer break after the Games of Ganthrea for students to work…*

"Ah, those are fine mircons," said an elderly voice behind Brenner.

He turned around to see a bespectacled lady with silvery hair flowing past her shoulders, approaching him with a quiet air of confidence.

"The quartz mircon works particularly well with red or orange elixirs," she continued, "and the oakbrawn mircon works well with all colors, but amplifies green spells, naturally."

"Interesting," said Brenner, "Where did they come from?"

"From our travels. My husband and I find and collect elixir-rich objects in their raw state, then come back to our workshop here to construct and refine them into premiere mircons."

"You own this place?"

"I do."

"Wow," Brenner said, his eyebrows rising appreciatively. "How do you know the objects contain elixir?"

"You want me to give away all of our secrets?" she said, chuckling. "Well, when you elixir-hunt for fifty years, you start noticing where it is likely to cluster. From there, it's just a matter of identifying the object with the most magic soaked into it."

Brenner noticed the amulet around her neck; it contained a triumvirate of green, indigo, and violet colors that were so dazzling, they seemed to put a spell on him. Only her voice brought him back to reality.

"Are you buying today, or just browsing?"

"I wish I was buying…" he began.

She nodded. "Save up then. We have what you need when you're ready."

The owner smiled and turned to help other spellcasters. Soon Finnegan bustled over to join Brenner, holding a jar filled with a clear jelly.

"Found some that I like," Finnegan said, pointing at the substance within that glowed like pale moonlight. After Brenner stared blankly at him, he added, "Remember? Lumarlin oil."

"Oh, right."

"It's exported from Aquaperni islands, and gives mircons a protective coating that prevents spell-leaks, and seals cracks." He held his mircon straight up, where Brenner could see a gash on it, and poured some of the blue oil on the tip, where it ran like honey around the edge of the wand until it covered the cut. "You have expensive taste," Finnegan said, looking at the mircons next to Brenner. "Don't suppose you have one hundred and thirty golders on you to pay Sorceress Corsmith?"

"No," Brenner said forlornly. "Any tips?"

"Hmm, no use trying to steal it—the door magician will incinerate you without a second thought. If I were you, I'd try to get adopted by a rich magnate family…or if that fails, just work without sleeping for three or four years, then you'd have enough golders."

Brenner laughed. "I'll see you after four years in the metal mines."

"Yeah, good luck with that," Finnegan said, holding up a wooden receipt token to the door magician, and then opening the door for Brenner, "After four years you'll have your golders—*and* you'll be a hunchback, so you can earn money in a traveling circus."

"And you can be my stage manager," Brenner retorted.

"You know it!" Finnegan said. "Come on, let's see how busy my Pop's place is."

They left Corsmith's, and began winding away from the center of the city, where foot-traffic thinned, and the monstrous trees were spaced further apart. Before, Brenner had seen the city guard patrolling once or twice an hour, but in the outer ring of the city he didn't see any. They passed a pub called Tallegrim's, with glowing letters on the restaurant sign that grew and contracted above patrons sipping beers.

"My Pop's friend runs Tallegrim's," said Finnegan, "he always says it's the only place that makes a spicier stew than his. If you want to burn your tongue off later, we could—"

Angry shouts from ahead cut him off. Someone from a gang of men dressed in orange had thrown a rock across the street into a group of tanned, blue-caped spellcasters, causing one to cry out, "So, that's your idea of honor then, you sand brutes?!"

"Go back to your islands," a man in the orange crowd mocked. "You stinking fishermen don't belong in the Games."

A flash of blue light slammed into the orange men. Someone shouted in pain and the man next to him shouted, "We'll have you arrested for that!"

"Cause you're too weak to fight!"

Each of the groups advanced to the middle of the via, and voices shouted from all sides.

"You can't battle here—" a fruit seller warbled from his stall.

"Like hell we can't!"

"—gonna smash your face in—"

"Enough!"

A tall man with a crooked nose, leather vest and a black cape held up his mircon and strode between the groups, which seemed to Brenner about as smart as walking between two broods of vipers. The stranger cast an Aura spell about himself, and just in time, as an orange spell crashed into the Aura and quickly fizzled.

"You spellcasters have two options," said the man, "you can either have a fair fight of Contendir that I'll be master over, or, I can report your brawling and spell-firing to the city guard and you'll lose the right to play in the Games."

"Hang on," said Finnegan to Brenner, pausing at the edge of the street, "This could be fun."

"You don't even know who we are," said one of the blue-caped men.

"Oh really, DiMarco?" said the tall man, "I saw you last year playing in Safronius."

There were murmurs among each group.

"I'll do it your way," said one of the orange-caped fighters of Arenaterro, stepping forward. He had long black hair tied in a tail behind his head, and a thin black beard tracing his jaw. "And you are…?"

"Silverman. And a silver from each man is what I charge. You?"

"Silverman…huh…I'm Majir. Do you even have the glowbes?"

"Of course." Silverman tucked a hand inside his leather vest and pulled out two glowbes. He animated them with a forked-wood mircon, and they levitated obediently above him. Next, he pointed his mircon to the far side of the dusty road, and a dark line appeared, running down one side of the street some hundred yards, then rounding and going back up the other side, forming a large oval. "Arenaterro has courage, what about you Aquaperni?" Silverman asked, looking at the blue group of islanders.

"I'll put the sand-rat in his place," said the biggest of the blue spell-casters, flipping Silverman a coin and advancing to the middle.

"Very good," said Silverman, who had caught the coin and now opened his palm to accept Majir's payment. "What are you spellcasters playing for? Golders? Mircons? Amulets?"

"Golders," said the island brute.

"Mircons actually," said Majir, smoothing his orange cape and looking over at his opponent's quartz crystal mircon.

"You may back out for the price of a golder," said Silverman to the man in blue, "or accept Arenaterro's higher wager for mircons."

"Get *his* mircon, Ranoa!" one of the blue men shouted.

"Mircons then," muttered the blue man, Ranoa, scowling at Majir.

"Spellcasters to their sides," Silverman said, as the two men paced to opposite sides of the oval.

"Brenner," Finnegan said, "you'll want to give them some space." He tugged Brenner back from the circle.

Silverman spun his mircon above his head, and around the ring a hazy dome materialized up from the oval around the two men and sealed shut in the middle some forty feet above them. Then Silverman directed a glowbe to both sides of the ring, behind each fighter.

"First to grab the other's glowbe, or otherwise incapacitate him, wins," said Silverman, creating a hole in the side of the dome and stepping out. Then he muttered something and closed the exit, sealing the men inside. "Contendir...begin!"

The blue spellcaster, Ranoa, wasted no time in firing *Arcyndo* spells, hoping to paralyze his opponent, but Majir had quickly conjured an Aura and the spells deflected harmlessly. Ranoa, seeing his spells did little to affect his opponent, began charging across the dusty road—Brenner sensed his strategy: brawn over brains.

Majir waited until the blue spellcaster was halfway across the ring, and then lapsed his Aura briefly to shoot a brown spell at the dirt in front of Ranoa—and quickly a trench formed, digging up the raw dirt and forming a ten-foot wall blocking his rush.

Majir then darted to the side of the field, as Ranoa called out, *"Persplodo!"* and immediately a small explosion ripped apart the dirt wall, flinging debris against the dome that Silverman had erected. It rained down the inside of the wall.

Through the cloud of dust and dirt, Ranoa pivoted his head quickly side to side, searching in vain for Majir, until he saw him sprinting twenty yards away from his undefended glowbe.

Ranoa squinted his eyes and yelled something, causing a strong gush of water to burst from the end of his mircon and block Majir's path, the force of which was too strong for the dome to withstand, and it ripped through the magical shield, flooding the storefront of a silk seller and causing shouts of surprise.

"Fix the wall!"

Silverman shot a spell to patch the dome, and at the same time Majir shot a flame spell back at Ranoa—who ducked as a streak of orange fire raced over his head into the dome above, which rippled like plexiglass.

Majir then shot a gust of wind at Ranoa's feet, causing the ground to spit dust into his face. Blinded, Ranoa cast *Arcyndo* spells in haphazard directions. He brought his other hand to wipe the grime out of his eyes, but as he did, Majir cast another flame spell—right into Ranoa's face.

"Arghhhhh!!" Ranoa called out, falling to the ground, using his hands and whatever dirt he could find to smother the flames out.

Majir calmly walked to edge of the ring and grabbed Ranoa's glowbe.

"Match over!" shouted Silverman, evaporating the dome-spell around the fighters. He shot a water-spell into Ranoa, dousing the flames from his face and shoulders. The blue spellcasters jumped into the oval, racing over to help their man.

Silverman sent one final spell that stretched across the ring like a long, wispy hand, lifted Ranoa's mircon from the ground, then zipped it across the street to Majir, who grabbed it with a grin.

The orange Arenaterro men clapped Majir on the back, who held up the mircon triumphantly. The blue fighters huddling around Ranoa looked mutinous.

"Come on," Finnegan said, tugging at Brenner's sleeve, "Ranoa was supposed to be a favorite at the Games this year, and his face looks beyond healing. This could get out of control quickly."

As Brenner followed Finnegan away from the oval, he saw Silverman disappear into the onlookers, and the charred cheekbones of Ranoa's face.

After twenty minutes of running through the streets, Finnegan paused to catch his breath. "You doing okay?"

"I'm alright," Brenner said, trying to think of something other than the ghastly black on Ranoa's face.

"That's why I plan to only stick with Agilis and Zabrani. My beautiful complexion just doesn't do black eyes and burnt-off cheeks."

"Do they always end like that?"

"Street Contendir often does…but in the official games, torching your opponent's face is generally frowned upon."

Brenner shook his head.

"Hey, cheer up. We're almost at lunch."

"I thought we'd go back to Valoria?"

"Not when we can eat here!"

Finnegan rounded a corner, and Brenner saw a restaurant sandwiched between two massive oakbrawn trees. It had a large replica of a mug atop a pedestal with blue fire crackling from the top of it. Underneath it was a sign: "Hutch & Son's – Brews, Stews and Singefire Ale."

Finnegan went around to a side door and pulled a key from his pocket. He clicked open the door and led them through a backroom filled with food crates and supply bins. Delicious smells of spicy tomatoes and garlic wafted from a kitchen to their right.

"Hey, Tarino!" Finnegan said, as they passed the line cook, a slender man with a black mustache the size of a woolly caterpillar.

"How are ya, Fin?"

"Just dandy. Pop here?"

"On a busy Saturday? He better be!"

"Thanks," Finnegan said, leading Brenner through another set of doors and into the bustling dining room. Near the front stood a handsome man with the same dark red hair as Finnegan, plus a trimmed goatee. Finnegan waited until his father seated a new group of patrons before guiding them over.

"Hey, Pops!"

"Fin, good to see you," he said, hugging his son and adding, "You up for lunch and afternoon dish duty?"

"I could help all day tomorrow—" Finnegan said, as his father raised an eyebrow, "but today I was hoping to take my friend around the city before it gets swarmed for the Games."

"Your friend?"

Finnegan pointed to Brenner.

"I'm sorry, where are my manners?! I'm Mick." He held out his hand jovially to Brenner.

"This is Brenner," Finnegan said, as Brenner's hand got pumped up and down, "He's a new conjurer at Valoria."

"Nice to meet you, Mick."

"Likewise!" said Mick, "Well I suppose one day of sightseeing is in order. Tell you what, Brenner, want to earn some extra spending money?"

"Maybe…"

"Come back with Fin tomorrow and I'll pay you a couple silvers for your help in the kitchen. And, of course, a free meal when you work."

Brenner thought about the mircons he saw earlier and said, "That sounds good. Thanks, Mick."

"Excellent!" he said, clapping Brenner on the back and then looking beyond him to the door, smiling. "Ah, new customers to seat. Fin, find yourself a table, and I expect you ready to make it shine around here tomorrow." He turned from them and practically sang to the husband and wife at the door, "*Welcome* to Hutch & Sons!"

"Let's grab a table," Finnegan said pointing a thumb, then directing them to the far corner of the bustling café.

"Your family owns this place?"

"Yep," said Finnegan proudly. "Going on four generations."

"Very nice."

"Now it's Grand-Pops, Pops, and me. Although Grand-Pops stops in mostly just to eat and gab with the regulars."

"Is your Mom here too?"

"No," said Finnegan, sighing. "She's passed on."

"Oh!" said Brenner, bringing a hand to his mouth. "I'm sorry."

"It's okay. You didn't know." They settled into a booth. "Happened just after my birth. Got an infection that turned deadly overnight."

"I'm really sorry to hear that, Finnegan."

"Thanks. Anyway, let's hear about you. What are your folks up to?"

Brenner felt guilty, sharing the concocted story that he and Windelm practiced, when Finnegan had been nothing but honest with him since they met. But he remembered Windelm's advice and kept his promise. Soon Brenner was biting into a toasted bryffalo steak sandwich, the day's special. He grinned as the salty, umami flavor hit his tongue.

Lifting the top of the bun he asked, "Is this a Rombell mushroom?"

"Only the finest," Finnegan replied, biting into his own sandwich.

As they ate, Brenner looked around the room: there were couples leaning close to each other and smiling, a group of rowdy men laughing at the bar, yellow-robed spellcasters blowing on hot stew, and by the front windows some white-haired regulars feasting on baskets of chicken drumsticks. What caught Brenner's attention was the argument coming from two men in the booth behind Finnegan.

"Don't give me that excuse," said a surly fellow, waving his arm in disgust. "You said that *last* week, Gespelti, and I need that money *today*."

Brenner's ears perked up. *Wasn't that Gemry's last name?*

"Just give me one more week—I promise I'll have it to you," said the other man, who sat with his back to them. "Our store's expecting a new shipment of Gelemensus Glass, and I'll have your money as soon as I sell through it. I swear it."

"Your promises mean next to nothing," the dark robed man said coldly. "If I don't get the money I'm due *in one week*—with interest now, for your delay—I'm going to collect more precious things next. For starters—your amulet."

Gespelti stood, and his words came quick. "I'll be by as soon as I get it."

"You better."

When Gespelti hastily made for his exit, Brenner saw he was a scrawny man, with unkempt brown hair and a jittery glance that didn't stay in one place very long; by the way he slinked between the tables and out the door, he reminded Brenner of a weasel.

The other man finished his amber drink, placed a stack of copper coins on the table and soon was gone.

"Aayyerrrrrp!" Finnegan interrupted with a full-bellied burp.

Brenner turned and stared at him. "What are you, part bullfrog?"

"Must be. Never met a bryfallo steak I didn't wolf down." He patted his stomach. "Now, want to see the tallest trees in Arborio?"

"Of course."

Brenner finished eating, went to pay, but winced as he patted his empty pockets. Finnegan waved him off. "Don't worry. This one's on me."

Relief flowed through him. "Hey, thank you very much, Finnegan."

Soon they were striding out into the city's vias. The forest air smelled fresh from oakbrawn leaves and budding fruits in the canopy. Finnegan directed them past shops, tree condominiums, and open markets. Along the way, Brenner saw something he had read about in books, but never imagined he'd witness. A crowd had gathered around an elevated stage with a simple wooden podium, behind which a stern man in the center gestured to someone behind him: the man was shackled in chains.

"For twenty-five years, do I hear five hundred golders?"

The group of adults watched him, but didn't speak. "Four hundred?" he offered.

A gruff voice from the crowd called out, "Three."

This seemed to satisfy the official. "Bidding starts at three hundred golders. Do I hear more?"

Another man countered, "Three twenty-five!"

The official acknowledged the counter-offer with a whack of his gavel, and then other thick voices called out. Behind the speaker, a chained man stooped on the platform, wearing a black robe, looking to be in his early thirties; pale skinned and frowning, he watched the auction with resigned eyes.

A moment later the official called out loudly, "Four hundred fifty going once…"

An uneasy silence clung to the air, as if daring someone to raise the bid.

"…going twice…sold!" He banged a gavel against the podium. "Five and twenty years bonded to Mr. Ratchkins."

Brenner was incredulous.

"Did he just…*buy* that man?"

"Uh, yeah," Finnegan replied matter-of-factly. "That's how the trading block works. Three times a week, sometimes more, slaves, servants or peasants, mostly adults, are sold for work."

"For how long?"

"Depends. Could be a year, could be ten, or as long as they live."

Brenner slowly shook his head. "Can they become free?"

"If their masters allow, but since they paid plenty, why would they? That man in the black robes was a different case. He was criminal, probably a thief or a swindler, and the Sovereign's Council ordered him to twenty-five years forced servitude."

Finnegan motioned for them to move on, his shrug indicating that they couldn't do anything about the sale even if they wanted.

"So, what do the sold people do?"

"The slaves? Depends on their master. Some work underground in the metallic mines, some in processing warehouses or harvest fields. From what I hear, those ones get worked the hardest. The lucky ones work for elixir magnates, families that are rich in magic and have their workers oversee production of garments, tools, or housing materials. If the government buys them, they get the luxury of building and maintaining forest-roads, or hauling away sewage and the city garbage."

"Couldn't people just use magic to get the work done?"

"Some could, but the wealthy consider elixir too precious to waste on menial labor. They'd rather stockpile their elixir, sell some of it for large profits, and use their extra money to buy more slaves."

Just before they rounded the corner to the next street, Brenner looked back, and saw the official snapping a thick, copper collar around the new slave, then fired a spell at it from his mircon. The man cringed as it clicked together like two powerful magnets, and then blazed fire-orange in what must have been a final seal.

They eventually found the tallest tree—over a thousand feet, and filled with wooden condos jutting off the side. At the base of it, exotic music filled the air, attracting a large crowd. Brenner heard the rhythmic beats of a man drumming taut animal skin, while three musicians behind him played a panflute, something like a mandolin, and an oversized guitar. The music transfixed him, and swelled as they strode past; someone bumped into him, and he felt a sharp tug at his belt. He went to grab his mircon and cringed.

It was gone.

"Hey!" Brenner shouted, noticing a hooded figure in gray robes hustling away from them, "Stop him!"

Brenner raced after the thief, cutting through the crowd, with Finnegan a few paces behind.

The culprit turned past a passion-fruit vendor and darted down an alley, dumping a barrel of food waste behind him.

Brenner and Finnegan sprinted to the end of the alley, jumped over the barrel, and saw that the thief had climbed a stack of crates. He jumped halfway up the back wall, and pulled himself up into a dark window.

"*Arcyndo!*" yelled Finnegan, pointing his mircon and sending a jet of light up the alley.

The spell hit its target—freezing the figure on the windowsill, who then started teetering back, and gravity pulled him down with a crash onto the stack of wooden crates.

"Nice shot!" Brenner said.

Brenner and Finnegan rushed up to the thief, who was still clutching Brenner's mircon in one hand. Brenner pried it free.

"What do think you're doing?!" Brenner asked roughly, pulling back the hood to get a better look at the thief. His brow furrowed.

He saw long black hair tucked into a pony-tail—and the face of a teenage girl, not much older than they were. Her beauty was marred by a jagged scar under her left eye. Around her neck was a copper collar.

"Stand back, Brenner," Finnegan said. "*Mobilus.*"

His white spell hit the girl, and she winced; then she slowly moved her arms.

"We should report you," said Finnegan.

"Please don't," the girl said, sitting up. "I'm sorry. I really am."

Her face had a look of desperation.

"You're just sorry you're caught, is all," Finnegan continued. "Tell us who you are, and who your master is."

"I'm Rinn, and my master…"

"Yes?"

"Please, *don't* tell him. I'll be whipped and sold to someone even worse. Promise me."

"Why should we?" Finnegan said.

The girl glanced around them, probably seeing if she could make a run for it. Finnegan held his mircon up.

"It's okay, Finnegan," Brenner said. "We won't tell him. Promise. In return—explain yourself."

"My master…" said Rinn warily, "is Gretzinger. Four years ago, I was sold to him, and I'm bonded for another twenty years. His plantation has been awful—I just lost my brother."

Brenner's initial anger was softened with a pang of pity for her.

"I don't want to die there, too. If I could get a mircon, or an amulet, I could sell it and pay someone to free me…" She rose to her feet.

"Easy now," Finnegan said, keeping his mircon trained on her.

"Please," said Rinn. "I must go. If I'm not back to his caravan in ten minutes, my collar will start the pain cycle."

Finnegan eyed her suspiciously. "What's in it for us?"

She looked earnestly at them. "If I can help you in any way…"

"Let her go, Finnegan," said Brenner, lowering Finnegan's mircon. "She needs a break more than we do." He turned to Rinn. "You can help us by not stealing anymore." He stepped back to the wall and motioned for her to pass them.

Rinn slunk by them through the alley with a slight hobble, before putting her hood up and slipping away into the crowd.

"You believe her?" Finnegan said, shaking his head.

"I do. She had the look of someone pushed to the edge."

"Maybe…but I've heard of people wearing fake collars to fool the city guards into thinking they were being controlled. Ten coppers says she's caught stealing again by sundown."

"Maybe. But if she's telling the truth, can you blame her?"

Finnegan sighed. "I suppose not."

The rest of the way back to Valoria, Brenner kept a tight grip around his mircon, giving himself a wide berth around other spellcasters.

The remainder of the weekend went by in a blur: Saturday evening he practiced levitation on rocks and twigs until his spells fizzled and the twigs started to smoke. When he tried the flight spell on himself, he achieved a few seconds off the ground, but then the bubble of air beneath him popped and he fell awkwardly on the floor. Sunday, he worked with Finnegan at Hutch & Son's, earning his first two silvers, and in the evening found a spot next to the river where he added to his journal.

Another week of academy training was about to begin, and with it, more confrontations with Sorian. But what was really making Brenner nervous was tomorrow evening's meeting with Gemry.

Does she actually like me?

Or will she fly even higher and fling me off Velvo?

Chapter Seventeen

Auras and the Love of Volanti

When Brenner went to breakfast on Monday, a strange thing happened. He gathered his food and was on the way to sit by his group, when the largest sage he'd seen stepped into his path.

"Fair morn, Brenner," said the portly instructor, who, from his shaggy, graying mustache to his bulging stomach, looked strikingly like a walrus.

"Oh—hello," Brenner said reservedly.

"The sages here have conferred about your recent accomplishments in class and on the Zabrani field."

Brenner shuffled his feet. "They were talking about me?"

"Indeed," the sage said emphatically, "It's our duty to watch for when spellcasters are ready for new challenges. I'm pleased to inform you that you've been promoted to a level five conjurer."

"Thanks…" Brenner smiled. "What does that mean exactly?"

"Why, new squad, new lessons, and new instructors, of course! Please set your food down, then come with me to get your belt."

For a man of such size, he moved with surprising speed, leading Brenner from the Banquet Hall down a corridor to a metal door. Sending a jet of light from his mircon toward the doorknob, he waited for a soft click; then he turned open the handle, and gestured Brenner inside. The room was cool and lit dimly by glowbes, until the sage raised his mircon and said, "*Brillium.*" Immediately the glowbes shone brightly across the surprisingly long storage room, and Brenner saw rows upon rows of silver and gold belts layered in front of hundreds of school cloaks, all different shades of green.

He wasn't sure what to do, so waited until the instructor lumbered to one side of the room before asking, "I'm sorry, who are you?"

"I'm Sage Ochram," he said, "and I teach Auras and mental magic to mid-level conjurers." He leaned in to a shelf filled with silver belts. "And this looks about right," he said, selecting one and extending it to Brenner; it felt like leather dipped in a thin layer of silver, creating a belt that was supple but not too heavy. Brenner slipped the belt around his robe and clasped it shut.

A moment later and they were back in the Banquet Hall, where Ochram said, "There are three groups of level five conjurers." He pointed to a middle table in the room. "Your squad is that one." Teenagers both younger and older than Brenner sat at the nearby table, a few looking at him as Ochram made to leave. "I look forward to having you in my class."

Without bothering to introduce Brenner to anyone, Sage Ochram turned and headed to the other side of the hall, which Brenner surmised must contain the sage's quarters.

*A whole new squad…*he thought with a mixture of surprise and relief. *I guess I got my wish.* He picked up his tray, but rather than walking over to join the new group, sought out Finnegan, who was busy regaling Maureen with a story.

"…and when these two Arenaterro soldiers threw punches at Silvalo spellcasters," Finnegan said. "My Pop thundered, 'Keep your brawls out of my pub! Or I'll have you stunned and thrown into the alley!' They straightened up real quick when they saw three of Pop's best mates pointing mircons at their orange cloaks…" Finnegan trailed off, his eyes flicking to Brenner's belt. "Well, we all knew that was bound to happen," he said in a voice of marvel mixed with jealousy, "but a week? Are you kidding me?"

"I'm as surprised as you are."

"I'll bet," said Finnegan. Then he joked, "You're just on a quest to break as many records as possible, aren't you?"

"As long as it isn't a record for quickest death on the Zabrani field, then sure…I guess I am."

There was an awkward pause as it sunk in that he wouldn't be training with Finnegan anymore. He smiled weakly. Finnegan must've realized this too, as he said, "Not to worry. You may have escaped Sorian and our squad, but you haven't escaped *me* yet. I'll see if I can find some time to join you for a shot or two during free periods."

Brenner grinned. "I'd like that very much, Finnegan. Hey, can I still work at Hutch & Sons?"

"Sure thing. The dishes won't wash themselves. Well they could with the right spell, but Pops doesn't want to waste elixir on it."

"Thanks. And hey, you'll probably be advanced to the next rank soon, too."

"Yeah, just as soon as I can cast spells without blurting them loud enough to wake a dozing dragon."

They both laughed. "You'll get there, Fin." Brenner didn't really want to leave his friend, but sensed from the shifting glances of his peers that he was creating a scene. "I should probably go and meet the captain."

"Yes, you should, you lucky conjurer," Finnegan said, and without bothering to lower his voice, added, "There's no way he's worse than Sorian. You know, I should melt some torch holders together and make my own silver belt."

Finnegan held out a hand; Brenner set down his tray and shook it.

When Brenner approached the new conjurers, he felt a strange sensation in his forehead, pulling at his thoughts. He glanced along the row of level fives and saw a girl hastily stow her mircon next to her lap and look away.

Here comes more mind games.

He set his food down and sat on the edge of the group. When he looked across the table, a boy with black curly hair and a large chin spoke up.

"Aren't you that guy who won the last Zabrani battle?"

"Well, my team won, and I got a couple—"

"Thought so. I'm Cad. Been here for a couple months. Ready to get my gold belt and move on."

"Nice goal, Cad. Say, who is the captain here?"

"Bianca. She's effective, but can get a little full of herself."

Cad pointed out a girl with blond hair cropped to her shoulders at the other end of the table.

"Thanks. What's the lesson for today?"

"Monday's it's Auras in the morning, then the afternoon switches to challenge games or woods training."

Brenner hardly had enough time to wolf down some scrambled eggs before the close of breakfast bell sounded and the groups marched for the exits like ants in a green, color-coded colony.

He followed Cad up a flight of stairs, down a corridor lined with tendril-snake plants rustling back and forth—Brenner kept to the far side—and into an open-air plaza. Warm sunshine flooded the plaza, and Brenner saw the fat, gray-mustached sage who directed him earlier approach the front of the group.

"Fair morn, spellcasters," the sage said.

"Fair morn, Sage Ochram," the class recited in unison.

"Please loosen your minds and prepare for our Aura training."

Brenner looked around and saw students closing their eyes. Some extended their mircons to their sides.

"Prepare for simple projectiles," Sage Ochram instructed, then flicked his metal mircon. "Auras up."

Large, translucent bubbles popped up and encapsulated each of the students, except for Brenner, whose forehead began sweating. *What was the spell he should be using?*

"Sage Ochram—" he called, but the instructor was looking beyond the students, directing something.

From across the courtyard, small pellets rose from the ground, and then they zoomed toward the group. Brenner dove behind the shell of the boy in front of him.

A barrage of marbles hit the student-bubbles, ricocheting off them like hailstones. Brenner covered his face and leaned toward the ground; the marbles felt like needles pelting his exposed back and legs. After several long, grimacing seconds, the hailstorm stopped.

"You may relax your Auras," Ochram said.

The bubbles around the students faded with a gentle *whish*. Students chatted with each other as if a sun-shower had just passed. Brenner raised his hand.

"Prepare for stronger forces," said Ochram, turning to cast the next spell.

Brenner urgently waved his hand. "Sage Ochram!"

The teacher finally noticed him. "Yes?"

"What is the shield spell?"

"Oh, dear me!" Ochram said, holding his hand against his head, "I just subjected you to a small torture, didn't I? So sorry, so sorry…" The class swiveled their heads to Brenner and many giggled as they realized he had been needled by the stones.

"The spell is *'Totum Aura'*."

Brenner silently mouthed the spell to himself twice. "Thank you."

"Would you like to practice out of harm's way then?"

"That would be great."

"Very well. Come by me."

Brenner strode through the ranks of conjurers, and found his place by Sage Ochram as the next projectile was unleashed on the students: jet blasts of water.

Brenner closed his eyes and spoke lightly to himself: *"Totum Aura"*.

He felt the air around him crystallize and warm a little, but when he opened his eyes, the bubble popped.

Ochram gave a knowing nod. "Good attempt. Now try thinking about your strengths." He then turned back to class and directed a flush of magic at the gushing blasts of water from large pipes in the wall, which reduced the water to small trickles and then to nothing. "Relax your Auras."

While the rest of the class took a breather, Brenner closed his eyes again and focused his thoughts on his knowledge, his ability to gather and grow new ideas, and his will to persist.

He opened his eyes, and let out a small gasp of wonder. Encapsulating him on all sides was a glimmering, translucent shield-bubble: his Aura.

"Now you're getting it!" encouraged Ochram. "Go stand in with the other spellcasters. Test the strength of your Aura. Go on."

Brenner felt a little reluctant.

"Come on now, no learning by being idle."

He lapsed his spell. As he joined the formation, the next command from Ochram made his heart jump: "Spellcasters, Auras up! Incoming flames!"

"*Totum Aura!*" Brenner shouted, not caring if he was the only one who had to speak the spell. He wasn't becoming charred ash if he could help it.

WHOOSH! From behind them, pure fire shot through the ranks like a savage wave.

Brenner cracked an eye open: he was inside a furnace, but thankfully, was not being burnt alive. All around his circular Aura raced orange flames.

*Please hold…please hold…*he thought, while all around them the fire turned red, yellow, and then white-hot. Sweat beaded on Brenner's forehead, but not because of the heat (surprisingly it only felt like standing under the early morning sun), but because the spell required his complete concentration.

Then, in an instant, as if a dragon behind them sucked in its plume of flame, the fire vanished.

Tentatively, Brenner lapsed his energy on the spell. His Aura dematerialized.

Small pops came from all around him: his classmates' Auras faded, and sighs of relief could be heard everywhere, except in the back row, where one student was crying.

"You'll be just fine, Alyssa," Sage Ochram called to a tall girl, channeling a blue spell at her that extinguished fire on her sleeve. "I daresay, the fire barely touched you, and my Aura addition put you completely out of harm's way. There's a soothing spell, and you're fine. Just work on concentration and endurance."

The girl sniffled a moment longer, and then, probably because of the unwanted attention, tried her best to compose herself.

"Conjurers," Sage Ochram projected his voice to the class, "recall that the fastest way to gain an Aura is by bringing to mind your greatest strengths, and the fastest way to lose it is by letting your attention wane *for even* the briefest moment."

"Sage Ochram?" An older girl called out.

"Yes?"

"Can we practice mental Auras next?"

"Kincay, you are overzealous as usual, but I like that in a pupil. Yes, we can conduct mental Auras now."

The students sprang into two lines facing each other, with Brenner shuffling into the formation.

"Face your partner and introduce yourselves," Ochram commanded.

A girl with canary yellow hair and a slender nose stood across from him, sized him up, and said, "Camira."

"Hello…I'm Brenner."

"Students on this side," Ochram said, pointing to Camira's line, "begin with a glimpse into your opponent's memory. Mircons at the ready…"

A memory spell? Brenner thought frantically, waving his arm at Sage Ochram, who again, failed to notice him as he turned and settled into an elevated chair overlooking the courtyard.

Ochram called out, "Begin!"

He didn't have time to shield himself. Camira shot a purple spell into him, and he felt like his brain was a book pried roughly apart. Memories of Earth and his old high school rippled into focus—his peers imitating his wheezes when passing in the hallway, getting fruit thrown at him in the cafeteria, finding the amulet in the tree tower, going through the portal—

"Halt!" Ochram announced.

The courtyard came into focus again. He put a hand to his head and looked across at Camira. She eyed him quizzically.

She'd seen too much!

"How many of you were successful in looking at memories?" Sage Ochram said from his chair, as students massaged their heads.

Along with the girl across from him, a quarter of the teenagers raised their hands.

"Decent," said Ochram. "By the end of the term, half of you will be able to peer at will, as memory gazing is both an art and a skill, where you must grapple with and overcome your opponent. Recall, when on the offensive with *Pervideas*, look at the personality and desires of your target spellcaster, then become like an army's advance scout, prodding their mind from different angles, combing over their Aura until you find soft spots or chinks in their mental armor. To block effectively, mask your emotions with neutrality, and think of the most solid wall or refuge, and of course, cover yourself with the *Psyche Aura* spell."

Students brought their mircons up to chest level.

"What's the mind-reading spell he just said?" Brenner asked the boy next to him.

"Memory-gazing? *Pervideas.*"

"Got it. Thanks."

If others can learn to do this, Brenner thought, *so can I.*

Sage Ochram spoke above the students, "Spellcasters, switch roles. And—begin!"

Brenner pointed his mircon at the Camira, who stared smugly back at him as if to say, "I *dare* you to try"—he had seen this look before in gym class, one of contempt and superiority, a trait he also read about in biographies of leaders who went on to lose both their supporters and influence—which made him a tad more confident.

I know how you think. He whispered softly, "*Pervideas.*"

A ghostly light shot from his mircon, and he felt like a rushing stream converging around a boulder. He saw that the former-girl-now-boulder indeed had a tiny imperfection on its side, a dark spot near its base. He pushed on it, but now the boulder became a great wall. He zoomed around it, seeing a dome cover the top. He tested the soil under the wall—it gave way. He focused the rushing stream on it and then he was in.

Images flashed before him—Camira was laughing with her friends after winning an Agilis course; snubbing a younger girl who was prettier than she was; he zoomed out and saw something else darkly rippling in her mind—her fears of wild jungle beasts, of drowning, and her largest fear of all, being jeered at by her peers, cast aside, unwanted—

"Conjurers, halt!"

A brief white light engulfed the field, and Brenner was back in the present.

Camira glared at him, as if he had just eavesdropped on a very private conversation.

"Switch mind gazers," Ochram commanded.

This time, Brenner was ready. *"Psyche Aura."*

When Camira threw her purple spell at him, she found a sturdy castle that deflected her rushing onslaught from every angle.

And on his next offensive, Brenner quickly sidestepped her defenses, found her weaknesses, and other dark secrets—jealousies, lies, regrets—that he guessed were likely shared with no one. When the session finished, Camira's pretty face blanched. Sage Ochram directed them to the Banquet Hall.

"Camira," he said, hustling to walk next to her before she joined her friends. "Your memories—I promise I won't talk about them. To anyone."

She looked at him as if he had something contagious.

"Will you do the same for me?"

Camira considered his offer, probably thought about the alternative, and said defensively, "Fine."

"Great...thanks," said Brenner.

Then she quickly turned back to some of the other girls, who gave Brenner a funny look.

That afternoon, their captain, Bianca, led them on an Agilis run through the thick forest on the eastern edge of Arborio—using no mircons, only amulets. Unlike Sorian, she declined the use of her own mircon, which was a relief. Although the squad climbed hundreds of feet into the canopy and jumped twenty-foot gaps between tree limbs, Brenner felt he was in his element.

At the end of the session, after averting two poison-coat python strikes (one which sent a peer to the infirmary), Brenner was in the leading group of climbers.

He ate his dinner quickly that evening and went back to the dormitories. As he had been thinking about his date with Gemry since Friday, there was no chance he would forget to shower beforehand. After toweling off, he dressed and headed back out to the eastern ramparts of Valoria.

On the top of the rolling green hills, Gemry was waiting for him.

"Hey, Brenner," she said, noticing his belt, and smiling at him. "How's level five treating you?"

"Apart from being pelted with hailstones and jets of fire, pretty good," Brenner said. "Where's Velvo?"

Gemry didn't answer, just held his gaze and flicked her mircon in a quick circle.

Brenner raised his eyebrows, but when he turned backward, it was too late.

The brown and green carpet had zoomed down from the sky and crashed into the back of his legs, bowling him over and onto its surface.

Gemry giggled, her hair waving as her shoulders bobbed up and down. "That *never* gets old!"

Brenner awkwardly propped himself up into a sitting position. "I'm glad *you* find it so funny. But can we call a truce on further sneak attacks?"

"I suppose…for the night."

"Thanks," he said wryly, smoothing out his robes.

Gemry hopped onto the carpet next to Brenner, sat cross-legged, and pointed her mircon ahead. The carrier carpet obliged, lifting the two of them up and flying over the forest next to the academy.

He looked over at her as a light evening breeze pushed against them. Gemry's long brown hair fluttered behind her, and small dimples formed on her cheeks as she smiled—her eyes caught Brenner watching her.

"Yes?"

Brenner looked away, his face turning a trace of red. "Nothing…just …you look nice tonight." The moment he said it, he became self-conscious. *Nice? Of all the words I could say, I chose 'nice'?*

Gemry didn't seem displeased—on the contrary, she gave a demure smile. "Thanks. You don't look so bad yourself, Conjurer. By the way— thanks for showering."

Brenner laughed. "Hey, for special occasions, and with advance notice, I clean up pretty well." Not wanting to linger on that topic, he quickly switched gears. "How was your weekend?"

"Definitely not the best. But not the worst. You go first."

As she steered the two of them past the Zabrani stadium, the walls of Valoria, around massive trees into the heart of Arborio, Brenner relayed the Contendir street fight, meeting Finnegan's father, getting his mircon nearly stolen, as well as his bungled attempts at levitating himself—Gemry laughed.

"I'm glad you're trying," she said. "Let's see if we can fix that tonight."

She landed them on a grassy bank overlooking a large river—"The Arborio River," Gemry informed him—big enough for boats to travel up and far down to the sea, with dark blue current foaming by boulders near shore. There was a splash by one boulder, and a large reptilian tail disappeared beneath the surface.

"Let's see your progress," Gemry instructed. "How are you doing with lifting inorganics?"

"*Levitulsus,*" Brenner said, and a collection of rocks by the water hovered waist-high and moved down the shore before falling to the ground.

"Good."

He then pointed his mircon at the wet soil, and a large clump obediently lifted and flew across the dark river, depositing itself with a loud *squelch* on the opposite pebble bank.

"Nice going. Now, let's see you fly."

Brenner thought hard and squinted his eyes: *Levitulsus.*

It was as though his feet became magnets and repelled a few inches up from the ground—but not for very long. Like brittle ice, the air under his feet cracked. He fell back to the ground.

"Not bad—you're getting there," said Gemry. "Two things: what spell are you using? Levitulsus?"

"Yes."

"That's what I thought. And second—what are you imagining?"

"Floating objects of course—sticks and mud hovering in the air."

"Ah… I see. Well, *Levitulsus* is best used for moving objects around you through the air—usually shorter distances. The spell you need is *Volanti.* You've been trying to fly using a short-range hovering spell. No wonder you've had trouble."

Brenner rolled the spell around in his mind.

"Remember our flight last week on Velvo?" she asked.

"Do you forget *your* near-death experiences?"

Gemry laughed. "Of course not. Okay, think of our whole ride. To fly, you have to visualize all parts of it, from lift-off to gathering speed to gliding, then maintaining flight…and maybe we'll hope for graceful landings *after* everything else comes together."

Brenner nodded.

"You ready to try?"

"As ready as I can be."

Gemry extended her hand toward the river. "After you."

Welling up inside of Brenner was excitement, fear and giddiness. *Would this really work?*

He faced the swift flowing river, and imagined mountain eagles taking off from cliff-faces over the forest, then pumping their wings.

Holding this thought he said the word, "*Volanti.*"

With an unexpected burst of energy, his feet jolted from the ground, and he was suddenly flying—if you could call it that. To all accounts he looked extremely awkward, like a baby bird unexpectedly caught in an updraft—plunging forward a dozen feet in the air, faltering, then shooting up and down in zig-zags.

"Does this count as flying?!" Brenner called out anxiously, then looked back at Gemry, who pumped her fist and let out a whoop.

"It's a start!"

When he turned forward, he realized with rising panic that he was well away from the safety of the pebble beach and now over the racing river—which was wider and more formidable than it had first seemed. He was now halfway across, and—*what was that?* Something large cracked its jaws open, then splashed and swam under the murky surface as Brenner lurched in a haphazard flight path. Whatever it was, it was not helping his concentration. Brenner felt himself losing his grip of the *Volanti* spell.

Oh no—not good.

His body started dropping toward the water, where river rapids loomed a dozen feet below. His heart beat frantically against his chest, as if seeking its own emergency exit.

"Volanti! *Volanti!*" he called out, falling fast.

For the final seconds before impact he did the only thing that came to mind: he flapped his arms maniacally, which, to onlookers, must have been quite comical, but to his dismay, did absolutely nothing.

Dark water rushed up to swallow him—

And then a green-brown animal swooped underneath, catching him like a taut trampoline.

"What?!" he yelled, as his thoughts raced—*How am I dry?!*—It took him a good moment to realize what had happened.

Velvo zoomed him back to the beach, where Gemry waited.

"You almost had it," she said casually.

Brenner didn't respond, as his chest was still heaving.

"Why'd you stop flying?" Gemry asked.

Brenner looked up at her with disbelief. "Oh, I dunno…maybe the crocodile circling me below? Or the rapids that would bash my head in? Take your pick!"

Gemry gave a small laugh. "None of which would have touched you if you had just focused on your spell. Here—come over to the grass. I'll fly with you."

He balked and turned his head to the side. "Don't I get a little break?"

"Tired already? How old are you again?" she pressed. "I thought you were sixteen—not six."

Brenner let out a huff. "Fine. But no over-the-river flights, right?"

"Right," she said reassuringly, "This time, focus on directing the flight—not on what's beneath you. And don't let the wind have its way. Come on."

"Okay…" Brenner said, following her up to the grass.

Gemry turned and held out her hand. "Ready?"

Brenner took a deep breath. He reached for her palm, which was softer and warmer than he expected.

"When I give the signal, we both launch the spell, okay?"

He nodded. *Here we go again.* "Alright…"

Gemry locked eyes with him and winked. "Now."

"*Volanti*," they said together. The same rushing sensation greeted him again, but this time Gemry was by his side, and her presence gave him a boost of confidence. They rose up together—five feet, ten feet, fifteen—as lightly as dragonflies fluttering by a pond.

"Woah!" Brenner shouted, feeling surreal and trying his best to hold tight to the thought of the spell.

Gemry kept them at about twenty feet high, and then, hand in hand, they began cruising above the Arborio streets and below the branches of giant oakbrawns and mahogany forest. The summer breeze felt refreshing, and sweet floral scents floated to them from red bromeliads on the trees.

"How do you feel?" Gemry asked.

When he didn't respond, she squeezed his hand. His mind registered her words, but when Brenner started speaking, he dipped from his flight.

"Keep the loop going," she encouraged him, "Remember, you're an aviamir, or a Pegasus, or a bird—you're meant to be flying. As long as you have that in the back of your mind, the flight will take care of itself."

Brenner visualized the eagle from the mountain peaks. He became it. He felt his chest puff out a little and his fingers and toes become lighter, as if they were really wings and talons.

As he flew more steadily, Gemry lifted her hand, and the two rose higher—forty, sixty, *eighty feet* in the air. If Brenner could have seen himself from a couple months ago, he would have stood wide-eyed and gap-mouthed.

Yet, here I am. Flying. With a girl. A beautiful girl.

Gaining enough confidence to look somewhere besides his flight path, he glanced over at Gemry, and smiled. Their speed increased, which made the wind sweep back Gemry's hair, and formed a light whistling sound. She saw him watching her, smiled back, and then, with a nod and a mischievous wink, did the unthinkable: she uncurled her fingers...and let go of Brenner's hand.

His eyes dilated and his heart beat madly. Grimacing, he expected to drop like a rock, but, to both his credit and immense relief, he remained in flight.

"Good!" Gemry shouted to him, waving over the wind current. "Now, let's have some fun."

She shot forward in front of Brenner, then turned her body to face him as if swimming the backstroke and called out, "Come on! Catch me—if you can!"

Suddenly she flew higher, up past a spiraling row of condominiums built on the side of a five-hundred-foot oakbrawn, up and up through the middle branches.

Be a bird, she had said...be a bird...

Brenner pushed himself forward, then up, like an eagle seeking to break through the clouds. One hundred feet…he saw her slender figure high above. Two hundred feet…she was fast!

But I can be fast, too.

Thrusting forward, he flew above the wooden condos, now below him like toadstools on a tree. Gemry cut through the tangled upper branches of the canopy. A moment later, as if shot from a cannon, Brenner burst through the treetops after her.

Intense sunrays blinded him.

Squinting, he hovered above the tree line and looked around, one hand blocking the sun from his eyes, the other gripping his mircon tightly. He hovered further up…so high that the canopy looked like a seamless green blanket.

Where did she go?

Small white clouds floated high overhead. *She couldn't have disappeared behind them so quickly…*

He lowered his gaze to the green foliage beneath his feet.

And then she hit him.

"Ah ha!" Gemry shouted, crashing into him like a tiger, grabbing his shins and shoving them backward, which caused him to flip forward uncontrollably.

"*What are you doing?!*" Brenner blurted as he tumbled from the sky back to the canopy, only righting himself from the somersaulting fall when he was within fifty feet from the treetops.

"Just helping you get your wings," Gemry replied with a grin, hovering upside down in front of him, gravity pulling her long hair down so that it looked like a chocolate stalactite.

"You seem to *forget* that this is my *first* solo flight! And we are something like a *thousand feet* up in the air!"

Gemry waved off his concerns. "Relaaax, you're fine." She turned herself rightside up. "You'll either adjust quickly, or you won't. Just choose the right option."

Brenner shook his head. "Oh, I'll choose the right option!" He zoomed toward her, nearly catching her ankle—but she nimbly zipped away, above the treeline.

Like hawks the two dove and raced through the sky.

Gemry always kept several yards in front—looping and spiraling and diving—and again Brenner almost grabbed her foot before she veered and wove down into the canopy. The two threaded above and below giant limbs and, at times, barely around other flying spellcasters, who threw their hands up and shouted, "Look where you're going!" to which Gemry shouted back, "We are!"

All the while, Brenner was learning her methods of flight—how to feint one way and carve the other, how to spiral and turn into a dive for extra speed, and how find and use thermals, rising up on the warm air currents to regain energy, instead of constantly fighting against gravity, air, and wind.

Finally, he surprised both of them. Guessing her next move down and around a large branch, Brenner beelined over it and tagged her ankle on the other side, calling out, "Gotcha!"

She smiled over her shoulder, then said, "Well look at you, conjurer. I suppose we can take a breather now. Come on." She pointed up and led them above the trees. Slowing her speed, Gemry shifted from a horizontal, face-first flight to a more casual, upright floating position.

"Not bad for your first flight," she said, waiting for him.

"Thanks," Brenner said, and unlike Gemry, was breathing heavily from all the mental and physical exertion.

"Let's cruise a bit more before the twilight sets in," Gemry said. She nodded to her left and said, "Those vultures will show us another thermal."

They followed the birds, and soon Brenner felt the warm air push against his body. "Ah…that's better," he said, soaring alongside Gemry as the orange sun dipped closer to the horizon. He noticed that flying slowly and riding the current eased the amount of energy he had to channel into the *Volanti* spell.

"Are you liking level five?" Gemry asked.

"When Sage Ochram remembers to tell me the spell names beforehand, it's fine."

Gemry laughed and then said, "Yeah, he always seemed to have too many things on his mind."

"I had the opposite impression. Like his routine was set on cruise control and he was spaced out."

"Cruise control? What's that?"

"Oh…" Brenner thought quickly. "That's just when you're…riding in a…boat…and you're keeping a steady paddle."

"Uh huh," she said with a raised eyebrow. "Must be something ordinary folk do. Spellcasters would just use a propulsion spell."

"Yeah. It is." Brenner nodded, hoping that was the end of it.

The evening breeze pushed her long hair back. "Well, now that you are capable of flying, the Games of Ganthrea are a little over a month away—are you going to try out?"

Brenner felt at turns thrilled and terrified at the prospect of playing a game hundreds of feet in the air. "I'd like to…but, isn't it difficult to get in?"

"Of course. But the prizes are great enough that most students try to compete. I am."

"Which event?" he asked.

"Contendir and Zabrani."

"That's cool. With your flight skills and spell ability, you can clearly handle it," Brenner said. He thought again about her question. "Honestly, do you think I could make it?"

"I've seen you play pretty well…I think you could do it. That is, first you have to make the cut for the Silvalo Zabrani team. Usually they don't accept any spellcasters below level nine."

"Oh," he said with a frown.

She noticed his expression and added brightly, "But the Agilis team accepts a few mid-level spellcasters each year. And if anyone at your level could qualify—you could."

"Thanks," Brenner said, feeling a surge of pride at her compliment. Then he wondered if there was a cost involved with joining the team...*and who would pay for that? Windelm?* The thought of money triggered an earlier conversation into his mind. "Hey, Gemry, does your dad go to Hutch & Son's?"

"I wouldn't doubt it. He doesn't usually say where he goes during the day—just that he has to meet with suppliers or negotiate business deals. Why?"

"I thought I saw him talking there with someone...and the guy was *not* happy..."

Gemry was quiet a moment before muttering, "Probably because my father owed him golders...which means my mother and I will have to work more to pay for his mistakes."

"Sorry to hear that," Brenner said, deciding not to mention the threat of the other man taking her father's amulet. "On the bright side, in a couple of years you can work for yourself."

"Yeah...that's what I want most. To be free of my family's business, and start saving for myself."

"That's a good goal," Brenner said, nodding.

The evening sunrays grew faint, then faded from behind the trees. As they flew onward, the suspended ball lanterns flipped on high above, glowing like yellow fireflies.

"Tell me," said Gemry, giving him a sideways glance, "why did you wait so long to come to Valoria?"

Brenner wanted to trust her...but felt Windelm's stern warning come to mind. "My family thought I could get along fine without it, and since I'm their only kid," he paused, feeling bad lying to her, "the harvests would be harder without me around for years."

"Huh," Gemry said, sounding not wholly convinced. "So you want to be a rancher then, once you're finished at Valoria?"

"I don't know yet...depends on what I learn, and what opens up for me."

"That's too bad," she said, giving him a teasing look, "I've always thought cattle-boys were kinda cute."

Brenner's tongue stuck in his mouth, and his cheeks warmed.

"Oh...really?" was the best he could muster.

Gemry cracked a smile at him. "It's okay—you can blush."

"I – uh...I'm not blushing..." Brenner said, the obvious lie growing as his face warmed. He looked away.

"We should head back to Valoria," she said. "I've got a modification class tomorrow."

"Right," he said, wanting to say something more, something witty or funny or a compliment—anything—but instead he just looked at his feet, flustered.

Together, the two flew back to the academy in the warm summer night—and when he happened to think about it, Brenner could hardly believe that he was still flying; a part of him felt the beautiful dream would end any minute. But after a flock of rainbow birds flapped from behind a tree in front of them, and one of their wings smacked Brenner in the face, and *still* he didn't wake up—he knew it was real.

They passed along the river again, Gemry flying gracefully at his side, and after much mental back and forth—*should I do it? No, she might flip out...maybe next time...although she did make that cattle-boy comment...*

He shifted his mircon to his left hand, and with his right, reached over and held Gemry's hand.

To his delight, she didn't punch him.

She didn't even shrug him off.

Rather, she looked back at him, squeezed his hand, and gave him another winning smile that made him feel like a firework had just ignited inside his chest.

If he had to guess, he was fairly certain he looked like a complete goof as he smiled back at her. And even though no more words passed between them as they flew through the night to Valoria, there was something else that did.

Brenner never grinned so hard.

Among the airborne spellcasters that Brenner and Gemry soared above that evening were two hooded men that had just flown past the Shell Towers before they were activated by nightfall, holding a conversation in deliberately hushed tones.

"Shivark told us to, that's why."

"But Silvalo? Why not another biome where we have more power? More soldiers?"

"Because, Fensk, you idiot, this is where all Ganthrea's talented and powerful are coming in five weeks."

"The games?"

"Of course."

"Do you think anyone knows about the missing scouts?"

"It's been a month—I'm sure they've noticed. But they don't know who caused it...and if our decoys worked, they'll think it was Safronius or Arenattero. This will give the other captains time to start the land scouring in Silvalo."

"Oh. Right. How many recruits does he want?"

"As many as possible. The more we gain, the more authority Shivark said he'd give us. You saw what he did to Paxton when he returned with too few recruits from Gelemensus."

"...his final cry was the worst...it still haunts me."

"We don't let that be us. Ever. We complete our mission, get rewarded, and when Shivark finally flips the tables on Rancor, we'll be the new elite. Now let's find someplace away from the arenas but near the heart of the city, where we can blend in. We'll start tomorrow."

Chapter Eighteen

The Package, the Plans, and the Roster

A week after the flight with Gemry, Brenner awoke and went to the Banquet Hall for his breakfast. He was in good spirits: he'd picked up the routine of his new classes…had better control of mental spells, knew more peers, played well in Zabrani games with mixed levels…and best of all, he could *fly*.

Every chance he got after classes, he soared with his *Volanti* spell across the forest behind Valoria, learning new tricks and maneuvers from Gemry. If Gemry was unavailable, he asked Finnegan to join him by borrowing a school carrier carpet.

As he bit into an apricot for breakfast, a sage arrived at his table.

"Brenner?"

"Yes?"

"This arrived for you," he said, holding out a brown package about a foot long.

"Oh…thanks," Brenner said, wondering what lay inside. *Who would send me gifts?*

He tore into the paper, unwrapping a long, brown case. Putting his thumb on the metal fastener, he lifted it with a soft click. Inside the case was a mircon: the body of it was a sleek baton of two woods spiraled seamlessly together, with the bottom end fused into a gleaming reddish rock, and the top end crowned with a purple crystal.

Woah…my own mircon!

The conjurers on either side of him let out appreciative whistles.

As he held the mircon, he looked back in the case. There was a loop of glass at one end and a folded note. Crinkling it open, he read:

Dear Brenner,

Two weeks into Valoria, and I heard you've already won Zabrani games and leveled up—not too bad! The school mircons are fine, but there's something to be said for a handcrafted one. I picked this up at Corsmith's. I asked the owner, Majelda, what mircon she'd recommend for best manipulating multiple elixirs, and she told me this one was the best: it came from volcanic rock, two trees—oakbrawn and conifer—and even has a tip cut from an amethyst gem. Said it took her over a month to fashion.

I hope you make good use of it. Just like your amulet, do everything but lose it, alright? I have a scouting expedition this week and next, but plan on being off for the Games of Ganthrea at the end of June—we can watch a few games together, or, who knows? Maybe we'll cheer you on at an Agilis match.

See you soon.

The Greatest of Your Uncles,
Windelm

P.S. Use the attached holster clip for your mircon when you'd like your hands free. The clip will remember who you are, and only unlock for you.

Excitement welled up inside as Brenner thought about what he would try the mircon out on first. He picked up the glass-like holster, and as he placed it next to his belt, the middle melted apart, stretched around the belt like hot glue, and fused back together. He brought the mircon to the loop, and a warm sensation met his hand; then the loop cinched around the mircon, holding fast.

When he wanted to remove the mircon, he simply reached down and touched his palm to the holster and it loosened enough to draw the mircon out. *This is cool...*

Finishing his breakfast quicker than normal, Brenner jogged outside the academy walls. He had a few minutes before his morning class. Blue skies and puffs of clouds greeted him, and a light breeze brushed across his skin. He held the mircon out in front of himself, looking a bit like a conductor striking up the forest to play a symphony.

"Apellatum," he said, and magic effortlessly shot out of the spiral tip of his mircon. From three hundred yards away, a fallen log lifted with a great squelch, and then zoomed at him in the air, bits of moss trailing from its sides as it flew.

He willed the log to go faster—it was more than halfway, making a whistling sound. He watched...waited...and let it get within twenty feet of ramming him before thinking, *Repello.*

The massive trunk froze as though blocked by an invisible wall. Then it obediently swung in a semicircle and flew back to the forest as lightly as a seed drifting from the canopy. Brenner guided it back to a clearing before letting go of the spell. The tree thundered to the ground.

Somewhere behind him in the academy came a familiar sound: dimly, he registered the iron bells. But he knew what he wanted to do next, and looked up to the cloud-checkered sky.

"Volanti."

Immediately his feet lifted weightlessly from the ground, and with only the slightest thought of a helicopter take-off, he soared above the rolling hills, over the dark treetops, higher and higher until he could see the full Valoria campus sprawled along the eastside of Arborio, its massive towers and walls stretching up and connecting to the colossal Zabrani stadium in the north, and the Agilis stadium in the south.

He flew higher still, up until he could faintly see the blurred edges of the city marked by the tall Shell Towers, then the major roads leading into Arborio, like rivers leading into a green ocean, up until his body chilled from the cold air currents, up toward his goal: the white cloud-line. Moments later and he could see the majestic curvature of Ganthrea stretching far on the horizon. *It really is as big as Earth…I wonder what else is out there…*

He kept pushing upward through the cold, with goosebumps prickling on his arms and legs, and couldn't help but thinking of how pet birds must feel when they are freed from their cage…and then, he did it: with his free hand, he touched the base of the clouds.

Looking down past his shoes, some ten thousand feet in the air, the sight was beautiful and in more ways than one, chilling. A gust of wind pushed into him, threatening to rip his mircon from his hand. He brought it to his chest as a shiver of panic rippled through him.

Brenner had always had a surreal idea that, up close, the clouds would feel like whipped cream, soft and smooth…but, as he put his hand into them again, they felt more like cold, dewy spider-webs.

With his other mircon, he had to keep telling himself to keep the *Volanti* spell spinning, but with the new mircon he felt different. He wanted to try something: could he separate the flight loop from the rest of his thoughts? He pushed the idea back, and kept his focus forward. And slowly…very slowly…yes…he found he *was* able to move the flight spell to another part of his mind, like simultaneously riding a bike and singing a song. Putting it on autopilot freed him to think and focus on his surroundings. Time flowed blissfully. He swooped around and dove through the clouds, perfecting his loops and barrel rolls in the sky.

Finally, he descended back to the ground with a broad smile on his face, and his new mircon gripped comfortably like a favorite pen. When Brenner walked back into the castle, he suddenly realized with embarrassment how incredibly late he was to Sage Ochram's class. He hustled to the open courtyard in the middle of Valoria, and waited in the archway until Ochram's mini-blizzard subsided and the snow melted on the flagstones. Then he quietly stepped into the formation along its side.

Brenner was dismayed to see that, for being absent-minded most of the time, Ochram's gaze had swept over to his side, and then onto him.

"Brenner," Sage Ochram said brusquely, "finally decided to join us, did you?"

"Sorry, sir," Brenner said quickly.

"See me after class for your work demerits," Ochram said, then shifted his attention back to the whole group. "Conjurers, prepare for the next physical assault."

The sound of balloons expanding filled the courtyard as Auras materialized like shimmering bubbles around each student.

"Fire assault—now!"

Brenner's mind pulled the green and crimson magic from the amulet as he thought, *Totum Aura*. At once a thick, clear cocoon of magic formed around him just as blue flames flickered across the field, creating a crackling furnace that changed the color of the flagstones from cream and light ochres to glowing dark reds. When he was certain the spell was locked in a loop, which like the flight, took less mental energy than usual, he opened his eyes and looked around. His peers looked most uncomfortable: their fists were clenched tight, most had their eyes closed and faces screwed up in concentration, some had even leaned into awkward, hunched-over positions.

Then Brenner decided to try something else with his *Totum Aura* spell: into the oncoming flames, and against the safe wishes from a little voice in his mind, he took a step forward.

Rather than crack open—and turn him into a charred piece of barbeque—his Aura maintained its strength and moved with him. Fire licked his forcefield on all sides, but could not penetrate it. He took a few more steps, and then, gaining confidence, began to move more quickly up and down between the rows of his peers, many of whom had beads of sweat trickling down their foreheads. The Aura traveled with him, and the flames channeled around it like angry lava around a stubborn stone.

Sage Ochram said something at the head of the field, and the tongues of fire receded back to the perimeter of the courtyard, fizzling with soft hisses.

After a couple more drills, Ochram dismissed the conjurers to lunch.

"Except you, Brenner," he said with a level tone. "Come see me."

Ochram was nearly as tall as he was large, and sternly watched as Brenner trudged across the courtyard, wondering dismally about his punishment—*Please don't let it involve tendrilsnakes.* Ochram waited to speak until Brenner stopped just below his bristled gray mustache.

"And where were you today?"

"I…" Brenner began, wondering if a lie might help him more, but deciding on the truth, "I got a new mircon…and I had to test it out. See how high I could fly."

Sage Ochram muttered something and Brenner felt a prick at his mind, as though a horsefly had nipped him.

"Indeed you did…" Ochram said, and Brenner realized with mild alarm how quickly the sage had checked his short-term memory. "Tardiness implies dishonor toward your fellow conjurers and your sage. Normally I'd keep you the length of your tardiness to scrub scorch marks and soot from the walls of the courtyard…but, I like to reward honesty…and also, from your classroom performance, I am impressed."

Brenner was dumbfounded. "You…are?"

"Almost any conjurer with basic knowledge of mental magic can project and hold a rigid Aura. But the ability to move with your Aura intact…that takes stamina, and, especially the first time, courage."

"Oh," Brenner said, hardly believing that he was receiving a compliment instead of a scolding. "Thank you."

"When typical conjurers move—or, try to move—with their Aura, it dissolves almost instantaneously. And since I was casting a firestorm spell on you, that would have been excruciatingly painful. Spellcasters don't usually attempt moving with Auras when they're under attack—so why did you?"

"Well…my Aura felt secure, and I wasn't aware it would fade through movement. I just figured it would continue as long as I focused on it."

"Hmm," said Ochram, casting a curious glance at Brenner. "Where are you from again?"

Having fielded this question quite a bit now, Brenner relayed the story behind his later arrival to Valoria in a more convincing manner.

Sage Ochram heard him out, then asked bluntly, "Are you trying out for the Valoria teams? For the Games of Ganthrea?"

"I might…although I hear they're dangerous," Brenner said.

"Well of course there's some danger. But there's prizes to be earned—last year's winners received a couple hundred golders—and, of course, prestige. Many of my former students who made it to the final rounds now hold powerful posts in government or merchant guilds—and they seem to enjoy treating me to dinners and gifts when they are in town,"—he patted his belly and gestured to jeweled rings on his hand—"Like them, you could make a name for yourself in Arborio, and beyond. Prosperous guilds from other biomes are seeking new talent to lead and protect their interests—and they don't pay meager amounts, they pay a *pre-mi-um*."

He let the words float like gold dust and settle around Brenner. While the money clearly appealed to Ochram, it was the prestige that hooked into Brenner. Prior to Ganthrea, he had never been cheered at a sport, never praised for his performances, his ziplines, his schoolwork…*what would it be like to be seen as a golden athlete?*

"Think about it," Sage Ochram said, cutting into Brenner's daydream, "and know that I can be of assistance along the way. Well, time for lunch then. Remember, next time you're late, plan on getting your robes covered in soot and grime."

"Yes, Sage Ochram. Thank you."

Ochram nodded and waved him off, then gathered odd stones from behind his instructor's pedestal and put them into a leather satchel.

Brenner quickly moved to the corridors, ate a light lunch, and then wound his way to the familiar outdoor classroom of his first instructor, giving himself fifteen full minutes before Bianca's afternoon Agilis regimen.

When Brenner crossed under a stone archway outside onto the dark geen lawn, he saw Sage Shastrel floating three feet in the air with his legs crisscrossed, his eyes closed, and a look of serenity on his face.

"Sorry to interrupt, Sage," Brenner said, approaching him. "I have something to return to you."

Slowly, Shastrel opened his eyes and peered down at Brenner, who was holding the wood mircon out to him.

"Ah yes," said Shastrel. "and I see you didn't break it. Very good."

Or lose it, Brenner thought with relief, thankful for Finnegan's help.

"You got a new one?" Shastrel asked, opening his hand.

"Yes. A composite." Brenner handed the carved wand to him.

"Must make the academy mircon seem slow in comparison, yes?"

"Yeah…this one seems to channel my magic better."

"One of the advantages of a composite, especially when one holds multiple elixirs."

Wordlessly, Shastrel flicked his own wand, and the old mircon hovered over to his satchel, and like a feather, floated inside his bag, which then primly shut itself. "Thank you for returning the mircon in good condition." He nodded and then closed his eyes again, which Brenner took as a signal that he desired peace.

As Brenner walked to the archway, Shastrel unexpectedly broke the silence. "Most spellcasters would call me a fool, but I have to tell you, it's not always in one's best interest to compete in the Games of Ganthrea. Prematurely, that is."

Brenner turned to look at his levitating instructor. "Why?"

"People don't just play for the love of the game: they play to win. At all costs."

Brenner considered his words, which seemed to go against the dangers he'd encountered so far. "I thought Valoria prided itself on producing brave spellcasters?"

"It does…and you certainly need that to play…but bravery does not guarantee emerging from the Games alive."

As Brenner considered this, the silver bells in the academy bell tower rang out with light peals, signaling the start of the afternoon session.

"Thanks for the advice, Sage Shastrel…I better get going."

"You're welcome. If you are offered a spot on the team, decide on your own whether you to play. Don't let the wrong reasons push you into it."

Brenner nodded, then joined his group of conjurers as Bianca led them toward the dense forest, carrying a chest of glowbes in her arms.

"Stow your mircons," Bianca ordered, "and prepare for Agilis. Play hard, but know the limits to your jumps. I don't want any unnecessary injuries before our next Zabrani matches."

Brenner placed his mircon in his crystal holster on his waist, and smiled when it automatically tightened. He turned his attention to the glowbes flying like silver hummingbirds through the forest canopy, then jumped on a thick bough of a nearby oakbrawn and began chasing his first glowbe, still thinking about the conflicting advice from Sages Ochram and Shastrel.

Three weeks later, and with extra flight practice with Gemry, Brenner had gained promotion into the level six conjurers. With the new gold belt around his waist, he played Zabrani as a flyer—a knight, as the rules called it—and was able to keep pace with some of the best of his team. While he didn't always capture glowbes in the scrimmages between spellcasters, he played well, which was good because the sages were using the inter-level games to decide which spellcasters would be asked to play for Valoria and the forested territory of Silvalo during the Games of Ganthrea.

Throughout his classes, his weekends working with Finnegan, or the occasional evening touring the city with Gemry, conflicting thoughts about the games swirled through Brenner's mind: *what sort of recognition could I get by playing? How much money is at stake, and what doors could open by winning? How dangerous were the other spellcasters? Would they be like Sorian, trying to cripple opponents in order to win?* The old Brenner had been limited to watching from the sidelines on Earth, but now that he was on equal footing, this new version of himself wanted to see just what he was capable of doing. And the games of Agilis and Zabrani, in spite of, or perhaps because of, the dangers, were just pure fun.

If the Games had been a common topic of conversation the month before the world event, during the last few days at Valoria they were the *only* thing discussed. For tomorrow, Monday, marked one week until the seven-day tournament began, and more importantly, was the day the athletes for the three teams of Valoria were finalized.

At his previous schools, Brenner had never been seriously considered for a team, let alone an elite one, and as a result his skin prickled on and off with anxiety and excitement.

Throughout Monday he absentmindedly ran his hand through his hair, eager to know if his progress over the last month was enough to earn a spot on the roster for one of the three sports. With more energy than usual he bounded from morning classes to lunch and then to afternoon practice with his cohort of level six conjurers.

Clouds rolled in after practice, and as his group trooped inside the castle for evening supper, news whirled through the squad: the rosters were posted. Brenner's heart beat louder, and his stomach felt like the time Gemry had tilted him sideways off Velvo.

Winding through the tunnels, they came to a standstill outside the Banquet Hall: all of Valoria's spellcasters crowded by the rosters just inside the doors, causing a bottleneck. Slowly making his way through the swarm of excited spellcasters, he saw some students squeal with delight and run off to find their friends, but many more consulted the lists and let out groans of disappointment.

At last, he made it inside the hall, then closer to the front of the line, until finally it was his turn to see the lists.

He checked the Contendir roster first—mainly to see if other spellcasters he knew were on it, since he hadn't even played the sport with his cohort. As suspected, he saw that of the thirty spellcasters, he was not listed as one to represent Valoria. But Gemry was. He stepped over to the Zabrani posting, scanning the names down…down…down…and felt a stab of disappointment: he hadn't made the cut for Zabrani, either.

Gemry, however, had been selected for both of the higher complexity games, and he felt a little ashamed of himself for being jealous of her. *She does have a lot more experience than me…*he rationalized, but deep inside he'd wanted to be picked, to be validated.

Moving to the last poster, for Agilis, he read the names of students…and his feelings of dejection grew as he neared the final names, but then, with a ripple of excitement tingling up in his spine, he saw that on the last slot of the chosen competitors was the name *Wahlridge, Brenner.*

I made it. I'm going to play. A huge grin grew on his face.

"Don't smile too hard, Brenner," a familiar voice jostled him.

He looked around, "Oh, hey Finnegan!"

"So, you made the Agilis team, huh? Crown me a sovereign—not bad for your first year!" Finnegan said, clapping him on the shoulder.

"Thanks," he replied, still feeling a bit surreal. As the two moved out through the crowd of students to the banquet tables, a flicker of light caught a strip of silver around Finnegan's waist. "Hey—nice job on your promotion!"

"They had to move me up sometime really," Finnegan explained, "And when I finally moved Shastrel's boulders without yelling my head off to cast the spell, I think that was the deciding factor."

"Way to go, Finnegan. That's got to feel good getting away from Sorian's squad."

"Like leaving a dunghill and moving to paradise."

Brenner laughed. "Will you be training under Bianca? You'd like her: she's straightforward and doesn't play favorites."

"Bianca could use a whip and run us into the ground, and she would *still* be better than Sorian."

They both laughed.

"Hey, you up for free time in the stadium later?"

"Count me in."

After dinner, Brenner and Finnegan practiced in the Agilis stadium, racing between trees and around stone ramps, and shooting glowbes with *Arcyndo* spells for target practice. Pausing to catch his breath, Brenner saw Gemry emerge from the archway entrance. He waved.

Walking up to him, Gemry said, "I saw you earned yourself a spot on the Agilis squad." She put her hands on her hips and gave him a glowing smile, which made him forget how tired he was. "I'm impressed."

"Thanks, Gemry. It's good, but not nearly as cool as your selection to both Zabrani and Contendir. *That's* amazing."

"Well thank you," she said, "but when you get to my level, you're pretty much expected to be selected to one or the other. So, for your Agilis, what obstacles do you think they'll include this year?"

"I don't know…huge snakes?"

"Dragons—they've gotta have some dragons," Finnegan cut in, before taking aim and shooting a glowbe in the distance.

"They haven't had dragons in ten years," Gemry said. "The last ones broke the protective barrier of the field and shot fire into the crowd at Montadaux. Sovereign Drusus would be reckless if he wants to risk dragon-fire in the heart of our tree city."

"Maybe," Finnegan said, "but my dad says that's why so many people are coming to the Games. They expect a higher level of danger now that they increased the prize winnings from last year in Safronius."

"Apart from golders, what can you win?" asked Brenner.

Both Finnegan and Gemry looked at him like he was an idiot.

"Only your choice of elixir, or a government post," Finnegan said.

"Have you won before?" he asked Gemry.

"I came close last year," Gemry said, looking out to the field. "My father—I mean, my parents—expect that I will place in the winner's circle in at least one event this year." She sighed and was silent a moment, which was punctuated only by the distant shots of other spellcasters.

"Let me know if I can help you prepare," Brenner said.

"It's fine," said Gemry, as if waking from a dream, "I'll be ready."

The following week swept by quicker than the previous three. The biggest change—and a welcome one at that—was that Sage Ochram seemed to be actively trying to not accidentally blast Brenner with deadly heat or hail spells. Although he did forget to de-ice the floor after the session before them, and several of Brenner's squad mates slipped past the threshold and suffered bruises.

Brenner found an official green Agilis uniform and garments next to his bed one morning, and the sages allowed him extra time in the afternoons to practice his sprints and aerobatics in the Agilis stadium. Unlike the Agilis and Contendir players, whose games depended on solo efforts, the Zabrani team was encouraged to practice together, so Brenner watched a few sessions of Gemry and the team practicing skirmishes and flight patterns.

Valoria's classes finished for the season on Friday; Brenner heard closing remarks that day in the Banquet Hall from Spellmaster Kinigree, who, Finnegan informed him, was the Chief Sage of Valoria. Spellmaster Kinigree, a shaggy, gray-haired man of average height but surrounded by a palpable glow of power, thanked the students for their hard work over the semesters, informed them of the outdoor graduation on Saturday for students that had reached the summer of their eighteenth year, and told them that he and the sages would decide over the week of the Games what levels, if any, the spellcasters would advance to for the fall session. Students were welcome to stay at the castle for the week of the Games and decide by Monday morning whether to go back to their families or off to summer jobs.

So, on Saturday, having no friends who were graduating and not having to wash dishes until the evening, Brenner and Finnegan explored some of the new merchant stalls from foreign biomes. Finnegan nearly got his finger pinched off when he got too close to an overgrown lobster scuttling across a butcher's table. For his part, Brenner enjoyed watching some of the street performers—jugglers throwing everything from steel machetes to live iguanas and even a couple of young kids from the audience—although he suspected another spellcaster was hiding nearby, assisting the act with a levitating spell.

Gemry had had to work Saturday and Sunday, but was allowed to have Sunday evening off since many customers were retiring early in preparation for the Games on Monday. And lucky for Brenner, she chose to take him for a ride. They sat together at sunset, high on her carrier carpet, Velvo, floating in the humid upper canopy along the western entrance of Arborio, talking about last week, the Games, and watching the throngs of travelers. Scores of spellcasters with amulets and colored capes flew past the Shell Towers, while thousands more without elixir pushed handcarts, rode animals, or traveled in caravans along the road of Via Arborio. Some of the walkers caught Brenner's eye.

"Hey, Gemry, those people holding the bridles of the camels, are they..."

"Slaves? Yes. You can tell by the collars."

Brenner looked more closely, and faintly saw some of the copper collars showing above their tunics.

"Doesn't that seem...wrong?" he asked, looking at her.

"Well, yeah," Gemry said, "but it's just part of life. It would take a decree from our Sovereign, and more than likely a major war among the wealthy magnates, to change it."

"Is that likely?"

"About as likely as a dragon hatching itself."

"So...that's a never, right?" he asked.

She gave him a wide-eyed look and spoke to him slowly, like a child: "As far as I know, it still takes a mommy dragon, and a daddy dragon—"

"Okay, okay," he said, rocking his shoulder against hers. He watched the owners sitting high on the cushions of their stagecoaches, while their slaves below slowly funneled past the towers. They ranged in age. Some were young, which reminded him of that girl from alley, Rinn, and how desperate she seemed to be free. He wanted to tell Gemry about where he really came from, and how slavery had been outlawed for over a hundred and fifty years. But instead he said lamely, "Well…that's too bad."

"It is," said Gemry simply. "But since the elixir magnates have the most power, use the most slaves, and have no reason to help eliminate slavery, that's how it will probably stay."

Brenner was silent.

"Hey," she said, nudging him. "Cheer up. Let's start with what we can control—our performance at the games. They only happen once a year, will lead to great things for us, and I, for one, am going to win." She smiled and laced her fingers with his own, creating a tingle that flowed from her touch up his arm. "Are you with me?"

Brenner couldn't help but smile back. "I'm with you."

Chapter Nineteen

The Games of Ganthrea

The early rays of dawn illuminated Brenner's dormitory, starting the June summer solstice, and with it, the Games of Ganthrea.

After breakfast, the sages ordered the Agilis team to meet at the southern stadium, which buzzed loudly with hundreds of thousands of spectators, all of whom, Brenner realized, would be judging their performance. Clad in a green and black uniform with a short cape on the outside, and feeling a bit queasy and jittery on the inside, Brenner sat with the other Agilis players in a designated section just above the field.

Seven teams were spaced around the field in a speckled rainbow configuration, with the biggest fans of their home biome seated behind them, waving banners, and donned with bright face-paint. Brenner's section of Valoria academy was centered between the golden yellow uniforms of Safronius players to the right, and to the left sat players in brilliant blue uniforms that seemed to shimmer like light rippling on water. *That must be Aquaperni,* he thought.

A loud clang of bells rang out across the stadium and the crowd grew quieter. An older wizard with a weathered, red beard strode out from an entrance on the stadium floor, then flew gracefully up into the center of the arena, until he was several hundred feet above the mostly flat dirt. "Spellcasters, Agilis players, and guests from the seven biomes of Ganthrea," he said in a strong voice that echoed around the stadium, "I'm Donavon Drusus, Sovereign Wizard of Silvalo, and the city of Arborio is proud to welcome you to the first day of the Games of Ganthrea." He spread his arms wide as the crowd cheered. "Please also welcome the sovereigns from the other six biomes."

Four men and two women from suites near midfield hovered from their seats.

"Roan Bondor of Montadaux, Calimus Palento of Safronius, Amal Jadula of Arenaterro, Kayla Vangetti of Aquaperni, Sari Sanati of Gelemensus, and Eckel Rancor of Vispaludem."

Some sovereigns raised their arm in a wave amidst the applause, while others merely tilted their head before flying down to their seats. Drusus pointed his mircon across the field, and a shimmering, rainbow flock of birds-of-paradise shot from the base of the arena up into the sky, whistling to each other as their plumage turned each of the seven Ganthrean colors.

"Today's first round of Agilis will showcase the academy spellcasters. As is custom for this sport, mircons may not be used, only amulets. Of the one hundred and forty players today, the top forty will advance to the second stage, with its four top finishers competing in the third and final stage, and earning their choice of golders, position, or elixir."

He raised his mircon and gave what sounded like a well-rehearsed benediction: "May the swiftest, bravest, and most cunning players win."

As the crowd began a thundering applause, Brenner brought a hand to his head. The nervousness and the noise combined to give him a sharp pain in his forehead. Using his mircon, Brenner cast a *Psyche Aura* spell, and found that the noise was reduced, and with it, the pain.

Drusus gave a signal to the side, and four white robed officials flew around the arena, scattering landform seeds.

This was the part that Brenner was most anxious to see: *what would the Agilis terrain and obstacles look like?*

Drusus took a gleaming seed from his own pocket, dropped it a couple hundred feet, and upon impact, a great oakbrawn tree started growing in the middle of the arena: its trunk bulged upward with huge limbs unfurling; its roots cut through the ground like gigantic ploughs; and within a few short moments, a five hundred foot oakbrawn stood like a skyscraper in the middle of the field. Drusus directed spells in a circle around the oakbrawn, and an enormous fissure ripped the ground, creating a canyon ring around the tree. In other parts of the field, officials were raising hills up from the ground. Drusus fired more spells—like fireworks from his wand—and all across the arena sprouted gnarled, tall willow trees, and large rock formations.

One of the officials opened a chest, and a swarm of bright glowbes rose together like bees and flew to the top of the center oakbrawn, hovering just above it.

"Spellcasters, you may enter the field and take your posts."

Brenner looked at his team of twenty. He stood and followed them down the rows of the stadium to the edge of the arena, and then down a carved stone staircase. One by one, they entered the field, and deposited their mircons in a black strongbox that, upon accepting his mircon, snapped shut.

His *Psyche Aura* spell gone, the noises and pain hit his head again. He had to do something...if his amulet could amplify his physical strength, and take away his asthma, it must do something for his mind...he focused on the red elixir in his amulet, and his leg and arm muscles rippled with a shot of adrenaline...

Brenner walked past some short poles, wondering if their whole team would be stacked together at the start, competing directly for the Agilis glowbes, when a girl in an orange uniform plummeted down from the sky and bumped against his shoulder. She gave him a look and said, "Watch where you're going, rookie," before turning and marching off to a glowing patch of grass.

He looked up, and saw athletes catapulting across the massive field, then landing deftly between poles. *The launch pad again...*

He joined the queue of Valoria teammates behind their pad. This must be like the launch before Zabrani...only this pad shot spellcasters in multiple directions.

Soon it was his turn; he walked into the center of the pad, and was hurled skyward. Without his mircon in flight, he felt naked, and wind-milled his arms as he crisscrossed air paths of other Agilis spellcasters, flinching as he flew within inches of them. He hit the apex of his flight, and for a moment admired all the rainbow capes and uniforms of players shooting up and falling down at the edges of the field, looking like a seven-jet fountain.

As he plummeted down to another launching pad, he noticed the solid ring of brambles around the entire arena that formed the outer barrier. The magic of the poles slowed his descent. He landed. Then Brenner jogged off the pad before another red Montaudax student touched down. The game would be starting soon, and his head still pounded.

Brenner and a mix of Agilis players gathered in a large section of glowing grass marking their starting zone; some jumped in place or swung their arms for last minute stretches. Focusing on the red elixir hadn't changed his headache, so Brenner focused on the green...thinking of the calming forest...and a feeling of tranquility rippled through his mind, easing the aches.

"Agilis players," the loud voice of Sovereign Drusus rang out, "the live creature obstacles have been released upon the course. Do your best to surpass them, but know that they will not hold back their aggression."

Brenner looked around at the twenty or so spellcasters around him, and was a little unsettled by how this remark caused little to no reaction from them. The crowd was still cheering, but strangely, with the green energy soothing his mind, their noise had dimmed. He smiled in relief: the elixir was working.

He could focus again.

Looking in the distance to the middle of the arena, he saw the flock of hovering glowbes above the humungous crown of the center oakbrawn tree. That was his goal.

"Finally, spellcasters," Drusus said, "race valiantly. Good luck."

Like antsy runners in a marathon corral, the group jostled forward in the holding pad. There must have been a barrier spell over the front of it, as none could put a toe past the glowing line—and then a clash of iron bells sounded; there was a soft *hiss*, and the magic barrier at the front of their pad dissolved.

"Begin!" shouted Drusus.

Brenner's amulet pulsed. His instincts kicked in.

Game on.

The wave of athletes in front of him surged forward, jabbing each other with elbows as they sprinted toward the tall brambles on the outer perimeter. Brenner joined the fray.

One of the players tried diving through a hole in the wall of brambles, but the thick, thorny vines closed shut on their own, denying him entrance. Another player found a gap, wedged herself into the wall—and without warning the brambles closed, swallowing her. Muffled cries came from within as she struggled to escape. Beyond the brambles, huge flying birds circled overhead.

Brenner slowed his speed and surveyed the bramble wall: it rose up a good twenty feet in front of him. Since he couldn't go through…could he go under? Or over?

Tentatively, he raised a hand to a branch as thick as a boa constrictor—and recoiled as it jerked against him, a sharp thorn cutting his skin. *Ouch! There must be another option.*

He backed away and jogged along the edge, seeing what looked like a willow tree, rising tall in the wall above the brambles, like a turret. He wasn't the only player to approach it. Two other spellcasters—of Aquaperni and Vispaludem from the looks of their blue and violet uniforms—leapt onto the trunk of the tree, nimbly ascending the willow.

Brenner approached the trunk too, when a shrill cry above made him freeze.

Looking up, he saw the bramble wall wasn't the only living obstacle: long sinewy vines flailed and whipped from the trunk of the willow tree, and one had lassoed the ankle of the violet Vispaludem boy, who covered his face as the vine slammed him against the other spellcaster. Both students tumbled from the upper branches, hitting the ground with sickening *thuds*. The fans behind him gave a collective groan.

He was about to back away when another tendril snapped onto his wrist like a whip.

He yanked hard against it, but it tugged back harder, looping another coil around his forearm.

The tendril started pulling him toward the willow trunk, where more sinewy vines snaked around in anticipation. Brenner's heart thumped rapidly. *This would not end well.* His eyes scrambled for anything—a rock, a root—something to stop the forward pull.

Spotting a large tree branch jutting out from the bramble wall to his left, he tugged the vine toward it as the tendril reeled him in. *It was now or never.*

He dug in his heels, and in one quick motion he circled his wrist—and the vine—around the thick bramble. He now had leverage against the willow, which kept tugging fiercely, its vine pulled taught against the bough. The pressure on his wrist intensified. He grimaced and kept fighting, but then the bramble branch pulled back too—trying to draw him into the wall like a Venus flytrap. The pressure mounted, and then—

SNAP!

He fell backward; the cut vine falling in a heap around him. The brambles tried to scoop him into the wall, but they weren't as fast as the willow tree tendrils, so he scooted away, uncoiling the vine from his red wrist. It felt smooth and firm, like rubber rope, and a four-foot section of it now lay at his feet, lifeless.

Other students were now trying their luck at climbing the willow tree, and a few had made it to the top while it had been distracted with Brenner.

He looked at his options: *do I want to try scaling the slower bramble wall, or dodging the fast willow? Considering their speed, I'd prefer the slower moving brambles…but how to climb them without piercing my hands on the thorns?*

Then he sparked an idea.

Grabbing the sinewy vine, he darted along the wall…searching…searching…*aha! That will work.* He found a long thorn, sticking up like a nail, and quickly used it to snap through the vine's midpoint. Stepping back from the moving brambles, he wrapped the two sections of vine around his palms.

With the improvised gloves, Brenner leapt onto the wall, and began climbing, now safely in his element. While the brambles still creaked and groaned around him, trying to dislodge him, his padded hands nimbly found hold after hold and, in a moment, he was at the top of the wall. He hopped across the large, crisscrossing branches—careful to avoid stepping on some of the larger thorns—came to the edge of the wall, turned, climbed halfway down, and then dropped to his feet, landing in a crouch.

Looking forward, he was met by a melee.

A thunder of hooves echoed around the hills, and bird screeches rang out from the sky. Other players had also trickled over the perimeter wall, and broke forward over the rocky crags, intent on summiting the oakbrawn past the chasms, in the middle of the arena. Brenner clambered over a rock pile, and shuddered when in the distance, a gray centaur galloped up to a yellow-uniformed Safronius girl, grabbed her hands, and then spun hard in a circle and flung her—shrieking—into the tangled thorns of the bramble wall.

Brenner's green cape billowed behind him as he jumped across a fissure, then, hearing heavy hooves pounding the ground towards him, he climbed to a rock ledge with a thin trail.

"Make one slip, and you're mine!" a centaur jeered from below, its brown hide emitting a sour smell of foamy sweat and mud.

Brenner edged forward, while the centaur kept pace below; twice his foot loosened a boulder from the path, nearly causing him to fall. He kept one eye looking forward, the other tracking the centaur, who stalked below him—and a good thing too, as the beast hurled a rock at his head—Brenner ducked and a cloud of dust rained onto him.

Brenner jogged along the trail, hoping to escape the beast, but soon was stopped short: his path dead-ended into a canyon. He was scanning both sides of the rock walls for the next best route, when something strong grabbed his ankle, yanking him off his feet.

"Now I've got you!" the centaur bellowed, hand clasped firmly around Brenner's ankle.

The weight of the beast scraped him toward the ledge—his hands desperately searched for a hold, while rocks grated against his skin. His hips slipped off the ledge—the centaur was laughing wickedly as he continued to pry Brenner from the cliff. *Oh, no…*

Brenner's fingers were slipping on the last stone of the ledge…he couldn't hold on any longer. He looked back at the centaur…and let go.

Falling, he kicked his free leg as hard as he could toward the beast—he connected with a crunch, causing the centaur to release his ankle—then wind-milled his arms toward the wall, trying to find a hold that would stop his fall into the canyon. His feet scraped against a crag, giving him a split-second to claw onto a rock, grab it with both hands, and hold on. *That was way too close!*

Panting hard, he looked behind him, and saw the dark centaur thudding down the sides of the canyon. *Okay…almost there. Keep going.*

Hand over foot, Brenner climbed to the top of the ridge, his legs bleeding from where the centaur had dragged him against the rocks. Reaching the top, he pulled himself up and wiped the sweat from his forehead. With a sigh, he realized the deep canyon ringed the entire oakbrawn.

He would have to leap across the fissure.

But his side of the canyon was far too wide for a jump. He would, at best, hit the other wall maybe halfway down. *There must be a smaller gap on the other side of the tree…*scanning both sides, he saw other spellcasters running toward the far side of the oakbrawn. *Yep, there it is.* A couple players had even made it to the tree and were climbing. He was behind.

Brenner started rock-hopping around the canyon, and was making good progress, when screeches from the sky caught his attention. He blanched, switching into defensive mode because these weren't just birds: they were aviamirs.

And one had spotted him.

Frantically, he looked for a stone to defend himself. *Come on, come on...* but the rocks were all fused together. Panic started to take hold of him. The aviamir, a giant, white eagle as large as a lion, screeched angrily at him as it dove down from the sky.

Brenner looked once more, but there were no rocks, and no cover.

He heard the wind whistling past the aviamir's feathers. Thinking fast, Brenner tore off his green cape. Then two things happened simultaneously: down from the sky the predator bird lunged at him with its front claws, and Brenner threw his cape into its face, blinding it. The beast jerked its head and tried ripping off the cloak, while Brenner quickly ducked around it and made a split-second, foolish decision: he jumped onto its back and latched on.

From the aviamir's earsplitting screeches and spinning bucks, Brenner could tell it wasn't used to this sort of human behavior, nor did it like it.

That makes two of us! He clenched the feathers along its neck harder, and didn't notice the loud applause and cheers from the crowd, who, like the aviamir, had least expected this turn of events.

Finally, when the aviamir decided that bucking and spinning wouldn't work, it flapped its huge wings and took to the sky. Brenner's heart thumped wildly: this was the part he hadn't planned.

The aviamir flew up, high over the canyon, and then up and up past the oakbrawn. Then it peaked, paused—and divebombed at the tree.

"Woah now! Woah!" Brenner shouted, as if that would help. "You're gonna kill us both!"

It was quickly looking that way. Wind whistled through his hair as the beast rotated its body to the right, and then Brenner understood the aviamir's plan: clothesline him against the huge tree trunk.

Thousands of fans shouted. The green canopy rushed closer. Leaves smacked his face. Seconds before he would smash against the trunk, Brenner leaned in, then used his hands and feet to push hard off the aviamir, leaping up toward the branches—*and yes!* His hand slapped and caught a bough. Hundreds of feet in the air, he dangled from it—the crowd hollered—then he grabbed on with his other hand. Adrenaline surged through him; he pulled up and into the safety of the bigger branches.

Shouts of "SIL-va-LO! SIL-va-LO!" rang around the stadium.

Well, he thought, catching his breath, *that's one way to get onto a tree.*

Brenner flexed his hands, and then climbed up through the dense canopy, jumping from branch to branch with renewed energy. Finally, the branches cleared away: he'd reached the top of the canopy. The flock of glimmering glowbes hovered almost expectantly above him, and he jumped up, grabbing one.

"We have our first Agilis advancement!" said the loud voice of Sovereign Drusus, "From Silvalo!"

The crowd erupted like a wave, crashing over Brenner.

*Wow…*he thought, smiling. *That feels pretty good.*

As the next spellcaster, an orange-cloaked girl from Arenaterro, grabbed a glowbe, a large, silver platform floated from the sidelines to Brenner. Thinking that this would be easier than descending the five-hundred-foot tree, he hopped onto it, and it gracefully flew him away from the tree and the flapping, screeching aviamirs, back down to the green banners of the Silvalo section.

So many spectators were clapping and whistling at him as he stepped down by the Silvalo dugout, how his friends and relatives met with him was a feat in itself.

Through the din, an amplified voice shouted, "Brenner! Up here!"

Forty yards away, Windelm and Sherry squeezed against the railing from the packed crowd, smiling and waving down at him. Finnegan and Gemry waved from behind them.

"Meet in thirty minutes at the northern doors!" Windelm called out.

Brenner gave them a thumbs-up, which, judging from their confused looks, must not have been a common gesture in Ganthrea.

"Got it!" he clarified. "See you then!"

He turned and retrieved his mircon from the team lockbox, then headed under the railing into the Silvalo dugout. The noise of the stadium dimmed as he walked through a tunnel, replaced with the peaceful sounds of running water. Steam and warmth met his face as he entered a large chamber illuminated by strange, glowing ferns all around the perimeter. There were three pools fed by rippling waterfall cascades, but, he frowned, no showers. *Ah well...* he thought, *when in Rome...* He changed out of his Agilis uniform, and noticed with a wince the jagged red cuts along his leg from being dragged on the rock ledge.

A tropical smell came from the one of the shimmering pools, not unlike aloe vera. He walked to it, and as he lowered himself into the water to clean off the sweat, the warm liquid relaxed him. He closed his eyes. When he looked down at his leg a moment later, the red cuts were already closing and healing over with new skin. He raised his eyebrows: *Okay, this is waaay better than a shower.*

Refreshed from the soaking pool, he climbed out, dried off, then put on new green robes he found at the end of the chamber, neatly organized by size. After walking through more stone-lined tunnels past the pools, he saw rays of light coming down a corridor, and followed them until he reached an exit from the stadium.

"There you are!" Finnegan said, clapping him on the shoulder as he emerged. "We thought you got lost."

"Brenner! Well played!" Windelm said warmly. "Your friends here suggested we go to *Hutch & Sons*. With the thousands of fans flooding the streets, we're surely better off flying. You all know the flight spell, right?"

Gemry nodded, but Finnegan turned red and said, "Actually—"

"We can walk," Brenner said, not wanting Finnegan to have to travel alone.

"Are you sure you're up for it?" Sherry asked, a concerned look in her eyes. "It's at least an hour with the crowds…and you must be exhausted from the match."

"Yeah, I'll be alri—"

"Excuse me," Gemry said, "if you can spare a few minutes, I have something that will help. Be right back."

She flew over the crowd in the direction of Valoria. Finnegan looked embarrassed that he was slowing the group down.

Sherry turned to Brenner. "How did you feel competing in your first Agilis match?"

A mix of emotions came to mind: "Well, nervous for starters…but then each task came so fast that there wasn't time to dwell on it… I felt hyper alert—probably because each obstacle was a must-win." A thought occurred to Brenner: he played today in a way he never could back on Earth, his body able to run, jump, and climb without limitations. "Once the landscape and creatures started attacking me, everything just…flowed…" He smiled. "And for the most part, that was fun."

"Your trick using tendril vines for gloves was impressive," Sherry said.

"That was good, but—" Windelm started saying, giving an annoyed look to a chubby man who bumped into him. Windelm cast an Aura spell around the four of them, then said, "That's better. I'd have to say my personal favorite was when you acted like a matador—treating the aviamir like a charging bull, using your cape to blind it, and then hanging on for the ride. I'd like to think I would have done that."

"Thanks," Brenner said. "I wished I could've ridden one sooner, then I would've been able to skip past the centaur."

"Yeah," said Finnegan, "That fall looked painful."

There was a tapping on the outside of the Aura. Looking up, they saw Gemry floating on Velvo.

"Capital idea," Windelm said, dissipating the Aura.

Finnegan and Brenner joined her on the carrier carpet, sitting cross-legged next to each other while Windelm and Sherry flew ahead, robes swishing in the light breeze. They hovered over the thick crowd on the streets and flew into the denser-than-usual current of flying spellcasters zooming high above the street.

"Thanks, Gemry," Finnegan said, looking over Velvo's side. "The vias are jammed down there."

"No problem," she said, then turned to Brenner. "Hey, nice plays in your Agilis match. Glad you came out on top." She slipped her hand into his, and to Brenner at least, her eyes sparkled.

A rush of happiness filled him. "Thanks, Gemry," he said, smiling back at her. He pretended not to notice when Finnegan looked over at them and made a gagging sound.

Velvo floated down for a soft landing at the entrance to *Hutch & Sons*, past a large replica of a mug on a pedestal, blue fire crackling from its top. A glowing green sign beneath it read, *"Arborio's Favorite Singefire Ale."*

"Looks like your Dad's reputation has spread," Brenner said, seeing an overflow of orange and blue robed customers forming a queue out the tavern's front door. Windelm went to join the end of the line, but Finnegan waved him back.

"Follow me," Finnegan said, ushering the five around the side, next to a massive redwood. Pots of steaming vegetables and aromas of grilled meat met them as they entered, and a startled cook who shouted, "'Scuse me! You can't come through there!"

"Hey Tarino," Finnegan waved over a counter covered with sliced tomatoes and grated cheeses, "They're with me."

"Oh...hey Fin. Hurry up about it."

They followed Finnegan and squeezed past other busy cooks and waiters through the extensive kitchen. Windelm looked ready to sample everything if it weren't for the watchful eye of Sherry—"Don't you dare, mister! It's not our cottage!"—and instead of leading them out the main door to the ground floor tables and packed booths, Finnegan took them up a circular staircase "These are the best seats in the house," he said, "where Pop and I like to eat."

The five of them slid into a corner booth, where chatter and laughter from the fans below wafted up and over the balcony. On the walls were iron statues of dragons and a few paintings of what must have been great Zabrani players, shooting spells across a huge arena. Brenner could see over the bannister to the packed tables below, where orange flames danced in stines before patrons blew them out and sipped their singefire ales.

Finnegan passed around thick menus, then leaned over the bannister and called out to a waitress, who looked up and waved to him.

"To celebrate," Windelm said with a flourish to the group, "order whatever you'd like. The meal's on me. Not only did Brenner win the first Agilis match, he won us a dozen golders, too."

While Finnegan and Brenner looked pleased at the invitation to eat to their heart's content, Gemry looked dourly at her menu, and Sherry crossed her arms.

"Relax, dear," said Windelm, "I never put down any coins I think we'll miss."

"So, you don't mind losing our golders then?" Sherry said with raised eyebrows. "Maybe you should balance the books this month and see what golders are left to throw away."

"Oh, come now, we both know he's good," said Windelm defensively, "really, with Brenner it was a sure bet!"

Windelm's words didn't erase Sherry's concerned look, but they created a glow of pride in Brenner. And it also made him wonder aloud, "Can anyone bet on the outcome of the games?"

"Sure," said Windelm, "There's gaming booths all around the stadium— I'll show you tomorrow at Zabrani—you can bet on teams, or, for higher odds, on individual players. That's one of the perks of the hosting biome, they get revenue from lodging and food of course, but the lion's share comes from all the gambling at the Games."

"Pop says there are at least a hundred bookies roaming the stands, too," Finnegan added, "I've seen a few here afterward, usually bragging about their winnings."

Windelm nodded. "For every patrolling city guard of Arborio, there are at least ten illegal bookies running their own odds. Sure, you could get better odds with them, but that's assuming they avoid a bankrupt payout, and worse, if you're caught, you could get a year with a collar around your neck."

"So the winnings must be good enough for people to risk getting collared," Brenner said. "Players couldn't bet on themselves, could they?"

"They can only bet *for* themselves, never against, or on a competing team," said Windelm, "even still, some do. But if they're caught taking money for throwing a match, they're banned from the Games for their life. And when the fans meet them in the streets, they're not kind."

A pretty, red haired woman sidled up to their table. "Hi, dears, I'm Ambry. All ready to order?"

As they did, she jotted down their remarks, then turned and walked back down the circular staircase.

Windelm asked about Gemry and Finnegan's families, listening politely, but with a crease in his forehead when Gemry said her last name of Gespelti. He brightened after Finnegan finished and said, "I haven't been to *Hutch & Son's* in years. Your father has a fine tavern here, Finnegan!"

"Thank you, kind sir," Finnegan said, beaming.

"Gemry," Sherry said, "How do you feel about tomorrow's match?"

"Mostly good," Gemry said. "The Game Keepers just posted the Zabrani schedule this morning, and we're playing Arenaterro. I think we have better knights than them. But I also hear they play dirty."

"For being neighbors of Silvalo," said Windelm, "you'd think they would show more decency...but you're right, I would expect the worst."

Soon Ambry arrived back with a tray steaming with five entrees and drinks, and they bit into hot sandwiches and roasted vegetables. Brenner smiled; his bryfallo steak was just as good as he remembered.

They finished their meal with cool ciders, except for Windelm, who drank a Singefire Ale, declaring its dark ale and spicy, honeyed taste as—

"One of the best flavors of the games!"—and then they left the tavern.

"A good morning, and a good game, Brenner," Finnegan said. He eyed the crowd of patrons sprawling out the door and added, "Pops could definitely use more help. I'll see you later."

"See ya, Finnegan."

With a wave, he turned and wove his way back inside.

"Well," Windelm said, "We are lodging at the Heather Heights inn— saves us from the long flight home each day—and you're more than welcome to join us...relax before your next Agilis match on Wednesday."

"Thanks..." Brenner said, looking over at Gemry, "I'll swing by later this evening."

Gemry smoothed her robes and smiled. "Thanks for the lunch, and it was nice meeting you today."

"And you as well!" said Sherry.

"I think I'll head back to Valoria," Gemry said, "rest up for tomorrow."

"Mind if I join you?" Brenner said.

"Sure thing, conjurer."

A knowing look flitted behind Sherry's eyes. "Windelm, I believe we have some sightseeing to do."

"We do?"

She nodded and tugged his arm. "Brenner," Sherry said with a smile, "we'll see you later this evening." Then she hooked elbows with Windelm and steered him down the street.

As an afterthought, Windelm pulled something from his pocket and said, "Brenner, catch!"

Brenner caught the airborne coin: a heavy golder.

"Extra winnings from your match," Windelm shouted. "Enjoy!"

"Oh. Thanks!" He waved back and then pocketed it.

Gemry sent a spell to the roof of Hutch & Son's, and Velvo appeared from behind a chimney and circled down to them. They hopped on.

"Valoria please, Velvo," Gemry said. "But take the scenic route."

The carrier carpet floated up, almost seeming to nod its front tassels.

"So…what's on your mind?" Brenner asked, as they whisked into the flight pattern of spellcasters.

"Well… the games of course. I've been working towards this week for my whole life. Winning will change everything."

"Yeah?"

She nodded. "With those golders, I can pay off tuition, make a name for myself, maybe do some traveling…see what the rest of Ganthrea is like." She sighed. "If I can convince my parents to let me."

"If anyone deserves to win at Zabrani, I think you do. You can read flight formations, predict offensive surges, you're easily one of the best."

Gemry's green eyes met his. "Thanks, Brenner."

"Of course."

She slid her fingers into his hand, then said, "You're blushing again."

"Me?" Brenner said, trying to laugh it off, "No…it's just…hot out…"

"Oh right," she said, "Up here in the breeze."

"Well…heat rises, and we're up in the canopy…"

"You're not fooling anyone," she said with a grin.

She was right, of course, but he didn't want to admit it.

For the next hour they swooped through the canopy hand in hand. Brenner was sure the curious looks they received from spellcasters looking down from their tree homes were because of the ridiculous grin plastered on his face. Soon, they soared into view of the ramparts and tree turrets of Valoria.

Velvo smoothly decelerated and Gemry directed it around the southern walls, then up to a large, open balcony with violet and pink flowers cascading over planter boxes. Brenner leaned against Gemry's shoulder, the light fragrance of her silky, dark hair floating into him.

"So, this is where the magicians live?" Brenner asked, already knowing the answer by seeing spellcasters inside reading on armchairs, but wanting to savor the moment.

"Good job, conjurer!" said Gemry, patting his knee. "Yeah, I like to come out here on the balcony to practice my spells…it's usually quiet and free from spellcasters, even though it has one of the best views of the academy and Silvalo…"

Velvo slowly rotated, giving them a panoramic view of the sweeping parapets and towers of the castle around them, then of the oakbrawns and lush, colorful foliage of the tree-city skyline.

Brenner's heart was thumping madly in his chest, as though urging him to do something…

He smiled at her, looked away…*just go for it already!* He closed his eyes, swung his head over to hers and kissed… her teeth.

Oh, no!

He pulled back, supremely embarrassed. "I'm sorry! That was not what I was going for!"

Gemry looked at him, eyes wide with surprise, and then she burst out laughing. Brenner felt mortified. *I blew it! That was horrible!* He covered his face with a hand.

Gemry's loud giggling drew some curious looks from the spellcasters inside. If he could have, Brenner would have sucked his head into his body like a turtle.

Finally, Gemry calmed herself down. Brenner pretended to be really interested in the distant woods, but he could feel her looking at him. She pulled his hand down from his face. "So was that your first almost-kiss then?" She chuckled again.

"Uh…yeah," he said, nodding and feeling like a thousand pins were pricking him all over.

She turned his chin to face her. "Here's another tip, conjurer: it works better when you keep your eyes open."

She leaned over and kissed him seamlessly: it was soft and golden and much, *much* better than Brenner's failed attempt. Then they drew apart, Gemry's eyes seeming to twinkle, Brenner's in a haze.

"See? That's not so hard, was it?"

Brenner felt numb. He nodded vaguely.

"And here I was starting to think we were only study partners…"

They sat a moment longer in a wonderful glow of silence, looking out over the city, as the sun drifted down through cotton-puff pinks.

"Alright," said Gemry, "I should be going." Her fingers pulled apart from his hands, and she nimbly stepped off Velvo. Brenner's senses returned to him.

"Will you be watching the Zabrani match tomorrow?" Gemry asked.

"That's a for sure."

She grinned. "Great. Do you want to borrow Velvo to head over to Heather Heights?"

"Thank you, but I think I have enough energy to fly back."

"Okay," Gemry said, giving him one last smile before turning back to her quarters. "As you're flying, don't let the tourists plow into you mid-flight on the airpaths. I've grown rather fond of you." She winked and walked inside.

Brenner wanted to say the same, that he liked her, too...actually that he loved her more than anyone he'd known, but those words seemed to escape him, and he simply held up a hand halfway in goodbye.

"Goodnight, Gemry."

He turned to the edge of the balcony, mircon out.

"*Volanti.*"

A rush of elixir swirled out from his amulet—matching the warm feelings that tingled out from his spine—his legs lifted from the smooth marble ledge, and he flew into the dusk, heading west over the academy turrets and walls, between the behemoth oakbrawns, toward the heart of the city, and the last glows of the orange sunset.

To avoid the clogged airpaths, Brenner flew above the spellcaster traffic. As Gemry had predicted, the rush of tourists and natives hovering between trees and shops made the forest look like a fast-flowing circulatory system. Subconsciously, he flew back toward Hutch & Son's, still thinking about Gemry and their shared kiss, when it dawned on him that he had no clue how to get to Heather Heights hotel. The ball-lanterns, floating by the giant trees, flicked on, casting shadows from all of the flying spellcasters.

He tried zooming down to the airpaths to find his exit to the familiar tavern, but was blocked when large groups of departing flyers nearly collided with him. He went further, then merged into the flow of spellcasters. He could read the shop names better now, but after a few minutes, Brenner realized he was completely turned around.

Below him, unfamiliar structures and shops whizzed by, with shouts and conversations buzzing up about the first games of the festival. He was about to give up and just head back to Valoria, when one of the illuminated shops caught his eye, and a familiar name flickered up to him: Tallegrim's. He could ask the owner about Heather Heights.

Brenner hovered down to street level and let his Volanti spell dissipate. To get to the entrance, he walked around a pair of orange travelers clearly trying to impress some young women with mind-reading spells. He brought his mircon to his side, and the molten glue of his crystal holster looped around it.

Pushing open the door, Brenner had to dodge to the side to avoid a red-caped man tottering off balance toward him, who stumbled into a group of adults that angrily pushed him away. The pub smelled spicy and dank—probably because of the stews boiling behind the counter, the many customers filled the tables, and their sweat and exotic perfumes that filled the air. Brenner squeezed his way next to one of the stewards at the counter, who handed out ale tankards to a group of men with turbans.

"Excuse me," Brenner began, but a shrill laugh from a woman at the table beside him drowned him out. Someone else stepped in front of him. Brenner waved at the barkeep for another minute before being noticed.

"Whaddya ordering then?" called the steward, a grizzled man with black stubble.

"Do you know," Brenner asked loudly, trying to combat the ruckus of the tavern, "where Heather Heights Hotel is?"

The steward gave him a curious look, clearly irritated to be wasting time on a lost teen. As he shook his head, an orange-cloaked, turbaned man next to Brenner roared with laughter and slopped some of his frothy beer on

Brenner's arm.

"A hundred apologies!" he said loudly, turning to face Brenner, and then, upon seeing him, did a double-take. "Hey! Aren't you the Valoria winner today? At Agilis? Marcom, look at this kid! You lost some golders on his match, didn't you?"

The man next to him, apparently Marcom, leaned over, frowned, and said brusquely, "Devil of a desert twister, I did! You pushed Arenattero players off the bramble walls—didn't you? Little hellion cost me a week's wages!"

Brenner hadn't done anything of the sort, but from the hatred in his dark eyes, Marcom was already convinced. "Uh...that wasn't me..." Brenner began, sweating through his shirt as more people turned to look his way.

"Bet you thought..." Marcom said, stepping past a stranger and uncomfortably close to Brenner, "...you's real clever..."

His breath reeked of beer. Brenner prepared himself to block a punch.

"Keep your hands to *yourself*," the steward butted in, banging a stine loudly on the bar, "if you've got a problem with Silvalo players, then you've got a problem with me—and the *rest* of our loyal patrons." At this, many adults in green tunics looked over at the steward, letting out supportive shouts. Others raised their cups and bellowed, thinking a toast was being made.

Marcom mumbled something and shuffled away. Brenner found himself breathing a bit easier.

"Here," said the steward, handing Brenner a glass tumbler. He poured a purplish liquid into it that bubbled. "Have some Moltifrute infusion—on the house. My apologies, I didn't realize you were competing." Noticing Brenner's hesitance, he added, "It's all energy and juices, nothing to slow you down for the games. I'm Hayward." He thrust out his hand.

"Thanks..." Brenner said, taking it and getting his hand pumped vigorously. "I'm Brenner."

"Let me take care of this spellcaster, and then I can tell you how to get to

Heather Heights."

Hayward poured and ignited a singefire ale, slid it along the bar, and launched into animated directions, "Join the airpath through central Arborio, above Via Azona, then fly on the second primary ring north—look for a statue of Salonin the Sorcerer defeating a hydra—turn onto Bottineau boulevard, that'll take you to Heather Heights."

"Thank you," Brenner said, replaying the directions in his mind before sipping the purple liquid, and puckering his lips as a sour grape and highly sweetened cranberry flavor met his tongue. He drank a quarter of the glass and said, "I better get going."

"And a good luck to yeh!" Hayward called from behind.

Brenner waved back to him, and as he did, saw Marcom quickly finish another beer, and give him a dark look. As Brenner brushed past the rest of the patrons, he felt he was being followed. He was nearly at the door when Marcom grabbed his sleeve and spun him around.

"You *owe* me some golders, you little—"

"That won't be necessary," a tall, blond man cut between Brenner and Marcom.

Marcom let out a startled yelp. Brenner saw the man's mircon pointed at Marcom's belly. He quickly scuttled back to the bar.

The tall man turned smoothly to Brenner, his calm eyes and cleft chin forming a concerned expression.

"Thank you…" Brenner began, relieved.

"Don't mention it," he said, extending his hand. "I'm Dalphon."

"Brenner."

"So I heard," he continued, giving Brenner a polite shake. "You had a fine Agilis match today, yes?"

"Well it was the first round…" Brenner began.

"It was," Dalphon nodded, "but it's still an excellent omen of things to come." He smiled. "If I may ask, do you have buyers yet for your services after the games?"

"No…" Brenner began, trying to mask his uncertainty as to what his services were. "Not yet."

"May I give you my card?"

The crowd was jostling against them—some green Silvalo supporters, and other orange Arenattero fans who looked like they were with Marcom; Brenner didn't want to hang around Tallegrim's much longer, and while he wasn't sure what buyers wanted his help, or what services Dalphon referred to, he figured saying yes would give him an excuse to go find Windelm and Sherry.

"Sure," he said, and Dalphon pressed an embroidered silver card into Brenner's hand.

"Excellent. I represent a guild of merchants that seeks protection and exploration services from the best players of the games. If you win the Agilis games, or place highly, we can offer more golders per month than any merchant here can offer you for a year."

Brenner raised an eyebrow. "Really?"

"Indeed. Our most skilled protectors earn up to a thousand golders their first year."

That hooked Brenner's attention.

"But I understand you have places to go," said Dalphon, "and this isn't the easiest place to discuss business—so, if you'd like to know more, you can find my enterprise at the central fountains of Arborio at the close of the Games."

"Thanks for the offer," Brenner said.

"Of course," Dalphon nodded. "I look forward to seeing you again. Best of luck for the remaining matches." He went back to his table.

Brenner stepped outside, ignited his *Volanti* spell, and joined the flyers in the airpath headed north. *Wow, a thousand golders,* he thought while flying through the night air, *that's a huge amount of money.* After soaring past a large caravan of carrier carpets floating with spellcasters draped in indigo robes, and almost mistaking two other statues for the one Hayward described, Brenner eventually saw the hydra and made the correct turn, swooping low onto the flagstone boulevard. At last, he saw the sign for which he was searching.

Walking into the well-lit lobby of Heather Heights, he saw Windelm and Sherry sitting and conversing by an elegant fountain that trickled into a pool with golden koi fish swimming just below the surface.

"Ah, Brenner," Windelm said, standing to greet him, "Glad you could join us."

"Brenner dear!" Sherry said warmly, rising, and giving him a hug before he could apologize for being so delayed.

"Try sitting in this one," Windelm said, "it's filled with sofitas feathers." He pulled a highbacked chair next to theirs, and as an afterthought added, "sofitas are like a distant cousin to a swan, only their feathers are purple and exceptionally soft."

Brenner relaxed into the plush seat, feeling like chocolate melting. "Woah, this is comfy, thanks."

The two regarded him with smiles for a moment, before Brenner asked, "What?"

Sherry looked from Windelm to Brenner, her eyebrows high and clearly entertained, "You didn't tell us you had a girlfriend."

Brenner felt like a spotlight blinded him. "Oh…Gemry?…uh…"

"*Relax*, Brenner," Windelm said jovially, "Sherry and I met at Valoria, too, you know." They looked at one another and laughed. "And it's a good thing we did, or I would've been stuck in level seven potions for all my teenage years," Windelm continued, "although I always wonder about that memory charm you whipped up for me."

"Oh—I had you wrapped around my finger a *long* time before that," Sherry countered, "that just ensured you'd say yes to all my requests. I'm sure Gemry has already developed similar strategies for Brenner."

Having never had a candid conversation with his parents about romantic relationships—or hardly anything, really—Brenner found himself turning beet red, and shielding his eyes with his hand. *And this is what it's like to have parents…*he thought, letting out a groan.

"Oh dear," Sherry said to Windelm, softening as she noticed Brenner's mortified position: he had slunk as low as possible into his chair. "I'm afraid we've embarrassed him." Then, as though she couldn't help herself, added brightly, "Brenner, we think Gemry's very nice, cute as a sunflower, and clearly has a smart head on her shoulders."

Brenner nodded, remaining quiet, hoping that the conversation would change to *anything* else.

"There is a two-month holiday after the Games of Ganthrea," Windelm said, "where students are free to return to their homes, or take apprentice-ships in Arborio, or jobs in the biomes of Ganthrea, or help the faculty at Valoria. However, I was wondering if you wanted to join my team on scouting expeditions around the perimeter of Silvalo for that time. The forest grows so rampant so fast, routes often get overrun, and we need to make sure the major routes are cleared. Our sovereign, Drusus, also wants to be kept abreast of any large dragon nesting grounds, and if occurring, troop movements of neighboring biomes. The job doesn't pay much, but you'd gain some valuable experience in the wilds."

"It sounds interesting," Brenner said, thinking of two months' travel around the biome...but would he get to see Gemry during that time?

"Windelm," Sherry said sternly.

"What?"

"You have to tell him the whole side of it."

"It's not a big deal—" Windelm started, but changed tack when Sherry glared sharply at him. "Alright, alright. There are natural risks that come with working in the wilds—you know, large predators—basilisks, dragons, wurms, but we'll go over evasive flight spells. You'll be fine."

"Anything else?" Sherry prompted.

"Well, there have been some disturbances on the fringes of Silvalo...but unless necessary, we try not to get involved with skirmishes—we leave that to the Biome Guard. Overall, it's no more dangerous than the games."

"So...deadly then, yes?"

"Well...yes. Sometimes," said Windelm. "There, dear," he motioned at Sherry. "Full disclosure. Brenner, what do you think?"

Brenner thought of the offer from Dalphon...with it, he would probably make enough to pay Windelm back for the mircon and then some...but that also involved going solo...and, either way, he would go months without seeing Gemry, which didn't sound entirely appealing.

"I'll need to think about it," Brenner said. "But thanks for the offer, Windelm."

"Certainly," Windelm said casually, although he looked as though he had expected a different answer.

"I'm sure you'll have plenty of opportunities," Sherry said, smoothing over the quiet interlude. "Now, let's get you some good food and good rest before the next match on Wednesday."

The three ventured to their hotel room, where Brenner discovered they had prepared a second bedroom for him to use. After eating a few helpings of roasted stew, Brenner wrapped himself in smooth sheets and, after thinking about Dalphon and Windelm's offers once more, fell into a much-needed rest.

Chapter Twenty

An Unexpected Opener

It was almost harder for Brenner to gain entry to the northern stadium that Tuesday morning than it had been to race in the Agilis match yesterday: tens of thousands of fans crammed around him, Windelm, and Sherry as they bought Zabrani tickets near one of the many entrances. After much jostling, they merged into the current of people converging through Coliseum-like archways. As a perk, Brenner was waved in for free by the attendant, as he wore his official Valoria uniform.

Once past the entrance, Brenner, Windelm and Sherry used their flight spells to skim above the crowd, steaming food stalls—Brenner smelled gyros—around pillars, through a twisting tunnel and out into the open-air arena. They spun a 180, then flew higher and higher and at last landed in their section. Brenner looked out over a vast arena too large to see all at once without swiveling his head from far left to far right.

Sovereign Drusus, hovering several hundred feet in the center of the arena, made the opening remarks for the Zabrani match, with clear relish introducing the twenty-one players from Silvalo's Valoria, dressed in green and black and flying to the tower at the far right side. Their opponents, Aserdian Academy spellcasters from the deserts of Arenaterro, did the same on the left, outfitted in orange.

Brenner wished he had binoculars, as he could barely make out Gemry, far in the distance, wearing a green uniform but a white cape, symbolizing her status as a healer. As the king for Valoria's team, Maverick had a gold and green cape, and flew to the middle of the field to meet with the other captain and game official. They struck shields, and then began the land transformation.

Both kings turned and made intricate flights, scattering what looked like pulsing red embers across midfield, and then sowing the green, blue and crimson landform seeds into their own territories. Rapidly the land gushed forth with two large, navy blue lakes on either side of the arena, a swath of forest ringing around the lakes, and a craggy ridge that stretched from the spiral tower on Valoria's side all the way to Aserdian's tower on the far left. At midfield an imposing, rocky range further dived the arena. Together, the two mountainous ridges formed a raised cross.

High on the ledge of the two opposing towers, players faced outward with mircons and shields, waiting to fly, while above them, mists of shimmering clouds appeared, swirling into a number for each team: 0.

The fans around Brenner began stomping their feet in steady quarter notes; the rippling thumps spread as hundreds of thousands of people joined, increasing the tempo until the stadium became a rumbling volcano. With a shrill blast from the official's mircon and the command, "Begin!" the teams flew off—all forty-two players seeking land advantage by soaring towards the middle, shields raised in one arm, mircons firing orange or green spells with the other.

Two orange Aserdian knights blazed over the middle mountains first, seeking position behind a large boulder on Valoria's near side, but were stunned midair by green spells. They fell to the ground some forty feet— their painful *thuds* drowned out by the crowd cheering for Valoria's sharpshooting. Valoria's score above their tower rippled from 0 to 2. The first skirmish ensued, and an Aserdian healer thawed them with a spell as other knights traded shots.

Brenner looked at Valoria's strategy: the three white glowbes for Valoria were staggered, two on Gemry's near side, and one on the far side, which meant more Aserdian knights flew across their mountains and forest, and over to the near side of the middle range.

Soon both teams had fortified themselves on either side of the midfield mountains. Aserdian began a barrage of orange spells against the knights hiding by boulders on Gemry's side of the stadium—some of the spells flew wildly up, directly at Brenner's section of the crowd—instinctively, Brenner muttered *"Totum Aura"* and his Aura materialized.

"No need for that," Windelm said, and motioned to something on the perimeter of the field that fizzled the spells. "Spellcasters have refined the game, and, for the fans at least, made it safer by adding a shield curtain."

Squinting around the arena, Brenner finally noticed a translucent lining, creating a humongous dome around the Zabrani game—shielding spectators not unlike a backstop at a baseball game. Brenner's shoulders relaxed, and he let his Aura dissipate.

Back on the field, Aserdian and Valoria continued their spellfire, with the scores above each tower creeping upward with every stun. Gemry was soaring behind oakbrawns in Valoria's territory, rejuvenating her stunned teammates as she flew in a circular pattern; apparently Maverick had instructed her to be a defensive healer this match.

After an hour, the score stood Valoria: 44, Aserdian: 32. Each team had captured a glowbe, but Silvalo knights proved more skillful in their shots, taking out two of three opposing healers, enabling them to control a third of Aserdian's territory. As a result, Aserdian's players were getting more desperate: they had one large cluster in a skirmish by Valoria's large lake, trying to move as quickly as possible toward the glowbes. The orange surge of ten knights and king feverishly shot their way through a couple of green sentries, gaining a strong advantage before Maverick regrouped, sending more Valoria knights back from midfield to bolster defense.

The spell fight intensified: more flyers got stunned, falling like flightless birds from the sky. Aserdian players slowed. Then they dug in, wedging behind rocks and redwoods. Having rebuffed the surge, Maverick took advantage of his strength in numbers to send a scouting party of two knights along the far back side, up the flank toward Aserdian's final two glowbes, which were, Brenner realized with surprise, completely unguarded.

The two flyers, a blond-haired, older teen Brenner recognized as Berlin, and a girl knight with a flight pattern that reminded him of a raven the way she swooped from tree to tree, flew down for cover behind a couple of rock slabs on the calm edge of Aserdian's lake. The next glowbe lay exposed on the opposite lakeshore. They paused, scanning the large lake and trees beyond for orange knights, then, satisfied the coast was clear, flew thirty feet above the waters toward the second glowbe.

Berlin and the other knight passed the middle of the lake, diving downward toward the beach and their open target, when something unexpected happened: the rocks themselves seemed to open fire at the two flyers. Orange stunning spells flashed; both flying knights turned shields to block—too late—and were hit in their sides. Paralyzed, they fell like rocks toward the lake.

Two loud splashes rang out as Berlin and his partner smacked into the dark water. Brenner gasped.

Where was the referee? Brenner thought desperately, his hands clenched tightly. Then he remembered Gemry's words: in the Games of Ganthrea, there were none.

"Windelm!" he said, yanking his sleeve, "Won't a sage stop the game?"

Windelm shook his head. "Unfortunately not," he said grimly.

No one else moved along the lake. The firefight back in Valoria's territory was still raging with sizzles and loud crashes; no one there could've seen past the midfield mountains to know two of their knights had sank into the watery depths. Brenner looked back to the lake.

The ripples subsided. The lake was still.

Aserdian's side remained eerily quiet, until a lone spellcaster crawled out from the rocks on the side of the lake—a last defender, who now flew

294

unimpeded across the edge of the lake and into Valoria territory.

After that, Brenner couldn't take his eyes off Gemry, praying she wouldn't be exposed flying over a lake.

Half an hour later, Valoria's better marksmanship and Gemry's strategic healing—rejuvenating at least a dozen knights—overcame the Aserdian blitzkrieg; they stunned the last orange healer, and a group of five flyers nabbed the remaining two glowbes, clinching victory, and sending the crowd into shouts that pounded Brenner's eardrums. Spectators flocked to the betting booths, with those betting on Valoria gleefully claiming their winnings.

A barrel-chested man flew to the middle of the stadium, and interrupted the cacophony of the crowd with an amplified voice, "A hard-fought match indeed, with Valoria gaining entry to the next round!"

Brenner recognized his voice as Sage Vicksman. Below him, officials clad in white uniforms flew around the field, unlocking players from their stunned positions. The teams began to gather around the midfield mountains, with Valoria players clapping each other on the back. Away from them, two officials came to the Aserdian lake and used a repulsion stone to part the waters. They floated the two knights out of the lake and toward a side exit, when someone on the Valoria team noticed.

Her face drained of color; she lifted an arm, pointing. Others looked. Their shoves turned to anguished shouts that carried across the arena.

"*No!* Berlin!"

"Phylia?!"

Maverick grabbed his hair. Then he flew at the other team's captain, who tried to turn and use his mircon, but not before Maverick slammed into him. Officials converged on the two fighting captains; Maverick landed more than a few blows before the officials, with difficulty, pulled him away, red-faced and screaming, still trying to pound into the Arena-terro captain.

Being across the stadium, Brenner couldn't hear all the heated words spewing from Maverick's mouth, but he could see and feel the pain. It seemed surreal…he had played Zabrani with Berlin before…and now both Berlin and Phylia…were dead. Right before him, and thousands of fans…

He started to notice conversations around him. And when he did, he was flabbergasted.

"Fun middle game, wasn't it?" someone was saying, "Aserdian sure used stealth to their advantage—did you see those knights sink?"

"Yah, they were fool-hardy to try the lake without scoping the sides. Rookie blunder. Should've just whittled Aserdian down before attempting the final push."

"I just lost *twenty* golders on Aserdian!" cursed a cauldron-bellied man, chucking a half-eaten turkey leg forward, "If they're going to shoot to kill, at least take out the king for more points!"

"They couldn't've killed him if they wanted," bemoaned his reedy-looking companion, "their shot was poorer than last year's. I'm surprised they drowned anybody."

Windelm elbowed Sherry and Brenner. "They've lifted the exterior stadium curtains," he said gently. "I suggest we fly over the back of the upper balcony."

Brenner whispered *Volanti* to himself, then followed their lead as they whisked over the heads of the other fans, who were now in a full-out brawl after another airborne drumstick smacked into an unlucky spectator.

It wasn't until after the match, when he was back at Valoria, sitting with Gemry in a stone courtyard, that he fully understood why Maverick was so livid.

"You mean the Aserdian players were supposed to help?" he asked Gemry as they sat together, hardly touching a small plate of beef sliders that, to Brenner, had largely lost their flavor.

"Exactly," Gemry said. "Players who stun opponents or sense impending death—especially in academy level games—are encouraged to save the downed player. If they can't, they should send up a distress signal with their mircons, so that another player can."

"I didn't know the Zabrani mircons could do that," said Brenner.

"They allow for a few types of spells: stunning, flight, and distress signals. Healers also have rejuvenating spells."

"So, that Aserdian player by the rocks..."

"Should've done *something* to help Berlin and Phylia...not sit spitefully and watch them drown..." She put her head in her hand. "If only I wasn't caught up on defense. I should've been there."

"Hey," Brenner rested his hand on her knee, "You played as hard as you could've, and helped the people around you. You made a difference. And you couldn't have known that would happen."

Gemry was silent.

"Were you close to them?"

"I've known them both for years. We weren't exactly friends off the field...but here, we were teammates." She closed her eyes. One tear, and then another, trickled down her cheek, making Brenner squeeze his mouth shut, fighting back tears of his own.

He leaned in and hugged her shoulder. "I'm sorry."

Gemry leaned back, giving a small shudder. She mouthed one word, "Thanks."

Gray clouds rolled in, and he felt the air of the courtyard cool. For some time they sat like that: quiet, somber, and still.

It was Gemry who finally broke the silence. She breathed in deeply, and her voice changed, trying to return to her old self. "Some of the biomes encourage that fierce mentality," she said, "thoroughly eliminate your opponents, and send a powerful message to the rest of the teams. Other knights think it makes them more valuable to merchants as explorers...or mercenaries...after the Games."

"That's...brutal," Brenner said, reminded of Dalphon's offer...*how many other spellcasters would be gunning for kills on the field? And if Zabrani was dangerous...what did that mean for Gemry's Contendir game?* "Hey, what time is your Contendir match?"

"I'm slated to fight tomorrow morning. Before your Agilis game."

"And there's no lakes involved in those matches, right?"

"Right…it's harder to die than in Zabrani…but there's other ways to get hurt."

Brenner didn't want to imagine that. "You don't have to play, do you?"

She gave him a look. "If I want to pay off tuition and be known as anything more than a pawnbroker's daughter, I do."

"Okay. But just…be careful out there," he said, giving Gemry's hand a squeeze. She squeezed back. "Tell me," Brenner said, trying to brighten the mood. "What's your favorite post-game treat?"

"Well…the honey drip-cakes from Benitillio's are really good, but they should be. They're way expensive."

"Hmm," he said, getting an idea. "When do betting booths open?"

Gemry stiffened. This was the opposite reaction he'd hoped for. "Not you too," she said, crossing her arms and glaring at him, "My father does enough gambling as it is."

"I just thought you are fully capable of winning—" he said defensively, holding up his hands, "—that's all."

She didn't speak for a moment. When she did, her tone was colder: "Two hours before each match. But don't be a sucker."

As she spoke, someone entered the courtyard.

"Brenner," a robust voice called out. Brenner turned to see Sage Vicksman walking toward them.

"Yeah?"

"I have something for you," he said, coming to a stop at their table, "An offer." He looked Brenner in the eye. "Due to your skills on the Agilis field, and the unexpected vacancies on the team, how would you like the honor of playing Zabrani for Valoria?"

Brenner inhaled deeply. A day ago, he would have leapt at the chance to join the elite team…but now, with the danger all too real…

Sage Vicksman tilted his head, seeming surprised by Brenner's slow reply. "Might I remind you the prestige and prizes of winning this year are higher than ever? They really should pay us sages more as your trainers… anyway, as one of the most junior level spellcasters Ganthrea has seen at this event, you'd make quite a name for yourself."

Brenner took a long breath. Was it worth it to make himself more marketable? Did he really need great wealth? After all, he had a new family, new friends—he could fly—and he had Gemry. He looked over to her, and she met his eyes. The carefree talk of the games a few days ago was replaced with a serious decision.

"You can do what you want, Brenner," Gemry said.

He nodded. And he knew...if something happened to Gemry on the field, when he could've helped, but instead could only watch...

"Count me in," Brenner said with newfound resolve, more to Gemry than to Sage Vicksman.

"Excellent," Sage Vicksman said cordially. "Your Zabrani uniform and game mircon will be in your conjurer chambers by evening meal. Meet with Maverick after his Contendir match later today to discuss strategy before Thursday's match against Vispaludem. And congratulations."

Brenner nodded, and Vicksman turned on his heels, striding out of the courtyard.

Gemry studied him. "You didn't have to join for me, you know."

"I know." He put a hand on hers. "But I wanted to."

That evening the Zabrani team held a memorial service for the two players they had lost. Amid burning candles, each teammate shared their respect for Berlin and Phylia, and their sadness at their passing. Maverick asked for a long moment of silence. When it was over, he praised the two knights' bravery, and let everyone know that dangers can and still would be present in their next matches, and if anyone wanted to leave the team, they were welcome to. "No questions asked. No shame in leaving," he said.

But no one did. On the contrary, the teammates stood closer to one another, lifted their chins a little higher.

Gemry turned her green-eyed gaze to Brenner. "Well, despite your rookie status, and brash desire to jump into harm's way, I'm glad you're on the team."

Brenner gave her hand a squeeze. "Thanks," he said. "But you're the one who taught me to shrug off close calls. Remember flight training?"

"So I did…" Gemry said, "and a good thing, too. You'll be using those skills soon."

Chapter Twenty-One

Bittersweet Battles

B renner awoke the third day of the Games jittery with excitement. He ate breakfast with both Finnegan and Gemry—the usual seating arrangements based on rank was lifted during the games—and then Gemry headed off early toward the north stadium for her morning Contendir match. As Brenner's Agilis match was in the afternoon, he was optimist-ic he could watch all of Gemry's performance.

"Before the game, would you mind taking me somewhere?" Brenner asked Finnegan, walking with him out the wide doors of Valoria.

"Sure, where's that?"

"The betting booths."

"Now you're talking!" Finnegan exclaimed. "Hoping to win a few silvers on your match?"

"Not mine."

The two made their way through the bustling streets, dodging great masses of fans wearing all different colors in support of their home biomes. Finnegan steered them to a stall on the exterior of the northern stadium, where already there was a huge line of spectators hoping to cash in on the outcome of the Contendir matches.

As the line ahead of them dwindled, Finnegan explained the postings on an elaborate carved board behind the trader accepting coinage. A familiar voice in the line ahead caught Brenner's attention. There was an argument between the booth trader, a tall, balding man, and a buyer with dark hair.

"…we only accept Ganthrean currency—coppers, silver sheckels, golders, and platinums—for betting. You can't bet mircons or enchanted ob—"

"Do you have any idea how rare these necklaces are?" blurted the buyer. "The glass is made from Gelemensus glaciers!"

"Well go sell it then and come back with the proceeds," the trader said bluntly, waving him away. "Next!"

"Worthless betting booths," muttered the man, rummaging through his bag, "Hold on! Here—" he hefted a large black satchel of coins on the counter. "A hundred golders on Gespelti."

The trader raised his eyebrows, his look of contempt replaced with annoyance. "You could've started with that," he said, turning to the giant chart of duels and their odds. He pointed his mircon and floated the buyer's satchel to a basket on the wall labeled "Wagers," where it flipped upside down and emptied the contents with loud clinks, then, from another basket came the sound of metal carving against metal, and out spit a gilded disk. The trader floated the disk on the counter to the man, who quickly pocketed it, turned and slinked past Brenner. He caught a glimpse of the man's scowling face. Brenner recognized him. It was the same weaseling man from several weeks ago at Hutch & Son's: Gemry's father. Pushing past spectators, he was gone.

The next person in front of Brenner quickly finished placing his bet of forty silvers on a Montadaux magician, and the trader motioned the two boys up to the counter.

Brenner looked at the giant wooden board behind the trader, which listed pairs of spellcasters fighting in Contendir matches. Each listing contained the Contendir ring, the spellcaster, their home biome, academy rank, and then the odds for or against them. Brenner's eyes widened.

Gemry, at ring number four, was paired against a level twelve sorcerer from Aquaperni, Rodick DePallo, and the odds, Brenner saw with dismay, were 7-to-1 that she would lose.

"Three silvers on Gespelti," he said, pulling the coins from his tunic and sliding them on the counter.

The trader gave a small laugh, amused at either Brenner's choice of combatant or more likely, the small wager. He pointed his mircon at the coins, which floated to the Wagers bin, plopped in with a soft chink, and then out from the other side of the bin came a small, metal arm, much like a record player needle, which sliced a short inscription onto a metal wafer.

The trader floated it to Brenner, then called out, "Next."

Brenner edged away from the counter, reading the smooth, polished metal: *Contendir, Gemry Gespelti, 3rd day of the Games, Wager: 3 silvers, Odds: 1-to-7.* He held tightly to it as he and Finnegan marched to the main entrance of the northern stadium. The crowds were thick.

Vendors at the gate saw Finnegan's and Brenner's robes with green Valoria crests, and waived them through the gate without charge.

"It pays to be an academy spellcaster," Finnegan said.

"Yeah," said Brenner. The free admission got him thinking. "Where does all the money from the gates go?"

"Where else? The Silvalo government takes all the money from admission, all merchandise tax, and betting on players. Then the council doles out prize money, pays stadium employees, the city guards…"

"So, who pays for yesterday's burials?"

"I dunno. I would hope the council."

"Hmm," Brenner said, his brow furrowing as he worried about Gemry.

The two climbed up to a green section of the stands, where a large segment of Valoria spellcasters had joined together to cheer on their peers. The mid-morning sun felt warm against his green, embroidered tunic.

The scent of fried meats wafted over to them from the chest packs of food vendors, who strode up and down the staircases of the stadium, their loud voices calling out like squawking seagulls. From their vantage point, Brenner could see the vast arena, its surface completely transformed from yesterday's Zabrani match, as if a giant had unplugged the lakes and heaved the ridges into their empty basins, then leveled the entire arena with packed clay. Drawn on the surface were four enormous, white rings—each larger than a city block—for the Contendir matches. Taking in the entire field, with each ring nestled in its quadrant, Brenner thought the pattern looked like four holes of a humongous button.

"Do you see her?" he asked Finnegan.

"Not yet."

A woman dressed in rainbow colored robes flew to the epicenter of the arena and announced in an amplified voice, "Welcome to the third day of the games, and the thrilling sport of Contendir!"

The crowd around the stadium hollered so loudly that Brenner felt a physical wave of energy push against his body.

The master of ceremonies opened a wooden chest, and eight shimmering glowbes flew out like pairs of hummingbirds to the four circles, then divided once more and flew to opposite ends of their rings. She called out,

"Please welcome the first round Contendir players: in the first circle, Baridus Silver of Montadaux versus Johanes Sparks of Vispaludem!"

The red and violet colored sections of the crowd bellowed their approval, as the two players flew, mircons in hand, to opposite sides of the first ring.

"In the second circle, Jerimani Warsett of Arenaterro versus Armelia Sommers of Safronius!" Again the crowd burst forth with cheers, as it did again for the third combatants—"Jardin Swarts of Aquaperni versus Darimond Toyli of Gelemensus!"—and loudest yet for the fourth ring, since it contained a home favorite: "Gemry Gespelti of Silvalo versus Rodick DePallo of Aquaperni!"

Gemry flew gracefully from the southern side of the dirt-packed arena and landed just in front of her glowbe in the fourth ring. Thankfully, Finnegan had used the betting chart to guide them to the side of the stadium closest to her ring.

The rules of Contendir, told to Brenner by Gemry while flying a few weeks ago, seemed fairly straightforward: using mircons, spellcasters won if they got their opponent's glowbe first, using any spell, land formation, or flight maneuver to get it. Players lost if they left the ring, lost their amulet, or died.

"Combatants, collect your landform seeds."

Attendants approached each of the eight players, offering silver plates with colorful pebbles.

Gemry collected the tiny seeds with her left hand, holding her mircon high in her right. Her opponent, Rodick, a muscular young man with long, sun-bleached hair, bent his knees and rocked forward in anticipation.

"Contendir combatants!" called the rainbow-robed woman with a flourish, floating high above and rotating to look at all four circles, "*Begin!*"

Sizzles of spellfire ripped across the four rings of the arena as the players sought to disable their opponents. Rodick was among the offensive sorcerers, blasting Gemry with a blue spell that she met with a protective Aura bubbled around herself. Sprinting forward, Rodick used the advantage of her pause to throw his landform seeds in front of himself, creating huge shafts of earth that pierced upward like gigantic rock crystals. Gemry used some of her own seeds to grow a forest in a semicircle in front of herself. A moment later, huge redwoods and firs towered on her side of the ring. Levitating up from the back of her territory and using the trees as shields, Gemry pushed forward, keeping one eye on her white glowbe, which floated in the back of her territory. The two combatants sent stunning spells from behind trees and rocks, blocked with Auras, and the game progressed equally for awhile, like chess players trading pawns, then bishops, then knights.

Then Rodick lashed out from behind a jagged rock, sending a red spell at Gemry. Brenner inhaled sharply—but the spell missed Gemry and hit the tree in front of her.

Then Brenner realized Rodick had intentionally missed: it was a scorching spell, and it quickly engulfed the great redwood. Gemry was forced to fly backward, retreating halfway back on her side while Rodick advanced past the center ridge. With a yell, Gemry cast a misty white spell at him. It hit him in the arm and stunned him momentarily midair.

Rodick clutched at his temples and plummeted to the ground, but at the last moment sent a spell to his face, purging himself of the mental damage Gemry had inflicted. Ten feet above the ground Rodick paused, hovering. Then he abandoned any defensive strategy of using trees for cover: pulsing through the air like a missile, Rodick fired spells at Gemry—*ratta-tatta-tat!*—with an intensity akin to a Gatling gun.

Gemry dove for cover behind a tall oakbrawn, sending counterspells at her opponent, but Rodick wasn't allowing her enough time to get a clear shot. He pelted forward, now in the final twenty yards of Gemry's field, rattling off spells as quick as his thoughts would allow.

Gemry cast an Aura over herself, floated out from behind her tree, and bravely flew straight at Rodick, lapsing her Aura for a quick moment to shoot spells back. Brenner realized Rodick must have had a large amount of elixir in his amulet, for he soon bombarded Gemry with a nonstop barrage of blue and red fire spells, each one shrinking her Aura. Brenner grimaced. And then, like a pane of glass cracking, a loud snap rent the air: Gemry's Aura shattered.

The crowd let out a sharp gasp and watched her drop, limp as a ragdoll. Brenner jumped to his feet, horrified, as Gemry fell and landed on her side.

Rodick flew to her unguarded glowbe, grasped it, and it changed to blue. He gave a passing glance back at Gemry, then raised his arm in victory, to which the blue Aquaperni fans applauded loudly.

Brenner went to fly from his seat onto the field, but Finnegan pulled the hem of his shirt back. "Hey, you can't get past the shield curtain."

Brenner made one more effort, but Finnegan was insistent. "Brenner, it's like trying to puncture diamond. I know you want to help her, but you can't. Let the officials below do their job."

Fuming, he let Finnegan pull him back down.

Two sages came to Gemry's ring and channeled a spell into her, which seemed to revive her. Slowly she stood up, and then with their assistance, shuffled off the field, holding a hand to her head.

Above the din of the crowd, a brazen bell tolled.

"Brenner," said Finnegan, "that's the ceremonial bell for Agilis. You've only got about twenty minutes."

He had completely forgot. Torn between his desires to support Gemry and meet the challenges of his own match, Brenner reluctantly hovered down to the exit, through the gates, and out of the stadium.

Wind whistled past him as he soared through the streets. He felt a bit selfish, leaving the Contendir match right after Gemry suffered a loss. But Finnegan was probably right. What else could he really do?

Descending to the players' entrance of the stadium, his feet touched down in front of a city guard who was posted at the stone archway.

"I'm here to play Agilis," he said.

The guard saw the tree insignia of Silvalo on Brenner's uniform, and the Agilis logo of a glowing, sun-like orb. He nodded, letting Brenner pass.

As Brenner hustled through the tunnels to the field, he realized he had a stronger reason to play than prestige: unless he could match the best spellcasters, those like Rodick who probably had large amounts of elixir in their amulets, he would always run the risk of being overpowered…of standing by helplessly if others, like Gemry, were targeted—on the field or off. Today he would play as hard as possible.

Jogging into the final corridor, he remembered a story he'd read long ago…how the Greeks, descending upon the shores of their enemy and being heavily outnumbered, did something unexpected to their boats. He turned to his own mental safeguards—of fears, escape routes, and what-ifs—and like the Greeks, set them afire.

There is nothing to go back to.

I must win.

I must.

As he entered the arena, a hundred thousand spellcasters in the crowd shouted and sang chants for their home players. But Brenner didn't hear them. He had entered into fight mode.

A white-bearded official came toward Brenner, motioning for his mircon to be placed in a lockbox. Brenner dropped it in, looking at the middle of the field, where four glowbes hovered next to an announcer.

"Get a move on," the old official said, pointing to the slingshot launch-pad, which was busy sorting the forty players around the field. As Brenner jogged toward it, he watched the game announcer scatter the landform seeds—and then a huge column of earth and rock jutted up from the middle of the field…up fifty feet…one hundred…two hundred…he looked away, stepping onto the launchpad, and was soon flung over the center of the peak, now looking a bit like Devil's Tower. The announcer commanded, "Release the malipedes."

Brenner fell to the other side of the arena, slowing through a pair of poles raised off the ground, fitting neatly into the last open position of competing players, equally spaced around the arena like forty spokes of a wheel.

Looking to the huge monolith, he noticed the black hind legs of some giant creature disappearing into the side of its steep cliff-face; in an instant it had burrowed completely inside.

The announcer, her long hair billowing behind her as she flew above the middle of the mountain, cast a reddish spell downward, and immediately four tubes of glass appeared at the peak of the monolith, growing upward about four-to-five stories high. She directed the glowbes to hover above each of the tubes.

Brenner looked at the rock face to plan his climbing route, but was interrupted when the announcer said, "Let the second round of Agilis—begin!"

Brenner sprinted forward—an orange-caped Arenaterro boy to his left, and an indigo-clad Gelemensus girl to his right—his nimble feet jumping over piles of earth and granite boulders that the newly birthed monolith had shed like snakeskin.

The peak rose steeply ahead, and as he darted up the lowest ledges, its severe incline would soon force him to switch from running to climbing hand over foot. He jumped the last boulders, then leapt onto the wall and heaved himself up, using the protruding shield-sized stones for purchase. Other spellcasters arrived at the wall just after he began his ascent. They, too, scaled the crag wall.

Soon beads of sweat rolled off Brenner's forehead, down into his eyes, as he steadily gained elevation…twenty feet, now thirty feet…the holds became smaller, forcing him to exercise caution…forty feet. He used a crack to climb to fifty feet…*keep going, come on*…he spotted a large jug hold, and soon was thankful to catch his breath and rest an arm while hanging from it.

The wall trembled.

Then the sound of TNT exploding nearly threw him off. He glanced up in time to see a barrage of rocks raining down. Quickly, he flattened himself against the red rock as boulders careened past him, with smaller debris whacking his head and arms.

"*AAAARGH—!*" an Arenaterro player screamed below him, as a bear-sized boulder struck him off the wall. Brenner closed his eyes, not wishing to see the final impact. A moment later he felt his whole body vibrate from the rocks smashing against the arena floor.

Looking up again, Brenner saw black, scaly legs of the culprits recede into the side of the mountain: malipedes.

He changed direction to climb away from the large, blown-out hole on the side of monolith, but was jolted a second later when yet another explosion rocked the wall—this one not ten feet to his right. A grotesque, black, ant-like head of a malipede protruded from the hole—judging from the size of its large head, the creature must be as big as a buffalo—then it pulled back inside.

Another loud bang came from the other side of the mountain. Brenner looked up. There were several hundred feet to climb to the top ledge, and now that the explosions were happening at a feverish pace, he didn't want to find out what would happen if a malipede blasted through the very rocks he was holding.

He needed to get inside.

Against the voice of his fear, he climbed across a crag, and flung himself into one of the blown-out tunnel entrances. He landed, stood, and then pressed his back to the side wall, listening attentively in case one of the creatures came back through this passage. The interior of the tunnel was dim, fairly wide, and tall enough that he didn't have to duck down. He moved along it, and as he came to a fork in the passage, followed the side going up. The tunnel became darker. Heavy scuttling noises echoed around the passage, causing his arms to tingle with goose pimples...*if those creatures can bore through rock...I don't stand a chance fighting them.*

The sound of dozens of legs scurrying on rocks came from a tunnel to his right—and for a horrible moment, his body froze. He forced himself to climb the walls and cling to the ceiling—just in time, as a thundering beast pounded through the tunnel, charged underneath him—its hardened, scaly carapace scraping against his skin—and then it was past. Brenner took a quick gulp of air.

He leapt down, then ran faster up the tunnel—at least he felt it was rising up—and prayed that more malipedes would not be charging down upon him.

Going away from the outside and into the center, Brenner felt the darkness thicken, and a couple of times he bashed his shoulder into the walls. Then the tunnel turned, light filtered in, and Brenner came into a nightmare chamber where he could see clearly: the inner hive of the malipedes. Before him scuttled a herd of black, scaly, ant-like creatures the size of rhinos, scurrying, nipping, and crawling over everything with loud clicks.

Then one saw Brenner.

It charged.

Brenner grabbed the first thing on the ground he could—a rock—and chucked it at the beast. It hit the malipede in the head, and it shrieked in pain—buying Brenner a moment to search for the closest upper passage—and jump to the wall, climbing up it for his life.

The malipede darted after him—snapping its jaws—but couldn't climb upward as fast as it could scuttle across flat ground. Brenner bouldered over to another tunnel, and, seeing another black armored beast rearing up at him, leaped towards a window ledge, catching it with his fingers, and heaving himself up. The tunnel was clear. He sprinted upward, following the path higher and higher to the growing light. Unfortunately, a dead-end forced him to backtrack, losing precious time.

Panting, Brenner pushed himself up…and up…then shouted with relief to find the blue sky above him. He was out of the mound, out of the clacking, cacophonous lair of the malipedes, and standing atop the granite plateau of the peak.

A final task separated him from the four glowbes hovering up high: clear tubes of glass, rising up another fifty feet.

What were those dark shapes in the tubes?

He grimaced. Those were three other spellcasters, each shimmying up to a glowbe. He dashed for the fourth—and only—empty glass tube. Ducking inside the archway of the tube, he ran his fingers across the smooth, opaque wall, hunting for climbing holds. As the tube was a little bigger than a manhole, his search didn't take long: there weren't any holds.

He tried another idea. Wedging his shoulder against one side, and his feet against the other, Brenner pushed against the tube-walls, using his hands against the sides to propel himself upward. After using much of his stamina on the initial climb, and then sprinting through the Malipede's lair, Brenner was tired; the ninety-degree vertical climb was slow going. And the sharp squeak of his feet and shoulders rubbing against the walls didn't help.

He was about thirty feet up the tube, and could vaguely see the other three climbers through the cloudy glass—one girl had just reached the top opening and looked to have grabbed her glowbe—when a hard yank on his leg jerked his body loose and sent him tumbling down. The glass walls screeched like banshees as his arms scraped painfully against them. He collided with a red-shirted Montadaux player on the way down, and then hit the hard bottom. The other player quickly disentangled himself from

Brenner, and gave him a savage smile.

"And stay down!" the burly teenager yelled, kicking Brenner's stomach. Brenner gasped and curled in on himself.

Sprawled on the ground, his arms scraped with wall burns, and a sickening pain pulsing from his abdomen, Brenner saw the other player leaping upwards, quickly propelling himself with hands and feet on either side of the tube…just as Brenner had done—soon he would emerge from the top, snatch the last glowbe, and eliminate Brenner from the finals.

It should have been mine.

Brenner's forehead burned: something primal inside himself ignited.

"Oh no you don't!" Brenner said, crouching low and then bursting upward with all his energy, using quick, alternating pushes of his left and right hands to ascend the tube faster than before.

The Montadaux player saw Brenner approaching, readied himself for contact, and swung a leg down at Brenner, trying to catch him in the head. But Brenner dodged, and using both his hands, grabbed the boy's foot and yanked down as hard as he could—slamming the boy's upper body against the wall.

As the two fell, Brenner pulled himself level and then above the other boy. Cursing at Brenner, the player jammed himself in the tube and tried grabbing at him…but Brenner kicked his hands away, thrust his own hands to the tube's side to lock himself in place, and then jammed his heel down on the player's chest, sending him tumbling to the ground.

Advantage gained, Brenner started climbing up again. When he was sure he had a clear distance between himself and the Montadaux boy, he looked down: the player was still in a heap at the bottom.

Brenner continued with renewed intensity, determined not to relinquish his position.

After another five minutes of continuous climbing, he had done it. The tube opened to the thundering cheers of the crowd, and Brenner, balancing on the glass rim, reached up and grasped the shimmering glowbe.

Panting, he sat on the edge of the tube, his legs dangling against the thick, rigid glass, as an announcer's voice called out, "Spellcasters of Ganthrea, we have our fourth and final Agilis player advancing to the finals—Brenner Wahlridge!"

Up in the stands of the Agilis stadium, a brown-haired man in green robes wove through the applauding fans as Brenner and the other three Agilis players jumped onto silver platforms and hovered down to the sidelines. He stopped next to a yellow-hooded fan who nodded slightly.

"Took you awhile to find me," said the hooded man, "And you're supposed be wearing robes from another biome…"

"Sorry, Dalphon, I was caught up at the academy."

"How many have you secured for me?"

"How much are you paying for each?"

"Depends on their ability."

"Well?"

"Thirty golders for inexperienced spellcasters…fifty for the upper levels …a hundred for the top players."

"I've got seven convinced so far; five lower and two upper, and I had one top player. But he died." He held out his hand.

"What?"

"Where's my advance? I'm running risks you know—other sages at the academy are suspicious."

"Then you're not doing your job right."

The two looked hard at each other. Finally, the brown-haired man glowered, let out a huff, and lowered his hand.

"You'll receive payment upon delivery to my caravan after the final day of the Games."

The green-robed spellcaster shook his head resentfully, before turning back to the crowd and saying, "So be it."

Chapter Twenty-Two

The Rookie Knight

To soothe his muscles and backache after the Agilis match—particularly from the fight inside the glass tube—Brenner spent a good amount of time after the game soaking in the stone baths of the conjurer's dormitories, where fresh scents of vanilla plants and aloe permeated the air. By the morning of the fourth day of the Games, he felt rejuvenated and ready for his first appearance on the Zabrani team.

At the western side of the massive northern arena, their king, Maverick, dispersed special mircons for the game—giving three separate ones and white capes to Gemry and two other healers, Dunn and Piltkins. Taking his regular mircon, Brenner strode with his emerald green team to the base of their stone tower, and followed the lead of his teammates, who flew to the top of the tower, waiting on an upper balcony for the match to begin.

There was something different about the field ahead: high in the sky floated dozens of oblong silver discs, ranging in size from a ping-pong table to a large billboard. They hovered above the territories of both Silvalo and their opponent, Vispaludem.

"Kings, collect your landform seeds," announced the official in the middle of the field. Maverick zoomed off.

"Haggerty, how much did you bet on us this time?" Girard called past Brenner.

Haggerty, an older teen with a crooked nose and long black hair, answered, "The booths think we're gonna get squashed, so I took advantage of the 4 to 1 odds against us."

"Yeah?"

"Bet my entire savings: twelve golders. So we'd *better* win this one!"

"Gutsy!" someone yelled.

"Begin land formation!" the official called. Brenner watched the two kings cast down red seeds all across the middle of the field, where immediately a spine of mountains arched up, rising almost as high as the silver discs. Then Maverick grew trees in a Z-shaped pattern back from the middle, with two large lakes on either side of the diagonal trees.

"Knights!" called Maverick, flying back to them. "We *need* to reach the midfield mountains first. Vispaludem has better aim than our last opponent, and if we let this game drag on, we will lose. If we keep hold of midfield, we win. Six of you—he indicated Gemry and several others—stay to guard our three glowbes. The rest," he called, motioning with a sweep of his arm, "get ready to follow me."

Brenner crouched on the edge of the tower wall, shield strapped over his left wrist, mircon clenched in his right fist. He turned to Gemry. "Promise to stay dry, okay?"

She nodded solemnly. "You too."

The official for the match, now hovering over the transformed field, called with enthusiasm, "May the Semi-final Zabrani match of Silvalo versus Vispaludem—" he raised his arm, and out from his mircon golden sparks shot into the air, "begin!"

Brenner no longer had to speak the word *Volanti*, instead he pictured a flying kestrel and started the spinning flight cycle in his mind, surging forward through the air with five of his teammates, shield held in front of his face to ward off incoming spellfire.

Purple spells sizzled through the air past them.

"Watch the flank from right!" Dunn called out, and Brenner zig-zagged, lowering his altitude as shots whisked above his head.

The squad flew in a curve, away from the right, toward the middle of the spiny ridge. Brenner's face fell. He saw advance Vispaludem scouts landing on top of the mountain, spotting them, and opening fire.

"Split in two!" Maverick called.

The double attack from Vispaludem forced them to take cover; Brenner soared down with two others behind a stone pillar, shielding them from the purple spells coming from the top ridge.

He returned fire with *Arcyndo* spells, along with Dunn and a girl, Kasha, while the other Silvalo regiment hunkered lower down the hill, trying to repel the knights advancing from the right side. *Not good,* Brenner thought. He'd played enough chess and Zabrani now to realize that they were in poor position: with two angles of attack, all Vispaludem needed was a scout to slip around the left side, and his crew would be picked off.

"Got one!" Kasha yelled next to him.

A tall Vispaludem knight keeled over from behind his boulder, then rolled like a lifeless log a dozen feet before dashing against a ledge.

"Dunn!" Girard yelled from the crew below them, "Arturo's hit!"

Dunn aimed a healing spell at the motionless knight downhill, missed, but on the second shot, revived him.

Then Brenner felt a hot spell blaze past his shoulder. He reflexively hunkered to the ground.

"Guys!" Brenner called, motioning to a Vispaludem knight coming over the middle ridge and hiding above a silver platform, "They're getting behind us! I'm going around!"

"I'll give you cover," Kasha said, eyeing the rocks. "Make ready… and— NOW!"

She fired a rapid stream of green spells, forcing the Vispaludem knights to take cover.

"Volanti!" Brenner thought in a rush, flying low with his belly nearly scraping the ground, his shield thrust toward the upper ridge, racing past

rocks and scrub trees, seeking the far left end of the ridge. Twice, his shield buckled against him from the onslaught of spells, metallic tings reverberating through the air as he flew over the final rock ledge, into the opposite side.

He landed, and then scanned the area for enemies wearing violet. Two from the upper ledge fired down in his direction, but since they were well over four hundred yards away, their spells hit the dusty ground away from him.

Brenner ran through his options: he could retaliate at the two knights on the middle section…but they knew his position and were well defended; however, if he could sneak further…

His thoughts were interrupted by close spellfire. Other knights had staked a location nearby, and their spells were within twenty feet of him. He looked at the upper ridge—and a blinding ray of sun caught his eye. *Where was that from?*

He noticed a silver disc had deflected light around him…and a strategy sparked.

Quickly casting his *Volanti* spell, he flew away from the middle ridge and into Vispaludem territory, toward a grove of poplar trees, weaving over rocks as spells ricocheted all around him. Once in the woods, he felt secure with the tree cover, so turned back to the fray. Brenner spotted a cluster of green spells whizzing over the mountain from the Silvalo side, saw a flicker of purple on top ridge, and calculated his angle.

Aiming his mircon not at the rocks of the mid-section, but at a silver disc floating between them, Brenner loosed a volley of spells like arrows.

"*Arcyndo!*" he called out.

His spells flew up toward a floating platform, hit the smooth surface at a sharp angle, and bounced down toward the top of the ridge—striking just over the edge like missiles. While he couldn't see if his targets were hit, the blasts of spellfire coming from that area soon lessened.

After a ten spells, Brenner paused, wondering if more Vispaludem knights would attack him now that he had revealed his position in enemy territory. He hovered to a new vantage point, about thirty yards away, behind a large willow tree.

He watched the middle ridge; there, two violet knights climbed back over the center ridge into Vispaludem's side; he cast another barrage of spells at a silver platform, which bounced down and caught one of the knights in the chest, and sent the other scrambling to a rock for cover.

Brenner smiled, remembering how his brother used to chide him about spending too much time on blueprints and angles, but it was that dedication to detail that now gave him the advantage in battle.

Not wanting to venture further into Vispaludem territory with an opponent at his back, Brenner scanned the mountain, and noticed some crumbling, chossy ledges just above the hiding knight.

Time to flush you out.

"*Arcyndo!*" he called under his breath, sending a ray of spells into the rockside, which started a small avalanche toward the knight's hiding spot. It had the intended effect: the violet knight dashed toward a new boulder, exposing himself for three long seconds, during which Brenner shot a barrage of spells into his path, succeeding in stunning him to the ground.

Brenner grinned. His back secure—at least for a few minutes—he pressed forward to Vispaludem's glowbes. *If I can get one, that will shift attention and allow for Maverick to gain the midfield.*

About two hundred yards ahead, through a thicket of tall trees, he saw three shimmering violet glowbes…spaced far left, far right, and right in front of the Vispaludem tower. Overhead, on either side of him, silver platforms floated in the blue sky.

A flurry of lilac color moving behind the trees alerted him to the several defenders stationed around the three glowbes. It appeared there was a tag-team of defenders around each glowbe, probably two or three apiece.

Knowing that a flight straight for the center glowbe would be suicide, Brenner decided on another surprise attack: two at once.

Running low, Brenner advanced to the edge of an open clearing in the middle of Vispaludem territory; then, as he had done earlier, he shot

Arcyndo spells up, but this time at two silver platforms in the sky, raining down spellfire on the left and right ends of the arena, and, he hoped, into the guarding defenders of the glowbes.

"From the middle! He's in the middle!" shouts rang through the trees.

He ignited his *Volanti* spell, flying left, away from the middle. To avoid detection, Brenner flew hard and low to the ground, but accidentally gashed his knee on a tree root. He winced, but kept flying.

Then he looked back. A swarm of violet knights converged on the clearing he had left. But thankfully, a small contingent of green flyers had made their way over the middle ridge, and were now engaging those violet knights. Green and purple jets of their spells blasted back and forth through the canopy.

Using the distraction, Brenner circled wide left, on the fringe of the arena, and worked his way through the trees behind the outer violet glowbe. There was only one sentry left watch over it, not two as he thought— and she was facing the battle, her back to Brenner.

He crept closer through shrubs, and let off two quick shots: the first hit the girl's leg, the second, her back, and she crumpled to the ground. He flew in, grabbed the glowbe, and made a wide berth back to the center tower, only briefly hearing the crowd erupting in its approval.

From the explosions and loud shouts coming from the tall oakbrawns in the middle, it seemed his teammates had fully engaged the Vispaludem fighters. He made his next approach, darting from tree to tree in the back of their territory, heading closer to his next objective: their tower, which stood high above their center glowbe. He skimmed toward the base of it— shield raised at his left side in case another sentry saw him—then pressed his back against the shadow of the stone tower.

"*Volanti,*" he thought, and quietly floated up the backside of the tower, keeping the structure between himself and his opponents. He soared to the top, where Vispaludem's score—31—shimmered in misty numbers above the circular turret; if he planned correctly, the middle glowbe was about seventy feet down from him. He braced himself, spun around the side of the tower, and jumped—plummeting down shield-first to the middle glowbe, and opening fire on the squad of violet knights below.

By the time he had flown down the first fifty feet, his green spells had hit two knights in their backs, which alerted the other defenders and caused a counterattack of spells. Explosions rang in his ears; his shield vibrated as it absorbed return fire. Only twenty feet left. He leveled toward the ground, feeling his leg tingle with the shock of a spell—ten feet left—his mircon arm and other leg were stunned—*just a bit further!* Like a baseball player stealing second base, Brenner lunged for the prize, his shield hand stretched out—*got it! I got it!* As he grabbed the glowbe, he was shot from both sides and collapsed in a heap.

Brenner couldn't move, but it didn't matter. His plan had worked: he had gotten two glowbes. Pain erupted in his sides, but the thrill of triumph filled his mind. The white glowbe changed to emerald green and hovered up above the field. Soon after, the melee on the right side finished, and his team rallied to grab the third and final glowbe.

"Valoria knights—you have won the game," called an announcer from the peak of the middle mountain, "Silvalo will be represented in the Final round of Zabrani!"

A white sage flew over to Brenner, sending an invigorating spell that thawed his muscles, allowing him to stand upright. A moment later, his team was flying over to mob him.

"Fantastic game, Brenner!" Maverick called to him.

"Great flying," Girard said.

The group flew back to midfield, where all spellcasters tapped their mircons to a lantern, which sent up a swirling billboard in the air, publicizing individual stats and the final results from the match: Valoria had won, 89 to 37, and, of that, Brenner had scored more than half, with 51 points.

A gentle hand touched his shoulder. He turned around, and Gemry gave him a grin. "Was that you shooting against the silver discs?"

"I figured it was worth a try."

"I'll say." She raised an eyebrow. "Traditionally, those have been used for defensive flight-posts. Not for offensive strategy. But, they sure will now."

Brenner could only smile, glad his angle shots had worked. "Hey, you racked up some nice stuns for yourself," he said, spotting Gemry's name with six points.

"Yeah, not my highest, but I healed our teammates over twenty times. And didn't get stunned myself."

"I'm glad you're safe."

"Likewise. Come on," Gemry said, leading him away from the tumultuous crowd. "Let's clean up and have some fun."

After the team changed at the stadium, they flew back to Valoria for a delicious dinner. Maverick held his glass up for a toast to the team, offering a few ideas of strategy for their next game, but mostly celebrating their win, as the academy hadn't advanced to the final round of Zabrani in years, and never, from the spirited shouts around Brenner, had a rookie knight led the team in points.

Back in the heart of Silvalo, on a balcony overlooking the central fountains, two men held their own discussion of strategy.

"You've got that idiotic smile on your face again, Fensk. There'd better be some good reasons to back it up."

"Between Ignatius and me, we're up to twenty-six recruits."

"Not bad. But I need more. How many are active players of the games?"

"Well…that's much harder," Fensk said, looking away, "They've got all kinds of post-game offers—"

"I asked how many."

"Alright, alright…three."

Fensk started to duck, but wasn't fast enough to block a blow.

"I expect better. I'll give you until Monday to prove your worth."

Fensk rubbed his jaw. "Thank you, Dalphon."

"Do they know they are to be troop leaders?"

"One of them wanted the privilege…the others will need to be washed."

"While you have been taking your time with recruitment of foot soldiers, I have seen to the...*enticement*...of some of Silvalo's more wealthy plantation owners, and a sage, which will afford Shivark scores of other conscripts in a few days' time. Do you have Rancor's chambers marked with our men?"

"Yes. The elimination will go through as planned."

"It better. You know what's in store for us if we botch the most important mission Shivark's entrusted to his vanguards." Dalphon watched the courtyard below, and tilted his head in interest. "There's one of the owners now." He hovered off the balcony, and then turned back to Fensk. His voice turned icy, "If everything goes to plan except the one part that is under your watch—I will personally see you collared and in the front lines when these Games are over, and the war begins."

Chapter Twenty-Three

The Fog Before
the Finals

A light rain misted against the walls of Valoria on Friday, the fifth morning of the Games, and Brenner was doubly glad to have a day of rest between events. He would avoid playing in a thick fog that had crept through the city on padded tiger paws, and also, he needed a long, proper soaking after Zabrani. With each step down to the Banquet Hall for breakfast his body sternly reminded him that ground collisions—even controlled ones—from seventy feet high would not come without retaliatory aches and pains: his sides felt as though hornets had stung them from the *Arcyndo* hits; his chest and legs had nasty, purple bruises; and his neck was stiff with whiplash.

Brenner filled his tray with colorful fruits, cinnamon oatmeal, and hot, sliced ham, then more hobbled than walked to join Finnegan at a middle table. The Banquet Hall was about half-full, and spellcasters of different ranks swiveled their heads to look at him; by the time he sat down with Finnegan, several boys had congratulated him on yesterday's plays, while the girls that did meet his eyes blushed and looked away, giggling.

Do they do that for all the players?" Brenner asked, sitting down.

Finnegan finished his bite of French-toast before replying, "Stare unabashedly? No. They used to look at you funny because you were new; now they look at you funny because no one's heard of a rookie level six conjurer advancing to the final games in two events. In their eyes that makes you...well...a freak."

"A freak?" Brenner repeated. He chewed a bite of oatmeal. For most of his life, he'd been ridiculed as a geek. Now he performed well, but was oddly treated the same. *Whatever the society,* he thought, *it seems people always judge those who are different.* He swallowed. "At least freaks get some respect."

"I guess you can call it that," said Finnegan, looking away. "You don't have some sort of third eye on the back of your head, do you? I don't eat with mutants."

"Not you, too," Brenner said, giving him a light shove. "Hey, seen Gemry yet?"

"Can't say I've been wandering through the upper girls' dormitory at this hour. Don't get me wrong, that sounds like a grand time, but I'd probably be stunned within a few steps past the threshold—first by their beauty, which wouldn't hurt, but then by their freezing spells, which definitely would."

At this, Maureen, Evie, and a few other girls on the other end of the table huffed, rolling their eyes at Finnegan. But they smiled at Brenner. Finnegan tried to mask his annoyance.

"All this time your Dad has been busy making singefire-ale," said Brenner, "when he should be constructing a stage at Hutch & Sons for your performances."

"For me?" said Finnegan. "We should put *you* up there, charge a bunch of silver shekels, and let people gawk and clamor for your autograph. More if they want a portrait painted with you. 'See the amazing freak boy!'"

"Uh-huh," said Brenner, a little hurt, and detecting more than a hint of jealousy, "Well...I've felt like a zoo animal more than once around here."

324

Finnegan shrugged. Then he ate his food in silence.

Brenner felt a bit peeved: *was he just supposed to lose so that other people felt better?* He took a deep breath, forcing himself to think about the whole situation. In doing so, he remembered how frustrating it was to watch students back at Clemson make more progress with athletics and friends, much faster than himself. He didn't want this rift to break their friendship.

"You know," Brenner said, "If you're free today, do you mind if I hang out with you? For target practice or board games?"

Finnegan gave him a look. "You'd deign to come down to my level?"

Brenner nodded. "All the others have a 'No Freaks' policy."

Finnegan sighed. "Well if I'm all you've got then…I suppose you can tag along. But no growing extra arms around me."

"I'll try, but I can't promise. Thanks, Finneg—"

"Strange you think so highly of your weird-self, Rookie," a mocking voice interrupted from behind Brenner. "Considering you used to have food thrown at you in your old school."

Brenner grew cold. *Camira had told others his memory…*

He turned around to see Sorian Seltick, arms crossed, standing smugly next to Travarius and a couple bigger magicians. "I'm not sure why the sages selected *you* to be on the Zabrani team," Sorian continued, "when scores of better spellcasters should have been ahead of you." The older teens on either side of Sorian glared at Brenner, bristling in agreement.

"Then you must be as blind as you are stupid—" Finnegan cut in, "because yesterday everyone else saw his double glowbe captures."

"Shut your poor mouth, Hutch," Sorian said snidely.

"In case your tiny brain's forgotten, Salty-tick," said Finnegan, "I've been promoted out of your squad, and no longer am required to tolerate your insults."

Sorian ignored this, flicking his eyes away from Finnegan and back to Brenner; Brenner could tell Sorian wanted to get a reaction from him. "I don't care what you think, flea," growled Sorian. "I just came to warn Wahlridge."

"Oh yeah?" said Brenner. "About what?"

"My cousin, Jarik, plays striking knight for Boldenskeep," said Sorian, enjoying the attention of more and more spellcasters, "His shot is *legendary*, which means you won't stand a chance on Sunday's Zabrani game." He pointed a finger at Brenner as though it had the power to shrink him, and sneered, "And when *you* are forgotten after your loss at the games—" he turned and gestured to his group, "—*we* will be paid handsomely to travel with merchant cartels." The boys next to him grinned.

"And then," said Brenner, "once you're done botching that job with the merchants—like you did as a captain here—you can slink back to Valoria, maybe with enough courage to fight battles by yourself, instead of trolling everywhere with your back-up's. But I doubt it."

Sorian's eyes practically crackled with hatred. "Wahlridge, I might have to accidentally bump into you after the Games…"

"Just like you accidentally shoot spells at your own players? Don't worry, I'll be ready for nasty punks like you."

Sorian muttered something, and the teens at his side drew closer; Finnegan stood; Sorian reached for his mircon, but Brenner had already drawn his own and activated a *Repello* spell, sending Sorian sprawling backwards through his group.

"What's going on there?!" an adult demanded, and Brenner turned to see Sage Vicksman hustling past tables, descending upon the two groups.

"Rookie here thinks he can shoot spells at anybody he likes," said Sorian, pulling himself from the ground and dusting off his robes.

"Just at bullies who need it," said Brenner, watching Sorian.

"Brenner," Vicksman admonished, "we do not permit spells as weapons against spellcasters in the academy. Change your conduct, or you will be pulled from the roster." Sorian gloated at him behind the sage's shoulder, but thankfully his win was short-lived. "Sorian," Vicksman turned to the teen, "Don't interfere with Zabrani players during the Games. All of Valoria is honor-bound to support our players, and I will not have one of our best knights harassed by another of our own spellcasters, especially so

326

close to the Finals. Be off."

Sorian scrunched his nose at him, then turned and sulked out the side archway, his allies plodding behind him.

Vicksman watched him go, then said, "Don't do anything else foolish, Brenner. Save your energies for the Games." He walked to the sages' table at the other side of the hall.

Brenner looked at Finnegan. "Thanks for having my back."

"Of course. You gotta stand up to the real freaks. Come on."

Brenner and Finnegan spent the rest of the morning at target practice, wondering what obstacles would be in the next Agilis match: *wolves? Nightshades? Serpents?* Finally, Brenner's muscles reached their limit.

"I need to hit the stone baths," he told Finnegan.

"Smart move," said Finnegan. "See you at evening meal."

He wound his way through the corridors, where several students asked his opinion on the final Zabrani game—"Are you scared of Sorian's cousin?" "Think you can beat your glowbe record?" "Can you sign my notebook?"—he escaped the conversation only by telling them he felt light-headed and needed a rest, then he quickly followed a passageway lower into Valoria, feeling the warm, humid air rushing up to him. He used his mircon to fend off a couple of tendrilsnake plants that hung above the entrance to the boys' stone baths, blocking anyone who couldn't perform a solid *Repello* spell.

Minutes later Brenner was alone, soaking in warm, bubbling waters, with shafts of muted light piercing the otherwise dark space. *Ahhh...* he thought, *that's better.* Effervescent plants by the upper windows emitted citrus scents, while large roots from trees on the sides of the baths gave off pleasant smells like ginseng.

Brenner floated quietly, but inside, his mind was loud with emotions: bright excitement, because he was only two games away from prize winnings; curiosity, because a new elixir color might unlock new spells; muffled anxiety, because he would be competing against three Agilis players that had smoked him in the previous game, and he'd be playing against even harder obstacles, and…whom else besides Sorian had Camira told of his memories? Finally, there was gray uncertainty, because he still wasn't sure what he should do once the games finished, and Valoria dismissed for summer.

Windelm had made the offer to join his scouting expedition…but it would mean months apart from Gemry, and the low pay would take longer before he could pay off the mircon. On the other hand, if he took Dalphon up on his lucrative offer for a couple of months, he could pay off the entire mircon and very likely have leftover money to help Gemry.

That reminded him, *where was she?* There'd been no sign of her all day…*she's probably stuck working during the busy influx of travelers.* He would have loved to hear her thoughts on all this. *If they won, what was most important: promotion after the games, golders, or elixir?*

What would she do after the games, anyway?

He hoped she could use her winnings on her tuition, but remembered what she said about family getting first rights to prizes for spellcasters under eighteen.

For several hours, Brenner floated in swirls of thoughts and hot water. When he toweled off, changed, and went to evening supper, Gemry still wasn't around. He hoped she was okay. He turned in to bed early that night, hoping his emotions would settle by morning.

If it was up to Gemry, she would've stayed at the academy on Friday, practicing her flight rolls and her *Arcyndo* shots, hanging out with Brenner, and taking an afternoon off to recharge before the Zabrani finals.

But it wasn't.

Her parents knew she had a gap in her games, and like the vast majority of her free time, they required her to work at the Gespelti Warehouse, and without pay. At least they would let her watch the finals of Agilis tomorrow, but only because nearly every customer would be, too. That morning Gemry tidied shelves as her father, Radmond, argued with a posh woman with emerald studded hair-braids.

"Eleven golders for this security door?" the woman asked. "Can't you do better?"

Radmond grimaced. "This enchanted door only opens under the weight of an adult dragon, or your key—it's worth every golder!"

"Ten?" she asked.

Radmond looked affronted. "Surely you can *afford* this luxury. The price is eleven."

Wrong move, thought Gemry. Instead of budging on price and making a sale, Radmond made the woman throw her hands up and tromp out of the store. Another customer left after her, despite Gemry's mother's attempt to give him a free quill.

Radmond was more angry than usual since Gemry lost her Contendir match—and any hopes of that prize money. At least her team was still in the running for Zabrani. It certainly didn't help that she'd overheard that her parents were behind on lease payments, and they bickered often about her mother's spending habits. From what Gemry could tell, Radmond had not saved enough profit from last year, and worse, had a stockpile of Gelemensus glassware: more than he could hope to sell.

For the first part of the day Gemry tied her hair back and went to work: prying lids off wooden crates (she stopped counting after fifty), coughing as the dust scattered into the air, wiping a rag and oil over dark blue goblets, plates, misshapen bowls, and spiral pieces she guessed were art. Her instructions were to buff them 'till they shone and set them in the shop windows, in the hopes that customers would be attracted to their faint shimmer and supposed mind-clearing properties.

But for as much as Gemry handled the glass that day, it didn't improve her thinking or clear her vision of the future.

Just another gimmick my father fell for, and now trying to pawn off onto others…

"Gemry!" her mother, Iris, called from the front of the store.

What now? Gemry thought, walking past shelves of mismatched merchandise. "Yes?"

"We're not getting enough customers," Iris said. "Carry this to the crowds, and do whatever it takes to get people in." She handed Gemry a huge sign that boasted of rare goods, great deals and magical talismans.

"Okay, but mother can we talk about—"

"Go now. Talk later," Iris said, pushing her toward the door.

A couple streets over were the food vendors, so Gemry set her sign up on a corner. She used her mircon to levitate glass and produce yellow-green sparks, all the while half-heartedly calling to the spectators, "Gespelti's Warehouse—you want it, we got it."

A couple of red-robed Montadaux magicians glanced her way, but the majority shuffled past like she wasn't there. She felt like an ugly clown. *I wish I was done with this second-rate business,* she thought. *And actually could use my talents. But it's two years before I finish Valoria and get to do what I want…*

When she returned to the shop hours later, her father was storming around the front of the store.

"Can you believe he offered me only seventeen silvers for that glass?!" Radmond fumed. "I bought it for twice that!"

Gemry thought about chiding him for making the deal in the first place, *why would people want to lug fragile dishes back to their biomes?* But she had something on her mind.

"Father," she said, putting her sign next to the front counter. "I was wondering if I could work a different job this summer."

"Absolutely not," said Radmond.

"I've worked here my whole life, and—"

"Have you forgotten who feeds you? And pays for your education?"

"And takes the winnnings from my games?" she countered.

"How else do you expect to pay back tuition?"

"For starters, a little at a time. There are loans. Look—what if I tidy the shop for an hour first thing in the morning, and then go develop a real skill?"

She had misspoken.

"Is this not a real skill?" Her father said slowly, his eyes narrowing. "What exactly do you think people do to earn money?"

She wanted to point out that he was betting and wasting their money more often than saving it, but she knew that would make him angrier. "I could use my spellcaster skills to build homes, or protect and escort merchants, or research new medicines, or—"

"You just want to get away from us, do you?" Radmond said testily, and his face changed. He looked at her as though appraising a new shipment.

"I just want to make use of my education. That's all. I still want to help."

"Then you can help us by selling more of *this*." He gestured to the shelves of merchandise.

"My being here won't help sell this because most of *this* is just junk."

"Gemry!" Iris jumped in, shaking a bony finger at her, "Don't insult us!"

Gemry looked away, and then added, "What would you call it?"

Her mother scowled. "It's…boutique…"

"Look," Gemry said, "If I win at Zabrani, can I just have some time off to myself? To try something new?"

"So you can run away, is that it?" her father said, raising an eyebrow.

"That's not what I said," huffed Gemry, folding her arms, "I just want to try a new job before I'm out on my own."

"Oh sure," her father said. "Well tough luck! You're working here."

That rankled Gemry. "Then I can play poorly during the last game…we lose and you get *zero* golders of prize money. What do you think about that?" She stared hard at Radmond.

Radmond was silent, clenching his fists. His next response surprised her.

"I tell you what," he said slowly, "If you play hard and *win* at Zabrani… I'll give you a month off from the warehouse to work elsewhere in Arborio."

It worked! Gemry thought, trying to suppress a smile.

"But your pay goes to me," Radmond added firmly. "And then it's back to work here with no complaining."

Gemry could hardly believe her good fortune.

"Deal."

That night, looking down at the ant-like spellcasters below, Dalphon waited outside a rented room.

Twenty minutes had passed since he cast the mark of allegiance spell around his balcony, something only his faction could detect. He watched for his leader to be drawn to it amidst the thousands of other tree condos in Arborio...*soon now.*

With panther-like eyes he looked over the balcony to the air-paths and streets below, where the multicolored flyers zoomed back from restaurants to their rented quarters on massive oakbrawns.

Then two of the shadows detached from the flyers, and flew up toward Dalphon.

Although he had pledged allegiance to this leader for three years now, had been promoted due to his ability to persuade and execute, and if all went as planned their faction would soon command their entire biome, Dalphon's heart always beat irregularly when the two had face-to-face meetings.

The figures drew close and landed on the balcony. Before Dalphon stood a handsome man with skin that seemed to radiate warmth, a canine-sharp smile, and thick, dark hair; next to him stood a brute that looked like he was used to getting what he wanted in few or no words.

"Dalphon," said the man in a pleasing baritone voice, "One of my favorite lieutenants. How is business?"

"Right on track, Master Shivark," said Dalphon. "Please, come in." He held the door open to the condo and the two men strode inside.

"Do we have Arenaterro allied to our plan?" said Shivark, finding an armchair and sitting back in it. His guard stood by the window at his back.

"Yes," said Dalphon, "The head of their city guard said they won't interfere." He offered Shivark a crystal goblet filled with a strong, amber liquid; Shivark waved it away.

"Not now, thank you. There will be plenty of time for that once we've won. What about the richest Silvalo magicians? Rocksmith? Gretzinger?"

"Completely controlled. They've been at the auction daily, with instructions to choose only the healthiest and strongest."

"Good. And your subordinates?"

"Actively recruiting. We have at least fifty spellcasters."

Shivark was silent, which Dalphon knew meant one of two things: he was considering how the new pieces of information fit into his plan, or, he was about to lash out.

Shivark raised a fist from his pocket, and then opened it, revealing a leather pouch stained with blotches of dark blood, which he put into Dalphon's hand. It was warm…and heavy with coins.

Dalphon raised an eyebrow.

"A bookie who failed to pay me my dues. His loss is your gain—for any bribes, recruits or needs you see fit."

"Thank you, Shivark."

Shivark nodded. "Continue to serve me well, Dalphon, and you may keep what you don't spend on your mission. My other lieutenants are under orders to continue the land draining during the games, when biome guards have their attention fixed on their sovereign wizards and political security."

"Very good. Any new developments with Sovereign Rancor?"

"Rancor…" Shivark said, and Dalphon felt him piercing his mind, as if trying to determine his loyalty… "I trust you have followed orders for his demise? You know I can't be near when that happens…."

"Yes, of course, master. Everything will happen as you've planned on the final night of the Games."

"That's why I like you, Dalphon," Shivark said. "You never disappoint."

"I just meant, does Rancor suspect anything?"

"That old fool? He lost his edge years ago, pacified with the luxuries of power so long as I give him monthly allotments of elixir—which, most disappointingly, have steadily decreased this past year, but only for him…" Shivark let out a laugh and Dalphon found himself joining in.

Shivark stood to leave, putting a hand on Dalphon's shoulder. "Even if he questions our loyalty, as long as *you* fulfill your duty, in two days time it won't matter."

Chapter Twenty-Four

The Water, the Wurm, and the Dragon

Why nobody had told Brenner prior to the morning of the sixth day of the Games there was to be—of all things—a parade for him and the other Agilis finalists, he didn't know. But as he ate breakfast in the early Saturday morning hours—he had tossed in his sleep most of the night—one of the sages, Vicksman, asked him whom he'd like to sit beside on his procession on Via Arborio, the major road of the city.

"Quite an honor—" Vicksman said, "making the final four of Agilis. You've represented Valoria most admirably. I'm sure there's more than one girl here who would be thrilled to be asked as your partner on the parade."

He looked around, indeed there were several girls—Maureen and Evie among them—who kept flashing looks at Brenner from nearby tables. But for Brenner, his choice was already made: "I'd like to ask Gemry Gespelti."

"I'll send her invitation to the magician's chambers. Do you have your post-games planned?"

"Not yet."

"Well, I can give you a few tips later. I've been here long enough to assist many graduates in finding prosperous and powerful positions."

"Thanks…"

"Don't mention it. Now, clean yourself up while I inform the games-keeper to prepare your mount. Meet me outside the doors at nine o'clock."

Your mount? What did he mean by that? Brenner puzzled over that, and the tips Vicksman might offer, over the remainder of his meal.

Once finished, he looked to the Banquet Hall clock. There was too much time to fill before nine, and Brenner couldn't stand the idea of sitting still, so he took a long walk behind the academy, and put some of his thoughts into his journal. Then he returned to his conjurer dormitory, changed into his official Agilis embroidered robes—green trimmings with a handsome cape—and walked the passageways down to the grand entrance.

Outside the large arched doors, in the morning sunlight, he saw Gemry standing in a stunning green silk dress.

"Thanks for accepting my invitation," Brenner said, and added in a voice he wished was more composed, "You…look beautiful."

"Well, thanks," Gemry said, "although I'd feel much more comfortable in my Zabrani uniform. How do ladies wear these outfits so often?"

"I am sure I don't know. But you pull it off very well."

She gave him a hint of a smile. "You're not looking so bad yourself."

Sage Vicksman approached them, sweeping his arm forward and saying, "Your ride is en route."

Brenner looked for some large-wheeled carriage on the stone street…but apart from a couple mule carts, he didn't see anything for them to ride. *Perhaps a carrier carpet?*

A large shadow overtook them, and then a full train of flying white Pegasi—whinnying with their manes blowing—swooped onto the boulevard, steered by a coachman that Brenner recognized as Caster Greaves. The Pegasi were even larger than draft horses Brenner had seen on farms, and he wondered how Caster Greaves so easily controlled them. Their hooves clattered to a stop. "This way then," Greaves said, beckoning to Brenner and Gemry and motioning to the open double seat behind him.

Brenner walked around the majestic creatures to the side of the coach, and held out his hand to Gemry.

"Oh really," she protested, "I'm sure I can climb three steps to a seat." Then she nimbly hopped past Brenner. He followed.

"To the Northern stadium, Pegasi," Greaves called to the winged creatures, who cantered forward, then flapped in unison, carrying the coach swiftly into the blue sky, arching away from Valoria to the grand stadium.

"I wish they'd dispense with the beauty pageant, and just let the players focus on the games," Gemry said as they passed between towering oakbrawns.

"But then," Brenner said, raising his eyebrows, "the crowds might miss your exquisiteness."

She punched at him, but Brenner got a hand up to block.

"Say that again, and I'll actually hit you," Gemry said, slipping her hand out of his grip. "You know I'm only doing this for you. I'd sooner be caught dead than parading about on my own."

"Well thank you for accompanying me," Brenner said, and then added more seriously, "I missed you yesterday."

"Likewise," she said.

"Were you at your family's business?"

"Yeah. My parents are trying to sell as much as they can during the games. It's more of a chore than usual, since my father's in a sour mood, even though I won at Zabrani, which I'm sure he bet on."

Brenner was reminded of the earlier Contendir match...

"Gemry..." Brenner began, "does he tell you how much he gambles?"

"No," she answered. "My mother argues with him about it, that he's wasting their money, but then he says she's the one spending too many golders on beauty lotions and her vase collection, that if he didn't win his bets they'd be out of business." She shook her head. "Let's talk about something else."

"Okay," he agreed.

"For instance, how are you planning on winning today?"

Her question brought him back to the upcoming battle. He thought of some of the great commanders he'd read about...Napoleon, who conquer-ed much but spread too thin and lost in Russia...George Patton, who achieved American victories through aggressive offense...

"It depends on where the glowbes are," Brenner said, "and what my opponents do."

"Well, I can guarantee the glowbes are not going to be right in front of you, and that your opponents are going to by running towards them." She elbowed Brenner, which made him break into a smile.

"Then I suppose I'll play to my strengths," said Brenner, "and pursue the ones I have the best shot at grabbing."

"Sounds like you've really mulled it over," Gemry said with raised eyebrow. She laughed and shook her head.

"I've got to see it to plan it."

The two flew over scores of people trickling from the side-streets into Via Arborio, like streams converging into one strong river, which flowed next to the massive northern stadium. While the crowds had to present tickets at the entrances, Caster Greaves directed their train of Pegasi to the upper, shimmering dome of the stadium.

Other spellcasters tried to enter through the glistening, semi-transparent curtain but bounced off its thick skin. The six Pegasi flew toward a mage waving his arm on the other side of the curtain. He channeled a white spell at the dome, and a small circular opening the size of a porthole formed and grew until it was as large as a whole ship.

Greaves steered the flying Pegasi toward this opening, and the entire train passed through, above the stadium seats, which were filling with excited supporters.

As they flew into the stadium, Brenner noticed something unusual below: instead of the bare surface awaiting transformation, it was already partially constructed into the challenge. A river flowed through the field, past a large section of giant pillars and colonnades stacked like ancient ruins, drifting through more and more land on the far side before flowing back along the vast wall of the stadium, wrapping into itself and forming a snaky loop.

Their transport flapped down to the base of the field, over thousands of chattering spectators, where a large group of officials and the three other competitors were meeting, including a red bearded man dressed in richly decorated green robes, which Brenner realized was none other than the sovereign of all Silvalo: Donovan Drusus.

Drusus was talking with the lead Agilis player from Aquaperni until he saw Greaves and the carriage touch down. He finished his conversation and headed over to Brenner, who stepped out from the carriage.

Tall and intimidating, Drusus had broad shoulders, a reddish beard, and below thick eyebrows were two sharp, green eyes that sized up Brenner. "So," he said, "this is the young knight that is the talk of the city." He extended a hand to Brenner. "For advancing to the highest level of athleticism, you bring our biome great pride."

"Thank you…" Brenner began, putting out his hand, which was gripped with warmth and confidence by the sovereign. He could have sworn that Drusus was attempting to peer into his mind, but in a blink the queer feeling vanished.

"And your lovely companion," said Drusus, "she's also a Zabrani player, yes?"

Gemry stepped forward, met the sovereign's gaze, and answered, "Yes. I'm Gemry Gespelti."

"Excellent," said Drusus. "You'll both represent Silvalo well—I'm sure. Well, the ceremony is about to begin. Good luck." He turned to the field, flying with a small attachment of the city guard to a section of the stadium that appeared blocked off exclusively for the leaders of the seven biomes.

Loud bells clamored; Caster Greaves beckoned them back to the coach.

In the middle of the field, Sovereign Drusus flew up, spread his arms wide, and announced to the packed stadium, "Spellcasters of Ganthrea, for the Final round of Agilis, we have four contestants from Arenaterro, Aquaperni, Vispaludem, and…*Silvalo!*"

Thousands of fans gave a hearty applause.

"Our first competitor, from Arenaterro—Armin Kandar!"

A darker skinned and muscular boy, sitting beside a long-haired beauty that easily could have been a princess, rose to the sky riding a griffin. The crowd, especially the orange clad fans, clapped with approval.

"From Aquaperni, Rodick DePallo!"

Flying up from the other side of the stadium on a giant carrier carpet was a familiar face: long, bleached hair flew back from Rodick's face and over the shoulders of his blue uniform. Brenner recognized him from Gemry's earlier Contendir loss. *Very likely my biggest competition...*he thought.

"Jace Sozol, from Vispaludem!"

A wiry girl with close-cropped dark hair, along with a surly, black-eyed boy, flew over the stands on a giant bat-like creature; their deep violet robes flew in the wind as the creature swooped high and low about the arena.

Finally, Greaves shook the reigns of the Pegasi, and the two took to the sky just as Sovereign Drusus boomed out, "And from Silvalo—Brenner Wahlridge!"

Together, Brenner and Gemry made their loop around the stadium—Brenner's nerves racing under his skin in an unpleasant tingle. He'd rather just get to the game, as this—several hundred thousand spellcasters yelling, the scrutiny of the leaders—was causing his stomach to tighten.

Gemry seemed to sense his discomfort, and squeezed his hand. "Don't worry about them. You've gotten this far, which is great in itself."

He gave a small smile.

"And even if they turn on you, or worst case, you lose," she added, looking him directly in the eye, "you'll still have me around."

He squeezed her hand in return. "Thanks, Gemry."

"Of course. Now just finish in one piece, okay?"

Brenner nodded.

"Good," said Gemry, "Come on. Time for you to smile with *aaaall* your exquisiteness, and wave to your adoring fans."

He laughed. As if coming out of a trance, Brenner raised his arm over the side of the carriage and did his best to appear like he was enjoying himself. Gemry's words strengthened him; now all he had to do was keep his end of the bargain…and live until the end of the match.

After ten more minutes of touring above the crowds, Brenner and Gemry touched down on the arena by the largest section of Silvalo fans.

A voice from above caught his attention.

"Brenner!"

He turned around, and saw Windelm wedged between a large cluster of people, leaning over the front row of the stands. Using his mircon, Brenner flew up to him.

"Thanks for coming, Windelm."

"Of course!" Windelm said, as though it had never occurred to him not to come, "You know, it's not every day my great-nephew competes in the biome's largest Mindscape course."

"This…is the largest?" Brenner said, gulping as he looked again at the river, the islands, and the marble ruins in the field.

"Well, yes," Windelm said, nodding, "but you've played in tough courses before and you can do it again. Don't let your emotions get to you."

"Uh-huh…right," said Brenner tremulously.

Windelm twisted his head to the side and said quietly, "Did you… happen to bring that Alacritus potion I gave you? From Vale Adorna?"

"The Alacritus potion?" Brenner repeated, thinking. "No…" he said, remembering the vial was still in his backpack, and all the way back at Valoria. "I wish I did."

"Not to worry," said Windelm, reaching into his robes. "I have a spare bottle here." He pulled out a glass flask with blue and green bits swirling inside.

"Is this allowed?"

"Sure. It's just for your mind. Not a steroid. But it only works if you focus your attention on one task. Go ahead."

Brenner looked from Windelm to the multitudes of people in the arena…to the special box of sovereigns…back to Gemry…then closed his eyes, focusing on the glowbes that would soon flit across the field.

He opened his eyes.

Windelm passed him the vial. "Remember, take one task at a time. And if anything, your entrance Agilis test was probably as hard as this."

Brenner uncorked the vial and drank; the liquid coursed down his throat, tasting faintly of green tea, he thought.

Brenner felt like his vision narrowed. He became less aware of the crowd chanting on all sides…the food vendors shouting in the aisles…"Thanks, Windelm."

"I'm here to help. Now, go get those glowbes."

Brenner nodded, then turned, and flew back to the Pegasi carrier.

"Feeling better?" Gemry asked.

"Yeah, I think so."

"Good." She leaned in and gave him a peck on his cheek. "Be amazing as I know you are."

His face flushed with warmth, and then the two reluctantly drew apart. "Thanks, Gemry."

She pulled out her mircon. "It's about time I joined the fans. Maverick and Finnegan said they'd save me a spot in the Valoria section, which, judging from the riotous volume there," she thumbed her finger backward, "I'd say it's safe to guess they're excited to see you play."

Brenner looked up, seeing a wave of emerald supporters. Wider in their green section of the stadium than a concert he'd once seen at Red Rocks in Colorado, the fans were singing an anthem:

"We fly fastest and longest,
We shoot and stun every foe,
We are greenest and strongest:
For we are SIL-VA-LO!"

"Agilis players," an official called in a loud voice that echoed across the whole stadium, "please head to the start of the course."

"That's my queue," said Gemry, hovering. "One last thing, Brenner: be sure you beat that punk sorcerer, Rodick."

Brenner smiled. "If I can, I will."

Gemry flew off to the Silvalo section, and he sat back in his seat.

"Ready, Brenner?" Caster Greaves said, reins in hand.

"Let's do it."

Caster Greaves shook the reigns, and the Pegasi flew from midfield toward the far side of the stadium, where the three other Agilis players were touching down.

"Officials," Sovereign Drusus commanded, "add landform seeds, and release the glowbes."

Peering over the side of the carriage, Brenner watched as five officials flew through the course, adding seeds that brought the land to life, while others opened chests, and seven bright white glowbes shot through the field, crossing over the flowing river, growing forests, islands, marble ruins, before hovering to the perimeter. One zoomed to the far side, stopping over a thin band of something a dull iron. *Interesting,* Brenner thought, *the glowbes were forming a six-sided Star of David pattern across the field...with the seventh glowbe flying to the middle, over the ruins.*

"Each of the four players," Sovereign Drusus said when the glowbes and land had settled, "will receive a prize for making it to the finals of Agilis, and that prize increases for every glowbe captured. The spellcaster who catches the most of the seven glowbes will be the champion."

Greaves' team of Pegasi touched down on an elevated platform, and Brenner jumped out, casting a glance at the other three players, who were pacing around the starting circle. Because of the height of the platform— about eighty feet—Brenner was afforded a decent view of the nearly three-mile stadium.

He turned back, and the combatants met his eyes briefly. A searing intensity radiated from Rodick, his long, blond hair pulled back above his dark blue attire and thick arms. An amulet with blue and red elixir hung around his neck. The orange-clothed teen from Arenaterro, Armin, bronze skinned and brown-eyed, gave Brenner a dismissive huff, while the girl from Vispaludem, Jace, who sported a violet cloak beneath her pure black hair, gave the curtest of nods. An attendant approached Brenner with an open chest. Brenner deposited his mircon, and the man closed the lockbox, then bowed and returned to the edge of the platform. Having grown accustomed to flight and his spells, Brenner felt different...naked... without the mircon. To refocus, he swung his arms, then balanced on one foot and stretched a quad.

"Officials, unleash the creatures."

There was a savage grumble, and from the center of the marble ruins burst an enormous snake, as thick as a semi-truck and longer than three of them from its tip to its tail.

"Should've guessed there'd be a landwurm..." said Jace to his left.

Coiling around one of the marble structures beneath a glowbe, the land-wurm opened its cavernous mouth, sounded a devilish roar that muffled into a hiss, before lowering its grey, scaly neck, camouflaged against the stone pillars.

A loud splash came from the river ahead, and a group of officials quickly backed away from water. While he couldn't see anything besides frothing bubbles on the surface, Brenner knew *something* was gliding in the river now. More noises came from the jungle below them. Then a shiver pulsed down his neck as a piercing roar and a flicker of orange erupted from the furthest end of a field.

I have to play against a dragon. With no mircon. He shook his head and gave a nervous laugh. He took a deep breath, and words he'd read or heard somewhere floated to the front of his mind... *It always seems impossible until it's done.* He let the air out. *There must be a way.*

He scanned the field for all seven glowbes. The island glowbe was central and closest; he could go for that first, then separate from the group and pick a side for two more...

"Lastly," said Drusus, "begin the repulsion process."

Officials came to three sides of the middle island, where a glowbe hovered. They threw down shimmering rocks into the waters—immediately a gushing noise like geysers erupting filled the stadium, and three reverse-waterfalls sprayed upward fifty-some feet, cloaking the island behind water-jets. The dense mist from them shrouded the middle of the field. If he weren't about to race through danger, Brenner would have enjoyed sitting and marveling at the wide water-columns shooting upward like grand fountains. The forest was almost done growing now, with several trees sprouting branches right up to and beyond the starting platform.

"Spellcasters, await your signal," Drusus said with solemnity, then rotated to speak to the crowds. Brenner's amulet pulsed with warmth against his chest. "Fellow Ganthreans, you have the pleasure of seeing this year's final match of Agilis. May the best athlete win." He spun in a circle, eyes resting on the four spellcasters. "Begin!"

There were two sets of stairs that rose up to the starting platform on either side, and while Jace and Armin raced down them, Brenner and Rodick leaped forward into the boughs of the tree canopy. Rodick then slid down his trunk until he could jump down to the ground, but Brenner took the high road, bounding like a panther across the giant limbs from tree to tree.

While he jumped through the canopy, he caught glimpses of the race below: the other three Agilis players ran ahead of him, elbowing each other when they came too close, Rodick lashing out with kicks.

They were getting too far ahead. Brenner started to clamber down to catch them when he heard deep, angry snorts.

"Ah!" someone yelled ahead.

He climbed to the bottom bough of the oakbrawn—then a dense pack of warthogs stampeded through the undergrowth. Busting through bushes, snorting, and tearing up dirt, the tusked-animals circled and charged back. Brenner reversed course, keeping to his route in the trees.

Less than a minute later, he saw Armin and Rodick sprinting sideways through the bushes, the sounder of warthogs rushing right after them, eyes raging red. Only when the players climbed trees and began racing along the boughs did the warthogs snort angrily and end the hunt.

Through the jungle-tops the players progressed, the roar of the reverse-waterfalls growing louder, until the forest thinned, and Brenner scaled down one of the maple trunks. The warthogs appeared to be gone.

Across the river, on the big island, Brenner could make out the pulsating white glowbe behind the upward coursing waterfalls. There were three small openings around the island that would likely be the best routes. Looking up and down the riverbank, he noticed something else: four slim boats a ways down on the bank…and further away, a cluster of rocky rapids that could be used to jump across the river.

He made a dash for the boat, but Armin and Jace suddenly burst from the jungle ahead of him, shoving one another. Armin pushed a boat into the water and hopped into it, pulling a paddle from below the gunwale and making deep strokes toward the island. Jace got a boat, too—and, looking scornfully back at Brenner, pushed the third boat hard into the water. The current quickly carried it downstream. That left one vessel.

Brenner ran the final fifty yards to the last boat, put a hand on it to heave it into the river, when sudden movement to his right caught his attention: Rodick body-slammed into him like a hockey player, rocketing Brenner off his feet.

"Feels good, don't it?!" Rodick yelled, then seized the fourth boat.

In a daze, Brenner scrambled to his feet. Rodick had just pushed off shore and was about to paddle when a tentacle slapped the water in front of him. Rodick shook his head, turned back to shore, and abandoned his boat, which floated downstream. He ran to the rapids on the right side.

Brenner had two options: chase after and fight Rodick to jump across the rapids, or swim through the river. The fight held zero appeal: he'd either lose the fight, or waste time and lose a glowbe. And the swim—he saw Armin was now using his paddle to both steer and fend off a tentacle—would be madness.

Those were both terrible. *What else can I do?*

He looked left. There was a glowbe past the water, but no rapids, and no stepping stones. The river channel was fifty to a hundred feet across: too far to jump. *But could I...run?* He remembered how his earliest attempt to run on water had ended in failure. *But today...I have the Alacritus potion.*

Grunting startled him from behind. Out of the bushes stomped a smelly warthog...and then another. He bolted left along the river, the herd crashing behind him. Bounding over roots, ferns and rocks, Brenner thought, *if Windelm could do it...it's possible!*

He brought to mind a nature documentary he'd seen long ago, with a green basilisk lizard running across the surface of a stream.

He pumped his legs hard, gaining speed as he made a cutting curve toward what he hoped was the narrowest section of the river. The tusks of the warthogs scraped rocks behind him. He was at a full out sprint. *Focus—on—speed.* Here came the last grasses, the sand, the edge, and then—

Like a thrown pebble, he was skimming across the surface.

His only thought was to keep moving: *be the wind across the water.*

The dark river blurred. His peripheral vision saw something slap the water, but he kept pumping his feet, the other side approaching—twenty feet—ten feet—five feet—solid ground—*made it!*

His amulet radiated heat and magic against his chest; far above, the crowd chanted; he panted, incredulous; somehow only his back and boots were wet. Then his goal came back into focus, and he ran toward the first glowbe.

While he wouldn't have to navigate around a reverse-waterfall to get the white glowbe in this clearing, it wouldn't be a cake-walk, either. The pulsing glowbe was hovering over the middle of a pit, black-as-night. And there were no trees, bridge, or rope around to assist him.

That left Brenner with a very long jump. Steeling himself, and pumping his legs into another sprint, he tore across the land to the abyss, then at the edge of the pit pushed off with all his might—time seemed to slow as he vaulted up, over darkness; just before mid-arc he hit the glowbe with his right hand, then, with arms and legs wind-milling, he descended down... down...and landed at the earthen edge of the other side, rolling into a somersault to reduce the impact. His body tumbled to a stop. His captured glowbe changed, and now shimmered green.

Vaguely, he could hear the rumbling applause from the crowd. He climbed a hill, and looked across the terrain: Jace had made it to the island before Armin, gotten past the reverse waterfall, and now that glowbe pulsed violet; on the far side, Rodick must have snagged a glowbe as well, as it shimmered blue. *Three glowbes taken…four left.*

He hustled forward. While he couldn't see the others as he rushed past trees, he sensed that all four were converging into the middle obstacle of the field: the stone ruins. Like the skeleton of a crumbled city, there were marble beams criss-crossing together above rows of colonnades, frames of pyramids, and pillars that looked like strands of DNA coiled on the ground. Although large, the ruins wouldn't have been too hard to climb through, if it wasn't for the giant wurm that was lying dormant… somewhere in the labyrinth.

Brenner entered the ruins from the left, and heard the footsteps and crumbling rock as the others entered off to his right. Jumping over a raised section of pillars, he made the mistake of trying to use a beam as a step. His foot slipped on its polished surface, and he landed hard on his side. A dull ache spread along his waist.

As he lifted himself up, he heard what sounded like tree trunks snapping, and then the ground shook.

Up ahead, columns smashed down into one another, causing clouds of dust that masked the field. He hastened to his feet and continued weaving through the ruins. He heard his opponents gaining ground ahead of him.

Dodging around fallen columns, Brenner advanced to the middle ruins, when out from the dust-cloud a wurm-coil came whipping at him. Brenner ducked—and it whistled over his head and smashed into a row of pillars, shattering them as if they were nothing more than bowling pins.

Brenner followed the outline of the thick coil another hundred feet until he saw the ferocious head of the landwurm. With yellow fangs bared, its dusty face looked like a wrathful cobra.

His opponents were near its head, in a triangle. They dodged in sync with the lunging head of the landwurm, getting closer and closer to the white glowbe pulsing behind the beast. Brenner climbed past rubble toward them, keeping one eye on the monster's tail, as every few seconds it whipped through the ruins, attempting to flatten him.

I could try to get this glowbe, thought Brenner, *but the odds aren't good: 1-in-4, plus potential death by landwurm...* With three other glowbes uncontested—by players, anyway—Brenner decided to pursue an outer glowbe, and raced to the edge of the ruins, out of the landwurm's territory, and not a moment too soon.

A cry of panic pierced the air—Brenner looked over his shoulder. The Arenaterro player, Armin, lay trapped under a marble column. Seeing a meal pinned beneath the rocks, the landwurm slithered away from its glowbe. Brenner was about five hundred yards away—there was no way he could get there in time to help.

"Over here!" Brenner said, hoping to draw its attention. The beast paused. But then with a shrill hiss from its reptilian mouth, it turned, reared back, and dove down—devouring Armin in two sickening crunches.

Brenner's eyes bulged. He felt sick. Yet somehow Rodick and Jace continued full tilt, grappling with each other to gain the center glowbe while the landwurm was distracted.

There was nothing else for Armin now. Brenner tried blocking the image from his mind. He jumped through the last passageway of columns, and then the stench of rotten mushrooms hit him.

Oozing, speckled marshland covered much of the next section. He walked to the edge of the muddy blob and put a foot in it—it squished, sucking his heel. He yanked his foot out. *Yikes...it's like quicksand.* Quickly Brenner climbed back onto a marble column, surveying the field. There were marshlands with far-flung glowbes to his left or right, or a thin, center isthmus running through the quicksand. Past it, the dragon guarded the seventh and last glowbe. Brenner wanted to take the isthmus, but it didn't have what he needed: a second glowbe.

He jumped down and ran left on the edge of dry land, searching for a route through the marsh. No trees…no big boulders…*but what were those?* Faint circles flickered in the bog as he ran past. He smiled. *Stepping stones.* They seemed to be magicked so that they only lit up when he came within twenty feet of them. When he passed, they dulled and blended back into the marsh.

Brenner heard Jace and Rodick scrambling over the ruins behind him, and knew he had to move fast. He drew on the elixir in his amulet, magnified his speed and jumped out to catch the next bright stepping-stone. As he came to land on it, three others lit up, and he hopped between them like burning coals.

The path of stones continued deeper into the soggy marsh, then forked. He had a split-second to decide: the left route coiled—*was it a dead-end?* Brenner banked hard right. A few jumps later the stones again divided, this time into three rock-paths. He couldn't afford to lose momentum by stopping, saw the center path aimed toward the glowbe—but then it disappeared into the bog.

He took the left path. Then Brenner panicked, as the stones arced away from his goal, growing further apart. He focused his mind: *one—jump—at—a—time.* Gradually, they spiraled back to the white glowbe, and at last rewarded him with a clear shot at it. He launched up and snatched it, then jumped through the last decision forks before escaping the stinking marsh.

Heart racing, he touched down on solid ground. He'd captured two glowbes. Brenner looked to his right, and saw Rodick sprinting to the last of the center isthmus, a blue glowbe floating behind in the ruins, while Jace jumped across stones in the far-right marsh, closing in on her glowbe.

That meant they were tied. *Whoever gets the final glowbe wins.*

Ahead, a roar and a stream of molten heat brought him back to the present. Now he simply had to outsmart and outmaneuver a dragon, which, as he knew about dinosaurs, was kind of like a Tyrannosaurus Rex, but with wide wings that flapped up dust devils, razor-tipped talons, and of course, a mouth filled with fire. He recalled what had happened with the last giant reptile.

Marshaling his courage, Brenner sped forward, closing the gap on Rodick, but was thrown off his feet by a tremor and sound of iron smashing rock—the dragon had stamped a clawed foot and triggered an earthquake. Pushing himself to his feet, Brenner again raced after Rodick through a stand of birch trees.

Waiting in the clearing up ahead, the dragon, armored in metallic, blood red scales, narrowed its vertical slitted eyes, snorted a black haze of smoke, and flattened its ears, ready to fight. Ringed around the dragon were maple trees and thick, marble columns. The two players wove through the birch tree grove, then right up to and past the circle of columns. The dragon wasted no time showing them its intentions: as Rodick and Brenner broke into its territory, it blew a jet of orange fire straight at the them, forcing them to retreat and dive for cover.

Rodick tumbled behind a stand of maples on the right; Brenner dashed behind a white column on the left. The dragon stomped toward Brenner, and the sound of iron scraping stone hit him. But before the dragon could cleave Brenner's marble column in two, it stopped.

Brenner peeked out. The dragon's wild eyes were still fixed on him, its scaly chest heaving, the fire inside recharging. He realized the only thing preventing the beast from diving at him was an iron band wrapped around its hind leg, which was anchored by a titanic chain to a stake in the middle of the clearing. Brenner estimated the dragon had about two hundred feet of movement around the center stake, above which hovered the final, frosted white glowbe.

To get it, he had to know the dragon's range—and what would trigger a reaction. Sprinting out from behind his column, Brenner pushed the limits of his elixir, running in a tight spiral around the creature.

But the dragon was not stupid. It only gave chase when Brenner came within reach—and was electrifyingly fast. Right around two hundred feet, it leapt at him, and if Brenner hadn't pulled out of the spiral immediately, the crushing jaws of the beast would have snapped him in two. He retreated to the far side of the ring, panting behind maple trees, watching Rodick to see what tactics he'd try against the red dragon.

Like a determined running back, Rodick charged out from the trees, then made a zig-zag pattern toward the center. But the dragon matched him move for move, and after a few close-calls, Rodick backtracked. As Brenner caught his breath, Jace ran to a stand of trees on Rodick's side.

Brenner realized a direct attack would never work. To win, he'd need to perform an intricate dance: pressing in, feinting back, and gradually gaining ground when the dragon was distracted with his opponents.

The dragon inhaled, its scaly stomach expanding to the size of a yacht, then it spewed a red-orange plume of fire, strafing twenty trees from Rodick over to Jace.

Rodick jumped through the blaze, and darted closer into the circle, while Jace blocked with a pillar, then ran counterclockwise into the clearing. The dragon zeroed in on Rodick, cutting off his access to the center. As Rodick feinted back, Brenner sprinted behind the beast—gaining half the distance to the glowbe before the dragon saw him out of the corner of its eye. It whirled around and charged toward Brenner, the ground quaking from its clawed tonnage. *No!* he thought, turning and sprinting back for his life.

A wave of fire flew over Brenner's shoulder; he cut away to the safety of the pillars, blood pounding in his ears, but the heat persisted. That's when Brenner realized his shirt was on fire. Beating his hands against it, he rolled to the ground, crying out. Dust and dirt whoomphed around him; it felt like he touched his shoulder to an oven's inner coil, until finally he smothered the flame. His shoulder stung, and an acrid smell surrounded him. He had lost his advantage, and nearly his life.

He walked to the pillar, forcing his attention back to the clearing, where Jace and Rodick looked on the verge of grabbing the glowbe. They had distracted the dragon on either side, cutting in and out from forty feet away; the dragon swerved its head back and forth, snapping its jaws in frustration. Then it blew a stream of fire at Rodick, who lunged over to

Jace's side. She pushed him away, pausing her run. The dragon turned to them both, reared up on its hind legs and whipped its thick-veined wings forward, generating a sudden squall that threw them airborne like seeds in a windstorm. It roared in triumph and trampled after them.

With the dragon's back to him, Brenner saw his window open. He pushed his pain aside, summoned his strength, and dashed to the center with all his speed.

Go!

Two hundred feet…one-fifty…a hundred…seventy…*misfortune.*

Jace and Rodick had escaped behind columns, and the dragon turned around, seeing Brenner darting toward the glowbe. In a thunderous fury, it crashed at Brenner on all fours, belly scraping against the ground as it opened its fanged mouth and gave a guttural roar.

The two sped headfirst at the middle, the ground crunching with each dragon stride. And suddenly Brenner knew the dragon would reach the glowbe first. But he was too close to pull away now.

Tilting his chest forward, Brenner lowered his center of gravity as he sprinted—like a king-cobra, the head of the dragon struck at him—and in that split-second, Brenner vaulted up as high as he could, front-flipping. He felt the tip of his boot hit its snout—a crunch of teeth gnashed beneath him—and then he was falling.

He wouldn't reach the glowbe.

Plummeting down onto the dragon's back, he saw the glowbe on the other side of the creature, and another figure sprinting full-out across the arena. Brenner landed in a sprawl on the hard scales of the dragon, cutting his hand. He shoved himself up, ran down the spine, through the wings— Rodick was racing from the other side unopposed, and would soon hit the glowbe first unless—

Brenner turned sideways off the dragon like he was running off a cliff, and dove for the glowbe. Rodick leaped forward, a hungry grin on his face.

But it was Brenner's outstretched fingers that skimmed against the glowbe first; it turned jade green; and midair Rodick collided into him with a loud *crack*. They fell to the ground in a heap as the dragon whirled around, jaws open.

Brenner tried scrambling to his feet to run, but knew, this time, he wouldn't be fast enough.

With a snarl, the dragon tore through the air at him—and a dozen white spells slammed into it. Brenner jumped back as the beast's head crashed to the ground, inches from where he'd been. Officials converged on the scene, shooting more spells at the dragon, until it became safely immobilized.

"Fans of Ganthrea," boomed out Sovereign Drusus from above, "we have our champion: from *Silvalo*, Brenner Wahlridge!"

He looked up, and the sounds of the arena came rushing back.

The cheers of the crowd rumbled in his chest.

He'd done it. He had won.

An official approached him, patting Brenner on the back and holding an arm forward. "This way if you please," he said, inviting Brenner, then Rodick and then Jace to follow him onto a stone dais that was, strangely, rising out of the ground. They jumped onto it, and then the granite tower shook and grew upward, like a lance pushing up through the cracked earth. Brenner felt like he was watching himself from above, the shock of winning overshadowing the dull pain coming from his hand and shoulder.

At the top of the pedestal, Sovereign Sorcerer Drusus alighted from the sky. "Although he did not live to the end of the final round," said Drusus to the crowd, "Armin Kandar from Arenaterro played bravely. Let us have a moment of reflection for that valiant player, lost while competing in the highest honor of Agilis."

The hundreds of thousands of fans stopped their shouts and chants. A peculiar calm swept over the stadium.

"Thank you," continued Drusus, then turned his attention to Jace and Rodick. "And for these two Agilis players, who tied for second with two glowbes apiece, we award their choice of two-hundred and fifty golders, or, admittance into their home government in the department of their choice. Jace?"

"I'll take leadership in Vispaludem," said Jace, "in the Department of Landform Planning." Drusus nodded at her, reached over to his side, and handed her a shimmering medal.

Rodick stepped forward. "I'll take the golders," he said, extending a hand.

Drusus nodded, and again reached down, giving him a large coin bag that looked to weigh at least five pounds.

"And for our champion, Brenner Walhridge, with three glowbes," Drusus said in a pleased voice, "the choice of five hundred golders, a place in Biome leadership, or an infusion of an elixir color."

An attendant flew to Drusus carrying a platter with a domed lid. Drusus took it, then pulled off the cover, revealing an elaborate golden platter, with seven bowls carved into its surface, each filled with a different rainbow color of the biomes, making the treasure appear like an artist's palette. "Brenner?" Drusus said, and he felt himself yanked back to reality. He didn't really want leadership yet, or know what he would do with that political power—so it came down to riches or more magic.

The five hundred golders looked very appealing. He could buy his mircon, and have some to help Gemry out, too…but when he considered what he was capable of now, and what might be unlocked with the addition of new elixir…he could always work to earn more money…

"I'd like the elixir, please," Brenner said, looking up at Sovereign Drusus.

"A fine choice," Drusus said in his arena voice, before reducing it for his next question. "And which color?" He looked at the swirling green and red amulet hanging from Brenner's neck. "Do you want to add to the colors you have, or gain a different source?"

Brenner gazed at the seven shimmering colors on the golden platter… recalling a passage from the book he had read about Elixirs, and which of them boosted mental magic, ingenuity, and persuasion…

"Blue elixir, please."

"Very well," Drusus said, then amplified his voice, "Supporters, please

355

enjoy the seven-colored fireworks, and the musical talents of the Silvalo Strings and Singers." He waved his hand at waiting attendants on the sides of the arena, and immediately fountains of fireworks shot from the sides, flying heavenward and bursting into shimmering colors and animated pictures above—red roses waving in the wind, purple and blue sailboats racing into the clouds, and yellow winged aviamirs that flew around the stadium before vanishing.

Music accompanied the magical fireworks, beginning with low base notes and surged into a mixture of the finest string sounds Brenner had ever heard, reminding him of crescendos in Beethoven's Ninth Symphony.

While the celebration of sights and sounds engulfed the stadium, Sovereign Drusus turned to Brenner and asked, "Would you like the blue elixir channeled into a new amulet, or would you like to see if it can be added to your amulet?"

Brenner hesitated, and Drusus added, "If I pour the elixir into your amulet, it will enhance your abilities, but, since it has two elixirs already, they could repel the new one, breaking your amulet and leaking out in the process. I will try and stop that before too much is lost."

Brenner looked over at Rodick, noticing his blue and red amulet... *I could be even faster than him, and produce superior spells...if I just...*

"Please...add it to the amulet."

"As you wish."

Drusus muttered an incantation to himself, pointing his mircon at the blue swirling bowl, and the elixir floated out like a gaseous vapor, and over to Brenner's amulet. He flinched.

The blue elixir spilled into the amulet, and as it did, he felt it growing warmer—*would it accept or repel the new elixir?* The amulet vibrated, as if in protest, then settled. Drusus slowed the decanting, his cautious eyes flicking from the source bowl to Brenner's; presently, when the blue elixir continued trickling in without complications, Drusus expedited the spell, and a great torrent of blue magic cascaded into Brenner's amulet. Then it was complete.

"Your blue elixir, freshly sourced from Aquaperni, now at your command." Drusus said, a smile hinting behind his red beard. "Use it well."

Brenner held his amulet in his hand, marveling at how the reds, greens and blues swirled around one another, but never mixed. The amulet felt only a tad heavier, but when he rested it on his chest, he felt lighter.

With a swell, the orchestra finished their symphony, and the crowd applauded. Sovereign Drusus presented the winners to the jubilant fans once more, and then a white robed official held open a metal chest to each of the three. They collected their mircons. As they turned to go, Jace said, "Good game, Brenner."

"You too, Jace. And good luck in your new position."

Rodick merely scowled at them, clearly disappointed he hadn't won.

Brenner cast his *Volanti* spell and, with less effort than before, flew to find Gemry, Finnegan, Windelm, and Sherry in the stands.

An hour later, after they had flown over the stadium and decided on where to have a celebratory feast—Finnegan had again insisted they go to Hutch & Sons for the afterparty apres—Brenner finally felt his nerves settle from the day. Sherry had sent a healing spell at his shoulder, and the skin closed together around his burn wound.

While munching on a ciabatta roll and sipping a refreshing lemon drink with his two friends and great uncle and aunt, he shared his thoughts of the match and listened to theirs—"I nearly bit my fingers off when you flipped over the dragon," Sherry was saying. "I don't know what you were thinking!"

"I felt like that at the beginning," said Brenner, "anxious, jittery...my nerves were all over the place." He turned to Windelm. "But thanks to that potion you gave me, I felt calmer and more focused for the rest of the match."

Windelm chuckled in a bemused sort of voice. "That Alacritus potion before the game?"

"Yeah. Thanks for having me try some."

"Oh, you don't have to thank me for that."

"Huh? Why not?"

"Because," said Windelm, "It wasn't anything more than tea leaves, water, and blue food-dye."

Chapter Twenty-Five

Wizard's Gambit

Having lived through the Finals of Agilis, Brenner no longer felt as queasy playing under the wave of sound and chants of the spellcaster crowds, which was good, because the Zabrani Championship between Silvalo's Valoria and Montadaux's Boldenskeep was hosted in Arborio's professional stadium, Evermax, which held five hundred thousand fans—according to Finnegan, anyway—packed in hexagon sections of the stadium that rose hundreds of feet high.

When Brenner and the team arrived to the interior of the stadium the afternoon of the seventh Games Day, the sight of fans flitting upward and downward, their hands full of greasy turkey legs and salted potatoes, flying some four hundred feet to family-sized honeycombs completed the resemblance to a massive beehive.

After Brenner and his teammates looked over the grand arena, their captain, Maverick, led them away from the field and through arched hallways to what Brenner could safely say was the most unique locker room he'd ever been in. Individual cubbies lined the perimeter of the large common room, and in the middle were two pools: one a cool, deep blue, and the other a bubbling, inviting hot tub. Attached to the main locker room were numerous chambers with personalities of their own: one filled with tall windows and glowing crystals, another with exotic ferns and plush grass, the next had ice caked on the windows and a closed door that appeared to be frozen shut, another had warm sand and ample light streaming from a charged glowbe and, finally, a room with rows of vats filled with brown slop that Brenner hoped was just mud.

"Francesca," called out Haggerty, "if we win, how's about you and me take a dip in the renewal pool?"

Francesca rolled her eyes and made a face that clearly said not-in-your-wildest-dreams, before replying, "I would say yes, if only to force you to take your first bath."

The rest of the team laughed.

"So, that's a yes then?" Haggerty replied, undeterred.

"Haggerty," called Maverick, "How's about you stop hitting on your teammates an hour before the most important game of your life?"

Haggerty went silent at the admonition. Brenner looked from the spa to Gemry, who seemed to read his mind, and gave him a shake of her head.

"As this is the professional arena, Evermax, there's one team room. But we will take shifts in the antechambers to give privacy to Zabrani teammates. Lady knights, you get the common room first. Guys, pick a Stimulus Chamber to prepare for the game, and don't come out for ten minutes, until I give the word. If you so much as put a toe out of the chambers, I will use a shocking spell on you from one foot away. Also, I don't recommend the Ice Chamber until after the game—we don't want you frozen stiff. Alright, get moving."

The teen boys obliged and each headed to a chamber. Brenner chose the green foliage chamber, and found a free spot to lie down on the wave-like grass, which wriggled against his back like silken tentacles of a starfish he had once touched at an aquarium. He closed his eyes in relaxation, and readied himself for the game. Presently, he heard Maverick's voice summon the boys from their chambers. Then the girls rotated, taking their turns in the antechambers, and Brenner changed into his uniform.

When all the Zabrani teammates were changed into their deep green

With uniforms, the healers and king in their capes, they met in the middle common room, and Maverick discussed strategy.

"Alright," he said, "Boldenskeep's known for their strong accuracy and aggressive surges. So, we need to divide into five squads of four to be ready for unusual or improbable attack routes. Also, they excel at maneuvering around the midfield mountains, so my plan is to create a buffer zone of a long lake between mountains and the forests of our territory—that way they'll have to make one surge at a time, which we can counter."

Most of the team nodded at this, but while Maverick was the official Zabrani captain, they also frequently looked to Brenner. Some teammates were elbowing each other—"Ask it, Lucas!"—"Why don't you?"—"Come on!"

"Alerio! Lucas!" Maverick said in vexed tone, "Do you follow or not? What are you jabbering about?"

"We were just wondering," said Lucas, "What does our Agilis champion think of this?"

Maverick turned a little red at the interruption, but decided to hear what Brenner might say. "Well then?"

Put on the spot, Brenner felt embarrassed. Nevertheless, he shared what was on his mind: "If Montadaux makes aggressive surges…wouldn't it be good to have a few covert guards hidden at the base of the midfield mountains, to shoot their backs when they pass by?"

His teammates murmured, and more than a few nodded.

"Not a bad strategy, Brenner," Maverick said, turning their attention back to himself. "Miggens and Brutnick, you each take a hidden alcove on each end of the mountains. Don't fire until the opponents are well past you; the other two players in your squad can patrol around the lake."

Shortly, Maverick finished explaining the rest of his game plans, and a reminder to fly in groups of three or more over water. The team formed a line, and walked from the locker room through a torch-lit tunnel. As they approached the arena entrance to Evermax, the low buzz from the crowd grew louder, at first like chattering in the background, but as they came to the sun lit entrance, it sounded like an entire army shouting in the build up to battle.

In front of Brenner, some of the players rubbed their fingers together, looking at one another with nervous glances. As they crossed the threshold into the arena, the chants, singing, and shouts of the crowd became a tumultuous crescendo. Following Maverick's lead, the team flew from the dusty entrance at midfield across half of the formless field to their stone tower. As he flew with his Zabrani team, Brenner's eyes widened at the mass of supporters packed around the stadium: everywhere he looked, more and more fans were sandwiched together, from ground level all the way up to the top of the combs.

Brenner also noticed silver platforms floating in the air—twenty or thirty of them, staggered at different heights all around the field. *Hmm…this might change Montadaux's strategy…*

The team assembled on the upper turret of their tower, an intimidating structure ten stories high, and looked across the massive field. In the far distance, Brenner could just make out flying red figures, about the size of moltifrute balls, descending down to the opposite tower: his opponents, the Montadaux Knights.

"Sorcerers, mages, and spellcasters of all of Ganthrea," boomed a voice from high in the stands, as a green robed wizard floated from the upper catacombs of the stadium, "Welcome to the final Zabrani match between Montadaux and Silvalo. Zabrani kings of Boldenskeep and Valoria Academies, come forward to establish your landforms."

Maverick and the Boldenskeep king flew to the middle, as the wizard floated down to intercept them. Soon rugged mountains erupted from midfield, and Maverick used all the water seeds to create a deep lake at the foot of their side, stretching several hundred feet toward them, then prairie grasses, then he blanketed the last third of their territory with seeds that quickly grew into gnarled oakbrawns, tall willows, and thick Douglas firs.

Another moment, and the creation of forest, prairie, lake and mountains was complete.

"Where do you want to station the three glowbes?" a knight by Maverick asked.

Maverick pressed his lips together, then responded, "This game, we are not splitting the glowbes."

"Why not?" Gemry asked him, frowning.

"Montadaux is our strongest opponent. We need a couple blockades, and then a strong concentration in one area, with our glowbes, to withstand a surge and maintain control."

Maverick ordered the glowbes positioned at the top of their tower, with two sentries by them, and another squad of six making the perimeter defensive ring a hundred yards out. Aside from Maverick, the twelve remaining players divided into four squads, two for each side of their territory, ready to block. Most annoyingly, Brenner was ordered into a separate squad from Gemry. Brenner also felt like Maverick was making a mistake to focus on hanging back, that they were practically welcoming a surge. But he didn't want to appear arrogant, so said nothing.

"Zabrani teams take your positions!" the announcer called from above the mountains. Above their team on the tower, magical vapors appeared, giving their starting score of 0.

The team fanned on all sides of the tower, shields and mircons ready, legs tensed to launch. He didn't like that he would be in a different squad than Gemry. Brenner looked again to the silver floating platforms, scattered through the sky like tiny, flattened moons. They seemed to be hovering on three different levels in the air—the lowest were the heights of church steeples, the mid-range as tall as airport control towers, and the highest discs at levels of skyscraper observation decks. An idea came to Brenner, which would allow him to keep an eye on Gemry, and plan for eventual attack.

"BEGIN!"

His teammates shot *Arcyndo* spells across the field—hoping a few would get past the midfield mountains and score an early hit; most flew down to the trees, skimming the tops as they split into five groups: the largest as the defensive ring, two to push right, and two to push left.

Brenner, however, broke ranks. He flew to the closest floating disc, a low-tiered one about a hundred feet above the field. From there, he paused, able to see over the mountain ridge, watching at the edge as the majority of Boldenskeep's knights flew on the right side of their territory toward the middle mountains. They were indeed making a surge. If he pushed himself, he could get to a higher disc ahead, past the middle of Valoria's territory. He brought his shield in front of himself, then thought, "*Volanti.*"

Air rushed through his sandy-blonde hair as he flew over the forest and prairie below, to a larger disc hovering at the secondary level. He skittered on top of it and quickly flattened himself.

Below, he heard the pulses of spellfire crashing into the mountains and trees, as each side vied for possession of the midfield mountains. He looked ahead: there were no red knights on the discs to his right, or above him…and then he saw movement on the far left of the field, on the first level of discs—below him. A knight had just landed on the floating platform and was firing brazenly at the green squads near the lake. Brenner raised his mircon. He had to make a decision: shoot now and reveal his position to the enemy—as the rest of the red players were still flying up the mountain like currents of wind—or keep his position secret for access to more targets later.

He lowered his mircon. It pained him, holding back his shot when he could help his team now, but he felt it would pay off with more stuns later. He laid low, keeping his shield in front so that the red knight on the other disc could not hit him, and, through a narrow slit between shield and disc, trained his mircon on the enemy player, ready to fire.

Brenner tensed and waited long minutes, while Boldenskeep surged over the left hills diagonally below him…the red knight knight kept firing from his disc to the ground green knights, unaware of Brenner above…

Then, his patience paid off: a cluster of red knights moved from the top of the midfield mountain, down to the base of the lake, firing heavily at Valoria. While boulders protected them from direct, frontal shots, their backsides—and heads—were completely exposed to Brenner in the air above.

Brenner waited for a second red regiment to get into range, but just as he was about to fire, the other aerial knight happened to look up—and saw Brenner's shield.

"Arcyndo!" Brenner thought quickly, loosening three spell-bolts toward the disc knight. The first shot was absorbed by the boy's shield, but the other two sizzled into his torso and legs before he could move it again, immobilizing him. Then shouts of alarm rang out from below: Brenner had been seen.

Let's rain fire, Brenner thought, swiveling his mircon down at the regiment of red knights huddled below by a boulder, and sending a barrage of spells into the cluster.

Thankfully, he hit two targets, and stunned the legs of the next, but this squad was smarter than others. Immediately, the surrounding teammates scattered like cockroaches to nooks in the hillside, casting *Arcyndo* spells pell-mell at the floating discs in the sky. That meant not all knew where he was.

In their confusion, Brenner flew to another disc. This secondary-level platform straddled the midfield mountains, so that he could see both sides of the colossal field. He flattened to it, and could see each team's tower with score pulsing above.

Silvalo had taken an early lead, 7 – 2.

He scrutinized his opponents' territory. Boldenskeep had a unique land formation: at the base of the midfield mountains on their side, a narrow valley separated the next section of hills, rising up a quarter way into Boldenskeep's territory like camel humps, with a dark blue waterway arcing through them, which flowed straight into the back half of their field, before finally wrapping around a miniature island, which stood out of the water like the eye of a long blue needle. The Boldenskeep tower was a bit further beyond the island. After the hills, there was a swath of trees, and then in both back corners, symmetrical rock crags connected endwall to the sidewall, fortifying the corners. From the faint red light emanating from behind the crags, Brenner concluded that that was where they stationed their glowbes…likely two on one side, and one on the other.

Then spells slammed into his shield, ringing out loud, metallic tings.

He scooted back from the ledge as more spells rocketed from below and shot past him like fireworks.

"Got one in the sky!" came a shout from below.

Judging from where the spells hit his disc, Brenner surmised there were two clusters of red knights firing on him: one on the far side of the mountain range, the other from the squad he had just broken up. It would be futile to return fire when both groups were shooting his platform with all the spells they could muster.

He looked back to his side…a white caped healer was advancing with green knights—*that must be Gemry.* She pointed to Brenner's position, motioned something to her squadmates, then pointed to another floating platform above the midfield mountains. *There was no one on that, was there?*

His teammates opened fire on the platform, and then Brenner understood: they were using the angle. Their spells hit the underside of the disc, and bounced down at sharp slants over the midfield mountains, right into the enemy squad.

And thankfully, it worked.

The barrage of spells against Brenner halted momentarily, giving him a brief window to fly back to safe territory, to a first level platform on the right side of the lake.

"Lake knights, charge midfield with me!" Maverick shouted below him, capitalizing on their momentum.

A second green platoon of knights flew up the side of the mountain—right into the nest of Boldenskeep fighters.

"Wait!" Brenner called down, but it was too late.

The squad of four flew up the side of the mountain, and immediately were stunned by knights hidden on the other side. Brenner cringed. With their king, Maverick, stunned, they just gave their opponents 20 points.

He looked across the field to the distant tower, and sure enough, Boldenskeep had just gone up from 2 to 30. *They must have gotten a healer then, too.* That meant only two healers were left for Valoria.

Another green squad of reinforcements must have seen Maverick's group go down on the ridge, as they were now flying over trees, grasses, and then over the lake to give reinforcement, when a shower of red spells sparked from midfield down to the lake. Most of the green knights blocked with their shields, but Haggerty was caught off guard, stunned over deep water.

Brenner felt his heart rise into his throat. He'd seen this play out before.

The other flyers split formation once the shots came. But Haggerty had been the last of their group, so they didn't see him immobilized, then plunge down...his splash into the lake drowned out by pelts of spells hitting rocks.

Brenner wasn't about to let someone else die—let alone one of his teammates.

He spun the *Volanti* spell in his mind, and launched off the side of his platform, diving down to the middle of the lake, spells sizzling past his legs. The white bubbles around Haggerty's impact site were now fading... Brenner braced himself. He shifted his mircon to his shield hand, saw the dark outline of Haggerty's body below the water, and dove after him.

The force of the impact jarred Brenner more than the cold water.

While his *Volanti* spell seemed to assist his swimming ability, stroking one-armed with a shield on was clumsy at best. A dark figure drifted ten feet below him. Pushing himself even harder, Brenner kicked his legs until he reached the sinking body of Haggerty. Haggerty was rigid, but his eyes flicked in fear. Slipping an arm around Haggerty's chest, Brenner turned, then kicked upward toward the light.

The dead weight of Haggerty slowed him immensely, and he still needed to push up the last ten feet to get back to the surface...Brenner's lungs were burning; he clenched his mouth tight against his body's desperate attempts to expel the carbon dioxide clogging his lungs... *nearly there, nearly at the surface.* Bubbles fled the corners of his mouth. His free arm thrashed madly to fight the pull of Haggerty.

The two broke from the water, and Brenner drew a desperate gasp. Then he reignited the flight spell, and with double the effort, pulled both himself and Haggerty from the water, frantically skimming toward the nearest shore. The sound of bullets piercing glass burst around them, as red spellfire ripped into the water.

You've got to be kidding me! Brenner thought angrily, as they flew toward the shore—his shield clanged with a direct hit, and Haggerty's body shuddered under the shots. The pebble shore came close—and then a spell hit Brenner's waist; he felt his grip on the flight spell slip, and the two flyers plummeted down.

THUD!

Just barely, they landed on the pebbled edge of the lake, frozen.

His body was crumpled in such a way that he faced midfield, and could see Haggerty next to him on the boundary of the lake: his legs in the water, his torso on the shoreline. *Come on buddy…get some air in there…*

Haggerty was still.

Brenner wanted to do more—turn him on his stomach, pump the water from Haggerty, anything. But all he could do was lay still and watch, like a felled tree.

And then a ragged jerk came over Haggerty's upper body, and he retched water from his mouth, exhaling and inhaling feverishly.

Brenner breathed a huge sigh. They were both stunned, but at least Haggerty would live to see the end of the match, even if it was a loss.

For several long moments, red and green spellfire blasted back and forth along the lake and mountains. It didn't look good for Valoria, as now the brunt of the battle was defensive.

Then, on the far edge of his vision, he saw two green spellcasters—one a knight, the other with cape, a healer—*Gemry!* The two flew down the midfield ridge and regrouped back towards the lake. Gemry scanned the area as she flew along the other shore, spotted the downed knights, and sent rejuvenation spells across the water. Fortunately, they were direct hits.

A surge of energy flowed up through Brenner's limbs. Haggerty sat upright.

"I..." he wheezed, "shot down in the lake...you..."

"You can thank me by heading for cover," Brenner said, as three red knights from the midfield mountains popped up and began shooting at them anew. Haggerty and Brenner made it to the edge of the forest as spells pelted the trees. Brenner chanced a look to the other rocky side of the lake—and with shock, saw Gemry and another knight struck down by *Arcyndo* spells. He made certain that they were immobilized on dry land, and breathing, before turning to Haggerty.

"We're in trouble," said Brenner. "We have to regroup and get a healer up here." Haggerty nodded, and they flew further back in their trees to a squad of Valoria knights stationed on defense.

"Nils," Haggerty shouted to the lead knight, "how is it back here?"

"Not good," Nils said sourly, "Not good at all. A red scouting party took out one of our defensive ring players. Unfortunately, it was a healer, Piltkins."

"Well just get Gemry or Dunn back to rejuvenate him," said Haggerty.

"We can't," said Brenner.

The two looked to him.

"What do you mean?" asked Haggerty.

Brenner pointed to the middle ridge. "I know there was a healer with Maverick that was shot at the midfield mountains...that must have been Dunn. And I just saw our other healer, Gemry, get stunned."

The other two let out groans.

"No healers?!" said Haggerty. "We're screwed. Montadaux still has two, which means they'll soon be at full strength."

Nils looked equally crestfallen.

"Have they gotten a glowbe of ours?" Brenner asked.

"No," said Nils, "our defensive ring held back their first advance."

"Well," Brenner said slowly, remembering something Finnegan had once said was ludicrous. "I have an idea then."

"Share it quick," said Nils, "'cause our tower sentries just signaled that more red knights are coming over the mountain. They're preparing for a final surge."

"I need three knights with me," said Brenner.

"Then we won't have enough to hold our defense."

"We're not playing defense anymore."

Nils scrunched his eyebrows together. "You don't mean to—"

"I do," said Brenner. "Wizard's Gambit."

His teammates looked as though they were watching a madman propose a mutiny.

"It hasn't been tried in over fifty years," said Nils, "You're crazy."

"It's our only shot," said Brenner, "otherwise they'll just whittle us down one at a time. We can either finish on their terms—or on ours."

Haggerty finally found his voice: "I'm not thrilled about it, but this crazy guy just saved me from death. He can lead as he sees fit."

"Thanks," Brenner said. "Nils? What do you think?"

Nils' frown slowly let up; he nodded a fraction of an inch. "Go ahead."

"Right then," said Brenner, "cover me while I go back to the tower."

He turned, hovered, and flew with arms forward to their tower, dodging tree branches along the way. Soon he was there, arcing up the back of the tower, and came to the top—he saw their score, 13—and two sentries standing by the glowbes. One had pointed his mircon at Brenner's chest; the other gave him a confused look.

"Why are you—"

"New gameplan," said Brenner between breaths. "Starts now. Your names?"

"Lucas," said a stocky, black haired guy.

"Alerio," began the second, who looked like a blond scarecrow, "but we were commanded to—"

"No time," said Brenner. "Maverick's stunned. All healers, too. Come with me, and stay as low as possible."

"What do you think you're doing with the glowbes?" one asked him, clearly agitated, as Brenner grabbed the three glowbes and cradled them with his mircon arm.

"Wizard's Gambit. And we need to go *now* before they realize the glowbes are gone."

"What?" said Alerio. "No one from Silvalo has ever pulled off a Wizard's Gambit at a Ganthrean Game."

"I told you, we're out of healers, and our king is stunned. We're going to lose soon in a war of attrition. Do you have a better option?"

Lucas and Alerio looked at each other—in the distance, Brenner heard the Boldenskeep knights shooting against the last strong squad of green knights. The two reluctantly shook their heads.

"Then it's settled," said Brenner. "Now, follow me."

He strode to the back of the tower, so hopefully any Boldenskeep scouts watching wouldn't see him leaving with the glowbes, and then dove head-first down—*Volanti*. The two knights flew at his heels.

Now, let's see if this actually works.

The trio whipped down the stone tower, past the rustling leaves of the tree line to the base of the forest, and then Brenner zoomed forward, snaking through the air around thick trunks.

Something bright was interfering with his vision.

He looked down and found that the three glowbes, held together against his chest, radiated green light, which undoubtedly made him a clear target.

He switched the glowbes from his right arm to his shield arm, and found that not only did the shield act as an extra support for keeping them in place, but it also cut down on the amount of green light radiating from the glowbes.

The trees began to thin, and Brenner saw Haggerty's fortification about a hundred feet away. Four green knights were engaged in spellfire with a larger Boldenskeep regiment across the lake.

"Haggerty!" Brenner called from the last stand of trees.

The older teen, back against a boulder as red *Arcyndo* spells zipped past him, looked over to Brenner.

"Tell your squad to veer left soon," Brenner said. "But you go with me."

Haggerty nodded, and while he was summarizing the order to his troop, Brenner turned to Alerio.

"You need to fly to the next disc above us."

Alerio's face fell. "You mean *that* one?" Alerio asked, pointing to a silver platform overhead, about twenty yards over the lake.

"Yes," said Brenner. "Sync it with Haggerty's movement, and you can make it. Once you're there, fly from disc to disc as able, and join us past the midfield mountains when you can. Hopefully we distract enough at ground level to give you some good shots."

Alerio looked less than thrilled with the order, but nodded.

"On my count!" Brenner heard Haggerty shout to his troop.

"Lucas," said Brenner, "get ready to fly hard around the right bank of the lake, as soon as Haggerty reaches us. But don't shoot."

"Wh—?"

"Troop disperse!" Haggerty shouted.

In a flurry, his group streaked left, firing across the lake as they did so. Simultaneously, Alerio flew past the canopy and up to the silver disc, and Haggerty flew to join Brenner.

"Now!" shouted Brenner. Lucas and he flew along the right perimeter of the lake, with Haggerty close on their heels.

As hoped for, the chaotic movement of the squad first diverted Boldenskeep's attention to Haggerty's troop speeding left, which sustained the bulk of the red spellfire, and while Alerio drew a few shots on his ascension, Brenner didn't see him plummeting. Alerio had made it to the superior vantage point. Their trio—Brenner, Lucas, and Haggerty—now rounded the final section of the lake, and only as they zipped past some crags at the base of the midfield mountains, did a few red spells flicker behind them.

"I told my squad to veer as far left as they could," Haggerty said, as the three got a few mouthfuls of air, "to buy us time."

"Good," said Brenner, "Okay, since they know we're here, we need to break apart again. Who would rather fight from the sky?"

"I'll give it a go," Haggerty said, catching Brenner by surprise. "As long as I'm over land, I don't mind making a target of myself."

"Thanks," Brenner said, looking at his routes up the ridge, searching for the biggest cracks. "Before Haggerty flies up, Lucas, you venture a little back to shoot from lake level, while I ricochet shots off the discs into the red encampment. That will give Haggerty cover to gain position."

"Got it," said Lucas.

Brenner nodded, and turned to the other knight. "Ready, Haggerty?"

Haggerty lifted his chin. "Ready to take down some Boldy Baldy's!"

"Okay," said Brenner. "Lucas, go."

Lucas zipped back boulder to boulder, soon signaling from near the lake.

"Okay…" Brenner said, waiting for a break in the spellfire…"*Now!*"

Brenner and Lucas burst-fired their *Arcyndo* spells from different angles, bouncing them off silver platforms, and causing a confused counter-fire from Boldenskeep's knights, while Haggerty flew skyward to a secondary disc.

"Lucas!" called Brenner between shots, "Keep giving cover, then join me on top!"

Red spells whistled past Lucas' boulder; he looked to Brenner and signaled with a nod that he understood.

Brenner paused his shots, and channeled his flight spell to speed him up through the crevices of the midfield mountain. By taking the shadowed route, he gained the advantage of surprise when he summited, shooting a look-out sentry and a red healer firing the other direction at Alerio, and then he skirted behind a rough-hewn boulder on the right. He shuddered as he saw a pile of stunned Valoria players not too far from him— Maverick's earlier surge. "Sorry guys," he said, checking to see if any needed emergency help. All were breathing, he was glad to see. Not being a healer, there wasn't much else he could do. He needed to press forward if they had any hope of winning.

Poking his head around one of the monoliths, he scanned Boldenskeep's territory. Both crags in the far back corners—where their glowbes were—looked to have three knights patrolling the tops…and the double hills across the river probably had guards, too.

As he was thinking of their next path, something cracked behind him, and he turned, ready to return fire—and nearly shot Lucas, who flew up next to him.

"Sorry," said Brenner, pointing his mircon down. "You're quick. Nice going back there."

"Thanks," panted Lucas. "There's one or two trailing behind me, so we'd best keep moving."

"Okay," said Brenner. "Let's hope Haggerty or Alerio gets close soon, or this next step isn't going to pan out so well." Pointing to the outpost on the hill across from them, he quickly explained his plan to Lucas.

They were just about to ricochet their *Arcyndo* spells off discs into the two-man outpost, when blasts from behind sizzled above their heads: they'd been discovered.

"Fly down!" shouted Brenner.

The two hurtled themselves down the crags into Boldenskeep's territory—as low as possible above the jagged outcroppings—and Brenner steered them to a cave next to the river. They skidded to a stop inside the dark opening.

"Hey, Jarik!" a voice called across the gorge. "Two by the river's edge!"

Red shots rained through the cave entrance, kicking up dust by their feet. *Jarik*…Brenner thought, stepping back, where had he heard that name?

The shots intensified, now coming from two directions: on the ridge above and behind them, and across the canyon from the hill.

Lucas looked imploringly at Brenner. "Any ideas?"

Brenner racked his brain…they needed to at least see the vantage point of their opponent…

"Give me your shield."

Lucas unslung it from his arm. Brenner set down his mircon and rested the three glowbes against the dark recess of the cave wall. Taking both shields, he moved toward the entrance, as *Arcyndo* spells continued to pelt through it. He held Lucas' shield from the base, turned it horizontal, then stuck it out from the wall so that his hand was still protected by rock. It clanged as though hail beat against it. Then he pushed his own shield underneath it, resting against it and the wall.

"Alright," said Brenner, "Now I need your help."

Lucas approached tentatively.

"See the opening between the shields?"

Red spells pelted above and to the side of the two shields, but between them was a triangular hole as small as an eye-patch, created by the shields and the cave wall. No spells penetrated the opening…for now.

"Look through the opening for a quick second," said Brenner, "and tell me what we're up against."

Lucas steeled himself, then stuck his eye to the hole.

In a flash, he pulled himself back. "Two knights are stationed just to the right of a large beech tree at the top, with a clear sight line down to us."

"Hmm," said Brenner. "How thick is the beech tree?"

"I'm not certain," said Lucas, "Probably three to four feet at least."

"Mind if I have a look?"

"Sure," Lucas said, taking his spot, and holding both shields out.

Brenner waited for the spells to wane, then put an eye to the opening.

Lucas was right; the tree was plenty thick, and the Boldenskeep knights had their shields in front of them in fine position, making it virtually impossible to hit them…unless…Brenner traced the outline of the tree…

"There."

He pulled his head back.

"There what?" said Lucas, confused.

"This will only work if we get some cover from behind," said Brenner. "You can pull the shields back for a rest. We need to hope Alerio and Haggerty catch up to us soon."

"They probably don't even know where we are."

Brenner hated to admit Lucas was likely right.

"We have maybe ten minutes before the knights on the mountain above us come in for a new angle and flush us out," Brenner said. "When that happens, be ready to create the shield cover. Then let me take first shot, and as soon as I say the word, we fly out, hugging the waterway around the hills."

"Okay," Lucas said, but a heavy sigh betrayed his lack of confidence.

Brenner's anxiety only grew as minutes passed, and he watched the angle of shots against them shift: the upper knights must surely be moving down for a clearer shot into the cave. Only then did Brenner realize how tired he was—the game must have been a couple hours in, and he had been channeling elixir for either flight or *Arcyndo* spells nearly every moment. He tried, without success, to relax his body.

Spells continued whipping through the entrance. *Where were Alerio and Haggerty?* There wasn't much time now. Something else nagged at him. *That name, Jarik…*he thought…*where have I heard that before…oh…that's right. Sorian. That's his cousin.*

The red spells were nearly level with them—soon the second squad of knights would have a direct shot. Brenner steadied himself; if he was going to get shot here, he would at least take a Seltick down with him. He scooped the three glowbes behind his shield arm and gripped his mircon, readying for a last ditch shoot-out. *Even if we do get past Jarik and the other sharpshooter on the hill, how will we get through the back territory of Boldenskeep, where more enemy reinforcements—?*

Brenner's thoughts were interrupted by the loudest and strangest war-cry he'd ever heard: "COME and GET SOME, *Bald-eeeeez!*"

Haggerty had arrived.

The pelting of spells outside their cave paused briefly, and Brenner looked urgently at Lucas— "Now!"

Lucas pivoted his shield out the entrance; Brenner put his below it, creating a larger slot to both see and shoot from, then aimed and shot his mircon across the river canyon toward the two knights, who were busy shooting skyward at Haggerty.

With pleasure, Brenner saw his spell hit: not the fighters, but the tree-limb above their heads. A loud snap echoed across the canyon—and the branch fell onto the red knights.

"Let's fly!" Brenner shouted to Lucas. "*Volanti*," he said to himself, and the two rocketed out of the cave, hugging the rocky right side, as the waterway led them around the hills into the flatter center of Boldenskeep's territory. An island formed in the waterway ahead, but then Brenner's shield pinged, and he tasted white froth erupting from the river: spells splashed into the water on both sides of them—a sentry was stationed at the highest tree on the island, shooting determinedly at them.

"Split!" yelled Brenner.

He banked hard right into a small grove of trees, while Lucas whisked left. He knew that they couldn't afford to hide out anymore—they had come through an exposed part of the river, and more players had probably seen them than Brenner had accounted for. As he snaked through the woods, flying at waist level around roots, rocks and trunks, he stole glances across the waterway, hoping to catch a glimpse of Lucas.

A flash of green flickered behind some trunks. *There he was.* Brenner sent a green spell ten feet above Lucas' head. Lucas looked through his trees and across the water. Brenner pointed ahead to the edge of the forest, before it gave way to the shrubs bordering the water and island. Lucas nodded.

The two stealthily flew to the last of the thinning trees. The red knight atop the island tree paused his spellfire, scanning the forest for his foes.

Brenner met Lucas' eye. He raised his mircon hand, pointed forward, and counted down his fingers…three…two…one…

They sprang from cover, fired *Arcyndo* spells from opposite sides of the island, and flew back to the banks of the waterway. The treetop sentry blocked Brenner's shots with his shield, only to be stunned by Lucas', and dropped into the foliage below.

Soaring quickly up the water channel, they soon flew around the sides and then back of the island—intermittent shots flicked past them, coming from the back crag corners—and then they glided into the last third of Boldenskeep's territory, which had one last large grove of trees in the center.

Zooming past the trunks so fast that the woods seemed a brown and green blur—more than a few times did low hanging branches swipe leaves across his face—Brenner and Lucas wove toward the backfield, and closer to Boldenskeep's tower.

The tree line thinned for the last time, and Brenner slowed to a rest behind a large trunk. A hundred feet of open ground lay between them and the stone tower, which posted Boldenskeep's score—52. Unfortunately, there were clear sight-lines up to the crags on both corners, where the last red knights stood, ready to shoot.

"Okay," Brenner panted, "Here we go. Last hurdle."

"I can't believe we got this far," Lucas said in a ragged breath. "Should we fly it together?"

"That's what they'll be expecting," Brenner said, pointing to the sentries up on either side.

Loud jeers came from the high ridges, and then, "You think two of you are going to get over our rock walls? Not on your life!"

"You're down your king and your healers," taunted another red knight, "you need all three of our glowbes now—you won't even get one!"

Laughter rang out from above. Branches cracked nearby as shots blasted into them. The Boldenskeep knights were trying to get them to act impulsively.

Not today, Brenner thought, eyeing the tower…*did it have one last sentry?*

Spells pulsed through the trees behind them; they'd been followed.

"Lucas, you need to distract them, far left from here. I'll take the last leg alone."

A shot burst into a tree about twenty feet behind them.

"Now! Fly!" Brenner said.

Lucas obeyed, hovering left through the trees.

*Here we go…*Brenner thought, breathing hard, waiting for the green spellfire. A dull buzz droned from above. He called to mind the image of aviamirs he had seen whistling through the sky—so fast they seemed like mini-tornadoes. *Any moment—*

Above his head, bark blasted off from a red spell coming from behind.

He jolted sideways.

"The treetops!" someone yelled. "There!"

He couldn't see Lucas, but saw the green *Arcyndo* spells hitting the crag.

Now! Brenner blazed forward with his *Volanti* spell harder than he had in his life: his body made air ripples as it carved forward and twisted—his back to the ground so that his shield could fend off spells from above—shots pelted around him, singeing the hairs on his arms. He curved neared the base of the tower, felt a spell shoot and tingle his foot, immobilizing it.

He began his ascent up the tower, arcing around it in a tight spiral like a serpent, so that neither side could get an easy tracking shot—thirty feet up—the air formed tears against his eyes—fifty feet—spells now rained down from above—eighty feet—he changed course, spiraled backward, then at last came up and over the tower wall, firing off his own *Arcyndo* spell—and freezing the sentry on the tower. Out of the corner of his eye, airborne knights zoomed to the tower from the corner crags, firing spells.

He ducked into the inner part of the tower, lunged toward the small well in the middle, flung wide his shield arm—the back of his mircon hand burned as it was shot—the three glowbes tumbled away from his arm, down into the black hole. Icy shots stung his back.

"Got him!" someone yelled triumphantly.

Brenner slumped against the center well, frozen.

And for a moment, nothing at all happened.

Then, the stones against Brenner's body started vibrating.

A great whistling sound rumbled up from the depths of the Boldenskeep tower; the vaporous score over Valoria's own tower shimmered, changing from 19 to 139 points; then a terrific fireworks display screamed past Brenner, skyward from Boldenskeep's tower, exploding in green clusters of forked-lightning.

With foot stomps and full-body cheers, the crowd thundered their applause; half a million voices rose into one deafening sound; above it all, in an amplified, giddy voice, an announcer hollered—as though he could not quite believe it himself—

"*Valoria* HAS IT! A *WIZARD'S* GAMBIT for the *WIN!*"

Chapter Twenty-Six

An Eve of Sweet Sorrow

Although his team had lost their king, three healers, and all but two of their knights—a crippling position—Brenner's gambit had given them a bonus of one hundred and twenty points—more than enough to clinch victory. After officials had sent healing spells to the immobilized players, Sovereign Drusus orchestrated the Zabrani awards ceremony, with each of the Valoria players given their choice of three hundred golders, a leadership position in government, or, for the top five scorers on the team, their choice of elixir.

As Brenner watched Gemry gladly choose the golders, he considered his options. He already had opportunities for work...which could provide ways to earn golders...but what he couldn't easily get, and would probably help bolster his skills the most, was the elixir.

He had two colors that complimented his physical magic—red and green—one that assisted with mental magic—blue—which meant he was missing one area of elixir magic: the Aura. Two colors provided that strength.

Drusus finished handing his peers contracts for positions and golders, and came to Brenner, eyebrows raised. "What do you choose?"

"I'd like the yellow elixir."

Drusus smiled, "A fine choice." He pointed to the palette, and amber yellow elixir from Safronius flew out, trickled into his amulet, then swirled mesmerizingly with the three other colors: verdant green, fiery red, and sparkling blue.

"Quite the collection you've got there," Gemry said, pulling him out of his temporary trance.

"Brenner," Maverick called to him over the din of the crowd, "I don't know how in the world you thought that gambit would work, but I'm glad you went for it."

"Thanks," Brenner said, "but it wouldn't have worked without these three." He pointed to Haggerty, Lucas, and Alerio. "And Gemry, for reviving us."

"Knights, Gemry—fantastic work out there," Maverick said, clapping them on the shoulders. Then he turned to address the whole group. "Team, meet with your families, and Haggerty—your new groupies—then meet at the midfield platform in ten minutes for a victory flight."

Brenner saw most of the team fly to the middle section of the crowd, and thought he saw a glimpse of Windelm and Sherry waving. He used his *Volanti* spell to fly him across the field. As he came closer to the section, people held out their hands to him and shouted from all sides:

"That finish was brilliant!"

"Haven't seen a Wizard's Gambit in *decades!*"

"Where'd you learn that speed?!"

Even more shouted, "Come to Murfayn's with us! We'll buy you as many drinks as you want!"

Before he could reach Windelm, a confident baritone called out to him.

"Brenner!"

He paused his hovering, looked over, and saw Dalphon floating in front of the crowd toward him. As he did, one of the fans reached out and grabbed onto Brenner's foot.

"Hey, leggo—" Brenner said, trying to kick him off.

"Let me help," Dalphon said, muttering a spell which encased the two of them in something like a bubble, cutting out the shouts of the stadium, and causing the fan to let go of Brenner's foot, recoiling with a shout.

"That's better," said Dalphon.

"Yeah…thanks," Brenner said, surprised and grateful for the spell.

"Allow me to be among the first to congratulate you, Brenner. That was quite the strategy out there. Well done."

Brenner smiled.

"Say, do you recall my earlier offer to work with my merchants?"

"Yes."

"After seeing that finish today, I'd like to multiply it. I can promise five thousand golders for a year's work with my men in Aquaperni."

Brenner's eyes widened to the size of his amulet.

"So, what do you say?" Dalphon asked.

"Well, that…that is *very* generous…" stammered Brenner.

"Only the best we can offer. You're a talented knight."

"It sounds excellent…only, can I have a little more time?"

"You can…certainly. However, my caravan is leaving the city tomorrow; we have business to attend, contracts to uphold. If you'd like to work with us, and develop a reputation for yourself, meet me by the central Arborio fountain within two hours of sunrise."

"I might just do that," Brenner said, nodding.

"Good," Dalphon said, and with a flick of his mircon, the bubble encasing them dematerialized. "Look forward to working with you."

Dalphon floated back to the crowd, and Brenner continued his flight ahead to the largest section of green supporters, where banners and pennants waved feverishly, and the spectators rose and fell in a giant wave of hands that swept around the honeycombed stadium.

"Brenner, over here!" a familiar, warm voice rose to his ears.

Brenner looked over to his left, and saw Windelm and Sherry waving heartily at him. He touched down next to them, and the crowd swayed towards him like the ocean's tide.

"Brenner," Windelm said, putting an arm on his shoulder, "we couldn't be prouder of you today. Not even in my glory days of Zabrani did I pull off a Wizard's Gambit."

Red warmth spread across Brenner's cheeks as Windelm spoke. It had been a long time since he'd received so much as a small compliment from his parents. "Thanks, Windelm."

"Brenner dear," said Sherry, giving his arm a pinch, "you had me worried sick when you flew into the lake—we'd thought you'd lost your mind—then we saw you rescue your teammate." She beamed. "*That* was your best moment on the field today…"

"Thank you, Sherry."

She smiled at him, and then Windelm said, "We'd love to host you at our cottage in Vale Adorna for the summer break. I know you have your celebrations at Valoria tonight, but you are welcome to come tomorrow after the Fall's promotions are posted and you finish packing."

"We've got your room spruced up and everything," added Sherry.

"Also," said Windelm, "what do you think about joining my Silvalo scouting expedition?"

A crease spread across Brenner's brow as conflicting emotions tugged at him. "It's very kind of you both. Only…"

"Yes?" Sherry said encouragingly.

"How much do new spellcasters make in a year?"

Windelm and Sherry looked at each other, and Sherry spoke. "You know we won't be charging you for lodging, right? One simply doesn't do that to family."

Brenner nodded, "Yeah, I know."

"Well," Windelm said, "low-level apprentices or laborers earn about a fifty golders a year. But a mid-level mage coming out of Valoria could earn probably around eighty to over a hundred golders, provided they obtained a good job in a Leadership Department, Biome Planning, or worked for a Magnate."

"I see," said Brenner. "I'd love to stay with you…it's just…I've been offered a job at five thousand golders."

Windelm and Sherry looked at Brenner as if he'd just sprouted wings.

"That is a *very* lucrative offer," Windelm said. "You'd do well to consider it. What's the job?"

"Merchant protection and scouting."

"That's fairly typical for winning Zabrani players. But wow, five thousand. Where?"

"With a company in Aquaperni."

"Hmm," Windelm said, looking as though a stormcloud was coming.

"Any of your teammates going?" asked Sherry.

"I'm not sure yet."

"I would be careful," said Windelm, "That biome is in the far east—"

"Brenner!" Maverick's voice shouted to the stands. "We're waiting on you! Come and join us!"

"Sorry," Brenner said. "I better go. Thanks for coming today."

"Of course," said Windelm, and Brenner thought he saw a fleeting, forlorn look in his eyes before they changed to their normal cheer, "Please keep us posted, whatever your choice. We'll be at Heather Heights until lunch tomorrow."

"Great job, Brenner," Sherry beamed, giving him a firm hug. "Your great-uncle and I couldn't be prouder."

Brenner grinned, then flew back to his teammates, who were waving to the Silvalo supporters from the center pavilion.

After the crowd at Evermax Stadium gave them a final, booming ovation—some folks shouting because their home biome had won the match, others cheering as they shook their coin purses, heavier from successful bets—Maverick led the team in a flight around the lower seats and then up the honeycomb walls. White-robed officials used their mircons to snip open a section of the magic, semitranslucent foil encasing the stadium, allowing the team to exit and then closing it so they wouldn't be swarmed by overzealous, flying fans.

The twenty-one Zabrani players flew back to the academy in the warm afternoon—Brenner quickly ensured he was flying next to Gemry, who looked over at him with a smirk, and, pretending to be royalty, loftily held her hand out for him to hold, which he gladly did. They weaved between ancient stone buildings and mammoth oakbrawns, where news of the victory spread like summer wind, and cheers and congratulations sprinkled down on them from upper balconies in the forested city.

The team arrived at the entrance to the western gates of Valoria, touching down under great victory banners that were eagerly rippling, and walking past rows of lanterns emitting green sparks that formed a runway to the mahogany doors.

"Wel*come* and well *done*, Zabrani team!" said Sage Shastrel, standing by the castle entrance, surrounded by a mob of Valoria students. "Let the victory banquet begin!"

The Valoria students clapped each player on the back as they walked through the double doors of the castle, and down through the hallways to the Banquet Hall. More than once Brenner was knocked off balance by hands thumping his shoulders.

After the long receiving line, the team was ushered into a rearranged Banquet Hall, where all the tables formed concentric rings around a forty-foot long high table, adorned with plush green runners, crystal chalices, and silver rimmed plates, all set around platters of savory food: hot roasted lamb, garlic chicken, buttered-cinnamon squashes, clusters of fruits that pulsed from blue to rich reds, vanilla custards, raspberry tarts, and a cake that shot green fireworks into the air, giving off frosting explosions that coated the Banquet Hall with a sugary-baked aroma.

The chief Sage of Valoria, Spellmaster Kinigree, swept over to the middle table as the spellcasters chatted and found tables—Brenner joined the rest of his team at the center table, first scooting out Gemry's chair for her, then sitting beside her. Kinigree levitated into the air, his shaggy mess of gray hair pushed back over his forehead, and a quiet hush filled the room.

"Valoria spellcasters," Kinigree warmly announced, rotating so that he could see the rings of tables, "it is with great pleasure that I deliver the closing remarks for this educational year, on the final day of the Games of Ganthrea.

"Tomorrow, many of you will join convoys back to your Silvalo homes and begin your two months of summer harvest with hopefully, some rejuvenation too, while others who have accepted contracts will use their talents to forge new paths in spellcaster leadership, biome development, spell safety, potion crafting, and many other rewarding careers. I congratulate you all."

A smattering of polite clapping echoed off the walls and tapestries.

"Now," continued Kinigree, "it has been four years since we last had a champion at any of the three events, and more than thirty summers since we had champions of two. Please give the entire Zabrani team, and our Agilis Champion, Brenner Wahlridge, your applause."

Shouts and cheers erupted nearly everywhere Brenner looked, giving him tingles of pride and goosebumps of embarrassment. Only one table in the back remained quiet, where Kendra and her friends instead glowered at the champions. Sorian looked to be absent.

Kinigree held a hand up to quiet the academy. "Your placement into next year's levels will be posted on Valoria's entrance tomorrow. And now," Kinigree said, waving his arm out before him, "enjoy the sweet taste of victory." He floated back to the ground.

Brenner and his teammates dug into the rich food in front of them. For a carefree hour, the team recounted the best feats of the Games, their stuns across the field, who scored the highest in each category, and eventually, even joked about Haggerty's near drowning—Francesca teasing him, "Your smell finally got to you, huh? Couldn't wait until after the game for your bath?"—Haggerty laughed, and then retorted, "Well, I had to do something drastic to get your attention. Now that I'm fresh and clean, we still on for our pool date?"

"Nope," said Francesca flatly, "Still a definite nope."

The team ate and made toasts until Brenner was feeling full and more than a tad drowsy. Slowly, the number of spellcasters in the Banquet Hall trickled down. Gemry poured sparkling red drink into Brenner's goblet, then her own, and nodded toward the exit. He picked up his drink, and together the two left the celebration, walking up through the corridors to the western ramparts.

"Not bad for your first year," Gemry said, as they strolled onto a balcony overlooking the sunset.

"Well, once I was instructed on how to fly properly, it certainly helped my performance," Brenner said, gazing at her with a smile. "Thank you."

"I wouldn't be surprised if the sages jump you up another rank or two in the fall, based on your performance at the Games," she said, leaning against the castle ridge as the clouds started to match the color of her crimson currant juice.

"If so, I'd be closer to your skills—it may even be socially acceptable for us to be together."

Gemry gave him a thin-lipped smile. "With your wins this weekend, you could talk with any rank of spellcaster here...and probably have a date with any girl at Valoria." She took a sip of her drink, looking away.

"What makes you think I want to be with someone else? I asked you to join me in the Agilis Parade, remember?"

He slipped his hand along the top of the rampart, finding hers.

Gemry's green eyes turned back to his. "I just thought...with your wins and all..." she trailed off.

"What?"

"Usually the top players go for beauty, money, or connections. Whatever will get them ahead." She looked away. "I don't have those. You know my background—"

"Stop," Brenner said, giving her hand a squeeze.

She sighed, pulling a strand of hair behind her ear.

"Gemry," he said softly and slowly, "You. Are. Beautiful." Delicately, he brought his hand to her face, and turned it to his. "And winning or losing doesn't change my feelings for you."

Gemry met his eyes…and smiled. "Thanks," she said quietly.

She looked down at her hands. "My parents spoke to me after the game today…hardly complimented the team on the win at all, just asked for my prize money."

Brenner frowned. "I'm sorry."

"I knew that would happen," said Gemry. "And they said they'd come this evening right after the banquet to pick me up."

"Why so soon?"

"My mother thinks the Zabrani win will draw more customers tonight. Father insisted they need me at the warehouse one more week while fans are in town, before I can work on my own for a month."

"They're letting you work somewhere else?" He squeezed her arm. "Hey, that's great! That's what you were hoping for, right?"

"Yeah…it is." Her lips tightened. "They were *supposed* to let me do that immediately since we won…but whatever. It's just one more week. I can stomach that."

Brenner thought back to his own parents briefly, wondered what they would say if they saw him winning at the games. *They'd probably react just like Gemry's parents…thinking of how to exploit it.*

"Enough about me," said Gemry, "what are you doing after today? I bet you got some great bids for your skills."

Brenner felt embarrassed at her blunt but accurate appraisal. For a fleeting moment, he considered not telling her about Dalphon's offer, that it might upset her or cause a sting of jealousy, which was the last thing he wanted. But he also wanted to be more honest with her, even if he couldn't tell her everything about his life.

"I've been offered a contract worth five thousand golders."

"What?!" She shoved him. "That's amazing—you have to take it. From what I've heard from graduates over the years, that's the most a spellcaster's been offered. Ever."

Brenner let out a sigh. "But then I wouldn't see you…and Aquaperni is a long way away."

"It's only one year…" she said hurriedly, although the way she avoided his eyes seemed to betray her true thoughts.

Twelve months away from each other…

"With that kind of money," Gemry said with renewed vigor, "you could come back at seventeen for a final year of education, then get hired anywhere. Or you could skip the end of Valoria and start your own business. Anything's possible with that many golders."

"Yeah," Brenner said, wanting to tell her how everything was happening so quickly…

He'd been in Silvalo three months, and while back on Earth he would now only have to think about how to spend the next months of summer vacation, here he was pressured to make decisions that impacted not only his education, but his entire adult career…Dalphon's offer would make him wealthy, increasing his self-sufficiency and forcing him to sharpen his business and protective magic skills, at the cost of a full year away from Valoria Academy. Was that what he wanted to do? For most of his life he'd wanted to work solo, either engineering cool structures or maybe doing some type of research…this wouldn't involve either of those, but he would be independent, and after it he could do anything. But if he took it, he felt his relationship with Gemry would wilt.

Brenner just wanted to take a breath, and press pause on life.

"Windelm offered me another position as a scout on his squad," he said, sharing the dilemma on his mind.

"That's good, but you can always do that. Any spellcaster that's reached the rank of conjurer or higher is eligible to join. And the pay would be a fraction of what you could earn abroad."

"Isn't the type of work more important than the money?"

"Maybe for the already rich. But not for most spellcasters. And not for me."

The orange sun touched the rim of the horizon. Gemry's determined attitude was starting to rub off on him…

"I'm sure they would give you leave every couple of months," said Gemry, watching the sunset, "Depending on where you are in Aquaperni, it would be a two or three-day flight from the islands and around the mainland coast to Silvalo. You could come and visit sometime…it's not like I'll be leaving Arborio anytime soon."

Brenner watched the way the summer breeze floated Gemry's long, brown hair around her shoulders…over her silky, smooth skin…*it would be hard to be gone for so long.*

Sensing his gaze, she turned toward him.

"I've never said this…to someone before…" Brenner began slowly, marshalling the courage to finally say what had been running through his mind for the past month, "it's just…I love you."

Gemry beamed like the sun. He could have sworn her eyes sparkled from green to turquoise. Before he fully knew what he was doing, Brenner put a hand on her side, leaned in, and kissed her red lips.

For a moment he'd gotten his wish: in the midst of her sweet fragrance and this kiss, the world indeed seemed paused. From the crown of his head, a thrilling prickle spread down to the tips of his fingers. His heart beat faster, pumping giddiness, pumping delight. Gemry put her hand on his. Their kiss probably would have gone on for a while—*forever, please,* his subconscious hoped—but a loud cough came from beyond the balcony, and then a curt voice: "Gemry. Time to go."

The two pulled apart, and Brenner turned to see the scowling face of her father, his arms crossed as he stood on Velvo. There was an awkward pause as Brenner wasn't sure if he should introduce himself, or wait to see if her father would do so.

He didn't.

"*Now,*" her father said, motioning to the carrier carpet.

Reluctantly, Gemry let go of Brenner's hand.

"Take the job in Aquaperni," Gemry said, stepping across the rampart to Velvo. "And stay safe for me."

"Okay," Brenner said, nodding, desperately wishing their moment could have been longer. "If I go…you know I'll come back to see you."

"I know," Gemry said. She smiled. "And I'm sure you'll have plenty of stories to share with me."

"Velvo, the shop," her father commanded, one hand on Gemry's arm.

The carrier carpet whisked down the ramparts, and Gemry looked over her shoulder, catching Brenner's eye once more. "Bye, Brenner."

"Goodbye…Gemry," Brenner said, his hand raised in a wave, as she vanished behind the curve of an oakbrawn trunk.

Head down, Brenner turned and shuffled back inside the castle. His hand absentmindedly rotated the amulet around his neck as he repeated her words. *Take the job…and stay safe for her…I think I can do that…* Although he was indoors, winding past corridors into the main hallways of Valoria, where groups of students laughed and talked loudly, Brenner felt like he was walking through a fog bank, and didn't notice Finnegan trying to flag him down until his friend was at his side, holding an envelope and punching him in the arm.

"So!" Finnegan blurted out, "what's it like?!"

Brenner slowly surfaced back to reality. "What's what like?"

"Oh I don't know—" Finnegan said sarcastically, "let's see…winning two of the three most prestigious Games, gaining elixirs that Valoria students see only a handful of times in their lives—let alone possess—having a feast thrown pretty much in your honor—do you need me to go on?"

"Oh…that," said Brenner. "I guess it feels good."

"That's a relief," Finnegan said, mockingly wiping his forehead. "I was starting to think that all the wishes we lesser mortals had about the Games of Ganthrea were completely misguided. I've already been asked by a couple mages if *you* were the one who taught *me* how to play Zabrani." He threw his arms in the air. "What is *going on* in Ganthrea?!"

When Brenner didn't reply, he added, "You know you're still allowed to smile, right?"

"Yeah," Brenner said, his voice feeling like someone else's. "I know, Finnegan. I was just saying goodbye to Gemry."

"Ah," said Finnegan. "You also know you can see her at her parent's shop anytime you want, right? Like, say, tomorrow?"

"That's the thing."

Finnegan lifted an eyebrow, and Brenner filled him in on the offer, and his departure. It felt strange, as though he'd accidentally taken an unmarked path into adulthood, saying he was going to be a contracted merchant escort.

Finnegan let out a whistle, then said, "Well, can't say I blame you. If I could turn a year into five thousand golders, I'd do practically anything: shovel dung in dragon stalls, be a tester for potion trials. Heck, for that much I could even tolerate working in the same room as Sorian. But you'd have to pay me another thousand not to choke him when the boss wasn't looking."

Brenner's mood finally brightened. "Maybe I can help land you a contract, too, and on our lunch breaks we can plan pranks for how to make this a summer Sorian won't forget."

"I've got just the thing," said Finnegan definitively, "Unbreakable glue, a rogue Pegasus, and a fake offer to be a captain of level five. He'll be stuck tight and sent to Gelemensus faster than he can bark orders."

"Nice. You get the glue and the letter, and I'll borrow a Pegasus from Rimpley's Sky-Couriers."

"I'm on it," Finnegan said, clapping Brenner on the shoulder. "Hey—I almost forgot, one of Rimpley's messengers stopped by the banquet and dropped off this letter for you."

He handed a piece of rolled parchment to Brenner, who uncurled the scroll to reveal a hastily scrawled message that read:

Dear Brenner,

Sherry and I wanted to tell you again how proud we are of you.

I realize that Valoria likely has celebrations for you and the team all evening, and we won't get to see you for some time if you choose to take the Aquaperni contract.

*Of course, I'd rather have you join my squad this summer, and
attend Valoria in the fall, but it's your choice, and you will earn and
learn much on your own in the islands of Aquaperni.*

Just be careful in choosing your companions.

*I know we are not your parents, but in case you're wondering, you
have our support, whatever you choose. If you do leave tomorrow, take
good care of your amulet, mircon, and foremost yourself, and **keep in
touch.***

With affection, your Great-Uncle,
Windelm

Brenner set the letter down, feeling encouraged by Windelm's words,
and better about his choice to accept the opportunity with Dalphon.

"So," said Finnegan when Brenner finished, "would you like to join me
for an evening of entertainment before you ship off?"

"Sounds good. What did you have in mind?"

"I heard the apprentices are holding a competition to see who can best
amplify their jumps across the river. Wanna watch?"

Brenner agreed, thinking that a final walk around the castle grounds
would be fitting. The teens meandered through the stone hallways of the
castle, down the green sloping east lawns, and followed the familiar dirt
track through the forest where before Sage Shastrel had led them, teaching
them how to summon stoncs. Soon they heard the gurgling sounds of
Valoria's river, which ran north before feeding into the larger Arborio
River.

"Watch Lemke!" a brash voice called in the clearing ahead. "Here he
goes!"

They walked past a thicket of trees just in time to see a wiry, dark haired
student leap through the air across a twenty-foot section of the river—and,
arms flailing, land with a splash halfway across the swift waters. A
chartreuse crowd of gawkers sitting around the launch point—mostly
second and third level apprentices—let out hoots as Lemke surfaced. He

sputtered and then doggedly swam back to the shore.

Already, another apprentice was stretching and then kicking pebbles over the side of the rocks, sizing up the stretch of river. He backed up, then ran, and then leaped from the ledge. Unlike Lemke, he went higher on the halfway point, kept falling, and landed neatly on the other bank.

"Nice going, Timothy!" a friend called, as the apprentices gave him approving claps and shouts. Brenner clapped, too, but stopped when he realized spellcasters were elbowing each other, pointing in his direction. For a short moment the evening air was still, and then a dozen girls and boys jumped to their feet, clamoring to be the next jumper to prove themselves.

A couple of the younger spellcasters were pushing each other toward Brenner. Finally, one got shoved right up to him. He blurted out, "Can you teach us how to jump?"

Brenner smiled. He knew he should probably pack and mentally prepare for tomorrow, but he didn't have much personal belongings, and he would not be around Valoria much longer. And, he thought, *it's kinda fun to teach something you're good at.*

"Okay," said Brenner, "to start with, who knows what the best jumping animal is?"

That night, after finishing his impromptu lesson with the younger spellcasters, Brenner decided a final flight around Valoria and Arborio would be fitting. In his mind he spun the *Volanti* spell. He hadn't noticed earlier, but now did with pleasure, that the fourth color of elixir caused his spell to be easier to ignite and sustain—and soon he was lifting through the treetops, then soaring above dark and light canopy greens and bright fruits that, like a patchwork quilt, knit together to form the eastern woods of Valoria. The river flowed below, looking like lapis blue thread leisurely unspooled, giving life to everything it touched.

The summer air was warm, and the stars twinkled.

He soared across the forest, over the hills, west around Valoria's ramparts, and hovered, like a hummingbird, looking at the giant city of Arborio: the night orbs had all flickered on, illuminating the trickle of flying spell-casters flitting to pubs and hotels; bursts of laughter and conversation echoed from tree condos at the head and eateries at the foot of massive trunks. Some dark clouds were forming on the far side of town, and he wondered if his journey tomorrow would launch under a storm.

Brenner turned and flew back, down to the balcony of his quarters, dodging a snake-like vine to land on the stone surface. He went inside. Packing only took about ten minutes. His inner-expanding rucksack made it easy to fit in the new sets of clothes and belt alongside his toothbrush, canteen, compass, knife, Essence of Spungelite and Alacritus potions, pen and journal.

After setting the dials on the side of his bed to wake with the sun, Brenner laid awake, thinking about the thrill of the Games…Dalphon and his new contract, Windelm's advice…Sherry's hug, leaving Valoria and the sages and Finnegan's jokes…but mostly, he thought of Gemry.

Am I making the right choice?

When Brenner finally drifted to sleep, his mind mixed the triumphant events of the week with his subconscious fears, bobbing through thoughts like icebergs in a foggy sea…of moving into unknown regions, fending for himself, going it alone. Strange dreams descended upon him, one moment filled with cheering green fans and brilliant blue waterfalls, the next with ashes, shadows, and strangers.

Chapter Twenty-Seven

The Morning of Mayhem

B renner awoke early on Monday to the gradual rumblings of his bed, grateful he'd finally figured out how to change the settings on it from jolt to gentle. Only a handful of the other level six conjurers were up, clasping their trunks and quietly leaving the dormitory. He showered, dressed, and picked up his rucksack. *This is it,* he thought, looking around, feeling a bit nervous now that he was truly leaving. He double-checked the contents of his rucksack, and noticed the shimmering blue Alacritus potion. He lifted it out. *It wouldn't hurt to start this job with a little boost.* He uncorked the bottle and took a small swig of Alacritus. It tasted awful. But he found his nerves did indeed start to calm, and that he was more in-tune with emotions. He went to the Banquet Hall, putting a couple of baked rolls and warm sausages on his plate—knowing this would be his last breakfast at Valoria for at least a year. Finnegan was not with the spell-casters in the Hall—no doubt he was still sleeping, as he wouldn't need to be at Hutch & Son's until lunch.

As Brenner took a seat at an open table and began to eat, he noticed students elbowing each other, and overheard them talking in worried tones with their heads down.

"—wasn't the only embassy to get burnt last night—"

"On top of that, I got an express post that says there's been murders—"

"My dad said he was coming to the gates as soon as possible. Said he doesn't want me to spend another moment in the city."

The news made Brenner's skin bristle. *Fires? Murders? No wonder merchants were hiring players for extra protection.* Then he felt the calming effect of Alacritus, and finished eating, feeling better. He slung his pack over his shoulder, and headed across the marble floors, through the passages, going to the entrance of Valoria. He was still puzzling over the conversations when he saw a couple of spellcasters stopped next to large bulletins hung on the entry wall: next Fall's Ability Levels.

While he wouldn't be back for the fall, he was curious to see where he placed. The chatty group of apprentices saw him approach, and politely cleared a path.

Brenner walked up to the middle, scanning the placements… he wasn't in the level six conjurers.

He wasn't in the level seven mages, either.

At the bottom of the next chart, he found his name: he was slated to join the level eight mages. A tinge of pride swept through him.

"Brenner," a husky voice called from behind, and he heard quick footsteps heading toward him.

Red-faced and a bit breathless, Sage Vicksman approached him. "Since it's urgent," he said, looking concerned, "I'll be blunt: there's been some fights and even some lootings last night. Your guardians asked me to escort you to their residence, immediately."

"What happened?" Brenner asked. "What did Windelm—"

"I'll explain as we fly—" he said, putting a hand on Brenner's shoulder and guiding him to the front entrance. "Have all your supplies?" he asked, his eyes flicking from Brenner's face over to his rucksack and to his belt.

"Yes."

"Good. Follow me." Vicksman walked through the large stone archway, levitated off the front steps of Valoria, and waved his arm quickly until Brenner was floating just behind him.

The morning sun was partly obscured by low, gray clouds, and the two flew forward through the major vias of Arborio. Looking down, Brenner saw something missing: the normal bustle of merchants and shopkeepers in the streets. Only a few vendors were out with their produce, while most stores remained closed with windows shut.

"Three of the biome embassies—Montadaux, Vispaludem, and Arenaterro—" Sage Vicksman called to Brenner, "had major fires last night. Sovereign Drusus has called for an immediate investigation to find the vandals, and for heightened security around the Ironclad Assembly, public buildings and banks."

Vicksman sped them toward the heart of Arborio, veering around ancient stone buildings and even taller trees, flying past few carrier carpets and an even scanter amount of spellcasters. Brenner tried to make sense of the vandalism—*were they just going after money, or was it something else? Political perhaps?*

"Sage Vicksman," Brenner said, as they passed Via Arborio, which would have led them to the Shell Towers, and beyond to Vale Adorna, "What has this got to do with me?" An odd feeling grew inside him.

"Down this way," Vicksman responded, turning off the major flight route, and flying down a less congested street. "Because," he said, looking over at Brenner, "You are Arborio's most valuable player, and if they could, these thieves would ransom you. Over here," Vicksman said, swooping to a stop at a grimy-looking doorway. Next to the door a rat scurried from one crate to another. Vicksman produced a key, fitted it to the door, and opened it wide. "Quick," he said, gesturing inside.

Brenner touched down, and was about to follow...but the Alacritus potion gave him clear thought, which cut through Vicksman's urgency... "Where is Windelm?" he said.

"He's coming," Vicksman said, looking at him with impatience, and then something much stronger: greed. He pointed his mircon at Brenner, whispering something.

Vicksman's spell enshrouded Brenner, and he felt his defenses weakening. Now he wanted to follow Vicksman inside...wanted to obey him by any means...to give him his amulet...

Brenner's feet marched him up to the door. His mind felt covered with clouds...he pulled off his amulet, extended it to Vicksman...suddenly, like a ray of light, the Alacritus potion burned through the mental fog; his thoughts within cried out, *Totum Aura*...then again, louder, and Brenner shouted, "*Totum Aura!*"

The spell of control snapped, and Brenner saw a look of malice flash across Vicksman's face as he muttered, "If that's how you'd like to get to Dalphon..."

Brenner pulled his arm back, clenching his amulet.

Vicksman bellowed, "*Torturi*—"

"*Repello!*" Brenner shouted, and Vicksman hurled backwards into the dark room, hitting the wall with a crack, his mircon thrown from his hand.

"*Apellatum*," Brenner thought, and Vicksman's mircon flew obediently to him; he caught it. He set it against his glass holster, which looped around it firmly.

Brenner didn't wait to see what Vicksman would try to do next, even if he was lying pretty still—immediately he cast his *Volanti* spell, and took to the sky.

He flew back through the alleys like a hawk; with every turn, he looked over his shoulder, but thankfully didn't see Vicksman...or anyone else trailing him. He sped behind a group of other flyers on a major via. *How much of what Vicksman told me was true? And how did he know about Dalphon?*

He thought back to last night...there were dark clouds over the horizon...*were those clouds...or could they have been smoke?*

Like a bullet, he shot past oakbrawns, mahagonies, and buildings, toward the fountains of Arborio. He looked to the eastern horizon; intermittently through gray clouds, he could see the sun was almost four fingers above the horizon—which meant he had about half an hour before

Dalphon would be departing...*but if Vicksman turned on me, who's to say Dalphon wouldn't be next?*

He slowed his flight by some giant sequoias, coming to the last corner before the fountains, and flew up to an empty balcony attached to an oakbrawn. He peered over the edge.

True to his word, Dalphon was near the fountain, his blond hair waving across his face as he marched between caravans, issuing commands to his orderlies who loaded people and cargo onto wagons. The faint smell of manure drifted to Brenner as he watched Dalphon climb up the lead caravan, which was attached to a team of charcoal-colored Pegasi that whinnied and jerked on their reins, ready to leave the ground behind. Most other caravans were attached to horses. People loaded wagons with barrels and wooden crates—many of which were stamped with the word Aquaperni—then began tying the boxes down with coarse ropes. There seemed to be a working hierarchy, where men and a few teens wearing silver necklaces ordered the rest to do the heavy lifting.

One of the teenagers scurrying around the caravans and giving out commands looked oddly familiar. Brenner tilted his head over the balcony to get a better look. The boy turned around to scold a subordinate for snapping a rope, and Brenner saw his familiar, rat-like eyes.

Sorian.

Sorian, who had swapped his green Valoria robes for ones the color of crude oil, and adorned with a silver necklace, smiled as he bossed the men and other teenagers around, most of whom had copper rings around their necks. From inside a caravan came yelps, which echoed off Brenner's balcony. As Sorian looked up to the balcony and around to the caravan, Brenner ducked his head down.

When a moment passed, he looked out again: Sorian was facing away from his balcony, and walked over to Dalphon, who was gesturing at two of the burly men to deal with their wagon. They drew their mircons and shot spells inside the caravan. The shouts within subsided.

Yesterday Brenner had been eager to claim a job for five thousand golders a year, but now, after seeing what the operation really looked like, and who they employed, Brenner decided the money, the risk, and the company was not worth it.

If Vicksman had been right about the lootings, and fire, would the vandals have stopped at embassies? Would they have attacked other shops as well?

Gemry. What about Gemry?

He had to find her.

Casting his *Volanti* spell about himself, he quietly hovered back from the balcony, and then, using side alleys, veered in a wide circle up and away from the fountains, over to the northwest side of Arborio, where Gemry had said her father owned a shop.

The majestic oakbrowns thinned, and the buildings sagged with a run-down look: flaking paint hung like scabs on the front of shops, crude graffiti boasted equally crude suggestions, and spellcasters traveled solo, glancing curiously at him as they passed, as if they couldn't understand why a Zabrani player would be caught in this part of the city.

He read the shop signs quickly as he passed…*Tyrane's Tattoos…Golders on Loan…Guard Beasts and Plants*…that wasn't it…*Spell Magnification and Curse Removal…Whisker's Wares and Saloon*…and then—

Gespelti's Warehouse & Pawn. The first two words of the sign looked worn from age, but the last one looked a little brighter, as if it was recently added.

The shop was more sprawling than the others around it. Its entrance had two large steel doors, and tinted glass windows on one side with a flickering sign that floated the letters: *Open.*

Brenner floated down to the collar of the street, cast one last glance around for anyone following him, then pushed the heavy door open.

Inside, the air was musty. Rickety sign posts hung from the ceiling every dozen feet or so, labeling aisles as 'Recent Imports,' 'Spellcaster Camoufl-age,' 'Cargo, Travel and Carpets,' 'Miscellaneous Pawn,' and a final sign labeled 'Sorted by Biome,' where different corrals held everything from Arenaterro animal bones and tusks to misty, glowing Gelemensus glassware.

Walking past the aisles, Brenner saw a frazzled-looking, dark-haired woman at the far counter, hunched over paperwork, face on her fist. As he approached her, he noticed her face had a familiar shape, and her thin nose appeared identical to Gemry's. But her eyes looked different—they seemed to have been surrounded by tired creases for so long they were permanently etched in, and they lacked the warmth of her daughter's.

"Excuse me," Brenner said, to catch her attention—she hadn't moved an inch the entire time. She tilted her head up. "What deal can I offer you?"

"None, really. Are you Mrs. Gespelti?" Brenner asked, knowing the answer but wanting to be certain.

She nodded.

"Oh good. Is Gemry here?"

Mrs. Gespelti let out a huff, as if Brenner was badgering her during a very important meeting. She fixed him with a pair of beetle-black eyes. "Who's asking?"

"I'm Brenner…"

She shrugged.

"I played with her on the Zabrani team."

This seemed to jog her memory somewhat, as she sat more upright and gave a slight nod. But then she went back to looking at her ledger.

Brenner pressed again. "So, is she working here?"

Mrs. Gespelti's blunt answer surprised him: "No. And if you're not buying anything, I have other business to do."

"Oh…" Brenner said, considering where else Gemry could be, "When will she be back this afternoon?"

Mrs. Gespelti looked down to her papers; her expression stiffened.

"She won't be coming at all today. And if you're here just to socialize, you can leave."

A sickening feeling rumbled within Brenner's stomach. *Is she lying to me? Gemry said she'd be here all week.* He needed to know what happened. Quietly, he pointed his mircon at Mrs. Gespelti. "*Pervideas.*"

Since she wasn't expecting a mind-reading spell, her defenses were easier to slip past. He skimmed the surface of her short-term memories, saw a room cluttered with brick-a-brack and furniture, a confrontation, Mr. and Mrs. Gespelti waving their arms at Gemry, her father saying "It's only for a year!"—tears sliding down Gemry's cheeks—a forced ride on their carrier carpet—a wooden pavilion, voices from a crowd calling out numbers—

"*Psyche Aura,*" said Mrs. Gespelti, pulling Brenner out of her mind and back into the pawn shop. "How *dare* you enter into my thoughts."

Brenner stared back at her, struggling to control his own anger from bubbling over. "How dare *you* sell your own daughter."

The truth of his accusation pierced her, and her seemingly strong facade crumbled. Mrs. Gespelti covered her face with her hands, saying, "You don't understand, my husband was about to be stripped of his business, his mircon—everything."

"You're right, I don't understand," Brenner said coldly, shaking his head. "Who bought her?"

Mrs. Gespelti looked like a guilty defendant wilting under interrogation. Looking away from Brenner, she muttered, "Gretzinger."

Brenner didn't know whether he should yell at her or storm through the rest of the warehouse in search of Gemry's father—the real culprit for the family's problems. Faintly, the Alacritus potion checked his anger.

"How much did he sell her for?"

Mrs. Gespelti seemed unable to speak. Finally, she said in a hollow voice, "One hundred golders."

Waves of pain, anger, and contempt crashed in Brenner's mind. *One hundred golders.* When he spoke again, his voice was low, and didn't sound anything like himself.

"So that's how much your daughter's love is worth to you."

He wanted lay into Mrs. Gespelti, to shout how any parent with any decency would never consider a bargain so soul-wrenching, how this could have all been avoided if Mr. Gespelti would have reined in his gambling addictions…but the Alacritus nudged him: if he yelled those judgments, she wouldn't cooperate anymore, and he still needed one last thing.

"Where is Gretzinger?"

"Gemry's already under contract—you can't undo it. He has full—"

"I said, *where* is Gretzinger?" he drew his mircon.

Her shoulders slumped; her mouth twisted; Mrs. Gespelti looked as though a guilty shadow had swept over her. She met his eyes fleetingly.

"I've heard he's on the southern side of Arborio."

Anger took hold of his feet, and Brenner turned and strode to the exit without another word, leaving behind the animal bones, the splintered crates, and the Gelemensus Glass, all now symbols of Gemry's parent's betrayal. As he pushed open the door and stepped a few paces outside, a surprising emotion came out of the nowhere: jealousy.

That's odd, I don't feel jeal—

"*Arcyndo*," said an oily voice to his side, and Brenner felt his limbs lock in place. *What the—?!* His balance failed and he started falling to the side, but was caught roughly from behind.

"Thought you went unseen, Rookie?"

Brenner's eyes widened. Frozen, he was being dragged around to an alley. Even before he could get a look at his attacker, he knew with a terrible feeling who it was.

"Now you see that winning isn't everything," said Sorian, shoving Brenner behind a dumpster and watching as he fell hard on his ribs. "Being on the most powerful side is."

Sorian kicked Brenner in his stomach, and he felt some acid come up his throat. "Dalphon has already rewarded me with troop command and plenty of golders, and once I bring you to him, he will give me even more. Oh yes, he was most interested when I told him about your previous school…you aren't from here, are you, Brenner?"

Being immobilized, Brenner could only glare back at Sorian.

Sorian pulled a piece of chain from his pocket and leaned down, tying Brenner's hands behind his back. "You will come with me to the caravans," Sorian said. "And if you try anything stupid—run or call for help—I will do more than stun you." The chains pulled snug, cutting into Brenner's skin. "Dalphon taught me an effective spell for dealing with slaves—*Torturium*. I went a bit overboard the first time I used it—that slave lost control of his legs."

Sorian yanked Brenner's mircon away, stood up, and pointed his own at Brenner. "*Mobilus*."

Brenner felt his strength returned, but without access to his mircon, he was powerless against Sorian.

"Stand up," Sorian commanded, pulling out a black cloak, and draping it around Brenner's shoulders, hiding the chains on his hands. "Cross the road quickly, and stay in front of me."

Brenner did as he was told, knowing that resisting would only encourage Sorian to use a pain spell.

"Stick to the side routes," Sorian said gruffly, directing Brenner into the next alley. The smell of garbage filled the air, and Brenner saw a man passed out in a crate.

"What makes you think Dalphon won't turn on you?" Brenner asked.

A hard blow to his back caused Brenner to stagger. He coughed for air, feeling like the wind was knocked out of him.

"Did I say you could speak? Do it again and it's time for *Torturium*."

Brenner trudged on, muted. As they passed people in the roads, Sorian discreetly kept his mircon poking against Brenner's side, guiding him into darker, more secluded alleys. They marched in silence for awhile, back to the caravans. *He had to escape…find Gemry…*

Entering a last alley, Brenner could hear the gush of fountains ahead. He was out of time…but he had no spells, he couldn't fight back, and his Alacritus only helped with mental emotions, it couldn't help him now…still, he had to do something. He turned to face Sorian.

"Please, if I give you my mircon and my amulet, will you let me go?"

"*Torturium*," Sorian said, and a burst of pain hit Brenner's chest. Like fire it spread to his limbs, driving him to his knees and then onto his side. Mircon still pointing at him and spell flowing, Sorian continued, "In case you forgot, I already have your mircon, and plan on selling your amulet for several thousand—"

Whack. The pain spell stopped. Sorian suddenly dropped to the street. Brenner could breathe.

Behind Sorian, a hooded figure with a club looked down and muttered, "Scum."

Brenner felt his chains being loosened, and he slipped his hands free, looking up. "Who are—?" he began, and then the vigilante flipped back her hood, revealing black hair and a scar on her cheek. He knew that face.

"Your mercy deserved repayment."

"You—" Brenner began, remembering the alley with Finnegan. "Thank you...Rinn." He looked at the mark on her neck. "Where's your collar?"

"I bribed a spellcaster to disenchant it," she said. "Sorry if I didn't exactly follow your advice." Rinn grabbed the mircon from Sorian's hand. "This yours?"

"Yes."

She flipped it to him.

"Thanks," Brenner said.

Rinn looked over at Sorian on the ground, and reached for his mircon, when Brenner heard movement behind them. Two of Dalphon's men with silver necklaces walked into the other end of their alley.

"Run," Brenner said. "*Totum Aura.*"

His shield spell bubbled around them, deflecting the stunning shots from the attackers. Brenner and Rinn darted back up the alley, then turned the corner. He lapsed the spell.

"We're even," Rinn called to him, pulling her hood up and sprinting down another side road.

"*Volanti,*" Brenner said.

For the second time that morning, he flew with an urgency he'd before thought impossible. Branches, spellcasters, birds, and carpets became brown and green blurry streaks as he navigated the major Vias, which had now become more crowded as the sun rose higher.

Other than flying south, he didn't know exactly where he was going.

Between openings in the treeline, he saw Evermax Stadium far off to his left, then past the inner heart of Arborio with its more extravagant shops, storefronts, and fountains.

Now he saw outlines of the Northern and Southern Valoria Stadiums, and still he kept surging south…past still more sequoias, redwoods, oakbrawns, and high-rise apartments built on their sides, past banners for the Games, past marketplaces. Presently, the larger oakbrawns thinned. The southern city came into view, and then the Shell Towers of Arborio, ringing the city. He passed one of the towers, and the land transitioned into yellow wheat and green crop fields, with castle-like mansions scattered around the fields.

He descended down to a stretch of shops clustered on the street before the Via branched into smaller, private roads. He wove between a group of customers, then landed and approached a merchant with orange and brown fur coats lining the sides of his stall.

"Do you know—" he began, but was cut off.

"Hey, you're that Valoria Champion! Brenner, isn't it?"

"Yes, but—"

"Knew it! You couldn't have picked a better place for furs!" The man put an arm around Brenner's shoulder. "Look around—I'll give you anything you see for half-off—you bring such pride to our city! What would you like? New coat? Gloves?"

"I'm sorry," Brenner said, peeling off the merchant's arm. "I need to find someone. Do you know a spellcaster named Gretzinger?"

"Gretzinger?" he said, mood clearly dampening as Brenner wasn't showing interest in his deals—other folks had now heard Brenner's name and were peering over at him and chattering—he continued, "Oh sure, Gretzinger. He lives at the white mansion down Via Montego, not too far over there," he said, pointing west.

"Thank you," Brenner said, making to leave.

"Wait!" the merchant said, steering Brenner to another rack with accessories. "You want these?" he asked, pointing to an embroidered scarf and fur-lined hat. "They're free! A gift from Vladmin to you!"

"Thanks…" Brenner said, accepting the hat the vendor thrust into his hands, if only to get Vladmin to let him go. Then he followed a winding road, past poplars, willows, and tall maples. He coasted lower for the final stretch, and saw a stone carved with the words *Gretzinger Estate* at the corner of a long driveway.

He flew up the ornamental brick driveway that had patterned purple and pink flower beds on both sides that looked like they were meticulously weeded each morning. Coming to a halt at the marble entryway, he landed and walked to the door, lifting a brass lion knocker, and letting it drop against the door.

There was no response. He knocked again, louder.

Still nothing.

He tried the handle. It was locked. Venturing down from the entryway, he took one of the stone paths around the to back, underneath trellises of ivy and blooming red flowers.

"Hello?" he said as he walked.

Mature trees lined the border into the back of the estate, and Brenner walked across prim green grass to the veranda and stone patio. A marble fountain in the distance gushed blue waters, and a large pyramid reflected the yellow sun—no doubt part of Gretzinger's mindscape.

He approached the back door, knocked slightly, and when no one responded, he tried the handle. This time he lucked out. It was unlocked.

Brenner walked into a large ballroom nearly the size of his entire house.

"Gretzinger?" he called.

Didn't Gretzinger have slaves and servants? Where was everyone?

"Gemry?"

He walked across the cold marble floor, down to a corridor. He was starting to feel anxious, and realized the Alacritus potion must be wearing off. Dozens of closed doors with bronze handles lined either side. Towards the end, one was ajar.

"I won't!" a man's voice shouted from within.

Cautiously, Brenner walked toward it, clutching his mircon tightly.

He heard a chair scraping against the floor and loud mutterings.

As he pushed the door open, he saw an older man in a rich, silver suit staring at him with desperate eyes.

"You!" he shouted at Brenner. "You did this to me!"

"What?!"

Before he could ask another question, the man leapt from his chair toward Brenner, brandishing a knife.

Brenner dropped his hat and raised his mircon, starting to cast an Aura spell around himself, but the man suddenly stopped, glared at Brenner, and pointed the knife to himself, hissing, "You are making me do this!" He made a quick cut across his throat and collapsed to the floor as scarlet blood spilled out.

Brenner was speechless.

Hands shaking, his thoughts raced in different directions—*Was this man Gretzinger? If only I knew a healing spell*—he edged closer to the man, thinking maybe he could use a piece of clothing to stop the bleeding, but as he did, the man whipped his knife through the air, as though warding off attackers. Brenner stepped back. The urge to escape pressed heavily on him. *Who else is around here?*

He scanned the room for anyone else—it was empty—and bolted back through the corridor, out of the mansion doors, and into the backyard.

Standing on the grass, heart beating rapidly, Brenner ticked through his options: *Should I call for help? Fly back to Valoria? What about Gemry?*

He was still eerily alone on the grounds of a giant mansion, which gave him another nauseating feeling: *If people heard those shouts…they will think the murderer…was me…*

Hands trembling, he decided waiting at the scene of a crime was worse than finding help. Brenner took to the sky, flying back over the entrance grove, racing along Via Montego, to the intersection of merchants.

"Back for another deal?" Vladmin called jovially to him as he flew to the ground. "Hey, where's your hat?"

"Nevermind—where are the Silvalo Guards?"

"The Guards?" Vladmin repeated blankly. "I gave you free gift, why—"

"Because," Brenner said between quick breaths, "'there is a dead man at the Gretzinger Estate."

The fur merchant's good-natured tone vanished. "What happened? What did you do?"

"I didn't do anything—I just went there to find a friend, and no one was around, and…" Brenner didn't want to reveal how he had trespassed, and thought quickly to if there was a window in that bedroom—yes he was quite sure—"I saw a man's body through a window."

"I'll summon the Guard at once," the merchant replied, striding to the street in front of his tent, and firing a green and red spell into the air, which gave off a tremendous explosion, creating a spearhead-shaped cloud.

The merchant squinted at Brenner, clearly wondering if he was the killer.

A few minutes later, two spellcasters in bright green capes soared into the plaza from the edge of the city: the Silvalo Guard. They zoomed down the trail of smoke to the merchant.

"Who produced the Commotion Cloud?" said the lead guard.

"That was me," said Vladmin, who then pointed at Brenner and said, "This spellcaster says there's a dead man at the Gretzinger Estate."

The lead guard fixed his steel eyes on Brenner and subtly flicked his mircon at him. Without warning, Brenner's memories floated to the surface of his mind—being shot at in the alley next to Rinn—the flight down Via Montego, the empty hallway inside the mansion—shouts of "You did this to me!"—Gretzinger crumpling to the floor—

He felt a hand on his shoulder, and the stream of memories stopped.

"I believe memory sifting is allowed only by a Mind Warrant. Do you have one?"

Brenner turned and was shocked to see Windelm at his side.

"And you are?" the guard said, clearly irked at the interruption.

411

"Windelm Crestwood, his guardian."

"I see." He turned back to Brenner, and took a small square locket from his pocket and clicked it open. "State your name, and your business at Gretzinger's."

"Uh…Brenner Wahlridge. I heard my friend was sold to Gretzinger… and I wanted to see her."

"Slaves are not to be visited, except by their master's permission. Did you have an invitation to the residence?"

"Well…not exactly."

"Pardon him, please," Windelm cut in, "He just wanted to see his friend. And he is not yet graduated Valoria."

The guard looked over and said simply, "Pardoning is up to the courts." He turned back to Brenner. "What did you see and do at the Gretzinger Estate?"

With his whole body sweating and his hands trembling, Brenner started relaying his trip to the mansion. His great uncle made pointed glances at him, and Brenner felt a mild sensation in his forehead: Windelm was subconsciously directing him to keep the story brief, his presence at the estate limited.

When Brenner finished, the guard nodded. He closed his square locket. "Now that we have his spoken testimony on record, we'd like Brenner to give us his memory of the estate this morning." He took out a glass vial.

Brenner gave an involuntary shudder.

"That's a breach of spellcaster privacy," said Windelm, "and only allowed in court when a jury votes in unanimous agreement."

The guard gave Windelm a glaring look, but put away the vial.

"My partner and I will inspect Gretzinger's estate. If what you say is true and there's a dead man there, Brenner is under investigation and may not leave his residence until granted permission from the Silvalo Guard. There will be a trial. Give my partner, Guard Otavio, your address."

Windelm did, and then the two guards streaked off, down Via Montego to the estate.

From their stalls, other vendors and customers had been watching the exchange between Brenner and the guard, and once finished, they began crowding round the fur merchant, peppering him with questions. Vladmin seemed to enjoy being the center of attention, saying, "One of the richest land-owners—yes, Nigel Gretzinger—he's been *murdered*... Although, I can't say I've been most fond of him; I hear he's made many trips to the icy lands of Gelemensus, but never bought a *single* coat from me..."

The crowd cast suspicious glances at Brenner, likely wondering, like the Silvalo Guards, if he was the killer responsible.

"Brenner," Windelm said, putting a hand on his shoulder, and steering him away from the merchants, "let's head back to home."

"Wait—Gemry," Brenner said, taking Windelm's hand off and turning to face him, "she was sold to Gretzinger!"

"I heard," Windelm said sadly.

"You did? How?"

"It's how I found you. I came to the Arborio fountains to give you warning and news of last night's events, but didn't see you with the trading caravans, so I checked Hutch & Sons, and when you weren't there, I tried Gespelti's warehouse."

"Where is she? Why wasn't anybody at Gretzinger's house?"

"There wasn't *anyone?*"

"No, the house was vacant."

"That is not good...then he may not have been the only person..."

"Only person who what?"

"Whose mind was controlled."

Brenner wasn't sure if he heard right. "Mind controlled?"

"Yes. Gretzinger had both clout and a large fortune to draw on...under normal circumstances there's no reason he would've been unprotected, or take his own life."

Windelm levitated and motioned Brenner to follow him. "Come. There is one more place we can check. Stay close."

The two arced back to the heart of Arborio, with Windelm selecting less busy boulevards on which to travel. Several minutes later, Brenner recognized the oval clearing, the podium on a raised pavilion, and scattered chains bolted to the stage: the trading block.

Windelm flew them to a small stone building bordering the stage, knocked sharply, and in a moment, a mole-like man opened the door.

"Auctions are closed now, come back tomorrow after sunrise."

"We seek to review the slave register."

The man let out a sharp huff, but must have been duty-bound because he opened the door, and, with eyes filled with irritation, led them to a thick leather tome easily the size of an anvil.

"Yesterday's and today's transactions please, if you don't mind," Windelm asked.

The records keeper opened to a page marked *Solar Equinox, 5,196 A.E.* Then he flipped forward six more pages. Windelm and Brenner peered at it—there must have been forty to fifty names entered, each with a master, price, and duration. But none of them were Gemry's.

Windelm turned the page to the seventh day after the equinox, and there, on the third line, was Gemry's name. *Sold from Radmond Gespelti, father, to Nigel Gretzinger. 100 golders. One year.*

There were lots of other names listed, and Brenner saw Gretzinger's name as the buyer for more than a dozen.

"But she wasn't there," Brenner said, confused. "Did Gretzinger sell her to someone else?"

They scanned the names, down until the final entries of the morning. Gemry's name didn't appear again. Brenner's heart sank.

"If he did," said Windelm, "it's not on the public market…"

The keeper bristled at this suggestion. "Selling on black markets is a crime that, if true, I will have the Silvalo Guard prosecute."

Windelm looked up. "You don't have to worry about prosecuting him."

"And why's that?"

"He's dead."

"Oh!" said the keeper, looking as though Windelm pulled a dagger on him.

"Don't worry, the Silvalo Guard is already aware," said Windelm. He bowed solemnly and said, "Thank you, we'll be going."

The keeper fumbled the book closed, and seemed more than willing to show them the door.

Outside, Windelm turned to Brenner with heavy eyes and sighed. He didn't have to say it. Brenner knew.

Gemry was lost.

"I'm sorry," Windelm said, putting a hand on Brenner's shoulder. "Come. We have much to discuss. And here in the open is not the place."

Despondent, Brenner triggered his flight spell once more, then followed Windelm as he flew past the stage, past the heart of the city, the fountains, the many oakbrawns, the Shell Towers, then the farmlands, and over the open wilderness. Thankfully, Windelm didn't look back much as they flew, because for most of the journey hot tears dripped down Brenner's face.

Finally, the town of Vale Adorna appeared in the forests, and Windelm guided them down to the narrow paths, spindling through the woods to Crestwood Cottage. Benner felt some security, landing at the doorstep to Windelm and Sherry's home, but, unlike the first time entering their cottage, this time he was cut deeply with the sharp pain of losing someone he loved.

Chapter Twenty-Eight

The Unjust Journey and the Known Knight

That day in Arborio, hundreds of thousands of pilgrims, caravans and traders formed long lines in a mass exodus from the Games, some going back to the green countryside of Silvalo, while many others began longer journeys to the other six biomes of Ganthrea. If someone would have asked Gemry yesterday if she'd be traveling away from her home city today—or anytime in the next two years—she would have laughed, and welcomed the chance to get away from the warehouse.

But inside her carriage, packed next to about two dozen other spellcasters, with chains on her wrists and a thick collar on her neck that made her feel like a common criminal, she would've gladly traded her current trip for many more years in Arborio.

For Gemry, the events of the morning were still hazy: the rude pre-dawn awakening from her father, the auction block, her amulet and mircon stripped from her, the cold finality of the collar snap followed by the heat sealing it around her neck, her mother's last look of disbelief and shame…then she was loaded into a caravan to an estate, herded out and crammed into another dark carriage with small air-slits on the top of the sides; a severe-looking, bald man ordered them onto four long benches, fastened their wrist chains to posts, jumped out, locked the doors behind him with a loud click, and the carriage jerked into motion. Away she had went, against her heart and against her will.

While everything had seemed like a bad dream at the time, it was the cold, metal chains on her wrists and the halo-like collar fused around her neck that confirmed the ugly truth: she was a slave.

There were twenty-three other people around her in the carriage ranging from late teens to late fifties: two other teenagers had eyes frosted over in shock; most of them middle-aged men and women, quiet and resigned to their fate; one woman, about mid-twenties if Gemry had to guess, stared at her hands, lost. Several of the men had dark eyes and muscular arms. The collars didn't faze them, which made her think they were sold criminals.

It was these men Gemry kept an eye on.

The other riders, indebted laborers who had been forced to sell themselves at the trading block, still tugged at their collars, as if they were as simple to remove as a necklace. Gemry had already tried slipping off her own collar, but it was unbreakable, and because of its small perimeter, wouldn't go past the underside of her jaw.

Judging from the loud canters of hooves in front, Gemry knew they were being pulled by a team of horses, and because they traveled by land only, the horses weren't Pegasi. Occasionally, because of her position by the front right corner of the caravan, and the slits in the upper wooden sides, which let in whiffs of air and hourglasses of light, she heard some of the conversation coming from the driver's seat.

"—probably round Arenaterro first? Then cut through Safronius—"

"We better have a mage with us, as it's breedin' season for dragons, and I do not want to come across one without magic."

"Of course we've got a mage."

"We used to have a mage, but Dalphon left."

"Ain't he a regent now?"

"Don't you listen? After Rancor's death—which I don't buy was natural at all—Shivark's our new sovereign, and Dalphon's one of his inner regents."

"Eh, as long as we get paid, I don't much mind who's our sovereign."

"That's 'cause you've got more mush than mind in your skull. I've been here longer than you, and I've had a lot more business since Shivark was given joint-control of our Guard four summers ago, and now that he's sovereign…business can only get better."

Apart from Rancor, Gemry didn't know the other leader they referred to. She wished she would have paid more attention in her Silvalo History and Biome Relations class at Valoria.

For the first hour of their journey, the carriage had a relatively smooth ride, so Gemry figured they were on a major thoroughfare heading out from Arborio. If indeed they were heading to Safronius, they were going south. The slaves sat facing one another in a tense silence. After another couple hours, one of the captives broke the silence, suggesting that if they worked together at a stop, they could overpower their drivers and have a shot at freedom. A couple of people murmured their agreement. But the drivers must have overheard the conversation, as all of a sudden their collars crackled. A sharp sting pulsed into their necks. After that the slaves kept silent. Presently, the drivers began talking again.

"—anyway, that leaves traveling through the fields of Safronius the next three to four weeks, and we should be crossing the Gorge next month if we don't get held up too long with other business, and then on to Vispaludem…"

Vispaludem. Of course she knew of that biome from school, and had heard some talk of its people from her father. They were known to be ruthless, lived near bayous, valued enchanted objects above money, and never forgot old grudges. If that's where their caravan was headed…Gemry didn't have a good feeling about it.

A gust of air jostled the side of the caravan, and Gemry heard a boy's voice call to the drivers in front. It sounded familiar, but there was something missing from it…arrogance. "You traders haven't seen any collared cargo in the bushes—have you?" The boy sounded winded, and like he was trying hard to mask his fear.

There was a pause.

"You lost a slave already?" a driver asked incredulously.

"He wasn't on *my* list," snapped the boy, "the other driver took his eyes off during a pit stop. Anyway—have you seen a collared man or not?"

"Not."

"Send up a summon spell if you do."

Something like a large flag rippled, and there was another pause before the two men resumed, this time in mocking tones.

"*'Send up a summon spell'*—pah! I'd just as soon claim 'em for meself."

"Don't know why Dalphon would give overseer's jobs to bratty teens."

"He looks nothing more than a new recruit himself. Dalphon must have gotten a load of new collars, more than our crew alone could handle."

"He seemed pretty pleased this morning. Hey, you heard the other overseers say how we're to take the cargo for sorting when we get there?"

"I did. Poor saps."

"I thought they wanted soldiers?"

"They do, but I've heard they are getting plenty, and they want others for testing. The regents are looking for new ways to make elixir."

"To *make?*"

"That's as much as I heard."

Gemry thought hard. She only knew of skilled sorcerers and lucky mages *finding* elixir. Not making. *Just how would they use people?*

The carriage turned sharply, causing Gemry to lurch against the front wall. The new trail had more holes and bumps than the last. Unfortunately, the sounds of the herky-jerky carriage and the clanking chains inside their compartment meant she couldn't hear the two drivers very well.

Gemry took stock of her situation.

She didn't have any amulet or mircon, so couldn't use magic. She didn't know—or trust—the other captives, but she was grateful that two of the laborers sat between her and one of the likely criminal-slaves. The only people who knew she was gone were her parents…and as they signed her up for this, they wouldn't be helping anytime soon. The thought of them made her heart beat with bitter anger…and sadness. If not them…would Brenner help? *Brenner will be on his way to Aquaperni now, and he won't have a clue that I'm gone, until maybe a month or so, if he comes back to Arborio…and sees I'm not there.* The thought made her more miserable— that he might think she hadn't cared enough to tell him where she'd gone. Unless her parents told the truth…which she doubted.

It was all so blasted unfair.

For the past month, and for the first time in several years, she had been truly happy with someone. She had hope to keep her going, more than just the far-off prospect of graduating from Valoria and making her own way in Arborio—*being with Brenner.* He was friendly, and less conceited than other academy boys—she hadn't met a Valorian guy who wasn't obsessed with self-promotion, or was just trying to get a taste of her. There was something about Brenner that she loved, how everything he tried seemed fresh and exciting…how he didn't care that she prized adventure and knowledge first, and looks a distant second, or third. And how, unlike many of the boys, he wasn't put off by her higher rank.

How could I reach him? She could try to slip a letter-post back to Windelm and Sherry…but she wasn't sure where they lived.

A small voice nagged at her…*Would Brenner look for me?*

Or would he move on…like everyone else? She hoped not—the warm way he had always looked at her, his kind tone when he spoke to her, their shared kiss—but she didn't know, and found herself pinching her eyes shut, stopping herself before the moisture pooled into tears. She didn't want to appear weak. Not here.

For now, that meant she only had one person left to help: herself.

Gemry took a deep breath, steeling herself. She would need to figure out the lax points of the overseers' schedule, locate the weakest link among them, hopefully break away, and if possible, pilfer a mircon and amulet from someone. She could run away without elixir, but that would make her exposed. *Exposed to beasts...traders...the elements.* And in the wilds of Ganthrea, survival without magic, or at least fellow travelers, was slim.

She knew she was slated to be a slave for a year—with bitterness, she recalled how her father had phrased it like a brief, exotic vacation, working under Gretzinger in the outer limits of Arborio. But she had been traded to a new master and going to one of the harshest biomes, and no one knew yet how cruel her new owner, or the drivers, would be. What if he'd tear up her contract and keep her *permanently* enslaved...or if, as she'd heard matter-of-factly said of many slaves in foreign lands, she'd be 'overworked' before her year was up?

Gemry vowed then that she would never be manipulated for another's folly, never be taken advantage of again, and if she would lose her life in the harsh work of the following months and even years, she wouldn't lose it without a fight. First, she would fight for herself...and, because a part of her wanted this last hope, their love, to endure—unlike everything else crumbling in her life—she would also fight for Brenner.

Before games, she used to pump herself up to fly fast and play harder. But she knew this ordeal would be much longer and *much* tougher than any game she'd played. Gemry modified the words she used to tell herself, but she wanted them more than ever:

Can't stop now. Battle on.

Brenner's morning had brought betrayals, escapes, death, and enslavement; his afternoon brought still more unexpected news. When Windelm ushered him inside the cottage in Vale Adorna, Sherry threw her arms wide and ran to hug him the moment she laid eyes on him, gushing all the worry she'd pent up while they had searched for him. When he told her about Gemry, her mouth dropped open in shock, and creases furrowed across her forehead.

Sherry tried to pull herself together, and insisted he have some ginger tea, which she claimed would help his nerves. His Alacritus potion having expired, he said yes. Windelm, Sherry and Brenner sat on the back patio underneath the monstrous oakbrawns and cottonwoods, which were dropping copious amounts of white, cotton puffs. Brenner was vaguely reminded of his old cottonwood, but these white seedlings felt less like summer and more like a winter snow: he was numb.

Sure, he had won the Games, elixir, prestige—everything a young spellcaster could want, but it had only taken one morning to lose everything, or rather, the one person dearest to him.

If only I'd read the signs… Gemry's father's bets, the threats against him, her parent's lack of pride at her Zabrani win, the grim escort by her father Sunday evening… I could have done something.

I still can do something.

Windelm and Sherry were quiet, waiting for Brenner to emerge from his thoughts.

He rose to his feet. "Windelm, Sherry, thanks for your hospitality," Brenner said, "but I should go now. I'll take some food, and I'll fly every major road from Arborio until I find her."

"That is certainly noble," said Windelm, watching but not moving to stop Brenner, "but, after the events of this morning, it may be the last thing you do." Brenner paused by the door. "Nearly everyone knows who you are, what power you've gained, and until we prove your innocence, the Silvalo Guard think you are connected to Gretzinger's death. There's also been fires, and the people who did that would certainly be glad to find *you*, steal your amulet, and leave you in the gutter to be found in the morning sweeps of the city guard."

Clenching his fist, teeth, and mircon, Brenner heard him, but didn't want to listen. "Every moment we delay," Brenner said, "Gemry gets further and further from the city!"

"But a wild goose chase fifty miles down and back up the major vias from Arborio would take well over a week," said Windelm, "and that's not counting the time sifting through thousands of travelers and caravans. Don't forget, many merchant spellcasters take to the skies when traveling back to their homelands. So, first we need to look for signs, for clues, of who has taken her, and then proceed cautiously."

Brenner was in no mood to wait and proceed cautiously. He started walking to the door. "How would you feel if Sherry were kidnapped and I told you to sit on your hands for a week?"

Windelm heaved a sigh. "I would feel as angry and lost as you do now, and you have every right to feel that way. But please allow me to share some of my recent discoveries, and the events of last night with you, before you take action. I want to find her too, you know."

When Brenner looked over at him, and saw the sympathy in Windelm's eyes, he stopped walking. Although it pained him to delay his frantic search, he nodded a tiny bit. "So…what do you know?"

Windelm motioned with his hand for Brenner to sit by them, and as he grudgingly did, Windelm said, "There were fires last night, at three of the visiting biome embassies—Montadaux, Vispaludem, and Aquaperni. Scores of people got hurt from the blaze, and thieves made off with platinums and golders from the embassy's treasury. Bad as that was, I don't believe it was their chief goal."

"What was?"

"They want the biomes to distrust each other. Starting fires and stealing coins and elixir from three embassy vaults has made certain of that."

Greed for money and magic sources, Brenner thought.

"On top of that," Windelm continued, "A biome leader with great power died last night—the sovereign wizard of Vispaludem: Rancor."

"How? Aren't sovereigns protected?"

"Yes. And that's the issue. The only people who had access to his chambers were his Royal Guards, and they're dead, too. The initial news is that one of the guards turned traitor, killed the other and attempted to steal the sovereign's amulet, then was killed trying to escape the embassy."

"Hmm…is that what you think, too?"

"Not yet…launching an assassination during the most patrolled event of the year is not a smart choice for an inside guard…but since all seven biomes are present, it is a very smart choice for a neighboring country…or someone looking for power. The new leaders of Vispaludem are accusing the four other embassies who didn't suffer fires that night, saying there's an alliance forming between them. You haven't lived here for very long, but there have been tensions running between the biomes for decades, and this murder has kindled old embers into flames. Now, spellcasters are going to rally around their home biomes…or those that they think have the most power. There is very likely a war coming. All of this means that city guards and soldiers of each biome—biome guards—could be hostile to travelers passing through."

Brenner was quiet a moment, composing his thoughts.

"Sage Vicksman, is he from another biome?" asked Brenner.

"Vicksman? No, not that I'm aware of. Why?"

"He tried to steal my amulet."

Windelm's eyebrows rose in alarm.

Brenner relayed the flight of the morning, and Vicksman's attempt to trap him and steal his amulet. Windelm shook his head.

"Amulet Extortion…from a faculty member at Valoria? I will send a message to Spellmaster Kinigree. If Vicksman has any sense, he will have fled the city by now. Once caught, he'll be stripped of his title, amulet and mircon, sent to jail, and his name will be blackened."

"He won't be stripped of his mircon," Brenner said, pulling it out of his holster.

"Nicely done," said Windelm, looking at it, then to him with concern. "If one of your instructors tried to steal your amulet, imagine what lengths others might go to."

Brenner knew Windelm was right. He would have to work on strengthening his Auras. He lifted his amulet from under his tunic, watching the afternoon sunlight highlight the four colors within. They seemed to have their own personalities, one moment keeping to themselves and the next, swirling together in pairs.

Windelm watched Brenner musingly. "That brings me to my next point:

your amulet. How is it working for you?"

To demonstrate, Brenner pointed his mircon at a giant boulder at the edge of Windelm's yard, and said "*Apellatum.*"

The boulder, a dark stone as big as a young dragon, immediately lifted with a loud squelch, and flew towards them as if nothing more than a wind-blown balloon. Halfway to them, Brenner flicked his mircon left, and the boulder obediently swerved to the other side of the yard, where Brenner flew it around an oakbrawn twice, and then flew it back to its spot, seating it neatly next to a large maple tree.

"Impressive," said Windelm. "We should soon work on using the strengths of each elixir color. Brenner, how many dual elixir amulets do you think there are?"

"I don't know. Ten thousand in Silvalo?"

"No, more like a couple thousand in all of Ganthrea. How about triple elixir amulets?"

"A thousand?"

"Probably no more than two-to-three hundred in existence, each guarded jealously and passed with care from generation to generation. So, that brings us to your quad colored amulet."

Brenner looked down at it again, and then up to Windelm.

"I've only heard of a handful that could hold four or more colors," said Windelm, "When Sovereign Drusus went to add your new elixir from the vault, I thought your amulet might repel the additional color, and Drusus would pour your new elixir into a separate amulet. But surprisingly, your amulet accepted the new elixir."

Brenner peered down at the iridescent red, green, yellow, and blue colors. "It's rare then?"

"*Extremely,*" said Windelm, "which means it must be guarded closely. "Additionally, it takes a unique personality to wield different elixirs, someone who empathizes with diverse people and diverse lands. Most people, putting on your quad-colored amulet, would have one of two reactions: they'd find themselves overwhelmed by the magic within it, like being pinned beneath the torrent of a waterfall, or would be unable to control themselves, their inner impulses driving them to steal golders, hoard power, or dominate others. The fact that you've remained steady and largely self-controlled under substantial elixir power is no easy feat, and a very good indicator."

"An indicator of what?"

Windelm fixed his deep green-blue eyes on Brenner. "I didn't tell you the whole story of why I recruited you to Ganthrea."

Brenner's neck hairs tingled like an electric current was running through him; his mind searched for motives. *What has Windelm been hiding from me?*

"For many years," said Windelm, "I have traveled around and out from Silvalo to other biomes, and wherever I go, on the outskirts of countries, I've seen portions of the land…fading. Not just the forests, but also spines of mountains, stretches of plains, and marshes. At first, I thought it was a coincidence, but then I became aware of something more sinister: the lands didn't grow back when I saw them years later.

"It was as if the elixir of the lands was permanently drained. Aside from my chief duties to Arborio, my side project has been for my scouts and I to search for the culprits behind the elixir losses." He stiffened. "Do you remember my friend, Patrick?"

Brenner vaguely recalled the conversation in the streets of Vale Adorna from some months ago. "He's your neighbor, isn't he?"

"He was, yes…"

"Was?"

"Sadly," said Windelm, "he's dead."

Brenner let out a gasp. "I'm sorry. How?"

"Spellfire. He and another spellcaster went searching for their friend, Philip McRorin…and were found on the outskirts of Arenaterro, their amulets and mircons gone. The land nearby was desolate, sapped of energy."

"Do you know who did it?"

"Not for certain, but three biomes are likely: Arenaterro, Safronius or Vispaludem."

"Have you told Sovereign Drusus?"

"I've told him my suspicions once, but as there was largely peace in Ganthrea, he shrugged it off. Whether he will mobilize Silvalo to fight now, I don't know, but it will take more than one biome army to fight this enemy, since they have been accumulating so much elixir."

Brenner wasn't sure he wanted to ask his next question, but he had to know. "So...what's this have to do with me?"

"Seeing the lands drained of their elixir confirmed something that I had read long ago, in the first few years when I came to Ganthrea. I was taken in by a spellcaster named DeFarras, who, apart from buying and selling potions and silks from other biomes, happened to collect ancient stories and scrolls of Ganthrea, some of which came from the Oracles in Gelemensus.

"His most valuable parchments, held together with early magic, were many hundreds, if not thousands, of years old, and contained prophecies about Ganthrea."

"Have they come true?"

"Of the scores of prophecies that antiquarians have found—most are still kept in Gelemensus—none have led to false fates. The Oracles have a saying that a prophecy will come to fruition when the harvest is ripe. And since the last prophecy that came to fulfillment was over four hundred years ago, and parts of others are fitting into place, it seems the time is now ripe again."

Brenner was getting an odd feeling. "So, where are DeFarras' scrolls now?"

"DeFarras didn't have any children. So when he died, he gave his collection of scrolls to me. And one of them," Windelm stuck a hand into his robes, and pulled out a scroll of yellow parchment that looked like it had once wrapped mummies, "is about the final days, and is also, I believe, about you."

He tapped the scroll with his mircon, and very gently, the two cylinders of it unfurled themselves. The air seemed unusually still, as if the forest itself was leaning in, and then Windelm began reading its words aloud:

"In what will be the final age,
from Ganthrea's grasslands will rise a king—
handsome, cunning, and cruel.
Gaining terrible power by promising peace,
no man will escape his rule.
Deepest magic he'll gather and use,
to enslave, erase, and abuse.
He'll plunder and drink
all beauty and strength
from Ganthrea's head, heart and hands —
unless a known knight from an unknown land,
against this false king, unites a true stand."

-The Elder Oracle of Saphyria,
Gelemensus

Windelm stopped reading, floated Brenner the prophecy to read its ancient scripture for himself. Then he summoned it back. He tapped it with his mircon once more, and the scroll rewound.

He fixed Brenner with a penetrating look, and waited.

"So, you think that knight from the prophecy..." Brenner asked, trying to discern the creases in Windelm's face, "that could be me?"

"We must hope it is," said Windelm gravely, "because it isn't me, and I don't know where else to look...and now we are running out of time."

"But, I'm not a knight, I don't know what—"

"On the Zabrani field, what are you called?"

"I'm not the king, I'm just one of the many—" Brenner stopped himself, remembering he was indeed one of the Zabrani knights. "I see. But what do you think it means by 'known'?"

"At its most simple, someone who is recognized. At its most profound, someone who is famous. And I haven't seen a Ganthrean Zabrani game won with a Wizard's Gambit in my lifetime…which has netted you more fame in one day than most players earn in a career."

Although it was nearly the middle of summer, Brenner was starting to get chills.

Underneath his swirling amulet, something inside of him was resonating. "And the unknown land," said Brenner in realization, "must be…Earth."

"Exactly. There is some quality or qualities that you've developed on Earth that's needed to fight against this threat to Ganthrea. And *that* is why I gave you a chance with your amulet, brought you into Ganthrea, and why I need your help."

Brenner felt like Windelm had placed him in a strange stone room, and just when he had familiarized himself with the hard surroundings, one of the walls melted away like ice, revealing a whole new wing to the castle.

He had only been in Silvalo and Ganthrea for several months…but already felt as if strands had been pulled from his soul and interwoven with the beauty of the lands, the magic, with people like Windelm, Sherry… Finnegan, Sage Shastrel, Maverick…and most of all, with Gemry.

And if all that was being jeopardized by what Windelm had seen, what happened last night after the Games, and the rise of this prophesied king…

He made up his mind. "If I can help, I will."

"Good," Windelm said, nodding to Brenner, and then to Sherry.

"With one condition," said Brenner firmly.

"What's that?" Windelm said, putting his palm out.

"We bring back Gemry."

"Of course," said Windelm smiling.

Brenner rose to his feet. "When do we start? And where do we go?"

"We start immediately," said Windelm, "tracking the possible transfers and routes of outbound slaves from magnates, and going to gain allies where we can.

"Along the way you must continue to develop your physical, mental and Aura magic, and perhaps learn to harness color-infusion spells. With a little luck, you might add more elixirs to your amulet. But one last thing."

"Yes?" Brenner said slowly, wondering what wall would melt around him now.

"The longer you stay on this side of the portal," said Windelm solemnly, "the harder it will be to go back to Earth. We won't be able to travel there once we start our next journey, and I'm not sure when, or if, we will get back. Are you sure you're on-board with this?"

Brenner thought of his past, which seemed so distant, almost murky compared to his new surroundings. A summer breeze swirled through the oakbrawns into Brenner, and with it, a purpose.

He didn't know who this cruel king was just yet, but trusted Windelm's judgement, knowing he had to do something to help Gemry, to prevent more deaths like Patrick's, more destruction of the biomes...recalling vaguely how the forests he knew long ago on Earth had almost seemed drained themselves...

Were they in some way tied to this place? To Ganthrea?

"I understand," Brenner finally said.

"And?"

"I'm still in. But first we get Gemry, then we tackle the rest."

"See, dear?" Windelm said, smiling to Sherry, "I told you he's my great-nephew."

Sherry put a hand on Brenner's shoulder. "I never doubted it."

Although Brenner was still anxious about Gemry, he felt his uncertainty and numbness melting away, replaced with a firm goal.

He had a plan to get back Gemry...had Windelm and Sherry...had new spell possibilities with his quad-colored amulet. And even though he had won Agilis and Zabrani, two of the deadliest Games of Ganthrea, he felt as though the most dangerous, the most important, journey of his life had just begun: finding Gemry, harnessing new magic and elixirs, and somehow uniting leaders against a corrupt king.

All of which would be easier, he'd come to find soon enough, if he wasn't a wanted fugitive.

About the Author

Andy Adams does his best to imitate Abe Lincoln: he cuts his own wood, grows his own beard, has a much-smarter wife, four kids, eleven chickens, and is wary of going to plays. He is thankful for his parents, siblings, coffee, friends, and the greatest gifts of all: kind beta readers & readers like you.

A magna cum laude alumnus of the University of Minnesota, Andy took enough Latin to know how to pugna dracones and carpe diem. While he came in 4th place for a poetry recital in 4th grade and *again* for an original, Monty-Python-inspired film in high school, Andy *completely redeemed* himself with an Ultimate Frisbee film in college, winning both the Judge's Choice Award and the affection of his future wife. **Booyah**, poetry recital!

An English teacher who equipped his 12th graders with swords to re-enact *Macbeth*, and unleashed his 8th graders to an outside Battle Room during *Ender's Game*, Andy has trouble sitting still. He lives with his family in Oregon: skiing Mt. Bachelor, rafting the Deschutes, improv acting, and, when tuckered out, reading at Roundabout Books and Dudley's Cafe.

The Games of Ganthrea is Andy Adams' first novel,
and book one of The Ganthrea Trilogy.

www.theandyadams.com

Made in the USA
Coppell, TX
08 June 2020

27179633R00256